THE MIDAS EFFECT

THE MIDAS EFFECT

Manuel Dorado

Manuel Dorado, *The Midas Effect*

First edition in Spanish: November 2016
First edition in English: September 2019

ISBN: 9781691920303

English translation by Laura Fitzgerald, 2019
Illustration by Эльвина Якубова (elvina1332), Pixabay
Cover design by Manuel Dorado

https://www.manueldorado.es/

For Mario and Pablo

"Destiny has two ways of crushing us –
by refusing our wishes and by fulfilling them."
–H. F. AMIEL,
From Amiel's Journal

"When the gods wish to punish us, they answer our prayers."
–O. WILDE,
From An Ideal Husband

Contents

PART 1 – THE CAPTURE

CHAPTER 1

Nobody feels pain in the center of their head. That's what the neurologists had told Miguel several times. But there it was again, that buzzing, like a constant electric pinching somewhere inside his head. His father wasn't a neurologist, but he *was* one of the best doctors in Seville: Dr. Benoît Le Fablec, a Frenchman who was almost entirely Sevillian. There was always a queue outside his clinic. Miguel could remember very clearly the busy waiting room of his father's clinic, where as a boy, he would stick his face through ladies' legs "so I can see my dad." And every time, he left the clinic with the same diagnosis: "The center of your head doesn't feel pain, Miguel." For many years after, the best specialists in France and Spain – friends of his father – would say to him, with their white coats and upturned noses, "*Ce n'est pas possible*," or, "Young man, this wouldn't be another excuse to skip class, now would it?"

But Miguel really was in pain. Now, after so many years, as he leaned on the bar in the university café, he thought his head was in more pain than it had ever been before. He imagined it must have been because of the preparations for his trip – saying goodbye, all of that – or perhaps it was because he hadn't eaten breakfast.

Miguel ordered a coffee. The students had packed out the engineering school's canteen. *My students always talk too much*, he thought. But the ruckus didn't seem to aggravate his headache.

Deep down, he had to admit he liked his unique, impossible headache, and the noise of the canteen.

"Your coffee," said the waiter, placing a cup in front of Miguel. "With warm milk, just like always. I heard you're leaving us."

"The United States. I'm going to try it out there for a few years. Here, for the coffee."

"They really have it down over there, in America. You know, the money. If they don't pay well here, then you've got to go somewhere else. It's the brain drain."

My brain isn't going to do me much good if it continues hurting this much, Miguel told himself as the waiter turned around to the cash register. Miguel stood there watching him. It wasn't worth the effort to try and convince him he wasn't going to earn much more in California than in his current position at the University of Granada. Miguel was leaving because he wanted to go back to aerospace research, return to his specialty. Well, that, and to live somewhere new. Different streets, different voices. It would be a little adventure in his routine-heavy life as a university professor – an adventure he would have embarked on many years before had it not been for Ana. He took a sip, the steam from the coffee entering his nostrils before fading away into his headache.

It was then that he saw her enter the cafeteria. Ana.

Miguel swallowed. Coughing, he turned around to set the cup down, and looked at her again. How on earth…? But it really was her. The pain pinched his head again. Miguel let his eyelids fall shut to try and mitigate the pain, but it remained.

No one gets this kind of headache, and this kind of thing doesn't happen to anyone, he told himself.

Ana was dressed exactly the way he remembered. Living with her for three years gave him an introduction to her entire wardrobe, he thought. But she was exactly the way he had imagined, down to the last detail. Her tight white jeans matched her white sweater, designer, also tight over a pink shirt. Her straight black hair fell loose, just the way he liked. Even underneath her expensive makeup, he could see her beautiful, impeccable skin, like glossy paper. It seemed Ana had dressed herself up in a way she knew he'd like. It was an image of her he had imagined and re-imagined many times since she left him a little over a month ago – Ana begging him to take her back, and Miguel rejecting her in an act of public triumph.

Ana spotted him and walked straight toward him, crossing the cafeteria at a diagonal. She walked with a confident gait, as though her body had made its decision to move and would overcome anything in her way. She smiled.

There's nothing to smile about, Miguel thought, picking up his cup again.

The scent of Chanel announced Ana's arrival to the bar. She smiled wider as she came to a stop in front of him and spoke. "Your second coffee of the morning? Third? We really don't change, do we?"

"I was just leaving."

"You look good..."

"I'm in a hurry."

Ana's smile disappeared like a puff of smoke. "I'll join you," she said. "I want to talk to you." Her voice was almost inaudible.

Miguel thought that if his fantasy was to come true, they would have to talk then and there, surrounded by dishevelled, noisy college students.

"I'm in a hurry," he repeated.

Ana pressed her lips together. She looked back towards the door, as if she were thinking of leaving, before exhaling deeply. Miguel watched her chest move. Her white sweater and pink shirt did not show much, but he could just make out the gap between her breasts as well as a subtle hint of their roundness.

Yes, just the way I like, Miguel thought.

Ana turned to him once more and lowered her head. "Don't go to America," she whispered. "Stay." She swallowed. "I want to get back together. I… I love you."

Miguel felt another pinch in the center of his brain. *Great. Here come the waterworks*. "No," he said.

Ana's expensive make-up began to run as tears left black, watery tracks on her cheeks. She looked exactly the way she did in his fantasies – tears staining her face like watered-down ink. Miguel reminded himself that it wasn't right to relish seeing those black tearstains, but he felt so good watching his dream become reality that he couldn't help himself.

"But I…" Ana trailed off, lifting her head and looking into Miguel's eyes.

Some of the students were staring at her. Some frowned while others smiled, and some even nudged their friends who hadn't yet noticed. Ana must have felt their eyes on her, Miguel supposed, as she hung her head. She patted her face with a handkerchief, which immediately became smudged. Dressed all in white and pink, immaculate, Ana fidgeted slightly with the blackened handkerchief, her face still damp. The students murmured among themselves, entertained. Perhaps this was too public. Miguel knew it would be wrong to do it then and there – too humiliating – but that was how he had fantasized about it. He could still feel a residual triumph. The ache in his head was constant now, a soft vibration inside his skull, so pleasant, so sweet. He suddenly remembered how he had wanted his final gesture to be: symbolic and dramatic.

"Ana." Miguel caught her attention, his tone serious and steady.

She looked up at him without moving her head, just enough to be able to see him. Miguel focused on her running mascara while he pushed back the hair that had fallen in front of his eyes. He took another sip of coffee without looking away from her and repeated himself. "No." A horizontal cutting motion with his right hand accompanied the word. A gesture fit for a Roman emperor administering justice.

Ana's lips trembled. Then, she lowered her gaze completely. She turned around and left faster than she had come in with short, quick steps, keeping her gaze firmly on the floor. She bumped into the students like they had all become obstacles in her path.

In just a few seconds, Ana's slim figure – black tearstains and all – disappeared. And so too did the headache. All that remained was a slight dizziness, like always. Nothing more. A little vertigo and a feeling of victory.

When he turned to place his cup down on the bar, he saw a boy quickly avert his eyes. It was one of his students. He must have seen Miguel get rid of Ana, reject her, make that cutting gesture with his hand. He lowered his eyes to his cup and gulped down his coffee. Maybe he had gone overboard. It would be useless to get back together with Ana. He just couldn't do it. She had never treated him right, ever. Maybe she deserved to be taught a lesson. But the sight of her ruined makeup smudged over her cheeks… No, he wasn't like that.

Miguel started walking towards the exit. He could feel himself being watched, and he quickened his pace. *Something about what happened just now*, he thought, *there was something strange about it.* Or perhaps he was just imagining it. He wouldn't blame himself. No, he had a… how to explain it? A supernatural hunch? Everything had happened exactly as Miguel had imagined it. Ana had followed the script of his fantasy to the letter. And Ana just wasn't like that. She had much more pride. Ana should have turned on her heel and marched out of the cafeteria with her head held high and a mist of Chanel following her when Miguel had told her that they couldn't talk in private. What she had actually done made no sense at all.

At that moment, Miguel left the cafeteria and the stares of his students before stopping in the hallway. He had no reason to feel proud of what had happened, but neither was he to blame for imagining it in the first place. The imagination was fanciful like that. And that... Look, it had simply been a twist of luck that reality had so closely coincided with his fantasy. That was it.

***

A Midas can make their imagination become reality, thought Vladimir Gorlov.

Seated at his desk, he unscrewed a plastic pen, disassembled it and then reassembled it slowly, carefully, like he was studying how it worked.

They could create storms, lightning, tidal waves... He placed the spring back inside the pen. *Stop a butterfly mid-flight, remove a planet from its orbit, turn seawater sweet, resurrect armies, turn honey blue, destroy the universe... Turn anything into gold. A Midas.*

Midas, Gorlov repeated to himself. He placed the now-reassembled pen beside his notebook. *A Midas could turn all the cows in the world green and yellow for a day. And make them fly.*

He took up his pen again, as if anxious to take it apart once more. The stupid cow example was the best one that came to mind when he tried to explain what a Midas was. A god—that was the best way to explain it. But Gorlov was on the verge of proving that a Midas wasn't all-powerful. There was one thing they couldn't do.

They can't destroy their own ability, he thought. *The Midas Paradox. The Midas subject can do anything they can possibly imagine, but they can't destroy their own ability.*

But how to describe it? Gorlov had to write about it using technical terms, but they wouldn't come to him. Or perhaps, deep down, he didn't want to find them. He stared at his bony hand lying top of the graph paper. His hands, now withered with age, had recorded more than fifty years of investigative research, but now it was like they resisted it. He began to move the pen with a strained, slow script.

Note 1067: The Midas Paradox.
The system of equations to maximize the Midas Effect could lack a solution. This could imply that, if the Midas subject existed, they would not be able to eliminate their power once used...

Gorlov filled a page and a half trying to clarify the implications of the paradox. Once he finished writing, he stopped and read over his final conclusion.

The Midas is damned by their own power.

Too melodramatic, he said to himself, crossing out the sentence with a thick, black line.

He removed his aviators, the only glasses with which he knew he could see well, the ones that had been with him since his years in Leningrad. Taking out a handkerchief, he wiped the lenses and the black plastic frames before placing them back on their specially-reserved spot on his nose. He re-read the crossed-out note. *Damned by their own power.*

Scientific notes shouldn't use such sensationalist language. But that was how he felt, deep down – sensationalist. Or, at the very least, restless, full of excitement, like a bright but unkempt college student presenting his final thesis. All that came to mind were stupid things like that final note and the example of green and yellow cows, lines that ran amok in his mind like giddy children.

Anyone would feel excited if they had finally found what they had spent their whole life searching for, he told himself. They were just about to capture a Midas, of course. It seemed, at least, that they had finally found one. Only once before had they ever been so close. But that candidate…, she had failed.

Gorlov didn't want to imagine what another failure would mean. He, in all probability, wouldn't live long enough to find another candidate. Looking away from the graph paper on the desk, he leaned back against the broad back of his chair. He watched the sunbeams, early risers like himself, crossing his study. Oblique bands of light on ochre walls. California had taken him in, had let him almost finish his investigation, the one he had started in the old Soviet Union. It was true that he missed his homeland – like anyone else in their right mind, he supposed – but he despised the cold. The Russian cold would freeze his knuckles, even when he wore gloves. He shivered thinking of it. But there, in his office located in NASA's south wing building, it was always warm.

But duty was cold. Duty.

Gorlov had his years in the KGB to thank for his Soviet sense of discipline, military in nature, and he managed to return his gaze to his notes. He exchanged his black pen for a blue one. Blue ink for mathematical notations, he reminded himself, writing out a system of equations, still incomplete, that tried to provide some meaning to the paradox. Once the formulae were finished, he noted the date. His movements stilled for a moment, observing the date with a serious look. April first.

Almost a year since we found him.

He remembered that the very same day he had started working on the equations, Eugene Barrett had appeared in his office with his mousy smile and announced that he had located a supposed Midas. In Spain. Eugene the hero, as ill-timed as his smile.

Gorlov eyed the blue equations of the paradox between his fingers, which were too slim to cover the formulae. The paradox was a problem that could not be avoided. He had even considered postponing the capture. A Midas was too dangerous, wielded too much power for one human being. And now Gorlov's blue formulae said something more – they began to show that activating a Midas was an irreversible process.

He closed the notebook. Nothing more to explain. His gaze returned to one of the diagonal sunbeams on the wall; one of them now touched the glass framing the periodic table of elements he had brought from Russia. For the sake of practicality, he had only brought with him his notebooks and that table. Irina, his memories, his past – everything else had been left in the cold. The sunlight left a glint on the edge of the glass that obscured his vision. The Midas dazzled him, drew him in, but wouldn't let him open his eyes fully. That very same sunlight had entered through his window and shone on the nape of his neck. A small, pleasant shiver ran through him. What he was doing had to be right, it had to. If not, it would mean he had sacrificed his whole life for…

The phone on his desk started ringing. The trilling sound woke Gorlov from his thoughts, from the Californian sun, and gracelessly dumped him back in his cold, damp office in

Leningrad. The screen showed that it was one of his secretaries calling him. He picked up the phone. "Karen?"

"Professor Gorlov," replied Karen's soft voice, "Dr. Barrett is waiting for you in the basement. He asked me to remind you."

"Thank you, Karen." Hanging up, Gorlov placed his notebook in his briefcase. He would have to visit the high-security floors. That was where the notebook needed to be, where neither his notes nor the documents scattered across his desk must be allowed to leave. He gathered them all together, almost sweeping with them. Americans, it was said, were very lax with security protocols. But Gorlov was grateful for that. He was too old to work all day locked away in an underground laboratory, as technical and conditioned as he was.

If old Karen knew what the "basement" really was, she'd never let me down there again, he thought as he shuffled through his papers.

One brown file didn't quite fit in the briefcase. It was the report on the pursuit of the supposed Midas. The rough folder represented the subject, represented everything they knew about him, and the plans for his capture.

Looking at the clock on his desk told him it was nearly sunrise in Spain. The first meeting with the subject would soon be taking place. That was the plan. Monica and Walter Castillo had followed him from Granada, and she would intercept him before he left for San Francisco.

Gorlov read the name of the subject written in black on the brown file. It was a half-Spanish, half-French name. Miguel Le Fablec. Then, he shut his briefcase and left the Californian sun.

CHAPTER 2

Monica felt stupid. Miguel Le Fablec appeared to be sleeping, not noticing her presence despite her efforts. In the middle of the gardens beside the Alhambra, disguised as a tourist with a backpack, map and baseball cap, she shook a camera about in her hand to catch the subject's attention. But, he appeared to be sleeping.

She observed him silently. He had dark, slightly long, straight hair. She liked it; it gave him a bohemian look. Romantic, in a way. She bit down on the right side of her bottom lip. No, that wasn't what she liked. *I'm not a romantic*, she told herself. In fact, she was quite the opposite. She hated sentimentality and preferred being practical. The Miguel she liked had been the one she saw that morning in the University of Granada; the one who had dismissed his ex-girlfriend with that cutting gesture with his right hand, like he was wiping her off the face of the earth. That had been particularly good. It was the best he could do, the only thing he could do. He had gotten rid of that madwoman with the tiny waist and exposed cleavage who did nothing but slow down Miguel's trip to California.

Monica crumpled up the map in her hands. It wasn't that she was particularly interested in Miguel's love life, far from it, but it was well that Miguel had resolved his personal issue in Spain. Ana. Yes, it was practical. She spread out the crumpled map on her leg, folded it and tucked it into the back pocket of her jeans. *Too many tourist props*, she thought.

It was practical to… Monica suddenly realized that she had spent several minutes completely absorbed in the subject's hair and his ex-girlfriend. Looking behind her, she spotted Castillo. He was watching her from behind some rose bush. She was not about to let Castillo report negatively about her.

The camera in her right hand had turned off. Pressing the power button, she told herself that she had caught other subjects before for the Project. She knew how to do it right.

Monica went over her instructions in her head while she focused the camera on the subject, adjusting the zoom and brightness. They were very basic, typical for the first phase of a capture. *Fake a chance encounter with the subject in their city of origin. Act nice and friendly. Tell him you'll be working in the same American university as him.* She adjusted the focus on Miguel. *What a coincidence! How lucky!* he'd think. *The first person I meet from my new world.*

She would be his first acquaintance in a new life he hadn't even started yet. The usual protocol: feign coincidence.

Clearing her throat, she extended her arm holding the camera and said, "¿Por favor?"

***

"¿Por favor?" Miguel heard a feminine voice speak, although it sounded distant. He paid it no mind.

Tourists, he thought. *The Alhambra, the Generalife gardens, all of Granada full of tourists in caps. In spring, all year, everywhere*. He touched the rough stone of the bench where he sat as he opened his eyes and pushed back the hair that had fallen over his face

In front of him, beyond the lookout, was the scenery he had come to say farewell to. That was why he had come. He had already said goodbye to his family and everyone else, but in order to begin his journey, he had to go through with the symbolic act of saying goodbye to his homeland. The church domes, the palm and cypress trees, the Alhambra, the white houses, the city. It all smelled like orange blossoms.

In California, they have orange trees, he thought, turning his gaze to California so he could smell it from there.

He imagined himself in a white and blue British Airways plane, an enormous Boeing 747, with a hump and four 60,000-pound Pratt & Whitney engines that would take him to San Francisco. His favorite plane. That was his future – the jumbo jet, the orange trees, the Californian sun…

"Please?" Miguel heard again.

Stupid tourists! He turned towards the voice.

It was a girl. Young. Right next to him. She smiled at him.

She had long, wavy hair, like an Italian actress. *Although an Italian actress would never hide such beautiful hair with a hat*, Miguel thought. Shining blue eyes. He stared at her for a moment, head turned slightly, watching her nibble the right side of her lower lip in a way that almost seemed sensual to him.

The girl showed him her camera and turned to point at the scenery. From one of the back pockets of her jeans, which had been tailored perfectly to her curves, Miguel could see a wrinkled map of Granada just at eye level. *Nice ass*. He looked up at her again as she removed her cap and shook her hair free. Miguel opened his mouth, but had no idea what to say.

"¿Por favor?" she repeated, this time in Spanish, with long, smooth Rs. She kept her hand still between the two.

Miguel blinked and looked down – the camera. It was a black reflex camera. Analog, with a good lens. It looked similar to one he'd had years ago, an antiquated thing he had loved. He smiled.

"Photo, yes?" he said in English, taking the camera.

The girl smiled too, and began to point behind her at the scenery she wanted as the backdrop for the photo as well as where she was going to stand. She spoke in rapid English with an American accent. She made decisive, forceful gestures with her hands, like an orchestra conductor. Miguel liked her. She seemed to have everything very clear in her head and made quick, practical decisions. Direct, that was the word. She wanted a full-body shot on the lookout, with the Alhambra and the light of the sunset behind her, which, by her approximation, was close at hand. And she didn't have bad taste, Miguel thought, but all that wouldn't be possible.

"The sun is still very high," he said. "You won't come out very well with all that light behind you," he added, handing her the camera.

But the girl didn't take it. She didn't even move. The look on her face faded as if a cloud had passed in front of the sun overhead. Her smile also disappeared.

It's not a big deal, I guess, Miguel told himself. But the look she gave him made him feel as if he had insulted her.

Suddenly, Miguel felt an unreal cold come over him, making him shiver. And then, in the middle of his head, a tiny pinch. He couldn't start his journey to a new life like that, denying the young woman such a small thing. Miguel turned the camera over in his hands, as if it would start to talk and give him an answer. *A photo in Granada... Nothing's easier than that*. He quickly remembered the photos he had taken with Ana at the Mirador de San Nicolás, the ones he had taken with his old reflex camera. Of course, that was it! He blinked, shaking off all thoughts of Ana, and looked towards the white houses all clustered together along the hill that was now in front of them. The Albaicín. Saint Nicholas, the church, the Mirador—Miguel could see all of them between the houses. He hesitated for a moment.

"I know the perfect place for panoramic shots," he said, pointing to the Mirador de San Nicolás on the other side of the houses. "We can get there before sunset if we hurry. Well…" he caught himself, "if you'd like me to accompany you, that is."

"Let's go!" the young woman exclaimed, almost militarily, her camera and her smile returning to her all at once. She seemed ready to run to get there.

"We can take a bus," Miguel said.

***

Thirty minutes later, Miguel stepped off the bus after the American girl. She smiled at him before taking her map out of her pocket and offering it to him.

But Miguel didn't take it. "It's over there," he said. He pointed to a tiny street leading away from the plaza. "We'll be there soon. It's Monica, right?"

"Monica Eveleigh. But my mother's maiden name is Graziano. Angela Graziano. She's Italian."

While they walked, Monica told him more about herself. Her mother had Italian heritage, and her great-grandparents were from Naples, good Catholic people – Miguel had already spotted the small gold cross hanging from her neck over her gray shirt – and her father was a scientist from New Jersey, working near Houston on something about embryonic cells, and she and her siblings had been born in Texas. Monica spoke in an uninterrupted stream of words. She was also working in research, but not in the same area as her father, since she wasn't all that interested in biology. Miguel tried to imagine her in Texas researching… he didn't know what. Although in Houston, he remembered, was the Johnson Space Center. Nothing less than NASA's Mission Control Center. It would be incredibly lucky, he thought, to know someone from the Agency. *NASA*, he thought. His childhood dream. The dream that had pushed him to become an aeronautical engineer.

"What do you do?" Miguel asked.

"I'm a psychologist and a mathematician."

Psychologist and mathematician? Americans are weird.

"At Saint Stephen's Catholic University," she added.

Of course. She had already told him she was very Catholic, Miguel remembered as they turned a corner. He hated priests. Their intimidating robes, the black flames of Hell, and the idea of an exclusive Heaven. Monica smiled suddenly, her whole face glowing. She really was beautiful. *Inhumanly so.*

In front of them was the Mirador de San Nicolás and its wonderful views.

"It's perfect," she said, still smiling.

The light was excellent – it had been a good idea bringing her here. The Alhambra and the Generalife on the hill, showered in the golden light of the setting sun, the white peak of the Sierra Nevada in the background, and the indigo sky above it all. Monica looked thoroughly impressed. *As anyone would be*, Miguel thought. Her eyes began to shine once more. He enjoyed watching her expression, like she was a little girl unwrapping Christmas presents.

"Would you like to sit?" Miguel asked, pointing to a white stone bench.

She nodded wordlessly without removing her gaze from the view. Then she turned and walked to the bench; the two of them sat down together.

Upon seeing her so entranced, Miguel began to fantasize about seeing her again in America. A little adventure, perhaps.

Don't be stupid! he told himself. *No one bumps into an acquaintance in a country the size of a continent. I'm going to California, and she's going to... Texas, or wherever.*

Miguel stood then. "The photo?"

"The photo," Monica repeated.

"We'd better take it before we lose the light."

"Of course." Her response was almost inaudible.

Monica opened the back of her backpack while nibbling her lower lip. Removing her camera, she pressed a few buttons and looked through the visor, focusing the lens. Miguel thought he could watch her for hours, never getting tired of her resolute movements, the feminine sensuality you'd find in a Russian army official. But she would be leaving soon. She would disappear, along with her backpack, her cap, and her photo, and so would he.

"I have an idea!" Monica exclaimed. "Get in the photo with me. We'll ask someone to take it for us. I'd like to have something to remember you by."

Miguel stood staring at her for a moment. "The people don't really fit the frame well..." he answered. "I'll take one of just you. If we ask someone else, they'll probably end up leaving our legs out of the shot, or worse, leaving out the Alhambra..." He trailed off as he looked around. He spotted a portly, jolly-looking man and approached him. "Excuse me, would you mind taking a photo of us, with this view in the background?"

"Of course!" the man replied in an Andalusian accent, taking the camera. "Stand over there!"

"He's going to destroy the picture," he muttered to Monica as he sat down beside her. She giggled.

"Alright, son, why don't you hug your girlfriend a little. Otherwise, you'll look like two strangers," the man said, gesticulating wildly.

Miguel was about to correct the impromptu photographer, until he realized his arm was already around Monica's shoulders, while she leaned into him. He supposed the man's instructions had caused his body to move unconsciously before his brain had time to catch up. But he liked it. She didn't smell like that perfume with the French name, like every other girl he knew. Instead, she smelled of something subtle, intimate, slightly salty. Droplets of sweat. The scent had a sharp aftertaste that excited him. Miguel felt his pulse quicken with the click of the camera's shutter.

"Wonderful!" the man said, turning his belly towards them. He returned the camera to Miguel with a wink. Miguel thanked him and wasted no time in moving away from her and giving instructions. "A little to the right… that's it… and… yes! Right there! Don't move." He pressed the shutter button.

The click hit him in the face like a freezing wind. For the first time, through the camera's visor, he looked properly at Monica's shirt. Squared dark blue letters spelled out an acronym on her chest in the shape of an arch. All very normal, except for the acronym itself – SJSU. San José State University. California. His new university.

He approached Monica. "How do you know San José State University?"

"San Ho? I have a research grant there. I work there."

Miguel looked at her, open-mouthed. Then, he smiled. A Boeing 747, he remembered, would soon transport him to California. To her. Behind her, the Alhambra began to darken. But before it disappeared into the night, it shone once more, an intense, fiery gold. Success.

CHAPTER 3

The flight from London to San Francisco had just reached cruising altitude, and with a ping, the light advising the use of seatbelts turned off. Many passengers started to get up and move around, but Walter Castillo didn't move. He watched. He kept quiet, his eyes hidden behind a pair of black sunglasses. He watched Miguel.

The ping seemed to awaken Miguel. He twisted in his seat before looking around, and then behind him. When his gaze neared where Castillo was, he leaned to the left to hide himself behind the seat in front. He watched as Miguel settled in his seat and fell back asleep. The cabin crew went about preparing the little blue carts containing breakfast.

Castillo eyed his own suit, his maroon tie lying over his seatbelt. The gray suit, along with his dark hair, made him look like any another Spanish executive flying from Madrid to London, and then on to San Francisco. He was sure he would fly under the radar. *Almost invisible*, he thought.

An air hostess passed him a breakfast tray, but Castillo didn't move. Instead, he kept his eyes wide open behind his sunglasses as he took in the hostess's dark blue British Airways uniform. She immediately passed a tray to the woman sitting beside him. Anyone, thought Castillo, would think he was asleep, his eyes closed behind his dark glasses. Good. His lips turned up in a smile with the barest of movements. It was easy for him to make others see what he wanted them to see. That was what he was best at. Huffing with pride, Castillo focused once more on the subject while the hostess passed by with the breakfast cart.

Miguel's brown hair was just a little too long for his liking. His sleeping posture caused it to fall over his left shoulder. He looked so… harmless. Castillo couldn't see Miguel's face from that angle, but he clearly remembered the soft, straight lines of his face, his deep-set eyes. He looked like a Romanticist poet. Or perhaps some soulless being.

Defenseless, he thought. *And terrifying.*

But above all, dangerous. Castillo couldn't lose sight of Miguel. He would follow him all the way to San Francisco. He wouldn't rest. This was his mission, and he would see it through just like he had done with every other mission before.

This was what he had left his Hispanic hometown for – distantly, he remembered that very few of his childhood friends ever made it out of Little Havana. But he had, in spite of his father, who had a fondness for rum. Despite no one ever believing in him. This was what he had gotten into Yale for, along with all those rich blonde bimbos, daughters of congressmen and expensive lawyers. This was why he had finished his law degree in three years at the top of his class before being accepted into West Point, among the best of the best. This was why he had been recruited to the CIA as soon as he graduated. This was why the Agency had sent him on this mission. Castillo breathed deeply again, smoothing out his tie as he felt the rush of pride and palpable success, just within his reach, filling his lungs.

There was still much work to be done. It was no longer necessary to feign sleep. He straightened in his seat and went over the report in his head – a result of the inflection in the University of Granada. He had been there, had seen Miguel's ex-girlfriend humiliate herself, crying and begging Miguel to stay. Miguel seemed to be the one who had caused it, through his imagination, through his will. He replayed the memory of Miguel's brown eyes lost in thought, the Romantic poet looking as if he was always just about to kill himself. But those eyes, Castillo thought, also reflected his fury, almost that of a demigod, as he humiliated that young woman. There had been the point of inflection. The quantum leap that the fool had caused went beyond all limits. It had almost been a Midas Effect. Now, they would have to find out for sure if he was the one who had caused it.

Miguel shifted in his seat, and Castillo leaned to the left to conceal himself once more. He looked back after a few seconds. The demigod appeared to have gone back to sleep. He would have to capture Miguel, Castillo told himself, for Gorlov and his scientists, so they could study him. For his mission, and for his country.

CHAPTER 4

Three days after arriving in the United States, Miguel still felt small. He always did in America.

Seven-thirty in the morning. He still had another half-hour to arrive at the university. His first day at San José State University. His grip on the steering wheel tightened. At that moment, he crossed a highway junction with criss-crossed lanes stacked on top of one another. Miguel tried reading the addresses plastered on the various billboards, but didn't recognize any of them. There were too many crossings like that one on Route 101. He was overtaken by an all-terrain vehicle with tires the size of a tractor's, and immediately the feeling of being tiny returned. *What if I've confused miles with kilometers?* he wondered. No, that couldn't be it. It shouldn't take more than an hour to get to San José from San Francisco.

To the left, beyond a thicket, a tent-shaped building appeared. It had rounded edges and was completely white, except for the black roof. It was colossal, a giant in a country of giants. NASA. Miguel had already seen pictures of it on the internet. It was one of the facilities for the NASA Ames Research Center—a hangar, or something like that.

None other than NASA, he thought. *That is a good sign*. It was only twelve miles from NASA Ames to San José, if he remembered correctly. Miguel relaxed his hands on the steering wheel.

Once he crossed the thicket, he took one last look at the hangar through his rear-view mirror. *They must keep special rockets in there. NASA. If only Dani could see this...* Miguel smiled as he remembered how his brother's face lit up when he told him he would be moving so close to the incredible engineers they had both dreamed about as boys.

The hangar disappeared from view, but the memory of Miguel's brother remained. Dani was the last person Miguel had seen in Madrid, before he left. He had visited him to say goodbye and to leave him his yellow Renault Mégane Coupé. *It's like a spaceship!* Dani had said when he took the keys.

Dani adored astronomy. He knew everything about the Space Race: the Sputnik, the Apollo missions, the Moon landing. He loved everything extraterrestrial. Even after the small accident...

Miguel remembered the accident. He and Dani were boys, in Nice, at the playground. Their father took great pains to bring them to Nice every summer to see their grandmother. They spent much more time together there, which, of course, meant that they fought much more there. Dani constantly picked fights with Miguel. They were fighting the day Dani lit a firecracker tied to a plastic rocket. He wanted to send it to Jupiter, he said. Then, the explosion. Dani's bloody ear. It was the type of game that always led Dani to disaster. Miguel saw in his mind's eye the scar on his brother's earlobe.

A blue sign on the highway appeared on the curve of the road. *Interstate 280 North, Downtown San José – Next Exit.*

He was already there. He put Dani's scarred ear out of his mind. *How stupid would it be if I got lost right about now and ended up in Silicon Valley?*

He took the exit to San José according to the sign and circled through the residential area on the south side of campus before entering the university parking lot on 7th Avenue. A simple route. After parking his car and making a short trip through the campus, Miguel arrived at the Department of Systems Engineering. He opened the door at exactly two minutes to eight.

But there was no one there. *It's time to start work, but this place is like a deserted island*, Miguel thought.

Someone cleared their throat behind him. "Good morning."

Miguel recognized the husky voice. It belonged to Professor Darl Branson, Director of the Department of Systems Engineering. All it had taken was a meal together following a conference in Granada for Branson to sign him up for his department in SJSU.

From behind an opening in a screen no bigger than a phone booth, Professor Branson came out holding a mug in his hand. His belly seemed not to fit in the opening. His white beard and long hair made him look like a cross between Santa Claus and a country singer.

"Hey, man!" he exclaimed. "Was it today you were starting? Yes, of course. Do you want some coffee?" Branson brought his mug to his lips, taking a sip. He gestured back towards the opening where he had come out belly-first. "I always need a cup before I start work."

"I don't have a cup," Miguel replied. He moved closer to the opening and looked through the screen. Behind it was a booth.

Branson walked away and entered an office, and Miguel watched as he opened a closet. The professor returned and gave Miguel a white mug with the NASA logo printed on it.

"But… Professor Branson."

"Take it, man! I have lots of 'em. I get them as gifts from the collaborators in the department. Consider it a welcome gift. And call me Darl! Everyone calls me Darl."

Miguel neared the coffee maker and briefly thought how Dani would give anything for a real NASA mug.

While Miguel served himself, Branson told him that he had received that mug from Vladimir Gorlov, a very good friend of his, a professor of Applied Physics at the university. *A very important man.* This Gorlov, it seemed, worked with NASA Ames. He was Russian, apparently, and was a psychiatrist on top of being a physicist and mathematician. And he gave NASA mugs as gifts.

Psychiatrist, mathematician *and* physicist. Miguel thought of Monica as he looked at his mug. *Mathematician and psychologist. She must work in the same department as the Russian. They're all wackos.*

Branson gestured for Miguel to follow him with a movement not unlike that of a cowboy leading a herd of cattle. Their walk was cut short by a short, dark-haired young man entering the department.

"Good morning," the young man said with a thick Indian accent. His bright smile was a sharp contrast to his dark complexion.

"This is Jagdish Lahiri, the computer engineer you'll be working with. He's Indian," Branson explained. "This is Miguel Le Fablec," he told Jagdish. "He's Spanish."

Branson continued walking while they shook hands. At the back of the open space filled with tables and computers, next to the windows that looked onto the campus, were two tables facing each other. Branson pointed them out with his coffee mug, and Miguel smiled when he noticed the tables were bathed in sunlight. One of them was covered with papers, CDs, books and a computer full of yellow notes. Miguel guessed they belonged to Jagdish. When they arrived, the computer engineer picked up a mug from the table and excused himself to go get some coffee, but not before Miguel spotted the words "IBM – Silicon Valley" printed on his mug. *Must be a gift from the professor.* Branson explained that the other table was his.

Miguel neared the table and set his own mug down, looking down at the campus through the window. The view pleased him: students hurrying everywhere under the warm Californian sun. His new workplace.

"The students have just gotten back from spring break," said Branson. Miguel looked at him out of the corner of his eye, but otherwise paid him little attention. "Exams start in a month's time, so I won't be able to give you and Jag much of my time. I'll give you the requirements of the project and we'll see how far you get by summer, okay?" Looking at his watch, he said, "We'll talk later. I have to go to class."

Miguel thanked him as he left. Then, he quite happily observed his NASA mug on the table.

CHAPTER 5

The dark wooden table stood between them in the NASA office. Monica knew the scientist was happy to see her, although his expression betrayed no emotion. The afternoon sun filtering through the window brightened the whole room. *The excessive light of Vladimir's study*, Monica thought, smiling.

"Sit," Gorlov said.

Monica did as she was told, laying the papers she had brought on her lap. She looked down and realized the jeans that now peaked out from behind her white lab coat were the same pair she had been wearing when she met Miguel. Nearly two weeks had passed since that day in Granada. Since then, Monica had compiled much more information about the so-called point of inflection of Miguel's in Spain. Ripple effects, direct interventions… She was even able to analyze some maps of isoinflexor curves, hoping to show them to Vladimir now that she had returned.

"I'll be with you in a moment," Gorlov said without looking at her. He was completely absorbed in something he was reading in a brown file.

Monica said nothing. She knew better than to disturb him while he was concentrating on something. She tightened the double knots on her white and blue sneakers. Looking around, she took a moment to observe the details in the room, the light there. She had missed it during her short stay in Spain. On Gorlov's left hung his framed periodic table of elements. On the other side of the table stood a blackboard on an easel. White chalk dust had collected on the floor. Only Vladimir could continue using such a relic for his writings. It was the same blackboard he had been using when he captured her.

Monica let her eyes wander over the blackboard as the memories came back to her. Back then, she had dressed the same way she did now, only without the white coat, and Vladimir had been her differential geometry professor. One day, he had brought her to his sunny NASA office to impress her with his mathematical achievements. It turned out that she impressed him far more than he did her, when she picked up the chalk and corrected the limits of an integral in one of his equations. Her hands were covered in chalk dust. That was one of the exceedingly rare occasions in which she had seen him without his square glasses. Gorlov had taken them off to see the correction with his own eyes. His student's straight, uniform script, correcting and improving his work, stood out against his own angular hand. Moments like that were what made her his main assistant.

"How was everything in Spain?" Gorlov asked, closing the file with a sudden thud.

Monica flinched. Gorlov's file, held in his bony hands, had the color of old wood. "Oh, you mean the capture report?"

Gorlov showed her the cover. It was indeed the capture report. She could make out Castillo's notes, as well as her own, along with all the information about the preliminary pursuit in Granada. There were also global calculations with data from the satellites and the maps of isoinflexor lines, but even still, she had much more information than that.

"Everything's in order," Monica said.

"Did you interfere with anything?"

"No," she responded quickly. Then she realized Gorlov had finished reading the report, including the report on Miguel's point of inflection. Everything that had happened. She *had* interfered, she knew, and the report showed it. What she didn't understand was why she had lied. She didn't mean to, or want to. "Well, yes," she admitted. Her right leg began to bounce up and down. "Maybe I interfered a little bit. I got too involved. Everything came to a head, and then that woman, the ex-girlfriend... I don't know."

"Monica." Gorlov's tone left little room for argument. His face remained expressionless, but Monica thought she could see some semblance of disappointment in his eyes. "You're the best we have. You could be my successor, the technical director of the Project. In time, I'm sure you'll outdo even myself. Don't ruin it." Monica looked down. "You cannot form a sentimental relationship with the subject of the study. You mustn't, and least of all with this one. He could be a Midas."

Monica chewed on the right side of her bottom lip. Vladimir's words vibrated in his Russian accent, his abrupt consonants only making themselves distinguishable when he got annoyed. Her teacher, her mentor, the one who had pushed her to become the best in the Project. He didn't deserve to be let down. Monica knew it wouldn't do to become emotionally involved with a Midas. She bit down harder. She supposed she must have been blushing, if the heat in her cheeks and ears was anything to go by, like Vladimir had just pulled on them as if she were a spoiled brat. She wasn't like that, she told herself; she was far too practical to do such stupid things. She always had everything under control. Always.

But Ana... What an insufferable woman. Monica told herself she had to act, for the good of the Project. Miguel sat there, indecisive, and that stupid, smeared mess of a woman, drowned in Chanel, only got in the way. Yes, she had slightly amplified Miguel's wishes, but that was all.

She looked into Gorlov's inexpressive, old, gray eyes behind his squared glasses.

"Do I have to follow the approach protocol? I'm completely sure of myself. You don't need to worry about that. But, Vladimir, if you think I should abandon—"

"You contaminated the records."

"Even still, the subject's inflection was very intense. The records can—"

"What about Castillo?" Gorlov asked suddenly.

Monica stopped. The heat from her blush vanished. "Then, can I assume?"

"Yes, continue the capture process. I need you, you know that. What happened with Castillo?"

Monica felt her lips stretch into a smile. Gorlov hated wasting time, and he wasn't about to start now.

"Castillo is a cheater," she said, inhaling slowly. She spent a moment finding the right words, trying to be as clear as possible. What she was about to tell him wouldn't show up on any report. That was why Gorlov had sent Monica to intercept Miguel – to observe the new agent sent by the CIA, the one everyone suspected had been sent to spy on them. She had thought of the mission as yet another proof of trust from Vladimir. No, she would not fail him again, she told herself. Never.

"Castillo has a thousand faces, all of them good," she explained quickly, "but there's one I haven't yet seen: his true one. He's very ambitious, but frustrated too, like the finish line is already upon him. I don't know what it is. His true objective blends in well with pep talks too noble to be believed by anyone other than a boy scout. His smile is perfect. He's the best car salesman I've ever seen."

Gorlov spent a long time gazing at the sunlight coming in through the window. "I think I'd like to meet this man as soon as possible."

Monica laughed. Gorlov didn't.

"You haven't met Castillo?" she asked.

"He and Fred are in Washington. When will you see him again? Miguel, I mean. It's been nearly two weeks since he arrived."

Monica shuffled through her papers, wondering if she had forgotten some data. No, it was all there. She chastised herself for that kind of staging with Vladimir.

"Tomorrow," she replied immediately. "Everything is ready. Jagdish has informed us that Miguel is hoping to see me again. It's already gotten late today, so there's no time. Tomorrow, at lunchtime."

CHAPTER 6

It was nearly lunchtime, and Jagdish had been gone for a while making photocopies. If Jag was eating somewhere else, who would Miguel eat with? He looked towards the back of the department, where his colleagues typed silently. The wait for Jag continued.

Miguel leaned back in his seat as he read on his computer screen an article about virtual interfaces for fighter pilots. It was very detailed, too detailed for Miguel's tastes. The coffee in his NASA mug had already gone cold. He turned to the window, looking down at the San José State University campus. "San Ho," as Monica had called it.

Monica Eveleigh, on his mind once more.

The psychologist and mathematician remained stuck in his head. Miguel tried and failed to return his attention to fighter pilots, to keep Monica at bay. But it was no use. Her words and her gestures from that evening in Granada all came flooding back to him. Her gorgeous hair, like that of an Italian actress, her shining blue eyes scanning the scenery, her half-bitten lips… and the map in the back pocket of her jeans. And of course, she had a nice ass. Why deny it? Round, pert, perfect… although he had no intention of actually saying that to her. *Or maybe I will*, he thought. *Who knows? Maybe one day…*

"There he is," Jagdish said from behind Miguel.

Miguel turned to respond.

And there was Monica.

"Have you already forgotten about me?" she asked.

Miguel opened his mouth, but no words came out. It was her! She wore a short, fitted, orange t-shirt – the neckline showed nothing more than the top of her chest – and a brown knitted cardigan, somewhere between slightly childish and Puritan, that covered her arms. Her t-shirt just barely covered her navel above her jeans. He forced himself to look at her face. It really was her. She had come; she had looked for him.

"I didn't... I..." Miguel managed to stutter out before standing up and approaching her, greeting her with two kisses, one on each cheek.

"How have you been settling in? I see it's going well. You already have your own desk and everything. You live in San Francisco, right?" she asked, the words tumbling out of her. Her eyes shone, her gaze darting all around. Out of the corner of his eye, Miguel spotted Jagdish's blinding smile.

"This is Monica," Miguel explained. "She's the girl I told you about, the one I met in Granada."

"Miguel's told me a lot about you," Jagdish said as he shook Monica's hand.

"Want to have lunch together, Jag?" Miguel asked.

Jag's smile vanished suddenly, as though eating with Miguel no longer fit his plans. "I've already made plans with a co-worker who's just arrived at the university," he said finally. Glancing at his watch, his eyes widened and he yelped, "I'm already late! I'll see you later!" He left sprinting.

Miguel turned to Monica. "Have you eaten?"

***

Minutes later, seated on a bench, Miguel and Monica each held a paper cup and a sandwich from one of the university cafeterias.

The cups and sandwiches, Miguel thought, did away with any sense of magic their reunion could have possibly had. But he didn't really care. There was a cheerfulness in the students all over campus. There always was, by Miguel's estimation, but in that moment, he felt it even more strongly than usual. The campus was full of students collecting money for their various organizations, playing the guitar, swapping notes, lying in the sun, or working on their laptops.

"I like it here," Miguel said. "Look at the students; they never stop moving. When do they study? Don't they go to class?" Monica shrugged, smiling. He pointed towards Tower Hall in the distance with his paper cup. "That's my favorite building. That's exactly how a European imagines an American university: ivy and arched windows." Monica stared at him, still smiling. "There aren't a lot of old buildings here in San Ho. Although… see this tree?" Miguel pointed behind them at the tree that shaded them from the sun. "It's an olive tree. It's almost like being back home, in the south of Spain. And over there are palm trees." He pointed at the towering palm trees with their slim trunks, just beside Tower Hall. "It's like being back home and being on a Hollywood Avenue all at once. I love it. And all that is just decoration. The best part is the people. The other day, when I was moving furniture, a guy I didn't even know – a friend of a friend – let me borrow his station wagon. He plays the concert flute in a symphonic rock band, or something like that. Yes, the people have been the biggest surprise."

"I'm glad you like us," Monica replied. "But I should warn you, not all of us play symphonic rock." She pretended to play the flute and somehow her lips seemed more alluring to Miguel than they had in Granada. He breathed deeply to calm the excitement Monica brought him. "And what about your grant?" she asked, taking a sip from her paper cup. She grimaced as she swallowed – she mustn't have liked the coffee, or the cup, or both – but to Miguel, she looked as if she had pursed her lips for a kiss.

"I'm working with Jag on a virtual interface prototype for combat missions. It's very interesting. It'll take us at least two years."

"Two years! That's quite a grant."

"It is." Miguel couldn't tear his gaze away from her mouth. Monica looked away, nibbling the right side of her lower lip. "Have you been keeping up with your photography?" he asked.

"What?" Monica's confused frown produced a wrinkle just above her right eyebrow.

"You know, the reflex camera. Do you use it often?"

The wrinkle on Monica's forehead remained for a few more seconds, as if she didn't know what a reflex camera even was, until a sudden look of realization crossed her face. "Oh! That. Yes, I do use it. How are things in San Francisco?"

Her sudden change of conversation topic was slightly disconcerting. Miguel shifted on the bench, shooting a quick glance at the olive tree. "I followed your advice and moved there. You were right, San José is far too quiet. You can get to know more people in San Francisco."

"Have you met many people?"

Miguel smiled. In reality, he barely knew anyone in San Francisco. He took a short sip of coffee. Monica and her questions – always so direct, so sharp and clever. "I know practically nobody, aside from my housemates."

She laughed. "I guessed as much."

"I share what's supposed to be a Victorian house with a Japanese girl and a girl from Arkansas. It's on one of those streets with the huge, curved slopes."

"Typical."

"My window has a perfect view of the bay. Right on Russian Hill…"

"Russian Hill? Which street?"

"Union Street, near the crossing on Leavenworth. Why?"

"Goodness, you must be following me! I can't believe it. You've come all the way from the other side of the world to work in the exact same university as me and to live in the exact same place I do."

"You live on…?"

"Leavenworth and Lombard, on the same side as you. We can come to work together."

The silence that followed dragged on for a few interminable seconds. *She gets more direct all the time*, Miguel thought.

"Well, if you want to, that is," she added. "Sorry, I didn't mean to put you in a difficult position. We hardly know each other, after all."

Monica was what interested Miguel most in that country of giant things. Two hours a day in the car with her—he couldn't have thought of a better idea himself. Taking another sip of his coffee, Miguel took a moment to just look at her. He loved Monica´s direct questions, her point-blank proposals. But what he loved even more were her round, parted lips that she so often nibbled.

The rough surface of the paper cup on his lips broke Miguel from his fantasy. He made a face, hoping Monica wouldn't interpret it as a "no."

"Yes!" he said immediately, before finishing the contents of that stupid cup with one big swallow.

CHAPTER 7

Gorlov sipped his coffee, trying to better process what he was reading. Castillo's report was too categorical. He didn't like it. Turning a page, he read on. The CIA agent was new to the Project, an amateur, but he already seemed so sure of his conclusions, as if he had been part of the investigation since the days in Leningrad. Finally, Gorlov closed the earth-colored file and stared at it in his thin hands. Monica had interfered with the details. Castillo had written a report that would have fit better in a sensationalist newspaper. Every piece of information in that file was contaminated. This wasn't going well. They were too careless. Were they not aware of what they were working on? Clearly, they weren't.

To make matters worse, the CIA had started getting involved. Gorlov straightened in his seat, set his mug down on the round meeting table in front of him, and looked at Frederick Windhorst.

"Fred," he said, "I was told there were problems in Washington."

Fred flipped through various pages filled with numbers, seemingly comparing them – Gorlov supposed they were costs, or something similar. He responded without looking up. "The usual. A couple of phone calls, a meeting.... Everything worked itself out." Fred smiled. His Anglo-Saxon features compressed with the action, his eyes almost disappearing between cavernous wrinkles.

"All under control," he added, a decisive nod serving as affirmation, before he dived back into his papers.

All under control? Gorlov pondered, watching Fred. He still saw in him the CIA agent sent to the other side of the Iron Curtain to help him escape. That was more than thirty years ago. Fred had always protected him, like an older brother.

Gorlov found himself staring at Fred's hands. The pages between his thick, strong, soft fingers looked like Bible pages. His calm expression. Ever since he had arrived in the United States, Gorlov recalled, the CIA agent had shared everything with him: his life, his home, his family. Fred's father, the old Reverend Windhorst, came to mind. *One day, you'll find God in one of those test tubes*, the reverend had said to him once, his smile cavernous like his son's. Gorlov remembered the late-night chats he had with the reverend about religion over a bottle of old whiskey, back when the reverend's health had been better, when he and Fred had visited him for Thanksgiving. A good man from Illinois. Frederick Windhorst had inherited the look of a colossus, an almost naïve goodness, as well as the beliefs of his father. What Gorlov couldn't understand was why someone with such strong moral convictions as Fred had worked for the CIA for so long. The CIA was as full of dirty tricks as every other intelligence service in every other country. As a young man, it had made sense, but now…. Fred turned a page over and scribbled something on it.

Maybe he's held out all these years because his only mission is to protect me and my project, Gorlov wondered. *And there's no dirty trick here. For now.* Gorlov left the file on the table, leaning his hand on it. "The CIA is starting to interfere in the Project, right?"

Fred immediately looked up from his papers. "If you're talking about Washington, it was necessary. But the intervention was minimal, I assure you."

"It's about Walter Castillo."

Fred's gaze evaded Gorlov's. He breathed deeply, his enormous, square chest, like that of a war hero from a Soviet monument, rose and fell like the cresting of a wave. "Yes. I know about Walter," Fred responded. "I think right now, we need him. I don't like him either, but that's the way it is." He finally looked at the scientist and showed him his papers. "Budgets, Vladimir."

Gorlov did not respond, and neither did he take the papers.

"Without Walter, I believe Washington would have brought us problems," Fred continued. "These projects aren't easily financed, you know. You need a direct line to the upper echelons of society, and that takes months. If it weren't for Walter and his contacts, we wouldn't have been able to do it in two weeks. We might have even had serious problems to follow up on." Fred pressed his lips together in a thin line and began to breathe slowly again, his large chest heaving. "But everything is in order now. Thanks to Walter, we can continue with our original plan, with the whole team, with the facilities and, most importantly" – a fat finger pointed at Gorlov's coffee mug – "with NASA as our cover."

Gorlov observed the mug and the space agency's red and blue logo, identical to the one Miguel had received. Fred was right. They needed all of it to continue the Project.

"Washington is a terrible place, you know that," Fred insisted. "Maybe I'm getting old…"

"We're both getting old," Gorlov said. The two men looked at one another. "Maybe this is starting to become too much for us."

"But we're so close to a Midas…"

"A Midas is a very dangerous thing, Fred. If the CIA tries to get involved, or if your agent gets it wrong, or if he does something we can't control…"

"I assure you, Walter is under my control."

Gorlov shook his head slowly. The fleeting memory of the blue, unsolved equations of the Midas Paradox flickered across his mind. It all spoke of danger yet to come. Looking at Fred, he spoke quietly. "A true Midas can destroy the world if they want. Nothing is under control, and you know it. Castillo is just another liability."

A knock at the door prompted Gorlov to quickly hide the brown file in his suitcase on the desk.

"It must be Walter," Fred said.

"Come in!" Gorlov called, closing his briefcase.

The door opened, and a serious-looking man in a suit entered the office. He looked like a Wall Street executive, barging in with military force, looking straight at Gorlov on the left at the opposite end of the room. His back was slightly turned and his shoes shone like black porcelain. Upon seeing the desk clear, he turned and smiled at the other two men before approaching the round meeting table.

"This is Agent Walter Castillo," Fred explained.

"Welcome to NASA," the scientist replied, standing and offering his hand.

"Professor Gorlov." Castillo stretched out his own hand in turn.

That hand was too limp for Gorlov's liking, too lifeless—so out of place for someone with such an aggressive presence. Confusing. That was it: Castillo confused him.

***

Castillo didn't like it when people grabbed his hand too much, least of all with such bony fingers. He didn't like the look of the Russian – everything about him was disagreeable to the senses, from his strange-looking, scrawny face to his outdated glasses. He didn't like the way the Russian looked at him either.

Gorlov invited him to sit and took out a brown file from his briefcase. He noticed the file contained the data he had collected from tracking. It contained his report. "Have you read it?" he asked immediately. Seated directly opposite Gorlov and Fred, Castillo felt like he was about to be examined. In reality, he knew that the document was his first real contact with the Project, his first test. He knew he had to win the confidence of the scientist, the real boss. That report, in all certainty, was the first step.

"Very alarming, without a doubt, but ambiguous," Gorlov said, opening the file. "We'll have to carry out more tests."

The words turned Castillo's stomach to ice. He clenched his jaw and his abdomen. Where was his report ambiguous? He had been very explicit, conclusive. Castillo silently watched Gorlov, but the damn Russian didn't appear to feel anything, reading the report as if it were the information pamphlet from a bottle of aspirin. Gorlov skimmed over it unimpressed, like he was reading something painfully obvious and mind-numbingly boring.

"I would say it's quite clear," Castillo objected, raising his chin. "Miguel Le Fablec's location coincides with the geographical co-ordinates and position of every registered point of inflection we've found since we started following him. I was there with him, with a sensor in my hands – it's all there in the report." Gorlov flipped through a few pages. "And I saw his face in Granada, when the inflection close to a Midas Effect occurred. I saw the look in his eyes. *He* produced the inflection in the university, when he exerted his powers on his ex-girlfriend." Castillo lowered his voice before continuing. "And he did it purely through the power of his imagination. I suggest we intercept him as soon as possible."

Gorlov breathed heavily before lifting his gaze from the report, looking right at Castillo. The massive lenses were like magnifying glasses, capable of seeing into every dark corner of Castillo's mind.

Gorlov turned to Fred. "See what I mean? This is just going to complicate things."

"Not necessarily, Vladimir."

"Well, I think it will. He doesn't know all the details, or the protocols." His Russian accent sharpened; he must have been offended. His face betrayed no trace of anger, or any other emotion for that matter.

"I assure you he is capable," said Fred. "I trained him myself."

"Then you didn't train him enough. What he proposes is beyond all logic."

Castillo was not about to allow this discussion to continue, with the two men talking about him without talking *to* him, as though he were a wayward child whose punishment had to be decided. He straightened and asked, "May I ask what's going on?" His own dry tone of voice made him flinch – picking a fight was not his objective. "Please," he added in a softer voice.

"Look, Agent Castillo," said Gorlov, "I respect you, and I don't want you to take this personally, but I didn't want you to join the team. Or rather, I didn't want anyone else to join the team. At least, not someone I didn't know and hadn't trained personally."

Walter Castillo was well aware that, whatever the Russian wanted, he had no decision in the matter. All three of them knew that. He adjusted the knot of his tie and straightened out his suit. There was nothing else to say.

"Vladimir," Fred said, "Walter is a very experienced agent. I trained him as hard as we trained everyone else. Alright, maybe he doesn't see every shade to every nuance, but he is more than ready to become part of the team. You have my word on that." Frederick Windhorst stared down at his own thick fingers. "Besides, you know I don't like it, but I must remind you that the CIA has demanded that we have another agent of theirs in our ranks."

Exactly, Castillo thought. Gorlov exhaled loudly, keeping his stony gaze on the agent. *I won't argue with you. We're not having it out here. Not now*. Castillo put effort into keeping his expression friendly, trying to smile without actually smiling.

"Dr. Gorlov, I think we all understand that the CIA doesn't want Fred alone in this Project. It was inevitable that someone from the agency would join your team sooner or later – that much is clear." He took a breath. "For my part, given the situation, the only thing I can offer is my experience and commitment to learn everything I need to." Silence. "And correct my mistakes, of course, whatever they may be. I believe that is the only problem we can solve right now, the only thing that matters."

Another silence. Castillo liked silence. He was better with silence than any other form of communication. He went on after a few seconds. "And what is this nuance I haven't understood that has caused this argument?" Leaning back in his chair, he splayed his hands over the dark wood of the table in front of him. There, now he had said everything he wanted to say. The silence returned as Gorlov watched him.

"Alright." The scientist appeared to have finally relaxed. His face was still expressionless, but the sharp Russian accent had almost disappeared. Castillo supposed he had managed to tame the beast.

"Let's analyze the situation." Gorlov began his explanation. "All the data points to Miguel Le Fablec being a quantum inflexor. He also appears to be a Midas-type inflexor – a Midas Effect. As you should already be aware, Agent Castillo, the Midas Effect is nothing more than a hypothetical theory, supported by mathematics and physics that have never before been tested since we began studying inflexors." Castillo nodded slowly. "The fact is that we don't know exactly what his potential is, and that makes him dangerous. We're facing a danger whose risks we are completely blind to. Prudence – and *that's* the nuance – would recommend that we move very carefully. If we were to intercept the subject, as you've suggested, we could panic him. And he's too powerful for us to control him. It would be like trying to shackle King Kong with a silk ribbon. His abilities, no doubt a mystery even to himself, could kick off at any time. Who knows what would happen then. He could strike every one of us down by simply wishing it. He could destroy all of humanity."

Castillo nodded again while Gorlov continued. "We must be clever. Interception is not an option, for now. What we must do is befriend him, gain his trust, get him close to our Project, and then study and control him. Break in King Kong."

Gain his trust... and then control him. Castillo turned the phrase over in his mind. That was, in essence, his entire mission. In most respects, he agreed with the Russian, although his mission was more difficult. He not only had to gain Miguel's trust, but also that of everyone around him, including those in the white coats. And he had to control them, King Kong and his handlers, as well as those who protected the handlers. Castillo turned to look at Fred, who was nodding along vigorously to Gorlov's explanation. He seemed inoffensive enough.

"There's more," Gorlov said. "We have to verify that it was indeed he who brought about the inflection. That was the ambiguous aspect of the report." He removed from the file a folded piece of paper and extended it to Castillo. Unfolded, it took up nearly the entire desk. The map of isoinflexor lines looked like a meteorological chart. He remembered that Fred had once told him what the lines were, a very basic explanation, not enough to interpret the map. The only reason Castillo had included it in the report was because Fred had told him to.

"Agent Castillo," Gorlov began, "I do not doubt the efficacy of your work, or the quality of the data you recorded with the sensor in Granada. But I know the precision of our measuring equipment. I designed them. And I can tell you with certainty that there is only one reasonable conclusion to be taken from this data."

"I don't understand."

"Did you see the recordings from the global detectors?"

Castillo looked from the scientist to the map. "The map of isoinflexors."

"The map is just a static photograph. The recordings are underneath, in the global monitoring stations. Do you know what that is?"

Castillo looked at Fred, who said nothing, before looking back at Gorlov's blank face. That goddamn Russian was starting to make him uncomfortable. Castillo cleared his throat and did his best to smooth his own expression.

"The satellites collect information, send it here to be processed, and then the isoinflexor lines are interpreted and shown on screens at the global monitoring stations, in the level -4 basement. From there, inflexors all over the world can be monitored."

Gorlov remained silent. It was a test, Castillo told himself, surely it was. And he had just responded like a child who had learned something off by heart without really understanding it.

"These lines," Castillo added, "represent the planet's inflexor activity." He had nothing else to say about the damn map and its hundreds of round, concentric lines that eluded all understanding.

"On level -4," Gorlov said, "we maintain global control of quantum inflection, or points of inflection. And yet, we use data from the satellites."

"Satellites with quantum sensors," Castillo replied, trying to improve the poor image of himself he was putting forward. He saw Fred shake his head out of the corner of his eye.

"They're not sensors," replied Gorlov. "The most powerful quantum sensors only cover a maximum area of three hundred kilometers, a little less than two hundred miles. The technology we use below, on level -4, is different. We use calculus algorithms to predict georeferenced data all over the world. The satellites don't have sensors. They're just simple communication satellites. Spy satellites."

Castillo shifted in his seat. Fred hadn't told him they were spy satellites, but he would just have to let the Russian's arrogance go. He didn't know all the details yet.

"Spy satellites, of course," he said, forcing himself to hide his surprise.

"What we do is predict states of reality and monitor how they change under the influence of quantum inflection. We steal data from communication satellites, meteorological satellites, scientific satellites – anything with data we might consider useful. Then we process the data, whether it's economic information, air traffic reports, meteorological data, solar radiation… all of it. We calculate millions of variables that can be predicted both on our planet and in space. The most advanced mathematical techniques in the world to predict the future: data mining, genetic algorithms, fuzzy logic…"

Castillo found himself nodding along to the scientist's explanations.

"It's simple," Gorlov went on. "When the inflexor acts, the world changes. We predict the world and the inflexor changes it. The isoinflexor lines represent changes in every corner of the world." He jabbed the map sharply with his index finger, right above Granada, where the lines seemed to pile on top of one another. "This map shows the world that Miguel Le Fablec changed during his point of inflection in the university cafeteria."

Really, Castillo thought, *the map only shows a small portion of the south of Spain*. In reality, Miguel had changed very little. "It hasn't changed very much," Castillo said.

"No, not much," Gorlov agreed, making a circular gesture with his hand that encompassed the entire map. The lines, concentrating on Granada, became more dispersed a few miles away. "A point of inflection with no notable consequences. Powerful, but not a Midas Effect."

"But I caught a point of inflection on my sensor that was off the charts—"

"This is much more precise," Gorlov said, cutting him off. "We're talking about a precision in the estimation of temporal variables of 385 milliseconds with a probability of 99.9%, up to four minutes. We can predict the future!" He then punched the map with his gnarled knuckles before taking up his coffee again. Castillo watched him silently. The Russian was good, he decided. Gorlov would wear him out with a tidal wave of mathematical details if he continued asking. He seemed to have everything under control. Castillo needed him on his team.

“If we’re accurate,” Gorlov went on, “then, according to the map, we could easily say that any inflexor within a two-kilometer radius of the University of Granada’s engineering school could have generated the quantum disturbances picked up on your sensor. You could have generated them yourself.”

“None of the things that happen to quantum inflexors have ever happened to me, so I highly doubt that I’m one of them,” Castillo replied, smiling at Fred, whose answering smile creased his entire face. “Besides, there are plenty of other signs that point to Miguel Le Fablec.”

“Of course there are; everything points to Le Fablec,” said Gorlov. Castillo’s smile widened. They were both finally in agreement about something. “But we must be cautious in order to obtain conclusive evidence, without any disturbances,” Gorlov added. “I should also mention, in this case, that there was an external interference.”

Castillo froze. “How?”

“Dr. Monica Eveleigh,” Gorlov said. “As you know, she’s a catalyst inflexor, capable of amplifying the abilities of others. She unintentionally amplified the effects of Miguel Le Fablec’s supposed point of inflection in Granada.”

“Monica?” Fred asked.

“Nothing decisive,” Gorlov explained. He retrieved a pen from the upper pocket of his white coat and began to disassemble it as he spoke. “She let herself get swept up in the moment. She wanted to bring the subject here as soon as possible, for the Project, and ended up slightly amplifying Miguel’s desire to humiliate his ex-girlfriend. Ana was the final hurdle for his trip to the United States.”

“Monica is usually much colder,” Fred wondered aloud, but Gorlov’s look closed his mouth.

From his seat under the microscope, Castillo observed the two of them in silence. He couldn't trust them. He had to gain their confidence, but there was no way he could trust those two dinosaurs. Monica's intervention in Granada was unacceptable. Gorlov should have taken her off the mission as soon as he found out. That stuck-up scientist was the Russian's favorite, and she would probably succeed him in the Project, according to what Fred had told him. Maybe that's why she had been kept on. Castillo briefly touched the bulge of his phone in his pocket. "Dr. Eveleigh should have been more careful," he said. Softening his tone, he added, "Although we all trust her professionalism."

Gorlov took a sip from his mug without moving his gaze, framed by those outdated glasses, from Castillo. *He's still x-raying me*, he thought, but none of it would do the Russian any good.

"For my part," Castillo continued, "I accept your criticisms, Professor Gorlov. My next report will be better." He stood up. "If we're all finished here, I have some matters to attend to."

"Of course," Gorlov answered.

Castillo smiled again – his Bible salesman smile, he called it – and left the office. Gorlov's secretaries watched him wordlessly, and he smiled at them too, quickening his pace. The second he left the building, his phone was ringing at his ear. "Agent Roth?" Castillo asked. "All good in Hampton? Good. Leave someone in charge there, and bring a team. Yeah, I need you in San José."

CHAPTER 8

The San José State University was almost empty. The campus was without its students, and Miguel's department was nearly deserted. Miguel was looking at his computer screen, his chin low and his eyes strained painfully. God had punished him by making him responsible for the mistake that now seemed to shine on the screen.

If there's one thing we have too much of in this world, it's religion, he had said to Monica earlier that day when they were in the car on their way to the university. *God is a great set-up for the privileged few to live well at the cost of everyone else.*

And now, God had punished him for saying that. That had to be it. He supposed that his ideas, his reasonable arguments, were not what a Roman Catholic wanted to hear. Monica was devout – if she wasn't, they would have never discussed religion in the first place, of course. She had turned her head away when he said that, staring out the window and refusing to listen or speak to him any longer. Miguel guessed he shouldn't have condemned the Church at all. The conversation left him with a sour aftertaste that had stuck with him all day.

He looked once more at the erroneous mathematical algorithm onscreen. *Concentration*, he told himself.

It had been a bad day, a bad week. It was Friday evening, and all his work would have to go in the trash. But what did God have to do with any of it? Monica. He was her Lord, after all. Monica.

He couldn't concentrate, that was it, that was the problem. She was always there, in the back of his mind. In his equations, inside his books, in the gaps of his keyboard. She had made a home for herself in each of his thoughts. If it wasn't religion, it was how her Italian-actress hair moved, her tight shirt, her neck, her eyes, her chewed bottom lip, the way she moved... *her ass*. Miguel looked over his desk, covered in disorganized pages filled with formulae and corrections. And the algorithm he had wrongly specified, which he had given to Jagdish. That was what had made them waste the whole day. The incorrect algorithm seemed to blink at him now from the screen, as if it was trying to record itself onto his retinas so he could remember it clearly for the entire weekend.

And all for a goody two-shoes Catholic, for the love of Christ! *From the parish of Saint Thomas*, she had informed him. *Saint Stephen's Episcopal School* – in the name of God! – *in Houston, Texas*. She had been a catechist for a time with Father O'Brien, an ancient man and close friend of the family who sang mass in Latin. Priests. The last thing he needed to argue with her about on the way to work was cassocks. A perfect plan to ruin the whole day. By Divine Grace. The mistake of the month continued blinking onscreen.

Looking to one side, Miguel saw that every other desk was empty. Only he and Jagdish remained in the Department of Systems Engineering. Jag was gathering up his belongings, sighing.

Maybe each of us should commute alone, he thought. *If we really are that different, we should just keep to ourselves. I don't understand her, and she doesn't understand me.*

"All good?" came Monica's voice from the doorway. "It's late, almost eight o'clock." Her eyebrows were raised, and her flat smile told Miguel that she already knew things weren't going well.

Miguel smiled as soon as he saw her. He hadn't meant to, but he did. Her dark, wavy hair fell loose over her too-tight olive-green shirt. Her tiny navel seemed to wink mischievously at him.

"Well," he started, trying to appear calm and unworried, to pretend that he had no problems. But it just made him feel juvenile, and he let the pretense go. "We didn't make any progress today," he confessed. "The whole day was wasted on a stupid mistake. *My* mistake."

Jag looked over at him while he turned off his computer, and then at Monica. "Take good care of him this weekend for me," he said.

Did Jag think they were going to spend the weekend together? Yes, he had just heard it. Miguel smiled again – he liked that idea. Jag smiled too, his perfect teeth gleaming.

"Come on, Miguel, stop worrying about it. We'll start again on Monday. Have a good one." With that, Jag was gone.

Miguel waved goodbye but said nothing. Looking at the error again, he shook his head. He pushed back the hair that had fallen into his face and turned to look at Monica. *Have a good one*. Jag's words reverberated in his head.

"Let's go back to San Francisco," said Miguel. "You must be tired."

"Why don't we go get dinner in San José?" Monica asked. "I know a nice restaurant near here that you'll like."

Miguel turned to face the screen again – not to examine his mistake this time, but to bite down on his lips so they wouldn't split into a huge smile. A date, with the goody two-shoes in the olive-green shirt! He wouldn't talk to her about priests again, of course. Not tonight. The algorithm looked like it wanted to blink again.

"We can relax and forget about work," Monica insisted.

Miguel turned off his computer.

***

All thoughts of work left him. Almost hypnotized, he rarely took his eyes off her. Her Italian-actress hair, her lips that she so often nibbled on… he could have sworn that even her eyes shone more than usual.

Sometimes, he looked down at the little golden cross around her neck. The shimmers on her collarbone seemed to call to him like Morse code. For an instant, Miguel was captivated by the shadow that fell in the gap between her breasts. He could just make out the edge of black lace. Perfect. His gaze returned to her lips. They seemed to want him to suddenly kiss her.

Monica kept her eyes on him, too. Miguel was certain of it. She watched him with a look of… desire, perhaps? The goody two-shoes in the olive-green shirt. They barely tasted the food placed in front of them.

Miguel watched as Monica placed her cutlery over her untouched *magret de canard* with oysters and pineapple. She looked at him with slightly parted lips, and he felt a jolt of electricity in his stomach.

Now. At that moment, the waiter came to take their plates and Miguel had to move his hand away, the hand that had almost touched Monica's. He felt like a soldier forced to retreat, cursing the waiter and his triangular plates. Monica never looked away.

A moment later, the *goddamn waiter* set their desserts down in front of them. Miguel held himself back, observing his slice of… whatever it was, his lips pressed into a line. Monica had already started her chocolate cake, and Miguel spotted a tiny piece of it caught on her lip. She began biting the right side of her lower lip again, like she always did, as if she could feel the chocolate on her lip and wanted to lick it away. But Miguel noticed how she couldn't quite get at it; it was just a little bit too high. The bite on her lip made her appear thoughtful, or perhaps excited. *Excited!* Miguel decided, feeling an urge to lick the chocolate away himself, his stomach tightening. Monica looked up at him then, and Miguel stopped breathing.

"Did you know that NASA—?"

"You have chocolate on your lip." Miguel's right hand reached out and he wiped her lip with his thumb in a swift movement. He watched Monica's blue eyes follow his thumb.

Miguel sucked the chocolate off his thumb. It tasted like her, like her lips. Monica froze open-mouthed, her lips forming a tiny O.

And Miguel brought himself closer to the O, in a chaotic kiss that tasted like chocolate. Instantly he felt a convulsion in what he called the middle of hyperspace, a place located somewhere between his stomach and the nape of his neck. He was crazy about Monica. There was no doubt.

The ride home to San Francisco felt like it happened in hyperspace, or something similar. Miguel teleported himself into the city, with just enough awareness to keep his car in the right lane on the freeway.

***

Monica watched Miguel's smiling face, as if the traffic signs were somehow funny to him. She gently placed a finger on his lips when he tried to speak, but he just kissed her finger, which excited her all the more.

She wanted him. And he wanted her too.

Miguel's desire! she remembered quickly.

Monica felt a pinch in her stomach. Miguel could be a Midas. He could be capable of making her fall madly in love with him just by wishing it. He could be doing it right now – dominating her will because he wanted to, just like he had done when he wanted to humiliate his ex-girlfriend.

Monica always followed the rules. But now, she had a mission she couldn't complete, rules she would have to break... simply because Miguel had kissed her.

Monica looked at him again, feeling like a marionette; she imagined an invisible string forcing her to turn her head at that moment. His stupid smile remained in place. *I can trust him*, she told herself, despite the fear twisting her stomach. Miguel flicked back a lock of hair with a sudden shake of his head, and Monica felt a shiver run over her skin, all the way down to her knees. What would sex with a Midas be like? Would he dominate her, overpower her body and mind? Her breathing sped up. She forbade herself from thinking about the Midas Effect. She forbade herself from thinking about anything other than the hot sensation in her chest, below her stomach, in her thighs.

Wait! Miguel's apartment is full of cameras, microphones, sensors!

"Let's go to my place," Monica said.

Minutes later, Miguel parked the car in front of her apartment complex. By the time they got out, Monica's mind was already filled with images of Miguel licking chocolate off her entire body. The almost electric shiver was now concentrated between her legs.

They entered the building with the resolve of an army searching for spoils of war, racing up the stairs. As soon as they were inside Monica's apartment, they started stripping. There was no speaking, just the same urgent chaos with which they had kissed in the restaurant.

Miguel froze when Monica's tiny black thong slid down her legs. He seemed to enjoy taking in her naked body, looking at her while Monica smiled and bit her lip. The gesture must have set him off, because Miguel suddenly took her in his arms and kissed her again.

Monica instantly felt her entire body begin to heat up. Between her legs, her breasts – everywhere Miguel touched her felt hot. And he wouldn't stop touching her everywhere – it was like he couldn't stop himself from grabbing and caressing her. It was all sweet torture for Monica. Her nipples hardened almost painfully when Miguel rubbed them, kissing and biting her neck and ears.

When Miguel sucked on one of her nipples, Monica felt a violent spark run through her that made her convulse out of his reach. Her eyes slowly ran over him – his chest heaving with labored breaths, his hard penis. *If this is what a Midas can do*, Monica thought, *I'll try it all the way to the end.* She leapt at him, kissing him forcefully, which seemed to excite him even more. He held her tight, as if he wanted to squeeze her. She felt his fingers grabbing at her ass, and she began licking at his neck, his chest, his arms. Miguel breathed heavily again, like there wasn't enough air in the room for the two of them. Monica closed her eyes, listening to his breathing. The sound aroused her; everything did. She licked his nipples before looking up at him. His back was arched and his hair had fallen back – she loved it, loved seeing his hair move like that of a barbarian. Then Monica picked up his smoky scent, like thick honey and old oak, like Miguel. This wasn't the first time she noticed it – she had picked up on it long before – but now she was surrounded by it as it overpowered all other scents in the room. She breathed in the honey and oak deeply, feeling her own wetness burn the inside of her thighs. Monica kissed and licked at his legs, feeling the same electric sensation from before in her hair, still enveloped in Miguel's scent. She found herself lying back against the rough fabric of her maroon sofa, unsure of how they got there.

Monica's sporadic breaths wracked through her chest several times before Miguel kneeled in front of her. Then, she looked at his penis again as a wild feeling overcame her. She wanted him, wanted to kiss him and lick him and have him all to herself. After a few seconds, she straightened and climbed over him. Kissing him fiercely, she lay back against the sofa once more.

Miguel lay on top of her, trying to cover her completely. He pushed into her as he kissed her. Monica's back arched, and she breathed him in until her lungs couldn't expand any more. The sofa's rough texture itched against her back. Reality came flooding back to her in a sharp, painful jolt in the middle of her lascivious daydream. It told her that this was the real thing, sex with a Midas, the most powerful man in the world. The thought aroused her to the point where she felt even her blood pressure drop.

Miguel and Monica spent the rest of the weekend together, never separating more than a few feet. They slept little and ate less, never leaving the apartment, far away from their schedules. What little rationality the two had left disappeared for those two days. Monica didn't want to think; she only wanted Miguel. She didn't want to worry about anything else, and neither did she want to face her fears. No, she wouldn't do it until after the weekend. Then she'd reconsider, maybe. Her decision was made. After the weekend.

CHAPTER 9

The weekend was nearly over. Monica caressed the dry, rough covering of her maroon living room sofa, and she began to come back to reality. Her life – monotonous, full of fear, responsibility, and judgment – remained stuck in her thoughts with the same stubbornness as that Sunday's sunset.

She drew her hand back as though the fabric had given her an electric shock. Touching her neck, she could feel her pulse beneath her skin, and reality faded away. Through the window, purple petunias swayed gently in the breeze. She had flowerpots underneath the windowpane—a custom Monica had inherited from her mother. *Something Mediterranean*, Mamma said. She felt a slight dizziness seeing the flowers move as if they were on a boat. Then she remembered – for the past two days, she had barely eaten. Deciding not to move from the sofa, from her little nest between the rough sofa and Miguel's body, she closed her eyes and let herself drift along a light tiredness, as refreshing as the morning breeze drifting in through the window.

Just then, she felt Miguel moving a finger through a wave in her hair. She felt it dig into her scalp, almost massaging it. The sensation made her fall deeper into sleep. A memory came to mind of her mother brushing and pulling her hair before school.

Like an empress, Mamma said one day after brushing her hair. It was the first time Monica had prepared breakfast for the whole family. She couldn't have been more than ten years old. Mamma smiled so proudly and spoke so softly, it didn't even sound like her voice; she always used a much more severe tone, as though she were constantly giving military commands.

But that day, she had just finished tying Monica's hair up in a high ponytail, with lots of ringlets coming down around her face. She gave Monica a kiss once her hair was done.

Like an empress. The Lord will reward you for being so early-rising, so diligent and obedient, Mamma had added, before going on to talk about good children going to Heaven, about little angels and things like that, all the way to the wooden front door of Sacred Heart College.

Mamma, a strong personality, Mediterranean. *Angela Eveleigh. Formerly Angela Graziano, Graziano of Naples*, she used to say, to state her origins clearly. She always said it with pride, even though she knew fewer than a dozen words in her grandparents' language and had only set foot in Italy once, to hear Papa give mass in Saint Peter's Square. Very Catholic, very devout, just like the rest of the family, who all had their own gold crucifixes. Saint Gemma guarded her childhood bedroom. All was harmonious and blessed by God in that house… Until the day the problems started – Patrizia and Mamma, and their fights.

Patrizia was fourteen and Monica was twelve. From that moment onwards, even the breakfast she prepared was enough to set off an argument, like enormous boulders of hate flung from a catapult. *You could try being more like your sister; she always gets her chores done early and makes breakfast for the whole family,* Mamma said. *My sister is perfect, like God, infallible…* Patrizia replied. *I won't allow you to blaspheme in this house!*

Monica felt a shiver run across her shoulders, as if a centipede was crawling along her back.

She truly hated those memories. The fights between Mamma and Patrizia. The two of them facing off, sometimes Monica too, and Papa – everyone except Paul, who just cried.

Paul was now studying with the Jesuits. He had always been the most impressionable and Mamma always hoped he would be ordained. Monica herself had always gotten along well with the Church too, but she didn't have the same vocation as her brother. And Patrizia… in the end, among many other things that infuriated Mamma, Patrizia was never able to stand the "crows in cassocks" as she called them. She wasn't *bad*, Monica was sure of it, but she couldn't bear priests. Or maybe she just couldn't bear Mamma. It didn't really matter. Patrizia went to New York, and she and Mamma hadn't spoken since. One thing was certain: religion had driven them part.

Monica lowered her hand from her neck and touched her small gold crucifix. It felt cold, metallic, absent, as if all that remained was her skin and an imperceptible piece of metal. Turning her head slightly, she opened her eyes and stared at Miguel's fingers running through her hair. Upon seeing his hand, the feeling of insects on her back, which had persisted somewhat, immediately disappeared. Completely.

It was incredible, the effect Miguel had on her. Miguel was a radical, anti-religious non-believer, like Patrizia. Patrizia sent centipedes across the nape of her neck, and Miguel made them go away.

She remembered how her time with Miguel had gone on Friday morning when they discussed religion. He had also brought up the "crows in cassocks," or something like that. At the end of that very day, they were naked on her maroon sofa. But Monica recalled how furious she felt that morning. *God is a great set-up for the privileged few to live well at the cost of everyone else*, he said. *No offense*, he added, as if it wasn't already offensive to call Catholics simple-minded, gullible suckers used by the Church to line their pockets. The typical self-satisfying ideas of an atheist. Miguel seemed liberated having spat out his words, scraping his palms. Monica had tried to make a meek defense of the Church, but Miguel started talking about multiple "Churches" and multiple "true gods" that "confirmed the believers' error." Typical atheist talk.

She and Miguel had managed to get over that morning's argument – according to Miguel, "making love and leaving theology to the priests." Monica smiled; he didn't know how to talk about religion without bashing the Church. He called it "ideals," but Monica understood it was one of his exaggerated and infantile stances. It wasn't worth arguing over. She had her God, and he had his ideals. All was peace.

Looking over Miguel's nude body next to her – toned, lean – she watched as he lay and played with her hair. She remembered the rush of sex, the rhythmic swaying of Miguel's dark brown hair. She gripped the arms of the crucifix so tightly they left indents on the pads of her fingers.

Various scenes from the past two days flitted through her mind. Feeling herself blush, she covered her chest and crossed her naked legs. She always – always! – felt ashamed after sex. Maybe her Catholic upbringing was to blame, she wondered, because of all that repression, but she was sure God would forgive her for. What had Father O'Brien called them? Ah, yes, "outbursts of luxury that must be cut short." He said things like that when Mamma invited him over for Sunday dinner, after mass. Father O'Brien reminded her of her adolescence. Monica curled up a little more between the sofa and Miguel's body. Back then, she had helped out in the catechism class in the parish of Saint Stephen. The impetuous love between fifteen-year-olds had squeezed her stomach and prickled her skin. She felt that way now, with a tight stomach and shivers running over her skin, as if the sofa was made of straw. Like a teenager… Monica touched her neck again, then her pulse underneath her chest, her crucifix.

Miguel opened his eyes then, turning his brown-eyed gaze on her; it was lewd, almost worn out. They looked at each other in silence. It was perfect.

"What are you looking at?" Miguel asked, smiling. "Do I look like a weirdo?"

Monica sat up suddenly, feeling a pull on her scalp as her hair quickly dragged through Miguel's fingers. *A weirdo!* she thought as she rose. Reality had pulled on her hair enough to wake her up properly. No, not everything was perfect. Miguel had just said it all – he *was* a weirdo.

"I'm thirsty," Monica lied, just to say something, while a storm of fears that she had kept at bay the entire weekend flooded her mind.

Turning away from Miguel, she walked over to the glass of water that rested on the round living room table, beside the window. Although he could no longer see her face, Monica kept up her fake smile. She took up the glass and drank its contents in one go. The liquid felt like caustic soda, burning her as she swallowed it, trying to clean out her faults and fears. But it didn't clean anything. The empty glass thudded against the table.

Miguel was still a possible Midas, the objective of her work, and she had not completed her mission. That was the reality. God, and even Father O'Brien, could forgive her for her luxury, and her mother could forgive her for sleeping with an apostate, the scourge of Christians… but Vladimir would not forgive her. This was the second time she had failed him. Monica realized her breath had caught in her throat. She moved over to the window, keeping Miguel behind her. *I failed*, she repeated to herself. She began bouncing her leg rhythmically, drumming her fingers on the window ledge. The cold from outside gave her naked skin goosebumps. Resting her crossed arms over her chest on the window ledge, she looked at the flowers. The soil had gone dry. She had forgotten to water it this weekend.

"You'll catch a cold standing there naked," she heard Miguel say from behind her. She couldn't respond.

I've ruined everything. Her mission was to talk to Miguel over dinner on Friday and encourage him to visit the NASA laboratories, not sleep with him. She hadn't thought about it all weekend, burying the idea in the farthest reaches of her mind, beneath solid blocks of passion, sex, shame from sex, fear of God; beneath her feelings for Miguel, beneath even her fear of Miguel and his ability to dominate her, beneath everything she had found. Monica saw various cars, heard them forcing their motors as they climbed up the street. At the end of the hill was a black truck. It was very similar to the ones they used to watch inflexors. She gripped the wood of the windowpane.

Her incomplete mission! The others would already know. Vladimir would dismiss her, possibly even remove her from the Project. She took deep breaths as the purr of the car engine that passed in front of the black truck drowned out the sound of the street. The petunia petals shook in the breeze and Monica shivered again. Then she turned to Miguel. He was still smiling, watching her from the rough, maroon sofa. He was still perfect.

Sex. Perfect. Miguel. What did she have to feel ashamed about?

She wasn't about to regret what she had done, she told herself suddenly. Why would she regret it? Once more, she was projecting more shame than she deserved onto herself, as she had done with the "outburst of luxury." She had simply acted like an adult, she thought. She wasn't guilty of anything. The mission could still be saved. *What does Vladimir care what I do?* She had to talk to Miguel about NASA, right? Fine. Now was as good a time as any. No one had told her whether she had to talk to him about it seated at a table in a restaurant or in bed, right? Or on a sofa. Fine, then she'd do it on the sofa.

She saw her wallet lying on the table, next to the glass. Picking it up, she picked out a piece of paper from inside it and made her way over to Miguel.

***

Miguel watched Monica approach him, almost naked, with a piece of paper in her hand. It excited him to wonder what new game she had invented. He sat up to receive her.

"Look," Monica said, handing him the paper.

Miguel looked at Monica's G-string, barely hidden behind the paper she was handing him. He thought his dreams could not have become reality more completely. Immediately after, his eyes focused on the paper. A red and blue logo. The NASA logo headed the letter. *My dreams*, he thought. "NASA?"

"I tried to tell you at dinner on Friday," Monica said, "but… you know." Miguel took the letter and read it before looking at Monica, slightly open-mouthed.

"You've been awarded a research grant in NASA Ames," said Miguel.

"I asked for it months ago. Isn't it great? With Professor Gorlov, the one who gave the NASA mug to your boss, remember?" She winked at him. "Maybe he'll have a job for you too."

Monica began explaining that Professor Gorlov knew a lot of people at the university, that he usually collaborated with other departments, that maybe the two of them could work in Ames… Miguel looked back at the NASA logo, his eyes half-shut, imagining that emblem printed on a white jacket. *His* white jacket.

“I’d love to go there,” he said in a whisper, never looking away from the red and blue logo of his dreams.

CHAPTER 10

The black monitoring truck stopped in front of a small NASA Ames building. Walter Castillo jumped out quickly. He had spent over forty-eight hours in that vehicle. It was early Monday morning, just after sunrise. He had barely slept, but he didn't feel tired. From that black truck, parked at the top of the street on the hill, he had been able to watch Miguel and Monica through the windows of her apartment. *Now isn't the time for sleep*, he thought. He should have ordered Roth to fill Monica's apartment with cameras and microphones. Stupid woman.

Taking long, forceful strides, as if trying to break the concrete with his feet, Castillo looked at his watch. Gorlov would already be in his office, waiting for the first sunlight of the day. In just a few seconds, Castillo had crossed the space between the truck and the entrance into the small brick building, shoving open the door. He abruptly realized he must have looked like a gunman entering a saloon in the Wild West and tried to moderate his pace. Then he stopped. Those scientists who played at being Secret Service agents knew plenty about atoms and quantum physics, but they wouldn't know a thing about how to lead an operation. *They have no idea!* Adjusting the knot in his tie in order to calm himself, Castillo kept walking.

He managed a smile by the time he found himself in front of Gorlov's secretaries. One of them looked up at him before silently typing something. Karen, Castillo remembered. The Russian's guard dog. She had been with Gorlov since he arrived in the United States. The other secretary, farthest away from the office door, was a young black woman named Sherry. She smiled back at Castillo.

Too pretty to be working in this dump full of worn-out scientists, he thought.

"Professor Gorlov?"

"He's expecting you," said Sherry. Her pale palm gestured towards the half-open door.

Straightening out his impeccable gray suit, Castillo drew himself up, lifting his chin, and tightening his tie once more. He let his half-smile fall and entered the office with two quick knocks on the door.

Gorlov stared at him as if he had been watching him before he even entered the room. As inexpressive as always, he watched him from behind his old glasses, sitting at the old wooden table with the same old look in his eyes.

Castillo shut the door behind him with a decisive movement, without slamming it. "She slept with him," he said.

Gorlov said nothing. He wordlessly gestured with a bony hand for Castillo to sit, but the CIA agent remained standing.

"This is hardly professional. She slept with Miguel Le Fablec," Castillo insisted. "Your protégée."

"She's not my protégée." Gorlov did not move when he spoke.

The Russian's apathy was beginning to exasperate Castillo. *Who cares what she is?* he thought. *She slept with him!*

"What are we going to do?" he asked. "Can we afford to allow someone who is so attached sentimentally to the subject to continue with the capture?" Castillo knew they couldn't. Monica had already broken several rules, like when she had amplified the point of inflection in Granada. But now she had completely crossed the line – that, Gorlov could not deny.

"We'll see," Gorlov said.

Castillo breathed slowly, deeply, trying to smooth his expression into something that concealed his rage. Gorlov had not only made the blunder of assigning an intelligence mission to a non-professional, but he also confronted the fact. Why? To protect his excellent student? Castillo didn't care why. Finally finding the calm face he had been searching for, he applied it like a mask. He couldn't see himself in a mirror, but he knew his expression revealed little more than the Russian's. Castillo could change his face at will and do so many more necessary things for his work. He was a true professional, and he had not failed like that amateur of a spy.

"She did capture him, in the end," Gorlov said.

Castillo did not let his face move a single millimeter. It was clear that the damn Russian would defend her again. Yes, she had indeed captured him in the end; she had sent a message to the laboratory informing them – the only thing she had managed to do well. She captured him, but that didn't mean she had to sleep with him. If their relationship failed, the subject could distance himself from the path leading to the Project. Was Gorlov not aware of that? Of course he was, but, from the looks of it, he would defend Monica to the end. It made sense. *She's the daughter he and his wife never had, a daughter he has with science*, or so Fred had told him. Nonsense.

"She captured him, that much is true," Castillo said. "But I want her off the mission." Gorlov said nothing. "I must go. We'll talk soon," he added, opening the door.

He would have to ensure that Miguel stayed on track, if need be. He could not be allowed to escape just because some ancient scientist wanted to defend his collaborators like they were his children. Castillo closed the door to Gorlov's office with a decisive movement without slamming it.

***

Gorlov sat staring at his office door long after Castillo had left. He could still see him there, fit to burst with reasoning against him and a rage barely contained beneath his poker face.

What was Monica thinking, sleeping with Miguel? the scientist thought. *Has she gone crazy?* It was inexplicable. He had believed so strongly in her serious nature. Inexplicable.

He picked up the phone. *Castillo knows*, he thought as he dialled Fred's number. The agent had finally revealed who he truly was – as soon as the slightest problem arose, he tried to take the reins on the Project. He clearly wouldn't let anything escape his control. Castillo had come to control it, the Project. And them, of course.

After several tones, someone picked up on the other end of the line. Gorlov heard the voice of one of Fred's secretaries.

"Director Windhorst is in the basement," came the response when Gorlov asked.

He dialled once more, this time Eugene Barrett's number. *Technically*, he thought, *Monica hasn't ruined anything. She's still in the wrong, of course, but her actions have served to unmask that tie-wearing hyena. That's good, to know exactly what we're up against with Castillo. He wants to control us. Fred has to know*. Barrett wasn't picking up either. *Where is everyone this morning?!*

Gorlov hung up. He could just about hear someone speaking to his secretaries on the other side of the door.

Monica was the most urgent problem. He would have to talk to her, try to see what was going through her mind for her to sleep with Miguel. The sun, as it did every morning, began to illuminate on the wall. Gorlov stared at the orange bands of light.

He remembered how Fred joked that the light made the office the most romantic spot in all of NASA Ames. Stupid things. Romantic spot. What if Monica had truly fallen in love? Taking up a white plastic pen, he began dismantling it, unscrewing all its pieces. If she really had fallen in love with him, perhaps he would have to distance her from the Project for a time – he hated admitting Castillo was right. Placing the spring back inside the pen, Gorlov screwed everything back together. Although, on the other hand, if he left her with Miguel, it would irritate Castillo's meticulous nature. It would infuriate him, and it would crack the greater part of his masks, his smiles, just like it had a moment ago.

Someone knocked on the door. Gorlov watched it but didn't respond, clicking the pen. But the tip didn't come out; he had left the tube of ink on the table while he reassembled. Then he realized what the problem was. He wasn't counting on her.

Gorlov picked up his pen and opened a drawer. Deciding he would have to speak with Monica as soon as possible, he paused thoughtfully for a moment and fiddled with the pen. Castillo wanted her out. Castillo didn't know what he was talking about! Monica was Miguel's catalyst. The knock came again, and Gorlov tossed his pen into the drawer. "Come in!"

It was Eugene Barrett. He did not enter but stayed in the doorway, observing the room from behind his small, round glasses. His rat-like smile that he always wore when he came to Gorlov's office was nowhere to be found. He was hunched over, as though the news he had weighed him down.

"Monica is with Fred on the lower levels," he said, clearing his throat and pushing his glasses up.

Why didn't she come and see me before? Gorlov thought. "Let's head down."

***

Monica decided to speak with Fred Windhorst first. The immaculately white, plastic walls in the meeting room on level -3 prompted an inexplicable heat to spread over Monica, as if she were a captive in an underground medieval dungeon. It was the same heat she had felt when she told about the point of inflection in Granada. Her first mistake.

She knew she couldn't confront Gorlov first, with his inexpressive gaze and his Russian accent sharpened in disappointment. Fred, on the other hand, had always seemed like a gentle giant from a story book. Well, nearly always – Fred looked at her between the cavernous wrinkles that comprised his forehead, coming down so low over his clear eyes that they were nearly completely hidden.

"We should discuss this with Vladimir," said Fred. His giant fingers were interlaced on the table and he looked Monica right in the eye.

She avoided his gaze, but he continued in a very serious tone.

"You may have ruined everything. Not only that..."

So, she thought, today wasn't going to be easy. Everyone would have some terrible future consequence to hurl at her with furrowed brows and deep voices, like an English judge. Monica felt a tiny surge of dignity – she hadn't *ruined* anything yet. Miguel's scent of honey and old oak came to mind, and Monica had to suppress the rising feeling of excitement. She straightened in her seat, ready to defend herself.

Barrett entered the meeting room in that moment, looking at her over his round glasses, and then at Fred. He didn't speak. Monica supposed he was here for the scolding, for the trial. Then, Gorlov entered.

Monica shivered. The scientist's face showed no emotion. Not even she, who had always been able to recognize some part of what the Russian felt from behind those glasses, could decode his thoughts. But she could guess.

Gorlov kept his eyes fixed on her while he and Barrett sat down. No one spoke, and Fred went quiet too. Of course, Monica concluded, she was the one who needed to explain herself. Looking down at her hands, she could feel the weight of their gazes. The Holy Inquisition had gathered here to judge her. And burn her. Her legs began to bounce in agitation. The impossible heat in that sterilized room began to cloud her vision. The dense, hot air felt like asphalt fumes. She couldn't stop her legs from moving. Where was her strength? She nibbled her lip.

The bite brought her back to reality, where she realized she had papers in her hand. It was the mission report. Her completed mission. She looked up. "Miguel Le Fablec has applied to come and see the NASA laboratories," said Monica. Her voice felt weak, but she forced herself to speak up as she straightened. "He will voluntarily come to where the test will take place. The objective has successfully been reached." The last sentence felt fake, like a pep talk from a soldier movie. But it was the truth, just like the report said.

Silence returned to the trial. Monica guessed there would soon be reproaches and accusations of lascivious, irresponsible, egotistical behavior. Sin. Bonfire.

"Do you love Miguel?" Gorlov asked. His accent was just barely noticeable. Barrett and Fred both turned toward him with the same crumpled expression one would wear listening to a genius spout nonsense.

Monica closed her eyes. The heat from the flames intensified. She felt like Gorlov was her father, or something awfully similar, asking her about her feelings. He didn't seem to care about anything else. Just her. Monica knew that couldn't be true, that Gorlov was trying to save the Project, his investigations, Miguel's capture, the results of an entire life dedicated to studying quantum inflexors. But in that moment, she was his main interest. Monica felt an urge to go over to him and kiss him on the cheek, like he was her real father.

"Yes," Monica said emphatically. A cold, stinging sensation blossomed on her face.

CHAPTER 11

Monica liked feeling fresh air on the tip of her nose. The sun was rising. The sticky smell of the Pacific in summer coming in through the living room window mixed with Miguel's scent. After two months, ever since Gorlov had allowed her to "continue her affair with the supposed Midas," the smell of honey and old oak permeated through the entire apartment. It had stuck to the maroon sofa where they had sex. Monica smiled to herself.

Her hands stilled on her laptop keyboard as she turned towards the open living room window. She recalled Miguel's wrinkled expression when he found her greeting the sunrise through the window – more or less how she did now – the first morning after coming to live there together.

Ever since I was ten, she explained to Miguel, *I've been getting up before sunrise to do some work and to prepare breakfast for everyone at home. Every day*. Miguel's face creased more in confusion as he told her it was inhuman to get up so early. *I've always been a little bit weird*, she told him. *I'm weirder*, Miguel had replied.

The screensaver activated, accompanied by a small popping sound. Monica opened her eyes, blinked, and saw her now blank screen. She hit the mouse against the table and the laptop immediately restored itself to the report she was writing. The clock above the refrigerator told Monica it was nearly six. She began typing rapidly.

Morning report: the supposed Midas subject slept well. His levels of static inflection are constant and elevated in recent hours (see measurements attached). From a psychological standpoint, he is ready for the experiment: he will be very receptive. The waiting period combined with continuous allusions to NASA, as was predicted, have created a strong feeling of childlike excitement.

She closed the report and attached it to an email, adding the measurements taken by quantum sensors installed in the apartment, her preliminary analysis, the psychological form; she encrypted everything and sent it to the laboratory. Turning off the computer, she stood and went to the kitchen. *Some of it is true*, she thought. *I have been doing this since I was ten.*

Monica turned on the coffee maker. She could see her younger self preparing breakfast for everyone at home – eggs, bacon, toast, juice, pancakes, coffee, cereal… overboard, like always. She tasted barely any of it, but she felt so good doing it. Her father, her mother, little Paul, even Patrizia all seemed so proud of the early riser of the family. Papa had once tried to send her to a psychologist a few months after this habit started. *Our daughter's diligence is a gift from God*, Mamma had said, putting an end to any more psychologist's visits. And Monica had been happy to be left with her gift.

The coffee began to drip into the pot, and its scent immediately filled the small rectangular space of the kitchen and the living room. Monica poured herself a cup before adding a drop of milk and taking a sip. She grimaced. *Why does everyone love coffee in the morning so much?* she wondered, throwing all of it into the sink.

She poured herself a glass of fresh milk, deciding that would be her only breakfast. No more ceremony was needed to start the day. She retrieved a frying pan from a low cupboard underneath the oven and placed it on top before adding oil. Why did people need so many routine protocols to start the morning? *Days have to start one way or another, right?* Miguel, on the other hand, was possessed by morning liturgies: insult the alarm clock, spend a lifetime in the shower, eat breakfast as if he would never eat again, drink a *lot* of coffee. *Eggs should be fried with oil, not butter*, he said.

But she liked him like that. Monica swallowed half the milk in her glass in one go and lit the fire cooker. She had someone to make breakfast for. Miguel's habits also made her job easier. Pursuing someone with a routine was easier, and the monitoring had been the most important thing for the last few months.

Monica took out some eggs from the refrigerator. The pursuit. She remembered what she had told Gorlov. She wanted to go with Miguel. *It's a perfect plan*, she had said, *I can monitor him more closely, observe him for longer, nearly twenty-four hours a day*. Vladimir had looked her in the eyes and replied, *A Midas is capable of anything. It's possible that you've only fallen in love with him because he wished it. You know that*.

One of the eggs nearly fell out of Monica's hand, but she caught it in time. She *did* know. The pan began to emit a thick smoke as the oil neared its boiling point. Monica cracked an egg and added it to the pan before covering it quickly, drops of oil spitting everywhere. Gorlov's words still provoked a disjointed prickling feeling, like the drops of burning oil bit her for real. If Miguel really was a Midas, he could do it. With just an almost imperceptibly small inflection, he could make her fall in love with him. Or he could make her hate him. He could manipulate her, just like he manipulated Ana, his ex-girlfriend in Granada.

Taking another sip of milk, Monica turned around and looked at her now shut-down computer. She had just finished writing her monitoring report. No, she told herself, she was the one who controlled everything, who wrote reports every morning, who manipulated Miguel so she could bring him to the secret NASA labs.

She constantly deceived him. It was not, of course, the type of relationship she had always dreamed of as a girl. No normal person dreamed of that, she thought. But neither Monica nor Miguel were normal. She lifted the lid of the pan to find the egg had burned. Monica shook her head silently. She was perfectly capable of thinking and frying an egg at the same time, she told herself. She could easily multitask if asked. It was nearly time to do away with all dishonesty – partly, at least, Monica thought as she scraped the burnt egg into the trash. Surely she would feel better if she made a huge breakfast, like the ones she made as a girl. Opening the refrigerator, she covered the countertop with food. The test was already prepared in the lab. Miguel wanted to go to NASA, and everyone was ready. She was ready. Everything would be fine. Bacon, toast, juice…

In that moment, Monica heard Miguel's alarm clock sound from the end of the hall.

***

Miguel hit his alarm clock, and it finally shut up. The June sunlight filtered in like a solid block of light to the bedroom, along with the Pacific breeze. The clock told him it was six in the morning, but Miguel felt much more awake than any other morning. The excitement was palpable in the air. The block of sunlight was filled with dust motes that danced in the air as if there were a party in the ether of the room. The day had come – he was finally going to visit NASA.

Miguel detected the smell of fried eggs as it wafted into the room from the kitchen, which rid of him of any residual tiredness. After taking a breath, he crossed the doorway into the small living room just in time to see an egg fall into the pan with a delightful crackling sound.

"There he is!" Monica exclaimed. Her smile sparkled along with everything else that morning, full of light and expectation and fried eggs. "Mr. Sleepy Head!"

"I promise I'll make breakfast tomorrow." He couldn't look away from the pan.

"I don't believe you," she said.

Miguel, just like every other morning, took the laptop from the table and placed it on the maroon sofa. Last night they had practiced their sexual games, and various positions, on that sofa. Breathing deeply through his nose, Miguel tried to suppress the excitement he felt from the night before. He recalled Monica chatting with him after sex, sitting in her usual position, with one leg folded beneath her naked body. They talked about NASA. In a single image, he saw Monica's breasts as well as the NASA Ames Center. The sofa fabric was so rough.

Miguel dispersed the images with a shake of his hand. They had to hurry. He began spreading a tablecloth over the table while he whistled *Silent Night*. It seemed like the right song to whistle, even though it was June. At that moment, all he could remember were Christmas carols and children's songs.

He stopped whistling as he sat at the table, smiling like a little boy about to leave for camp. He wolfed down half a fried egg and a piece of toasted bread the size of three of his fingers, which he had not quite swallowed by the time he asked Monica to repeat the plan.

She insisted that all of it might disappoint him, that the NASA Ames complex was nothing more than a collection of old, austere-looking buildings – most of them built in the sixties – and that, best case scenario, there would be a small lab, a wind tunnel, and maybe a simulator. The offices took up the most space, and he was unlikely to find any spaceships, or test pilots, or astronauts walking around talking about the avatars of their latest mission with their helmets under their arms. It wasn't the space dock for the Starship Enterprise.

The Starship Enterprise. Miguel felt like a five-year-old again being told a story. After swallowing a mouthful of buttered toast, he spoke. "Are we going to where you work?"

Monica smiled. Miguel guessed she would love to show him what she did there. The SSRC, Space Survival Research Center, as Monica had called it. They investigated how to survive in space, she had told him – space station simulations, colonies, things like that. It all sounded so interesting. "To the SSR Center? Yes, of course," she answered.

"Good."

Monica's smile widened, and she turned to look at the clock above the refrigerator. "Houston, we have a problem."

The child that was Miguel that morning swallowed an entire slice of bacon and got up from the table. He noticed his sleeve had gotten slightly stained from the bacon grease. *Houston, we have a problem!* he repeated to himself in his head in a metallic voice, like an astronaut calling Earth.

An hour later, in the car, Miguel continued trying to clean the small grease stain on his sleeve. Looking up, he began to hear astronaut voices when he saw the gigantic NASA hangar appear to the left of the highway. When they arrived at the Ames Center facilities, a stocky man in a suit gestured to them with enormous, claw-like hands to park in the outer parking lot. Monica told him it was Fred Windhorst, the director of the SSR Center. He recalled her description of Fred, like a gentle giant from a storybook; but to him, Fred seemed more like a bear who wanted to play with them.

As they got out of the car, the bear shook his hand, squeezing his fingers, and spoke in a booming voice. “Welcome to NASA!”

CHAPTER 12

By the end of the morning, Miguel was filled up with NASA. He walked aimlessly under the sun, following Fred Windhorst. They had already visited the majority of the facilities, and by now, he was afraid to open another door and find a new scientist trying to explain to him the principles of their experiment, their project, their laboratory… Small talk upon small talk. All morning. Only one thing had caught his interest: the wind tunnel complex. Supersonic wind tunnels, pressure tunnels, hypersonic wind tunnels… Miguel had never seen so many in one place. Dani, he thought, would die of envy when he found out.

Miguel saw in his head the scar on Dani's ear, the mark of the astronaut accident. If Dani could see that cathedral of space journeys, he would love it. It occurred to him that a visit like that could be a good incentive for his studies. He thought back on the largest wind tunnel – one hundred and twenty by eighty feet of test sections, he was told. A tunnel with an F/A-18 inside! Dani needed something like that. Miguel imagined his brother walking along the tunnels and aerothermodynamic laboratories. Both of them there, like they dreamed of as boys. He saw once more the scarred lobe of Dani's ear and his head began to ache slightly. It had been a while since the last time Miguel felt that ache in the middle of his brain, that impossible, sweet pain.

"Let's get something to eat," said Fred. As soon as Miguel heard him, the pain disappeared. "What do you think of the center so far?"

"Lots of scientists."

Fred barked a laugh. He really was like a gentle giant from a storybook.

"Although I would love to bring my brother here one day to see the wind tunnels," Miguel added.

"Of course…"

The canteen wasn't very far. They soon arrived at the single-storey building.

Monica and Fred were looking at the daily specials in the self-service queue when Miguel set eyes on a man who must have been nearing eighty. His eyes, framed by enormous, outdated, reading glasses stared pointedly at him from the table where he stood. He was like a frozen gargoyle looming over him.

***

At first sight, Gorlov thought, Miguel didn't seem terrible or powerful. He left his food tray on the table and remained standing, staring at him. Of course, no inflexor did. And it was silly to expect Miguel Le Fablec to be superhuman – athletic, stony, mysterious. Gorlov had seen him before, from afar, spying with Barrett in San Francisco and the lookouts on the Golden Gate while Miguel walked with Monica. But up close, for some reason, Miguel was disappointing.

A Midas *was* much more, Gorlov told himself. A phenomenon just barely supported by hundreds of blue equations, dozens of squared notebooks, and all mathematical and physical theory. After years of looking for someone as living proof of the phenomenon, he thought, it was normal that he imagined someone less common than a young, distracted-looking man with long hair like a rock singer. He looked like a dreamer; the worst thing to expect.

Doubts began to creep back in about whether he was doing the right thing in pursuing him. Miguel didn't seem very sure of himself. But Gorlov needed someone strong. He recalled his annotations about the Midas Paradox. If the paradox was correct, an indecisive person could become their worst nightmare. It was likely that someone insecure would not be able to handle the power of a Midas. Gorlov picked up a tablespoon and squeezed it between his bony hands. It bent as if it were made of tin.

In that moment, Gorlov realized Miguel was staring at him and he thought, finally, he could see something strange in him. Maybe that was the sign they had been waiting for, the proof that Miguel was special – his look. Overly cool, oddly warm ochre in color, like unusually dark wood, or dead wood. So calm. *Unlike any color in the world.* The Midas Effect.

As if of its own free will, the spoon jumped out of Gorlov's grasp as he waved in Miguel's direction. Whether it was him or not, he had waited half a century for him. When Miguel's eyebrows furrowed in confusion as he saw Gorlov's gesture, Monica waved back. She said something in Miguel's ear that made him smile. He seemed more decided now.

***

Miguel left his tray on the table and extended his hand to the gargoyle. Up close, Gorlov's face and glasses were even more horrible.

"Vladimir!" Fred called. "This is Dr. Miguel Le Fablec."

"It's a pleasure to meet you, Professor Gorlov," said Miguel, shaking his hand. Gorlov had a tight grip. Not one muscle moved in his face. Perhaps, Miguel thought, Monica had involved the scientist so that he could help Miguel during his visit, and that's why his expression was so blank. "I've heard so much about you, sir."

"Please, take a seat." Gorlov's response was stilted, with just a slight Russian accent coming through, some consonants that reminded Miguel of spy movies set during the Cold War. "How is Professor Branson? You work with him in San José State University, right?"

And the Russian began to ask questions. First, little by little, he asked for information about the south of Spain, his doctorate, his experience as a professor in Granada, disconnected questions; then, a barrage of questions. Gorlov was like Dani, asking about everything he had done during his years of absence. Miguel could only respond. He enjoyed Gorlov's attention.

When it seemed like lunch was over, the scientist stood and invited everyone to follow him to the SSR building. Monica, Fred and Miguel got up after him. Picking up his tray, Miguel looked at his pasta salad (barely touched) as well as his apple pie (one bite missing) and his bread (intact). But it was worth it. He liked talking to Gorlov, despite his frozen gargoyle look.

But he liked the SSR even more. Nothing like the labs and dishevelled scientists from this morning. Miguel was welcomed by a forty-something-year-old executive in a blue pinstripe suit. Dark-haired, perfectly styled. He looked like he had just stepped out of the most expensive law firm in Boston.

"Good afternoon, Dr. Le Fablec. It's a pleasure to have you here in the Space Survival Research Center. Welcome," he said in Spanish, with a Cuban accent. "I'm Walter Castillo, assistant to Director Windhorst. Please allow me to introduce you to our collaborators…"

One by one, Castillo introduced all of the scientists gathered in the meeting room. The looks, sometimes lost, sometimes grim, suggested to Miguel that Castillo didn't fit there.

After introducing Miguel to everyone, Castillo introduced himself as the newest member of the team, unfamiliar with the matters dealt with there and "humble prop assistant" of all of the "renowned scientists" to whom, of course, he immediately gave the floor, since he had already said everything he could. Miguel watched as the white-coated men's faces relaxed, while others smiled. The tour ended with a small round of honorable mentions of each and every doctor – prizes, publications. Castillo knew how to sell, that much was clear. Gorlov was the only one who didn't soften. The scientist squeezed a pen in his hands like he wanted to snap it in two.

When Castillo finished, the technical presentations began. Miguel counted as everyone sat down – there were twelve scientists there. Inside that one room was the biggest unfolding of white coats ever seen in NASA. There were some good things too – an impeccable meeting room, like new, very neat, a projector ready for use, white folders with the NASA logo printed in card on top containing papers, articles, SSR pamphlets. It was like they were preparing to receive the President of the United States. Miguel supposed such attention to detail could only be attributed to Monica. He thought about how to thank her as the projector turned on.

The SSR doctors talked about means of survival in space, problems in human behavior, lack of gravity and living conditions, physiological adaptation, simulations on Earth of space colonies… Everything was very clear. The presentations were easy to follow, very colorful, full of videos, like they had all been prepared by a publicist. And the talks: organized, understandable, with just the right changes of tone needed to keep the audience's attention. Some of them were even funny. It seemed the SSR building was lucky enough to gather all of the doctors with public speaking skills in NASA. There were too many of them, and they were too convincing. It was like they were trying hard to make sure no one suspected anything strange was going on. Like they were hiding something. It didn't make sense. Miguel must have been tired. Too many talks throughout the day.

The last person to speak was Dr. Eugene Barrett, the youngest of the scientists. He appeared to be in his fifties. The bowtie and small, lively eyes behind a pair of round glasses reminded Miguel of a New York psychotherapist. Barrett claimed to be a psychiatrist. He presented a project in which cases of schizophrenia were studied to… "see their influence on the environment."

What environment? Miguel wondered. It was the only thing in the room he didn't understand. The physical environment or the human one? The human one, of course, anything else would be nonsense. Miguel frowned. Barrett interrupted his own explanation and asked him if there was anything he didn't understand.

"Don't you carry out medical tests to select members of the team?" Miguel asked. "How can a schizophrenic patient access this?"

"Someone with that kind of illness cannot pass the medical tests in any level of NASA, much less the tests to become an astronaut," Barrett clarified. "But, in this case, we evaluated the influence of the environment on a healthy individual," – *the environment, again*, Miguel noticed – "that, due to stress and under certain conditions that could be found during prolonged periods spent on a space station, could trigger temporary episodes of paranoid delirium psychosis. We must not ignore that possibility. Even if it's only a passing episode, it could cause changes in the closed, limited and, let's face it, oppressive environment of a space colony…"

Right, Miguel thought, he was referring to someone sane who could pass the medical evaluations, not a lunatic. But what about the environment? Barrett could not explain himself as well as the others.

"Then the environment you're referring to, Dr. Barrett, is the group of people who cohabitate with the affected party, isn't that right?"

Even the hum of the projector's fans seemed to have been swallowed up by the silence that fell over the room. Everyone looked at Miguel very seriously, with pursed lips and shaking heads, like he had uncovered some terrible secret. Miguel imagined them as Chicago gangsters from the 1920s who took on the weight of finding out whatever he knew and wondered whether to eliminate him or not.

Barrett turned ever so slightly to look at Gorlov silently. Gorlov's eyes moved to meet Barrett's gaze and he nodded almost imperceptibly. Miguel didn't understand what he had said to warrant such expressions; everyone had been quite friendly up to now. Barrett turned towards Miguel and frowned, not understanding what Miguel was saying; as if Miguel, in his grasp of the word "environment" as a group of people, was radically out of touch with reality.

"Maybe it's my English..." Miguel said, clearing his throat with a cough, like that would help his English. "It seems to me that certain subjects who suffer psychotic episodes can influence their immediate surroundings – matter, physics, laws of the universe."

Silence and the hum of projector fans.

"Yeah, yeah, I know," Miguel continued, "it sounds stupid. If it really refers to... people. Or..."

The silence stretched on for another few moments. For a second, Miguel thought they would tell him yes, that there were subjects who could change the laws of physics.

"Human environment!" Dr. Barrett exclaimed, smiling so widely that instead of favoring his appearance, his small chin deformed to the point where he looked like a demented imp. "I was referring to people, of course. A subject who suffers from episodes of paranoia generates a collective psychosis on the spaceship."

The smiling faces returned, and Miguel observed them from the corner of his eye. Everyone seemed to have buried the gangster they had inside them.

And that's where Dr. Barrett finished up. He turned off the projector and turned on the ceiling lights.

Miguel remained seated with a bitter aftertaste in his mouth. He couldn't quite fit Barrett's talk with the rest of the SSR presentations. He couldn't even understand why he couldn't explain himself. *The environment.* No, he didn't understand it. The scientists said goodbye to one another, offering friendly smiles and firm handshakes, catching their white coats on the way out.

When the room was nearly empty, Miguel began collecting his papers, as did Fred and Monica. Fred was pressing the tiny buttons on the projector with his huge fingers while Gorlov and Barrett talked by the door. The Russian, blank-faced as always, listened as Barrett, who was much smaller than him, talked away looking over his round glasses. Castillo neared them, tightening the knot on his tie.

"I propose we go to see a space colony simulation," said Gorlov, looking right at Miguel, who nodded. "Or we could go see Dr. Barrett's experiments," Gorlov added. "Since our guest seems so interested."

The environment.

Barrett's smile split his face again. "I'm just about to finish one of them up. He'll love seeing it. Let's head down!"

CHAPTER 13

The elevator doors did not open. Miguel looked around at his companions: Castillo and Fred, both in suits, Barrett and Gorlov in white coats, and Monica, in jeans and trainers. No one said a word, choosing instead to look at the roof, the walls, the doors. Gorlov had brought them to an elevator with white doors – clearly too technological for the old brick SSR building, probably stolen from a spaceship – with a security guard standing nearby. Gorlov had pressed the button for level -1. The elevator had begun descending and had stopped at -1. There were no more levels. Just 0 and -1. Nothing above, nothing below. And the doors did not open.

Miguel looked again at the control panel. Below the button for level -1 were four horizontal slits, like four slits on a piggybank, stacked on top of one another. He realized that the slits corresponded to four more underground levels.

Secret labs! Suddenly Miguel's mind was overcome with technological intrigues, scientists giving life to biomechanical beings in inaccessible basements… the kind of silly things Dani loved. The excitement made his nostrils flare.

"We won't stop here," Gorlov said slowly. "On this level, there are only common experiments. We would bore him. People imitating life on Mars. Space colony simulations…"

"People locked up for months," Barrett explained, "little more."

Space colony simulations. Little else?

Barrett fished out from his pocket a polished black card about as thick as a microchip. The card was connected to a metal string that originated from somewhere in Barrett's coat pocket. Clearly, it was something he did not want to lose. It appeared to be made precisely for the slits on the elevator control panel.

In a movement that looked quite mundane to Miguel, Barrett inserted the card into the top slit, which corresponded to level -2, and placed his thumb on a black plate beside the control panel. In that moment, everyone took out cards identical to Barrett's. They all had their own metal strings attached from their pockets.

"Now we must pass through a new security measure," Gorlov said. "Don't be afraid, Dr. Le Fablec. There are soldiers at the door."

"Soldiers?"

"The projects carried out on the lower levels" – *the hidden basements!* – "are of a certain… national sensitivity. Some are financed by the Department of Defense, while others are secret" – *secret* – "or prototypes that should not yet be used. All of them are too important to be on a level open to the public, even to the NASA staff."

Secret labs... Miguel took in Gorlov's words, tasted them. *But I'm*... he remembered, *I'm the public.* Were they going to allow him to access military secrets, secrets hidden even from the Agency's own personnel? Just because he had badgered his girlfriend into bringing him there… to see astronauts and spaceships, and buy a NASA cap like every other tourist? It made no sense. Four secret underground levels guarded by the military, and all to investigate the best way to survive in space. That didn't make sense either. Something wasn't right.

Miguel looked over at Monica, but she was still observing the roof of the elevator like she wanted to know what material it was made from. It was absurd, all of it. The scientists' gangster faces sprang to mind.

Then they reached level -2, and the doors opened.

Two huge soldiers appeared, equipped with helmets, bulletproof vests, blue camouflage U.S. Air Force uniforms, or so it seemed to Miguel, and facial expressions that spoke of having to kill someone soon. Their rifles, hanging across their shoulders and tucked under their arms, pointed to the elevator. It was impossible to know whether the guns were pointed at them or if they just rested that way naturally. Miguel began to scratch his palms.

Miguel was just about to raise his hands in a sign of surrender when his companions exited the elevator. Castillo adjusted his tie once again. Behind him, Fred moved heavily, like a bear. Barrett beamed at the soldiers with his odd smile. They passed between the guns without even looking at them and inserted their black cards into two slits beside a set of glass doors.

Miguel watched them, his arms tense. Monica gestured for him to walk forward and wait with her. She told him not to worry, that the access routine was slow and that was why the others had not waited for them. She said nothing of the rifles.

Upon stepping out of the elevator, Gorlov took out one more black card and handed it to Miguel. "Use this to get in," was the only explanation the Russian gave.

A short while later, Miguel, watching the soldiers from the corner of his eye, proceeded to open one of the doors. Access required the black cards, fingerprint verification, and a retina scan. Each door also, as Miguel noticed, only allowed someone to enter through two contiguous sets of doors; the second set only opened when the first set closed. *Like in a bank*, Miguel thought. *Or a prison.*

Once inside, the group walked through a scarcely lit open space with dark matte floors, walls and ceilings. Gorlov and Barrett headed the group. Their white coats stood out against the dark surroundings. The entire area was full of consoles with lots of screens and keyboards, like control posts. Scientists controlling parameters, Miguel supposed. Nothing out of the ordinary, really. A few steps behind, Castillo and Fred followed him silently, as if watching his back. Miguel recalled the guns. Monica walked beside him.

"Was that necessary?" Miguel asked in a whisper. "The soldiers."

"Security measures. Vladimir warned you."

"Yeah, okay, he told me about the cards and sensors and all that, but guns! No one's ever pointed a gun at me before in my life."

Monica smiled at him. "They weren't aiming at anyone."

The group stopped when they reached the border of the control post area. Miguel looked back, eyes widening. His palms started itching again.

The rest of the dark surfaces on level -2 were occupied by immense black blocks, like dark flat-roofed houses. The blocks were completely covered in sharp, angular peaks, no more than a few centimeters long, distributed in a thick but uniform pattern. Like cubic hedgehogs. Miguel stared at them with half-open eyes. They looked like streamlined prison cells.

"These are the chambers," Barrett said.

Miguel's sight gradually adjusted to the darkness and his surroundings became clearer. The chambers – some of which were the size of a whole floor of a medium-sized three-bedroom house, while others were no larger than a student apartment – never came so high as to touch the ceiling, and were separated from the ground by black, spiked cylindrical supports.

"They're completely isolated from the outside," Barrett added, eager to speak. "Nothing can go in, and nothing can come out, not even sound, light, any type of radio frequency, or any known form of communication."

"Faraday cages," Miguel muttered. But they didn't quite look like Faraday cages.

"Something like that, but much more complex. It's a near-perfect isolating mechanism," Barrett explained. "It has to do with not interfering with the experiment…"

"And how is the data collected?" Miguel asked suddenly. He didn't really need to know, but he couldn't overlook such an obvious inconsistency. "What I mean is that all those control panels are monitoring what's happening inside, right? The information has to come out somehow."

Barrett cleared his throat, peering at Miguel over his small glasses before pushing them up on his nose. "The data is taken and collected inside the chamber." He looked over at Gorlov before continuing. "Every chamber has a computer that manages its functioning and collects data from the internal sensors, the cameras, the microphones…" Another cough, accompanied by a wiggle of the nose. He looked like a scared imp. "There is a device, by means of a watertight mechanism that…" Barrett's explanations turned messy again. Once more, Miguel had a feeling that he was being lied to.

But they wouldn't keep showing Miguel the rest if he continued bothering everyone with his questions. He decided not to cause any more fuss. He had not braved the pointed guns to be thrown out now, not when he hadn't yet seen everything. While Barrett continued with his incomprehensible chattering, Miguel turned to observe the nearest spiked wall. Extending his arm towards it, he looked back at Monica, who nodded. His fingers met one of the angular spikes that formed the surface. It felt spongy and soft, but also dry as sandpaper. The texture made him cringe. But he liked it too. If he could just see the inside of the chamber…

“Well,” Gorlov said suddenly. “Let’s enter the large chamber.”

“It’s possible to go in?” Miguel asked.

“The most important data has already been collected,” Barrett said. “The experiment is almost finished.”

“But… wouldn’t we be interfering?”

Castillo, Fred and Monica were already making their way towards a chamber on the right, which seemed like the largest one of all.

“From the interior observation deck, one person interferes very little,” Barrett responded. His impish smile widened. “In fact, people are always coming in to observe directly.”

“An observation…?” Miguel put an effort into not frowning any more than he already was and letting another question slip out. He understood less and less of the type of tests being carried out there, of the isolation the scientists hoped to achieve if they simply let people come and go from the inscrutable chambers.

Castillo went in first. Entry for everyone would require a few minutes, according to Gorlov. They had to process the cards, fingerprints, retina scans, double-door mechanisms… just like before, with the soldiers. Gorlov proposed that he and Miguel enter last – it would allow him to tell Miguel about the experiment.

Miguel nodded silently. He asked nothing. He had to see inside.

“Five healthy subjects have been locked in here for three weeks with a schizophrenic…” Gorlov said.

A lunatic? Miguel immediately spun around to face him.

The scientist went through the explanations without showing any semblance of emotions, as if he were in his kitchen explaining a newspaper statistic to his wife. But Miguel could feel an imaginary hand, like that of a demented psychopath, grab his stomach and pull. He knew it was far from rational. It was just a poor, sick man. There was nothing to fear. Miguel watched Barrett enter behind Castillo. He wouldn't ask. He wouldn't ask anything, he told himself. But he asked.

"Is it safe to lock people up in a room with a schizophrenic?" Miguel's hands turned to fists as he scratched his palms.

"The subjects of the experiment are not locked up," Gorlov answered. "Isolated, yes, but not locked up. They can leave the experiment whenever they please."

People from outside can go in and people from inside can leave. I don't understand any of this.

Fred Windhorst turned his enormous body towards the door to the chamber.

"If they feel unwell," continued Gorlov, "or threatened, they can leave freely. There are no security measures involved for leaving, no mechanisms to force them to stay for the duration of the experiment. A fingerprint scanner opens the doors and registers that they have left." Monica entered the chamber, winking at Miguel before the door closed behind her.

Miguel scratched his palms now with such force, it was like he was trying to create new lines with his fingernails. Everyone except for he and Gorlov had entered. A green light turned on beside the door.

"But…" He had to ask. He didn't know what to ask.

"This subject, the schizophrenic," Gorlov went on as he operated the security mechanisms, "believes he can communicate with others through his thoughts. He is in no way dangerous, but he does hallucinate that he can read minds and communicate telepathically." The outer door to the chamber slid open. "We've placed him here with five other people that he has tried to convince to hold telepathic conversations using his own mind as a nexus." Miguel entered the middle space between the doors. "We'll see now if he has managed a collective psychosis of telepaths." And the door closed behind them.

Miguel stretched out his hands – all the scratching made them burn – and looked down at them. He had to see what was happening inside those rough chambers, but... an experiment with a schizophrenic, with soldiers aiming guns at him...

Several identifications later, the second door opened and Miguel finally accessed the interior of the chamber. The first thing he noticed was an acrid, oppressive smell. Artificial air. The temperature, too, must have been one or two degrees above the outside. A slight dizziness washed over Miguel.

"You don't look so good," Monica said. "Are you okay?"

"The air here... A little dizzy..."

"It happens the first few times. It'll pass. It's happened to all of us."

Monica brought over a chair for Miguel, who was relieved to hear that he was not the only one who had gone through this dizziness. But he still felt something more than the strain of being in the closed space. He remembered small shacks in Granada where the smoke and heat had been overwhelming, but they had never provoked a feeling of strangulation like this. Fred Windhorst, smiling so wide his eyes almost disappeared, encouraged him to be brave, like a Spanish matador.

You're being ridiculous, Miguel told himself. With or without dizziness, he would not miss the experiment. He straightened, rejecting the offer of Fred's hand and Monica's shoulder. Castillo and Gorlov backed up to give him space to breathe while Monica sat beside Miguel. Everyone stared at him.

"I'm okay," he said, smiling. He swallowed some spit to mitigate the nausea.

Then they all turned towards a glass screen. Miguel looked around. The chamber was gray on the inside. Almost all gray. It reminded Miguel of the suspect identification rooms in cop shows. The observers – they – were situated in a lightless room before an enormous piece of glass that allowed them to see the conjoined hall. On the other side were two women and four men, between thirty and forty, seated around a circular table. They were dressed in black overalls.

"Can they see us?" Miguel whispered to Monica.

"It's a mirror," she replied, out loud. "They can't hear us either, so you don't need to whisper. We, however, can hear everything they say."

However, nothing could be heard. No one spoke to each other on the other side.

Miguel looked around intently beyond the mirror, scratching his palms. Those in the black overalls were completely silent… but they gestured to one another constantly. They smiled, looked at one another, nodded, shook their heads. They were like children playing at some quiet game.

"What are they doing?" Miguel asked, not daring to look away.

"They're talking," Barrett said.

Miguel felt himself tense up. Barrett must have meant something else, but… Miguel didn't know if he did it on purpose, but Dr. Barrett always shocked him with his responses. The nausea returned.

"Are they talking or do they just *think* they're talking?" Miguel asked. He didn't have the energy in that moment to let himself be tricked by the imp's half-suggested mysteries.

"At first glance, they think they're talking telepathically. It appears the paranoid psychosis has extended. Vincent has influenced all of them."

For the first time, Miguel thought, *Barrett is explaining himself clearly.*

"Vincent is the one with his back to us," Monica added. "The schizophrenic."

Schizophrenic. Miguel scratched harder. A shiver ran through him when he looked at Vincent. He couldn't see his face. Miguel then realized everyone was looking at him; not all at the same time, but all with the same intense look. Of course, they thought he was their telepathic nexus.

When Miguel *really* looked, he saw that the group's gestures didn't seem like the disconnected expressions of six people maintaining six individual conversations. No, he thought, it seemed more like something he had once seen looking at a movie playing on a TV behind a store window. He couldn't hear anything, but the gestures and expressions almost suggested a coherent, flowing conversation. Like they really were talking.

The chamber was too much. Miguel began to sweat, small droplets prickling his forehead and back. And the experiment started to seem like one small part of an overwhelming, strained atmosphere.

It's grotesque! It's already done, isn't it? he wondered. *They're all being controlled. When does it end?*

Barrett appeared ready to prattle on a little while longer with his nonsensical chattering. The group in the black overalls looked at Vincent over and over while Miguel scratched his palms once more. He looked over at the door as if it would let him escape. As he turned back to the telepaths, the scratching intensified. *Have to get out. Have to, but...* Instantly, Miguel wished he could enter the conversation too. Squeezing his nails against his palms, he wished desperately that he could just disappear and also that he could hear what they were saying. His head began to ache, right in the center, like always, a tiny pinch. *No, not my head, not now!* It was the chamber's fault, surely. He had to get out, but before… Miguel didn't move, he looked at Vincent, get out, hear, disappear, listen. *I have to leave. What are they talking about?*

And right at that moment, everyone stopped gesturing.

They looked over calmly at Vincent.

Miguel stopped breathing. He felt his body lean back, separating his face a few inches more from the glass. It was like they had heard Miguel get into Vincent's head and suddenly quietened so he couldn't eavesdrop. The nausea, the headache…

All of them turned immediately to look at Miguel behind the glass. Yes, they were looking at him. Miguel took a step back. His pulse thrummed against his sweat-soaked shirt. This couldn't be happening. *I can't breathe!* The last one to turn around was Vincent. He did so slowly, very slowly. Miguel felt his skin prickle. A fat drop of sweat slid down the line of his spine.

Vincent – black hair, slim, fair-skinned, and too-dark eyes, too opaque, otherworldly. Swallowed up in his black overalls, he almost seemed disturbingly beautiful, somehow sinister and seductive at the same time… He didn't look like a schizophrenic. *A dark angel*, Miguel's imagination suggested.

The two men stared at each other from opposite sides of the mirror, like they knew each other. Like two old friends. Like they knew what was about to happen.

A sudden pain burned Miguel's palms. And in the center of his head. He opened his mouth, just about to speak…

Hello, Miguel. Vincent's greeting was remarkably clear in his head. *Welcome to the Project.*

PART 2 – THE POWER

CHAPTER 14

Walter Castillo cast his gaze over the laptop screen. He had just parked in the residential area just south of the university, in the shade of the enormous trees. It was hot inside his Pontiac Solstice, but he didn't dare remove his hood. No one could see what he was doing. The car's black paint must have been trapping all the sun in California. Loosening the knot of his tie, Castillo clicked on the images from the secret cameras. Only he and Agent Roth knew the cameras existed. He clicked on the one watching the campus.

The image wasn't very sharp, the camera having been installed on an office desk in one of the university's administrative buildings. The desk faced a window looking onto Tower Hall. The glass must not have been very clean.

The image began to focus – on Miguel, sitting on the grass, in the shade of Tower Hall. He seemed distant, completely absorbed in contemplating the ivy wrapped around the building.

Soon, Castillo told himself, Miguel would be in the Project. *Trapped.* His vigilance would become much easier. Just then, Monica approached Miguel. *Let's see what the Russian's "nice girl" can do,* Castillo thought. He turned up the air conditioning in the Solstice and picked up his phone.

"Professor Roth speaking," Castillo heard on the other end of the line.

"Roth, it's Walter Castillo. I haven't received your report. Is everything going okay?"

Castillo watched Roth turn towards the camera, taking up almost the entire screen, before turning away to look back again. Through the phone Castillo could hear two feminine voices in the background. Roth looked at the camera again and spoke. "Yes, thank you for reminding me, Professor. I was just about to send it. Everything is fine here. Our friends are having dinner at the Russian restaurant."

***

To see Gorlov? I'm not going to see Gorlov. Miguel's response on the phone a few minutes ago played now in Monica's head. He had called her at least ten times that morning. She had already told him all she could about the Project. It was time to talk seriously, with Vladimir. Miguel walked now alongside her as they crossed the campus towards the parking lot. They were going to see Gorlov.

Perhaps Miguel would not admit it, but he was still scared. Monica only needed to look at his scratched palms, how he fidgeted on the grass in the shade of Tower Hall as he waited for her. He must have been afraid of seeing Vincent again in the SSR, even though Monica had already explained that Vincent was a quantum inflexor, not a telepathic schizophrenic. Someone with *different* mental abilities. Like him.

But he didn't believe her. Miguel stopped, looking back at the thick, tangled ivy of Tower Hall. He kept walking. Maybe he was scared of entering a secret project, Monica wondered. She had spoken to him about the CIA and the DoD, who were financing the project but did not intervene. Not like the KGB had done. Secret scientific investigations. She had told him that she had been working there for years, that Gorlov was the one who hired her, that Gorlov had been in the KGB and had begun to discover quantum inflexors in Leningrad State University. She told Miguel that NASA was just a cover. *Secret facilities near the city. It means we scientists don't have to live locked up in a forgotten military base in some desert in Nevada or New Mexico.*

They entered the parking lot. Spies, secret projects, covers, great scientific discoveries… It was the kind of thing that thrilled Miguel. He should be excited. Of course, it had only been a day since the telepaths. His point of inflection had been very strong. He had fainted, and, when he woke up, was faced with the task of trying to understand the new world Monica explained to him. His new life.

Monica nibbled her bottom lip as the pair got into her Ford. She gripped the steering wheel. *His new life*, she repeated to herself. More lies. Monica lied and lied, all to see if Miguel truly was a Midas. That was the hardest part. She had caught other inflexors before, but with Miguel… She had to make sure he entered the Project. She could not fail now. Convince him Vincent wasn't dangerous. Everything became so complicated. Monica couldn't explain everything to him, of course. Vladimir would help her. She turned the key in the ignition.

"Vincent isn't in NASA Ames anymore," Monica said suddenly. "He'll be outside for a few months. He's going to a clinic to rest and recuperate. He's a good guy, he's worked very hard."

***

A good guy! Miguel thought. Vincent. He hoped he would be very far away. For a long time.

He could still hear the words reverberating in his skull. *Welcome to the Project.* A chill sent goosebumps over his arms.

Miguel had always imagined that the voice of a telepath would sound deep, gravelly, like it was coming from imaginary earphones. But no. He had heard his own voice, his own thoughts, not Vincent's. *How would I hear his voice anyway? I have no idea what it sounds like!* His own thoughts, usurped, welcoming him to Project Who Knows What.

It wasn't long before they saw the gigantic hangar of NASA Ames Center. In the security-controlled entry, they gave him a permanent pass. It was obvious he had already been included in the Project, he thought, fidgeting in his seat. He wanted to know more about the new world Monica had told him about, but he felt uncomfortable.

When they arrived at the SSR building, they went straight to Gorlov's office.

"Hi, Karen," Monica said to the older secretary. "We're here to see Vladimir."

Karen smiled at Miguel. It reminded him of his grandmother in Nice, like she was about to invite him in to have a snack of chocolate and cake. It was the first thing to make him feel good since seeing that crazy telepath.

"He's waiting for you," Karen said warmly. "Go right ahead."

Walking past the smiling secretaries, Monica and Miguel were greeted by Gorlov's stony gargoyle expression and his bony handshake. His office was filled with light, like a greenhouse.

"Dr. Le Fablec, please have a seat," Gorlov said. It sounded like a Soviet military order.

Miguel sat where the scientist has gestured, in front of his desk, in a dark leather seat worn out at the armrests. Monica sat in an identical seat beside him. Sunlight filtered in through the gaps in the partially-closed blinds, forming oblique golden stripes on the books piled up on the shelf on the far wall. It smelled like old furniture. Miguel began to relax.

"I'll be with you in a moment," Gorlov said, sorting through the papers on his desk and stowing some away. He seemed in no hurry.

Miguel looked around the office. A round meeting table sat behind them, at the back of the room. To the right, in front of them, were two walls set with windows forming a south-facing corner. Light, lots of light. On an easel beside the table was a blackboard, illuminated with sunlight. A white NASA mug sat on Gorlov's desk. A framed periodic table of elements hung on the far wall. The yellowing paper – as well as the absence of gallium, germanium, and scandium – spoke of its age. A table from the end of the nineteenth century, one of Mendeleev's firsts, Miguel guessed. The square corresponding to gold was marked with a circle. *Au (ЗолоТо)*. Gorlov must have used this in his work. He was probably very proud to hang it there, proof that he gave classes in Saint Petersburg – Leningrad, Monica said – the same university where Dmitri Ivanovich Mendeleev had worked. The inventor of the periodic table, Miguel remembered, had a large, wispy beard. The table was a method of categorizing the entire world, made by Mendeleev. *The world as observed by those outside the Project*, Miguel thought.

Gorlov's filing cabinet let out a metallic screech as it closed, pulling Miguel from his thoughts with a flinch. "Well, Dr. Le Fablec," the scientist said, "you already have an idea of what we do here, in the Project."

"The Project. Yes."

"Dr. Eveleigh is authorized to tell you some of the details once we've completed certain verifications."

Miguel looked at Monica, who nodded and smiled. In that moment, he much preferred Karen's chocolate-and-cake smile.

"We believe you are a quantum inflexor," Gorlov continued. "Do you understand what that is?"

That damn Russian. Before, he wasn't in any hurry, but now he didn't want to waste a second on preamble.

"Someone with mental powers," Miguel responded.

Gorlov observed Miguel silently for a few seconds, expression blank, as it always was. Miguel thought he must have been missing some nerve ending in his face. His glasses reflected the sunbeams on the wall. "Let's move onto the general aspects of the investigation," Gorlov said. "The details, you'll have time to get to know them when you enter the Project…"

"You seem to take it as a given that I want to join."

Gorlov turned his gargoyle stare back at him. His stony face revealed nothing. He wouldn't get scared, Miguel decided. "I don't take anything as a given," Gorlov replied after a few seconds. "But I think the explanation will interest you, in any case."

"Of course."

"Quantum inflexor," Gorlov went on, not wasting another second. "Quantum physics states that the state of elemental components of a given material depends on probabilistic functions. I'm sure you're aware of the typical example – the location and velocity of the electrons in the atom. The electron finds itself in many places at once, with more or less probability of being in a specific place depending on that place, correct?"

Heisenberg, Miguel recalled. A consequence of the uncertainty principle. Gorlov wasn't telling him anything his science students wouldn't know. For now.

"It is as if the electron existed in multiple different realities with more or less probability of existing in some than in others," Miguel said. "Like Schrödinger's cat, dead and alive at the same time." Miguel smiled. "Stuck in its quantum box of probable realities."

"Reality. That is the key concept. The inflexor, however, can control the probability of state of these elemental particles. They manipulate the quantum state of matter. They control reality, in short."

Miguel narrowed his eyes. The implications of what Gorlov was saying went much farther than what Monica had explained to him. Controlling reality.

Gorlov went on. "We call the process quantum inflection. It's easier to understand with concrete examples – telekinesis or telepathy, for example." Miguel nodded. "In the case of telekinesis, inflexors don't move objects with their mind. They simply change the quantum reality enough to make an object move. With just a small modification to the state of reality, the object moves by itself. Something similar happens with telepathy. The inflexor doesn't read minds" – Vincent. Miguel rubbed his palms on the leather seat of his chair – "but instead changes reality so that the information contained in the brain is reproduced in someone else's mind."

Miguel didn't move. Gorlov picked up a pen and began to toy with it. His explanation continued. "Once we admit that someone or something can change the quantum state of matter, and thus change reality, the question then becomes, how can a person do it? The answer is quite simple." *Simple?* Miguel asked himself. "As you know, the brain function of animals is based on the electrochemical response of the neurons to outside stimuli." Miguel nodded again. "A stimulus from the outside world activates our neurons. Take light, for example." Gorlov opened his arms wide, as if trying to gather up all the light in the room, and then threw it up at his glasses with his bony hands. "Light activates the sensors in our eyes, which then send an electrochemical impulse to the brain, which activates a response. And we see the light in our heads." Gorlov tapped his pen against his temple twice.

"On the other hand, we know that humans, at least, have something more – the ability to generate responses in the brain without outside stimuli. This process is the biological basis for thought." He stood the pen on the table before Miguel. "Imagination, for example. We could imagine that this pen is a tree, couldn't we?" Miguel nodded again. "A tree with blue leaves, that we've never seen before." Miguel could see the tree in Gorlov's gnarled hand. "Our brain describes the tree, its blue leaves, imagine – vivid indigo leaves, swaying in the wind… Can you see it? You can, can't you? But your eyes have never seen it. They've never seen a blue tree. So where does it come from? From your imagination, or, in other words, from your brain's response to the electrochemical activation of your neurons. Voluntary and internal activation, not external activation."

Gorlov took a sip from his NASA mug. Miguel's eyes rested on the red and blue space agency logo, but it barely registered in his mind. He thought about his imagination, and about how it created images from nothing. A blue tree.

Imagine new realities. Create new realities. That was too much for Miguel to say out loud; he almost barred himself from even thinking about it. His hands ran over the leather seat of his chair.

The scientist left his mug on the desk before putting his pen away in the pocket of his white coat. "There are some humans who, for reasons we haven't yet determined, have developed the ability to go far beyond this with the voluntary activation of their neurons. The phenomenon is very simple – in these people, the neural response is quantum, not electrochemical." Miguel coughed, but Gorlov did not let it stop him. "As a result, their brain does not see an image created by the imagination; they change reality to *show* the image. Quantum inflexors see the blue tree outside their head. They make us all see it. They don't imagine reality, they change it. That's all."

Miguel waited for applause, but nothing came. It all seemed so coherent to him, so mundane. The gaunt, wizard-like scientist's explanations left no room for mystery. The answers were all so simple, as clean as his white coat. *The most valuable scientific theories usually are*, Miguel reminded himself. $E = mc^2$.

"Do you understand?" Gorlov asked. "I assure you, I could overwhelm you with infinite details I haven't even gone near in my explanation. I don't think now is the right time, but…"

"It sounds so simple," Miguel said. He looked at Monica, and she smiled back. Chocolate and cake. She was beautiful. "But is all that empirically demonstrable?"

"Almost all of it has been proven with experiments and measurement equipment developed within the Project. An enormous display of mathematics also gives theoretical support to the theories I have described." Gorlov presented a small notebook with squared paper, Russian and English annotations written in black ink alongside handwritten blue-ink formulae. It all looked like some sort of codex. Gorlov must have been far older than he was letting on. "Everything has been postulated and much more verified with specific experiments."

Miguel cleared his throat before furrowing his brow. "But the implications you've told me about go far beyond the phenomena of telekinesis or telepathy. If I've understood correctly, a quantum inflexor could make anything imaginable a reality."

Gorlov's face quirked slightly, as if the question upset him. But his expression remained as fixed as the squared shape of his glasses. Miguel couldn't interpret anything from his face.

"You can see pretty well, yes?" Gorlov asked.

Miguel sat back in his seat, frowning. "Me? I've never had any problems. But what does that have to do with—?"

"Do you use glasses?"

"I can see just fine. I don't need glasses."

"But you can't see ultraviolet or infrared rays."

Miguel shrugged. "No one can. Those rays are outside the visible spectrum of light for humans."

"That's it." Gorlov began toying with his pen again. "Something similar happens with quantum inflexors. They *see* better than everyone else, but they don't *see* everything."

Miguel half-smiled. He began to suspect what would come next, and he liked it. This was a good scientist who seemed to have answers for everything.

Gorlov continued. "Just like how natural evolution designed us to perceive only the colors between red and violet, it also designed us to have a range of limitations when it comes to quantum inflection capabilities."

Gorlov clicked his pen rapidly, like a crazed seismographer. Miguel couldn't quite understand what unnerved him so much, while his expression remained so calm. "The inflexor is a slightly more evolved human," Miguel said suddenly.

Gorlov hit the pen against the desk, the sound causing Miguel to flinch backwards in his seat. "That has not been proven," the Russian said, adjusting his glasses. "The purely evolutionary argument, I mean. The abilities we study seem to be present, on one level or another, in the entire species, although the majority of us are too weak to bring about a point of inflection that actually changes anything. But there are so many abilities, and all very diverse. Don't reduce it to something so simplistic…"

"I wasn't trying to—"

"… contained, simple, but many. I can list them off to you, if you'd like, all known types of quantum inflexors, categorized by abilities…"

In effect, Miguel told himself, Gorlov wanted to categorize the world, just like Mendeleev. He turned around, while Gorlov talked on about categorizing inflexors, to look at the periodic table on the wall. A little to the left was the door to the office, which was now partially sunlit. Just beyond that door lay a new world – secret labs, the SSR basements, quantum inflexors. The elevator with white spaceship doors.

***

Gorlov watched as Miguel turned towards the door and wondered if he wanted to leave, to escape. He seemed restless. Perhaps he had awoken more fear than interest in Miguel.

"Dr. Le Fablec," Gorlov said, calling his attention. "We would like to propose something to you."

Miguel looked back at him gravely, his eyebrows low on his face, eyes half-closed, as if he were annoyed.

That moment was the most crucial of Gorlov's fifty years of research. The proof from the previous day said that Miguel was a Midas, or something very similar. Some clean readings, detected by the quantum sensors, had registered an unusual ability to produce a point of inflection. Now he had to join the Project voluntarily. Gorlov cleared his throat and tried to speak with the best English he knew.

"With the data we took from yesterday's experiment, I have come to the conclusion that you are a quantum inflexor." He breathed slowly, fixing his gaze on Miguel, who kept his eyes narrowed. Miguel had already seemed reluctant to enter the Project. Gorlov had to offer him something that would interest him. "I would like to offer you an opportunity to form a part of the Quantum Inflexor Research Project."

Miguel did not respond. Gorlov looked at Monica, but she only shrugged.

"Please don't misunderstand," Gorlov added as he started disassembling his pen. "I don't mean to turn you into a subject for experimentation…"

"A guinea pig," Miguel said.

The pen snapped in Gorlov's hands. He tossed it into the trash and picked up a pencil from the desk. "Of course, you would take part in experiments. But I'm offering you a chance to actively participate, to be a member of an investigative team, if you would like…"

"A scientist," Monica added.

"A scientist," Gorlov repeated. The damn Spaniard wasn't yet convinced. He'd have to lure him in. "Laboratories, secret technology, the works… You must know the experiments will be harmless, so at all times—"

"When do I start?" Miguel interrupted.

"The team of scientists…" Gorlov stopped. Monica was smiling, although Miguel kept frowning at Gorlov. *Did he say yes?* "Start? Does that mean…? Dr. Le Fablec, it's an honor for the Project…" Miguel's frown remained. Suddenly, the pencil snapped with a crack. "Are you worried about something?"

"Your glasses are blinding me," Miguel said. "They're reflecting a lot of sunlight. I can't see your eyes."

***

Without them, he's even uglier, Miguel thought as Gorlov removed his glasses to stare at him silently.

Miguel turned to smile at Monica. It had been worth it to endure the fear of meeting Vincent. All of it. Now he knew. And he owed it all to her. Monica smiled too, and she seemed to shine, sitting in that old office seat. She was incredible. Chocolate and cake. "What kind of inflexor am I?" Miguel asked, not taking his eyes off of Monica.

"I'm not quite sure," Gorlov answered, adjusting his glasses again. He stood and began lowering the blinds. "Your case poses many interesting questions. The ease with which you got into Vincent's head—it is rare."

The office had darkened a bit, but it retained an orange light. Gorlov sat at his desk. "What you did can only be done by a catalyst."

"A catalyst?"

"Common inflexors take a long time to control their abilities," Gorlov explained. "They can usually master one or two abilities during their lifetime. The catalysts, however, are the only ones whose control mechanism is based on amplifying other people's points of inflection. When they develop their ability to amplify points of inflection, they also develop many other abilities as their own, and they do it very quickly. They cannot develop all abilities, of course, because of incompatible neural processes."

"This seems much more complex than what you've told me up to now," Miguel interjected.

"It is much more complex and unusual. Since we began researching quantum inflexors, we've only found two catalysts including you, if you really are one."

Miguel couldn't help feeling exceptional, superior. Only two. But... "Who is the other one? Are they here, in the SSR?"

Gorlov looked over at Monica, and Miguel squeezed the leather armrests of his seat. The orange light gave Monica a supernatural look.

"The other one is Dr. Eveleigh," Gorlov replied.

"You?"

CHAPTER 15

Miguel opened his eyes. The well-lit interior of the chamber reminded him strangely of the abundance of light in Gorlov's office. It was already almost a month since the scientist had offered to let Miguel join the Project. Gorlov's office was warm, but the light in the chamber was a cold white. It gave the experiments a clean, more scientific, less supernatural quality. It was a far cry from the lab shrouded in darkness and the dark, spiked exterior of the chambers.

Miguel looked at the clock on the door's control panel. He had spent fifteen minutes standing in the chamber with his eyes closed. Dressed in the black overalls of every quantum inflexor, he was sitting in the sole gray, plastic chair with his hands laid on the table, also made of gray plastic. He had waited for the chamber's neural inductors to set his brain to work, doing some relaxation exercises while he waited.

Miguel felt the coarse plastic beneath his fingertips, almost numb from his relaxed state. The soles of his feet felt the same, his entire body tingling. Dreaming consciousness—that was what they had called this mental state. He was ready.

Looking up at the ceiling of the small inner cubicle, Miguel saw a collection of equipment gathered where the walls met, all pointed at him. Visible light cameras, infrared cameras, thermal sensors, micro-radars, barometers, microphones, laser meters – there was just about enough room for all of them along the border of the ceiling. He studied the most important ones, the quantum sensors. They were devices very similar to video cameras in appearance, surrounded by a blueish halo of light. There were three of them on the ceiling, with a camera beside one of them. Miguel raised his hand to signal that he was about to begin.

Like always, on the table was a yellow piece of paper containing the test instructions. Everything he had to do was right there on the other side of the page, deliberately placed face down. Hidden, like always. Miguel wondered why they never told him anything about the experiments until the actual test itself. He never knew what he would be doing until he was faced with the yellow page. In fact, there were many things they never explained to him. Then again, he wasn't participating in the Project as a scientist. *I'm just a guinea pig*, he reminded himself.

He shook his hand in the air as if waving away a fly, willing the thought out of his head. With his other hand, he turned the page over. Even just thinking about the fact that they were using him as a guinea pig was enough to make him lose his concentration, and he was there to carry out a test. Everything else – being a researcher – would have to wait, at least until he left the chamber. He slapped the yellow page on the table as he turned it over. Fly squashed.

The instructions lay before him. Closing his eyes, Miguel visualized his relaxed body, and instantly felt a prickling in his hands and toes. Totally relaxed. He read the instructions and focused on committing them to memory. *Easy*, he thought.

When he had finished, he pushed the page away from him and looked at the block of steel that lay in the center of the gray, plastic table. This was his test object: a rectangular prism, so polished, so perfect, that it reflected the intense light in the room with dazzling glimmers. It almost hurt to look at it. The block was the same size as an ingot; it must have been very heavy. *How much would an ingot weigh? A lot. I don't know.* How much it weighed did not matter. Miguel would not even touch it. He concentrated on the steel. He had to move it using telekinesis, like he had done already with other materials.

Miguel remembered when he moved his first block of wood after entering the Project. He smiled, recalling how much he had sweat, how the electrodes all over his body had tingled. After an enormous effort of concentration, of imagination and sweat, he had managed to move the wood a few centimeters before slumping in his seat. *But it moved!*

Now, Miguel could move things with barely any effort. He just did it, sometimes, to warm up his brain like an athlete, before the real test. *You'll train your inflexor muscle little by little as time goes on*, Gorlov had said to him, gesturing to the woodblock with his head. *And Monica will help you.*

He felt his brain start to bubble, and then the pain – constant, aching, sweet – in the center of his head. Now he knew that the pain, deemed inexplicable by the doctors, was caused by his being a quantum inflexor. Inflection hurt.

He had already started. Where was Monica? She always helped him from another chamber. Then he felt the impulse, her catalyzing effect. There she was. The steel block began to move.

Miguel settled in his chair and let the world reproduce what he saw in his head. Slowly, the steel moved away from him in a straight line, towards the opposite end of the table. Then, it moved closer to him again, moving back towards the center. It made the same straight movements from left to right, and then right to left, before sliding back like an ice cube to its starting position in the center of the table. It stopped there for a moment. Then, it lifted up. With the same calm movements that took it across the table, the metallic block levitated until it reached Miguel's eye level. The warm-up was over. It was time for the real test. Miguel re-read the yellow paper and carried out the rest of the instructions.

> *Cut the block into two halves using molecular disaggregation. Leave a space of ten centimeters between the separated halves. In the same way, cut the two halves into quarters. Leave a space of ten centimeters between each quarter. Swap the positions of the first and third quarters. Use molecular aggregation to fuse the two quarters on the right-hand side into a single half. Fuse the two remaining quarters in the same way. Cool the two resulting blocks. Return the two blocks to the table at the same time.*

The two perfect, gleaming blocks of steel lay on the gray, plastic table. Their edges were cleanly filed, with no visible soldering edges, like two irrefutable children of the original steel block.

Easy, Miguel repeated to himself. Standing up, he disconnected a device from a small rectangular jack, where the tangled mess of wires from the multiple sensors Miguel wore on his body culminated. He removed them from his arms, his legs, his abdomen, as well as his face, careful not to hurt himself. The wires must have made him look half-man half-machine. But he was already used to it, and in reality, he wasn't really aware of them until he disconnected them and began removing them.

Miguel approached the control pad beside the door and began tapping, initiating the disconnect protocol. He stopped removing the electrodes for a moment; the protocol required some care. Neural disconnection, he was told, was dangerous. Miguel lowered the power of the inductors by one point. Immediately, he felt somewhere in his brain his slow return to reality. It felt clearer, like he was breathing in fresh air.

The truth about the chambers flooded back to his memory. They weren't isolation rooms, as Barrett had tried to explain the first time Miguel saw them, back when he wasn't part of the Project. They were psychic induction mechanisms, an aid for beginner inflexors. And there was danger within. The experiments were not as harmless as Gorlov said they were.

A countdown behind the control pad screen told Miguel how long he would have to wait until he could lower the power again. It would be a few minutes. As he sat, he recalled Monica telling him that he had to adhere to the wait time protocol very strictly. It was similar to decompression for divers, she had said. He could damage his brain if he did it wrong. That was why, he had been told, he got dizzy the first time he entered a chamber, the day Vincent greeted him telepathically, even though that chamber had been at the lowest power setting. Remembering that day still gave Miguel chills. Luckily he had had no more run-ins with Vincent.

He looked back at the countdown. One minute to go.

Quantum inflexor abilities, he thought. X-ray vision. Superhero powers. He could fly if he wanted, put on a cape and…

Turning around, Miguel looked over at the two pieces of steel he had broken and combined. They were perfect. If his ability to control molecular integration evolved like his telekinesis, he would soon be able to do it without the help of inductors. He could do it outside the chambers. He could split and fuse anything.

Build… Create a perfectly-soldered bridge, an exact copy of the Golden Gate, he thought. He breathed slowly through his nose.

The countdown announced that it was time to change the power setting. *3... 2... 1... 0.* Miguel stood up and lowered the power, feeling his vision and hearing sharpen. The countdown told him it would be another six minutes until he could lower it again.

He sat down again. He would be able to do so many things with his powers when he learned to control them. Of course, the scientists didn't like the word "powers." *"Abilities" is the correct term*, they told him. He liked "powers" better. As a boy, he had always dreamed of things like that. Like every other boy, he supposed. He had tried so many times. It was a game. He may have even accomplished it sometimes without knowing.

Play, he thought while observing the blocks. What if he tried to move them with the inductors at a lowered power? Why not? Miguel smiled. It wasn't in the instructions, he shouldn't, but… He bit down on his tongue, still smiling. *I can now*, he told himself. *This is what I'm here for, right?* Without giving himself time to rethink it, he made a V with the index and middle fingers of his right hand, pointing right at the blocks lying on the table. The prickling feeling instantly returned to the center of his head.

The blocks began floating again.

Miguel started to raise and lower his fingers alternately, making the metallic blocks dance in the air – one raised while the other lowered, like a seesaw in a playground. Then Miguel began curling and stretching his fingers, and the steel blocks swung in the air like a swing. Miguel laughed quietly. A playground with swinging steel blocks instead of children.

Abilities usually develop and present themselves in adolescence, Monica had said, *but they're not necessarily tied to physiological changes. There have been cases where, in infancy…*

While the steel blocks hung in the air, a vivid childhood memory sprang to Miguel's mind. The playground in Nice. He and Dani.

Their father always insisted on the family spending the summer in Nice with their grandmother. That way, they wouldn't lose contact with France, with their origins, he always said to them. That wasn't Seville, obviously. They had fun on the beach, but in Nice, he and Dani had to go everywhere together, and Dani spent all his time annoying and bothering Miguel. Miguel even had to let him into the Secret Hole Club just so he wouldn't tell everyone where he and his friends hid and played. The steel blocks kept swinging. Miguel remembered clearly what happened the day after he let Dani into the club. They were alone together that day. They went down to the playground and fought over a swing. *You don't know how to swing*, he told Dani. *Yes, I do. You've been doing it for an hour. It's my turn... It hasn't been an hour!* Dani said when Miguel grabbed the swing handles. He almost fell. *Idiot*, Dani said to him as he walked away. *Stupid. It was my turn*, Miguel replied, already swinging. His brother walked over to his lunchbox and took something out. It was a plastic rocket filled with firecrackers, the one he brought over from Spain. It didn't matter, he couldn't make it fly to Jupiter like he said he'd show Miguel in secret that morning. He didn't have a match. *I'm going to be an astronaut and you're not*, Dani said as he took his father's lighter out of his pocket. He must have taken it from Dad when he wasn't looking. Dani was his little brother – he had just turned six and Miguel was ten – and he shouldn't let him play with fire, but... *You're stupid. You'll never be an astronaut, but I will*, Dani sang, flicking the lighter. Everyone said Dani would become an astronaut. He was so cute, so funny, so clever. No one ever said anything about Miguel. *I hope your rocket explodes!* Miguel thought, swinging his legs out extra hard as Dani lit the rocket.

The steel blocks fell to the gray, plastic table with a sudden, metallic thud.

Miguel's eyes widened. The image of the exploding rocket stuck in his mind. The wounded earlobe, Dani's bloody ear.

It wasn't my fault, he told himself. *My head didn't hurt that time. Or did it? No. I don't remember...*

Destruction, he thought then. *Creation and destruction. This isn't a game.*

A blinking zero on the screen accompanied an insistent beeping. The countdown. Drawing himself up, Miguel lowered the power of the inductors to the lowest setting. Feeling returned quickly to his entire body, to every one of his cells. The bewilderment caused by the chambers disappeared completely, but the image of the bloody ear did not.

Miguel sat down once more for the final wait. *No, it's not a game*, he reminded himself. After the firecracker incident, he had fought with Dani plenty more times – they were children, after all – but he never again wished something bad on him. Nothing so bad he could remember. Was it him? His abilities? He couldn't know. This wasn't a game, his powers had to be controlled. But what exactly did he know about his own powers? Very little. Nothing. Gorlov had informed him of the basics, general things. Monica explained her catalyzing effect to him, as well as the chambers that inducted alpha waves or something, which disturbed the psychometric cerebral activity, sensory activity... *It's a question of cerebral frequencies and perceptive threshold – numbing the senses helps the imagination and points of inflection.* A short, minimal explanation, just like everything else Miguel had been told up to now. No one, not even Monica, had explained anything to him like they would to a real scientist. They still couldn't tell him anything more. *Then when?* He rubbed his hands over the rough gray plastic of the table.

Destruction and creation. He needed to know, not only because he wanted to be a researcher for the Project, but also because he had – he looked down at his hands – a power he needed to master, understand... *use*, a voice said in his head.

They promised me!

With a quick jerking motion, Miguel ripped off the rest of the electrodes stuck to his chest and threw them onto the table. He was nothing more than a lab rat, he told himself as he buttoned up his black overalls. A rat with power. He was the inflexor, he'd investigate himself by himself if he had to. But of course, Miguel didn't have access to any of this equipment, but he could create them. No, that was a stupid idea. But that was his ability, wasn't it?

The final countdown reached zero on the screen. Miguel could leave. He tapped his thumb on the fingerprint scanner, and the doors opened. Leaving was easy enough; and the experiment had gone well, that was good news as well. All his tests went perfectly. He would ask to be assigned to a project where he could research himself and they wouldn't be able to tell him no, he decided. There was no reason to say no. He pushed back some hair that had fallen into his face, clenched his jaw, and with one step got himself out of that *damn rat cage*.

***

Monica felt like an electric current had been running over her brain, and now someone had disconnected her. Opening her eyes, she looked around the gray interior of her chamber. Miguel must have finished his steel block experiment. The point of inflection she had been amplifying disappeared, and as it did, so too did the constant tingling in the center of her head.

According to what Miguel had told her, he could feel it when she activated her catalyzing effect. *An impulse that pulls my thoughts out of my head and brings them into reality*, he told her in an outburst of emotion. An indispensable help, Miguel assured her. Although soon, Monica thought, he wouldn't need her help. Just like he wouldn't need the chamber's induction. Nothing. He wouldn't need anything from anyone. Monica put her white and blue sneaker on her right foot, tying it tight – double-knotted, of course, like she had been taught as a little girl. *Now try it all by yourself*, her mother would say.

Very soon, she thought, putting on her left shoe, Miguel would be able to do everything by himself. She liked being barefoot when she produced points of inflection. She could feel the ground better that way, when she wasn't so separated from reality. The reality she and Miguel warped. Monica only put herself in these chambers so she could take off her shoes as she wished, no other reason. Her chamber wasn't even powered on; she could bring about points of inflection without help from inductors. All of them.

All except the ones she couldn't, of course, with or without inductors. Like the ones Miguel had just produced – break and combine matter. Monica had never gone that far. She tied the laces on her left shoe. One knot, two. She could amplify Miguel, but the disaggregation of matter was impossible for her. When she tried it for the first time, while they investigated her, she nearly collapsed. She couldn't even go through the disconnect protocol properly and had to spend a few days in hospital.

Monica looked down at her sneakers for a moment. They were the most comfortable things she could use, as she was on her feet all day, walking down underground corridors. Fred, always suited up with shiny black shoes, military in style, used to tell her when she entered the Project that she wasn't dressed appropriately for an SSR doctor. Monica smiled. *Those little marathon shoes won't help you become a better scientist*, Fred said to her the day they gave her a white research coat. Then he reached out and gave her a clap on the back with his enormous hand. It was shortly afterwards that Monica failed the steel block disaggregation test, after leaving the clinical unit.

Monica nearly jumped up from her sitting position, straightening her coat. An electrode pulled at the skin on her arm. Then she remembered: the electrodes. She wouldn't take as long as Miguel had in taking them off. Only a few had been placed on her to monitor some of her parameters. If she hurried, she could arrive in time to see the results of the experiment in the control post before Miguel finished disconnecting. Without wasting a second, Monica removed a belt with four electrodes from her head, four more from her abdomen and four from her arms. Miguel would be busy for a few more minutes. *A catalyst. That is what you are and that is what you will study*. That was what Vladimir had told her the day she received her white coat. *The most important of all our achievements up to now*. Now Miguel would be the most important. She would just be the person who discovered him. The discoverer of the Midas; if Miguel didn't fail, of course. She had failed. Fred never said anything else about her shoes.

She impatiently pressed the fingerprint scanner and left the chamber running towards the control post that monitored Miguel.

When she arrived, Monica observed the monitoring screen. She ran a finger over the monitor following a magenta line on a graph. The measurement of the quantum differential, the best variable for a quick analysis. It was good, very good, but… there were a few peaks at the end! Was there inflexor activity in Miguel's chamber? The experiment was over. "What is that?" she asked quietly.

The controller in that particular control post looked at her, blinking twice. "The subject," he said, pointing to a screen showing two metallic blocks floating in mid-air, "has started playing with the steel blocks while he waits. Those are the peaks." He stood staring at Monica, who was open-mouthed, and blinked again. "Right?"

"Yes, of course…" Monica said, nibbling her lip.

She didn't like this. Miguel was starting to produce points of inflection without her amplifying them. He was acting of his own accord. Well, she wasn't his nanny after all, Monica thought. Sooner or later he'd have to use his powers by himself. But… playing? You can't play with quantum inflections. Monica had discovered him. She was the one responsible for his capture, his training. *Playing!* she repeated to herself wondrously. *The power of a Midas is very serious*. Those were Vladimir's words when he told her that she had been a candidate. She memorized Gorlov's face from that morning, informing her that she had been on the cusp of being omnipotent. His sunny office, his inexpressive face framed with Mendeleev's periodic table. It was slightly disappointing for Monica. She would have liked to have been capable of a Midas Effect. But she felt relieved too; she didn't think herself capable of handling that much power… *The power of a god. In my hands. To be a god.* Monica chastised herself inwardly, asking the Lord for forgiveness for thinking such a thing. Just imagining it sparked fear in her. She felt a chill on her neck that made her shudder. This was something very serious. You couldn't play with that kind of power. Dancing blocks of steel! And she was responsible. She had to control him. In that moment, Miguel exited the chamber.

Monica put an effort into smiling and walking over to him quickly. He seemed tired, pushing his hair back as if he were overwhelmed, or resentful. But Monica didn't care about his gestures. Taking him by the arm, she practically threw him out of the lab, towards the elevator.

"You were perfect!" Monica muttered excitedly. "No one has ever accomplished that before, breaking up matter! Although at the end… I should tell you, the thing with the blocks dancing in the air…"

"Yeah," Miguel replied dryly.

Monica blinked. "What's wrong?" They stopped in front of the lab exit doors. Just beyond were two soldiers standing guard over the entrance to level -2.

"Nothing… Well, there is something. No one has given me any research tasks yet," said Miguel. "And don't tell me I'm being too melodramatic."

Monica looked at him seriously. There was a time when she had wanted to be a researcher and continue carrying out tests, but it was not meant to be. She wasn't a Midas, and he… He wanted more than a white coat. He had abilities other humans could only dream of, and he also wanted the coat.

"I want to investigate my experiments, my abilities," he insisted. "All I'm doing now is… stupid magic tricks."

No other inflexor, Monica thought, had ever accomplished what Miguel called a *magic trick*. "I'll talk to Vladimir," she said. "Tomorrow we'll see what can be done about getting you that white coat."

CHAPTER 16

Castillo typed on his laptop, seated inside one of the anti-inflexor safety rooms. He looked up. The room's interior was long, with a low ceiling he could touch if he stretched out his arm. The walls were a metallic gold color. It looked like a fancy microwave.

He liked it there, on level -5, the lowest basement in the SSR Center. It was soundproof and spy-proof. It was even protected from interference from inflexor telepaths. The most secret location in the world. Inaccessible.

But he wasn't sure if a Midas would be incapable of breaking the quantum distortion barriers and start sniffing around.

The room's distorters gave off a feeling like static electricity that made his hair stand on end constantly. Castillo straightened his suit jacket with the palm of his hand, a movement which caused the pinstripe material to spark. But there had never been any Midas who could enter that room, of course.

We'll have to put some pressure on the scientists.

Fred, who was seated at the metallic table in the center of the room, was examining an isoinflexor map, glancing at his watch every so often. Castillo guessed he was nervous because Gorlov had arranged for them to meet there. In fact, if they were in the microwave at all, it meant that whatever the Russian had to tell them was important. Castillo hoped it was. He was tired of waiting for results in tiny gold boxes, like pieces of jewelry. He tapped a key on his laptop, and the video footage he had been watching stopped.

The video footage showed Gorlov's office. It was the day the scientist explained to Miguel what an inflexor was. Castillo enlarged the image until he got a close-up of the subject. Gorlov had just asked him to join the Project, and Miguel, eyes narrowed, seemed to hesitate.

"Vladimir isn't as young as he used to be," Castillo said.

"What was that?" Fred looked at him. Two cavernous wrinkles creased his forehead.

"Look." Castillo turned the laptop around so he could see the screen. He pointed at the footage. "It almost slips out."

"Ah, Walter, you know Vladimir is a professional. The light reflecting off his glasses got in Miguel's eyes; he said so himself."

"He should have let us in the room with Miguel during that talk."

Fred's lack of a response told Castillo the discussion was over. Looking away, Fred turned back to his map, scrutinizing the round, concentric lines. Thousands of isoinflexors. He looked at them as if he were a real scientist who could understand them.

"Every one of those lines costs our country hundreds of dollars," Castillo said. Fred did not move, but he did look at Castillo through the corner of his eye. "The satellites, processing teams, communication networks, the information we buy, the information we steal. Everything on that map comes at a price," Castillo explained.

"Of course," Fred replied, returning his attention to the map.

"This place comes at a price," said Castillo, looking up.

Fred looked at him head-on. "I know it does—"

"We spend millions of dollars on the Project, Fred. And what does Gorlov give us?"

Fred said nothing. He stared at Castillo silently, jaw clenched.

"Nothing," said Castillo.

"Nothing?"

"The Project isn't yielding any results. Millions invested. When are we going to test the Midas?"

"We can't just—"

"Yeah, yeah, sure. The protocol. Following those outdated protocols nearly gave the game away."

"No—"

"Gorlov's old anyway."

"I won't allow you to disrespect…!" Fred stood up from his seat, like an elephant out of control. "You're too new here. Too young. You may have plenty of nice medals, but you don't have the experience or knowledge to criticize the professor—"

Then Vladimir Gorlov opened the door, and the two men fell silent.

As he sat, Fred shot Castillo a look. Castillo thought he saw Fred's fake sense of authority in his tense lips and tiny blue eyes, which were nearly completely hidden by his wrinkled brow. He decided to pretend to respect that authority, shutting down his laptop. Miguel's image disappeared from the screen. Gorlov reached the metallic table in the middle of the room. He didn't grab a chair, or sit. He simply retrieved a black folder of experiments from his briefcase and lay it on the table before speaking. "I have good news."

Castillo got up from the corner where he had been sitting with his laptop and approached the metal table. He sat beside Fred, not taking his eyes off of the black folder.

"Miguel has passed all of the preliminary tests," Gorlov explained. "And he also reached the maximum level of inflexor ability we've ever recorded."

"Has he done the last exercise?" Fred asked. "The one with molecular disaggregation?"

Gorlov reached into the pocket of his white coat and took out two blocks of steel, throwing them onto the table where they rolled and clinked against each other. It was a happy sound, like bells, Castillo thought. The bells of success. Happiness swelled within him for a moment as he took in the small achievement, until he remembered that success – *real* success, the kind of success he wanted – had still not come. That kind of success would still be a long time coming.

"Not even Monica was capable of this!" Fred said, looking amazed as he picked up one of the metal blocks.

Castillo picked up the other block and examined it, turning it over in his fingers. It was a perfect prism, with cleanly filed edges and yellowish specks in the surface that glittered under the golden light of the anti-inflexor room.

"He split the block into four parts. And he fused them together after," Gorlov said, turning to Castillo. "There's no way to tell that these pieces of metal were once separate halves of the same block a few hours ago. Not even an electron microscope could tell. The Midas Effect is just a step away," he concluded.

Castillo left the steel block on the table. "A step that's never been taken." He and Gorlov stared at one another silently. Castillo was still seated, while Gorlov stood tall, wiry, hunched over like a wizard.

The Russian took a breath before answering. "There's a first time for everything." His face, as always, was blank. His accent became thicker, full of cutting, aggressive sounds.

Castillo didn't care if Gorlov got angry. He had his own worries. "Yes," he responded, "but the fact is that we've spent the past month carrying out tests, and we still haven't determined if Miguel is the Midas we're looking for." Picking up the black folder, he leafed through the papers containing the results of the last experiment. "I've read the reports from nearly every investigation carried out since the beginning of the Project. And I'm worried."

Fred intervened then. "There's no reason to—"

"There is no procedure to detect a Midas," Castillo continued. "We've never gotten that far. Is that not reason enough to worry?" He threw the folder on top of the steel block before flattening out his tie.

Fred opened his mouth to say something but ultimately held back, looking to the scientist. Gorlov opened his briefcase and took out a yellow page, identical to the one used for listing instructions in the experiments.

"This is the step we'll be taking," said Gorlov. Castillo straightened slowly in his seat. "No one but me knows about it." Extending his arm, Gorlov placed the yellow page within Fred's reach, where Fred immediately picked it up. Castillo followed the page with his eyes. "I've had the idea since before Monica ever tried molecular disaggregation. She failed, and I've been safeguarding this ever since. Of course, it's not something that could be taught without an appropriate candidate. A useless material. Until now."

Gorlov kept his gaze firmly on Castillo as he spoke. Castillo escaped by nearing Fred and the yellow page that seemed to contain all the answers.

He read the page heading. The experiment code was MIDAS-000. Too suggestive, Castillo thought. It would undoubtedly capture Miguel's attention. He read down through the experiment. It seemed to be a… yes, a transmutation. But that was included in the category of classified abilities. It certainly wasn't a very common ability, but it was considered control of matter, just like what Miguel had done with the steel block. You didn't have to be a Midas to transmute elements from the periodic table. Castillo read on. Miguel, in this exercise, had to turn an ingot of lead into…

"Gold?"

Fred, perhaps because he knew Gorlov better, understood instantly. He smiled as if the yellow page told him a piece of gossip.

"Magnificent!" Fred exclaimed, slapping the paper with the back of his hand. "As elegant as always, Vladimir."

Castillo looked at both of them seriously. He couldn't understand whatever new dirty trick had come to the two survivors of the Cold War. But he was not about to give them the pleasure of showing his ignorance. Getting comfortable in his seat, Castillo crossed his arms and kept his mouth shut.

"As you can see, Walter," said Gorlov, his accent disappearing, almost mocking his ignorance, "the objective of the experiment is not just for Miguel to turn lead into gold. We don't want him to reorganize the atomic make-up of lead – any common inflexor can do that." Castillo arched an eyebrow. "Fine, I'll admit it, none of the inflexors that we have found could do it. But if Miguel could do it, that would not necessarily mean he is a Midas."

Castillo nodded, his expression unchanged. He still couldn't see where Gorlov was going with this explanation.

Gorlov continued. "What we want from the experiment isn't the result, but the process, the way he does it." *Gold!* It all made sense now. Tilting his head slightly, Castillo focused on the Russian. Gorlov seemed excited. "That's why the experiment is called MIDAS-000, so that Miguel reads it and thinks that what he's going to do has mythological connections. He'll lean more on his imagination than on reason." *Imagination…* "That's also why it's an ingot instead of a cold, unevocative block. Miguel has to think that the ingot corresponds to the form of gold, instead of thinking about atoms." Gorlov began to raise his voice. "And that is why Miguel must touch the lead ingot instead of looking at it and concentrating on it – and I remind you that he has never touched the objects in the experiments – because he must feel like King Midas, touching lead and turning it into gold!" Gorlov nearly shouted like a lunatic, his face still expressionless. "It must be his will that changes reality. That will fire up his ability, and show us that Miguel is a Midas Effect," he finished, resting his bony knuckles on the table.

Midas Effect! echoed around Castillo's head.

"That, and the parameters of inflection, of course," Gorlov added in a lower tone of voice. "This is still a scientific experiment, gentlemen."

Castillo half-smiled at Gorlov in mutual understanding, perhaps for the first time since they had met. He felt something similar to respect as he looked at the Russian. Turning over the yellow page again, his eyes found the sentence he was looking for. *Touch the lead ingot and turn it into gold.* Of course. The experiment not only evoked memories of King Midas' actions, but also required an imitation of those actions, and it did so concretely. It was clear, but…

"What if, despite all this invocation of King Midas, Miguel decides to forgo fantasy and reorganize the atomic particles?" Castillo asked. "He's an engineer. He knows the fundamental laws of physics and chemistry that govern the universe." He was sure Gorlov would already have an answer for that.

"You studied science, didn't you?" asked Gorlov.

"I studied law at Yale, but I have a bachelor's degree in science from West Point. Top of my class." Castillo raised his chin just a bit as he spoke.

"Have you ever studied elemental transmutation? Atomic transmutation, I mean."

"I know the basics."

Gorlov removed a notebook from his briefcase, ripped a page out and placed it on the table. He slid it over to Castillo before taking a plastic pen out of the upper pocket of his white coat and placing it on the page.

"Could you please explain to us the details of converting an atom of lead into an atom of gold? What elemental particles would need to be added or removed? What energetic contribution would be necessary? What residual radiation would be generated? The whole process."

Castillo looked at Gorlov silently, and then looked down at the blank squared paper in front of him. He did not reach out for the pen. Returning his gaze to Gorlov, he thought the scientist might tell him it was all a joke. But Gorlov, too, remained silent. He seemed to be awaiting a response.

"I can't do it," Castillo admitted. "I know how it's done, but right now, I can't remember all the details. I have the training, yes, but it's been years since I last studied this. With the right books, with time, I could try—"

"You needn't excuse yourself." Gorlov cut him off. "You'd have to have had some training in physics or chemistry to be able to describe it in such detail, unless, of course, you worked in a closely-related field. And Miguel does not work in that field."

Castillo nodded. Gorlov, evidently, had it all figured out.

"No," Gorlov went on, "it's unlikely that Miguel Le Fablec would so quickly remember all the details of the process and laws that apply to atomic transmutation. This experiment is not like breaking a steel block in two. With the block, the inflexor can imagine the molecules of the cut which separate and reorder themselves in each of the new blocks. They could do it without knowing anything about physics or chemistry. But with transmutation… Miguel cannot visualize anything on an atomic level. He cannot imagine how to replicate a complex process he knows nothing about or barely remembers. The only thing he can do is will the ingot to turn into gold. A miracle."

Castillo nodded, looking back down at the yellow page of Experiment MIDAS-000. "I just hope Miguel doesn't back out," he said. "The test seems absurd, as I'm sure you'll both agree."

"I've thought about that too," Gorlov replied. Castillo was unsure whether the twist in the Russian's mouth, although it remained perfectly straight, was a smile or not. "Miguel yearns to join the research team, and we've been denying him for almost a month. He has just spoken to Monica and *demands* to be a researcher."

"He demands?" Fred asked.

"It was to be expected that he would want to investigate, we knew that. But it suits us very well that he does it now. It will prompt him to hope the test will be a success."

Castillo stared at the scientist. Gorlov was a professional. There wasn't a single crack in his plan. Not one. For the first time, he felt admiration for the member of the old Soviet secret service. Straightening out his suit, Castillo felt several discharges of static electricity and smiled.

"We will propose to Miguel that this experiment be his first investigation," said Gorlov. "Gold, and he will have his white coat."

CHAPTER 17

The refuge of white coats. It was Miguel's first time on level -3, the basement of offices dedicated to secret research. He looked all around, rubbing the palms of his hands over the white table in the meeting room. He had left the door open and from there he could see the endless bustle of scientists. The tapping sound of keyboards accompanied the smell of warm, fresh printer paper. Just like every other office, Miguel told himself. There was nothing out of the ordinary like on level -2; no induction chambers with spiked surfaces, or control panels, or unknown technology. There were just offices and meeting rooms as white and clean as laundry rooms, but it was such a thrill to be there. Miguel scratched his palms slightly. Level -3.

Levels -4 and -5, he had been told, were dedicated to machinery, supercomputers, repair rooms for the spiked chambers, things like that. He hadn't yet had a chance to visit them, but they didn't really interest him. Miguel was only interested in level -3: the level for scientists.

Monica had finally convinced them to assign Miguel a project, although he did have to press her somewhat. Perhaps he shouldn't have. Monica wasn't the one who wouldn't give him a research job. He smiled. Now he was finally here. Miguel stopped observing the tables and computers on the other side of the door and picked up one of the manuals he had brought with him.

Before opening it up, he glanced at his watch; it had only been five minutes. He had arrived half an hour early to the meeting. The meeting room, of course, was still deserted five minutes later. White, noiseless. Miguel had already read – several times – all the documents they had given him. Lowering his eyes, he decided to read the manual one more time. At that moment, Castillo appeared at the door.

Castillo smiled, as he always did. His spotless shoes shone, as they always did, just like Fred's. Gleaming CIA shoes. Castillo tightened his navy tie underneath his dark gray suit as he approached Miguel. He sat beside him, and Miguel smiled back.

"You've come very early," Castillo said.

"It's my first investigation."

Castillo's smile widened. "I understand. I came to organize some papers in my office before the meeting." He picked up one of the manuals in front of Miguel. "I saw you as I passed by. Have you already read all of this?" He folded the book over in his hands, letting the pad of his thumb flip through the pages.

"More or less."

Castillo set the book down and smiled again.

"I read this one too," Miguel added, pushing the other manual over.

Castillo took it in his hands and laid it on his right hand, moving it up and down as if checking its weight. He let out a short whistle as his eyebrows raised.

Miguel liked Castillo. He knew that a lot of people didn't get on well with him. Monica, especially. Of course, Castillo came across as very pretentious in his expensive suits and matching ties. The half-spy half-auditor of the Project. Castillo straightened the knot of his tie. For all his smiles and commercial qualities, it was understandable that he'd run into problems with all those stubborn scientists and their experiments. They weren't particularly interested in anything of the outside world, much less the CIA. *Or anything about how a project is financed*, Miguel thought. Someone had to do the dirty work, the paperwork, get the funds, and he was convinced that Castillo did it all himself.

"You must be very interested in being an SSR researcher," Castillo said, leaving Miguel's other manual on the table.

"Being a researcher in a secret lab. Imagine it…" Miguel laughed. So did Castillo.

"An almost childlike dream, right?" the agent replied.

"Something like that." It was easy for Miguel to be sincere with Castillo. "But so much more."

"More?"

"I'm an inflexor."

"Right."

"I want to know what I am, what it is exactly that makes me… a weirdo, or whatever."

"I see."

"And maybe control it."

"Of course."

The CIA agent touched the words TOP SECRET written in red ink on the front cover of the manual with his index finger. "How is everything with your secret?" Castillo asked in Spanish.

"*¿Qué...?*" Miguel asked, switching back to his native tongue. *What...?* He usually spoke with Castillo in English.

"I've also gone through it." Castillo placed a hand on Miguel's shoulder. He continued in Spanish, his Caribbean accent sweet. "I'm in the CIA, nearly everything I do is secret. It's tough in the beginning: you can't tell anyone about what you're doing, what you're feeling, you know…"

Miguel got the feeling that Castillo, despite his storyteller cadence, was interrogating him. He must have been trying to check if Miguel was trustworthy. It made sense – they had given Miguel confidential documents, much more so than any material he had seen before, until the two thick manuals with TOP SECRET printed in red on the covers. It seemed that the agent was checking that he could trust Miguel with those types of secrets, those papers. Miguel smiled. That meant that whatever he was about to investigate was important.

"I'm not going to reveal anything about the Project to the outside world," Miguel said in English, "if that's what you're worried about."

Castillo smiled too. "Do you think about your family at all, in Spain?" he asked in English. Miguel frowned. "Do you miss them?"

Castillo unsettled him. He wondered if he was really interested in him or if he simply prowled around.

"I'm not evaluating you," Castillo said, breaking a few seconds of silence. Miguel looked down, and then looked him in the eye. Castillo's smile remained. With his perfect suit, impeccable hairstyle and his smile, he looked like he was about to sell Miguel a new Chevrolet. "I miss my family, in Miami. That's all. My people in Little Havana. They barely hear from me anymore, because of work."

Miguel did not respond.

"But I understand why you won't answer. Lots of people don't trust me. Nearly everyone, in fact. That's also because of work." Castillo's smile widened even more. He flattened the lapels on his jacket. "I'm a professional. It doesn't bother me. I don't care if you don't trust me."

"It's not that."

"Well, it doesn't matter. But if you've had any problems with all of this – the secrets, the double life," he looked up at the ceiling, "entire days working underground without seeing the sun – you can tell me. I get it. It's all so new and fascinating right now, but one day it'll bore you."

Miguel pressed his lips together and breathed deeply through his nose. The two men stared at each other silently.

"I think about my brother sometimes," Miguel confessed. "Dani." Miguel visualized Dani's right ear, the tiny scar on the lobe. Then he imagined him in Madrid, wasting his time instead of studying aerodynamics. Miguel, in contrast, was there, in NASA, living the dream they had both had as boys, still unable to do anything for Dani.

"I think about my two sisters too, sometimes. I think about the whole family."

"Dani would really love all this."

"You can't tell him anything, you know."

"Yeah, yes, of course. I wasn't talking about the basements. What's above ground in the NASA Ames Center would be enough to blow him away."

"You think he'd like NASA Ames?"

"He's trying to become an aerospace engineer, but he's not a very good student. He imitates me, he always has, and that makes me feel a little bad that he didn't make it. I think about him a lot, y'know? Underneath it all, I'd like to have him close so I could help him, even though when we're together we're always fighting. It's a sibling thing, we've always been that way. I don't know, maybe I'm just feeling nostalgic about my life in Spain."

Castillo shrugged. "Bring him here," he said.

Miguel stared wide-eyed.

"Sometimes, you need someone close who isn't part of this world. I know from experience. You have Monica, but she's part of these basements, part of this stale air. It would be good for you, and it might motivate your brother. He could work here under a grant in NASA, I guess."

"But…"

"I could take care of it if you want."

"You could?"

Tightening his tie, Castillo gave Miguel a serious look. When he spoke, his voice came out deep. "I took care of your grant in San José University."

Miguel remembered: Jagdish, Professor Branson, his grant to design virtual combat interfaces, all of it. He had barely been paying attention lately to his job at the university. He imagined Dani in San José.

"That's what I'm here for," Castillo continued, "to figure out those details. To make your lives easier. Even though all of you think I'm just here to spy on you." Just then, Fred and Gorlov's voices came from beyond the door of the meeting room. Castillo looked towards the door and added in a lowered voice, "We'll talk later. For now, we should focus on this." He tapped his index finger twice on the manuals before smiling and pushing the secret documents back in front of Miguel. Miguel smiled too.

Gorlov and Fred entered the meeting room. Gorlov stared fixedly at Castillo while they sat. Barrett entered afterwards and closed the door behind him. The blank walls in that room must have been very thin – the tapping keyboards was still audible through the partition. As Barrett sat down, Gorlov adjusted his glasses while he stared at Castillo. He wasted no time at all before he began to speak.

***

Gorlov couldn't take his eyes off Castillo. What was the agent doing there, with Miguel, the two of them in the meeting room? He wasn't pleased to see Castillo alone with the Midas.

"Good morning," he said to Miguel. "Have you read the manuals?" Miguel nodded jerkily and Gorlov continued speaking before Miguel could say anything. "Dr. Barrett will be your project manager." Miguel looked at Barrett, who removed his glasses quickly. "As you have probably deduced from the manuals, this is not a normal experiment. In fact, it's quite novel, which is why I advise you to always follow Eugene's instructions."

Gorlov's stare caused Barrett to speak up. "Okay, Miguel, I'll explain to you the importance of your role in the experiment." From Barrett's arched brows and his fidgeting with his glasses, Gorlov feared he was about to launch into another one of his messy explanations. But Barrett actually explained himself well. "We'll be carrying out a series of experiments that have never been tried before. The results will be difficult to interpret, given how new they'll be. However, we hope that you, as the subject of the experiment and researcher" – Gorlov saw Miguel's barely contained smile upon hearing the word *researcher* – "can help us interpret them.

"The operation description of the tests, like always, will be on a yellow page inside the chamber when the experiment takes place. Everything else will be the same – follow the protocol, pause the experiment if there is any ambiguity regarding the instructions…" Barrett stopped then and cleared his throat. Miguel stared at him, eyebrows pinched together. Gorlov was about to speak when Barrett continued. "I should warn you that in this case it wouldn't be convenient to halt the experiment once it has started. The psychic inductors are functioning at maximum capacity within the chamber."

"That's a bigger risk for me," Miguel replied, wearing a false, wrinkled smile.

"We're going to be starting a new line of experiment and you'll be the one investigating it," Gorlov said.

They had to motivate Miguel. Gorlov pulled out a sheet from his briefcase listing technical specifications. The various pages stapled together did not explain the test, but they did include team configuration details for the experiment, all prepared by Barrett. He could surely show that to Miguel. He thought Miguel would like to see one of those sheets – they were, in effect, a job for a scientist. Gorlov quickly checked the data before giving it to him: the inductors were operating at maximum power, the security measures were also at maximum, and the unfolding of sensors was much higher than usual, almost triple.

He handed the sheet to Miguel, who read it in silence. "It seems like there are a lot of means at my disposal," Miguel said after a few seconds.

"It's an experiment of great significance," Gorlov replied. "Eugene has already warned you that this is the most important of our recent accomplishments."

Miguel ran his hand over the manuals while he re-read the sheet. Gorlov watched how he moved his hand over the gray, sanitized cover. The words TOP SECRET written in red were just about visible between his fingers.

"We're testing a new inflexor ability with you," Barrett added.

Miguel's head snapped up. He looked at Barrett. "What ability?"

"That's part of the operative description. We can't talk to you right now about… It'll all be on the yellow page, of course" Barrett began fluttering through half-sentences. He smiled, but his mousy eyes belied his fear. "You cannot fail, Miguel," he finished in a whisper.

"He *must not* fail," Gorlov corrected, fixing his eyes on Barrett before turning to Miguel. "This is *his investigation*, Doctor," he added, taking out a perfectly folded white coat from his briefcase. The NASA logo was stitched into the top pocket.

The silence that fell allowed the tapping from the keyboards to filter through the entire room. Gorlov looked at the two men, one by one. They both looked serious. He watched Miguel stare at the new coat, inhaling the level -3 air slowly. The one for scientists.

"I won't fail," Miguel said.

CHAPTER 18

Miguel failed.

Monica, from her chamber, had just felt the electric buzzing in her head come to an abrupt halt. Miguel's inflection disappeared, but the experiment had not yet finished. She stood up immediately, barefoot, and left the room without her trainers. She needed to see what was going on.

As she exited, she saw Eugene Barrett standing at a control screen. His small eyes behind his round glasses were glued to the parameter monitoring screen as he shook his small head. Monica ran over to him, her eyes following the fall of the magenta line that represented quantum differentials. The power of the inductors was falling too. The parameters were falling apart.

A medical team ran towards Miguel's chamber, pushing a stretcher.

The door to the chamber opened and a beam of light shone into the room. It illuminated the shadowed area of the lab as if a ghost had escaped the chamber. From the light emerged Miguel's silhouette, and Monica ran to him. He looked like a desert survivor – he was sweating profusely, his face red and his steps faltering. Then, Miguel collapsed.

The words "brain damage" filled Monica's mind. She had been told it could happen. It had nearly happened to her. Miguel could be a zombie now. The inductors, the exit protocol, they had all been breached. Monica felt the air turn solid, like it stuck in her throat, but she hurried her pace.

She was just about to reach him when a member of the medical team stepped in front of her.

"You can't touch him," the doctor said. "Not until we've finished with him."

Monica watched them pick Miguel up and place him on the stretcher before injecting him with a syringe full of blue liquid.

Analgesic sedative, Monica thought. *Like what they gave me.*

They took Miguel away to one of the medical units, while she and Barrett followed a few steps behind. They would have to wait outside, the doctors told them. Monica nibbled her lip as she approached the glazed door of the clinic. She hated the mini-clinics on level -2. They were gloomy, full of electric robot-like equipment, with matte black walls like the spikes on the chambers. The day Monica failed her first test, she recalled, they put her in one of these mini-clinics. She did not like it then, and she certainly did not like it now. The doctors began placing some headgear on Miguel.

Flat encephalogram, Monica thought. She felt a block of air enter her body with a spasm and her throat closed over again. She took her gold crucifix into her hand and squeezed. The doctors kept attaching Miguel to different pieces of equipment. Miguel lay still.

Almost mechanically, Monica bit down on her lower lip. Ever since Miguel did the steel block experiment, things hadn't gone well between them. They fought over nearly everything: over his obsession with getting a white coat, over his use of his abilities. He would continue playing with his abilities once the experiments ended, investigating what he could do by himself. He called it exercising his right to utilize his own abilities. Miguel seemed to think himself the only inflexor on Earth, and he hadn't even been told he could be a Midas yet. Monica almost wished that he'd fail for once, that something would happen to make him lose that petulant attitude… But now that something *had* happened…

The doctors studied a monitor pointed away from Monica with expressionless faces. No good or bad news. She was about to do away with all the warnings and enter the clinic when the doctor finally opened the door.

"He's okay," the doctor said as the rest of his team filed out. "He's conscious now, but he'll be asleep in a few minutes. We'll keep him asleep for at least an hour. You can go inside, but please don't touch anything. Or him," he added.

Monica was already inside the room before the doctor had finished speaking. She went inside and sat right by Miguel's side. She leaned forward to touch his head, but quickly remembered the doctor's warning and froze, her fingers hovering just a few millimeters above his thick mane of hair. *Shhh!* she whispered to herself, and drew her hand back as if she had been whipped. She felt so clumsy, so lost. Barrett seemed to feel the same; he stood a few paces behind her between the door and the bed. Monica was grateful for the intimacy he left them. A little bit of space, just enough that Miguel wouldn't feel scrutinized by everyone and could be honest with her. She gestured to Barrett with the palm of her hand not to move. Barrett nodded his small head, and Monica turned back around to Miguel.

"Miguel," Monica said quietly, trying to cover up her worry with a neutral tone. Miguel barely moved his head to be able to look at her. "Are you okay?"

Miguel looked at her for a few seconds before looking at the medical equipment. "I couldn't do it."

"Some experiments don't go well the first time; it's normal—"

"No, you don't understand!" Miguel exclaimed. Suddenly, he clenched his jaw and grimaced with his eyes shut tight. "Shit, my head!" Monica knew all too well the effects of rapid disconnection, as well as the pain Miguel was going through now. The center of his brain would feel as if it were squeezed in a fist. If he got worked up, the pain would get worse. But Monica also knew that he wouldn't feel anything in a few minutes, when the analgesic sedative flowed through his body.

Fred came into the room then. Monica and Barrett turned toward him, but neither spoke. Barrett gestured with a finger to his lips that he should keep quiet, and, gesturing with the same finger, that Fred should wait alongside him. Fred approached Barrett and wordlessly handed him a black folder.

When Monica was sure neither of them would speak, she turned back to Miguel. "Don't worry," she said, "the pain will be gone soon."

"I read the instructions," said Miguel, looking at Monica. "The yellow page. I can't do that… Turn things into gold!" His face crumpled again, his suffering clearly less intense than before. The sedatives must have started working. "That's not science."

"Try not to overexert yourself."

"I got nervous when I saw that I couldn't do it. I lost my patience. I think I messed up the disconnection protocol. I went too fast."

"Way too fast. But it doesn't matter anymore. You were lucky, it's nothing serious. It'll fade soon," Monica insisted. She waited a few seconds before asking what she really needed to know. "What happened with the lead ingot?"

"I couldn't turn it into gold." Miguel huffed. "It sounds even more ridiculous when I say it out loud. MIDAS, an experiment named after the king from the story. I had to," Miguel smiled, "touch the ingot with my finger and turn it into gold. What does Gorlov want? To become rich, or what?"

Monica sat back.

"Sorry," he said. "I'm still nervous." Miguel looked over her shoulder at Barrett and Fred. He greeted them with a small wave of his hand.

"It's fine," said Monica. "Try to relax. The test required more effort, yes, but you've already done similar things before, like breaking steel blocks and fusing them. You've played with matter before."

"No, it's not the same." Miguel clenched his jaw again, just a little. "Breaking things apart and putting them back together is just moving molecules. Moving things is easy, and…" He faltered. "And you have a physical sense of what you're doing. But touching something and turning it into gold… I don't know what to tell you. I don't know how something can be turned into gold, whether I touch it or not."

It was clear that Miguel could not believe in the experiment. Monica looked over at Barrett, who opened the folder Fred had given him and began to look through the pages inside. She went back to the questioning.

"Did you feel that boiling sensation in your brain when you touched the ingot? You know, that sweet pain in the center of your head, the buzzing…"

"No, I don't think so," Miguel answered slowly. He began to appear tired.

"Nothing?"

"No, nothing."

Miguel's eyes slid closed before opening again. *The sedative*, Monica thought. *It must be kicking in, in his brain.* The headache vanished, just as quickly as the blue liquid had put

Miguel to sleep. There wasn't much time left. She looked at Barrett again.

Barrett handed her a graph showing the magenta line representing the quantum differential, although Monica couldn't quite read all of the details from where she was sitting. He pointed a finger at Miguel, and Monica guessed he wanted to ask a question. She nodded.

"Miguel," Barrett said, "did you imagine the lead turning into gold? Did you earnestly wish to see it turn into gold?"

"No, no, I… I couldn't," Miguel responded, eyes closed.

A few seconds of silence passed, and it seemed he had finally gone under. Then his eyes opened again, ever so slightly, a thin line between his eyelids so small no one could tell who Miguel was looking at.

"I thought it was… impossible," he said, before losing consciousness.

***

Gorlov studied the numbers they had just given him. Preliminary results from the MIDAS-000 test. He looked carefully at every figure, every fact sheet, every number. But it wasn't enough. He would need the final graphs, the black folder.

Miguel had failed. The experiment had not failed, but Miguel had, he told himself. He was almost sure, but he couldn't prove it. The figures, the moment of failure, were confusing. Castillo tapped his fingernails on the metal table in the anti-inflexor room. The rhythmic tapping, like that of a bolero, seemed to reverberate against the metal walls. Gorlov looked at the agent.

"Have you found the problem yet?" Castillo asked. The tapping stopped as he lifted his hand to straighten his tie. He did not smile.

"No," Gorlov replied. "But I would appreciate it if you could stop making noise. I can't concentrate."

Castillo nodded, crossing his arms silently while Gorlov took out a pen from his coat pocket. He began clicking the top of the pen, leaning over the records of the quantum differential. The differential fell just before Miguel produced the Midas Effect. But Gorlov didn't have the graphs. The folder. Miguel had not managed it, but…

At that moment, the door to the anti-inflexor room swung open.

***

Monica entered hurriedly. She felt the static electricity of the quantum distorters and inwardly cursed the room. Gorlov and Castillo were already there. Good, she was in a hurry.

"Eugene and Fred are coming now," she said, leaving on the table the black folder Eugene Barrett had given her containing the results. "I think we're done with this experiment."

No one responded. But she, in effect, had concluded that useless test. Barrett entered then. He sat beside Gorlov.

"Are there conclusive results?" Castillo asked, placing his hands on the table and drumming his fingertips on the surface.

Monica thought he shouldn't have been the one asking questions, but she answered, "Yes."

"No," said Gorlov, almost simultaneously.

The two looked at one another. In that moment, Fred walked into the room.

"We have less than an hour until Miguel wakes up," Monica told them as Fred sat down beside Castillo.

There was no time, she thought, to start a fight with all of them. She didn't want to start it either, least of all with Vladimir.

She looked down at the folder in her hands. The results of the experiment failure were there, along with data about the disconnection that had left Miguel badly hurt. Monica pushed the folder on the table, sliding it over towards Gorlov.

"Let's see," Gorlov said.

While Gorlov picked up the folder and leafed through its contents, Monica sat and observed the others. The static feeling from the walls still felt uncomfortable, but what was inside was worse. Castillo. He was looking at her cautiously, his right eye squinting as if he were looking at her through a microscope held between his eyelashes. His fingers continued drumming on the cold metal. Music. Or a silent machine gun. She couldn't like a single thing about him.

Castillo kept his eyes on her as he asked, "Is it normal for an inflexor to enter an inflexor-proof room?"

Monica grimaced disgustedly before answering. "Of course it's not normal! Investigating Miguel isn't normal—!"

"Monica is part of the team researching Miguel," Gorlov interrupted. Monica fell silent. "There's nothing more to say about it. Eugene?" he said, handing Barrett the folder. It was clear that Gorlov had laid the matter to rest.

Straight to the point, as always, Monica thought. She was glad he was like that. She had no interest in wasting time arguing with stupid Castillo. Crossing her arms, Monica smiled at him.

Barrett opened the folder and put it on the meeting table. Everyone stopped paying attention to Monica and looked at the page Barrett was showing them. It was the same page he had shown Monica in the mini-clinic.

"This is the problem," Barrett said. "The quantum differential falls here." He pointed on the graph to the magenta line falling abruptly to zero. "Miguel interrupted his inflexor activity when he had to imagine the lead turning into gold."

Looking at Gorlov, Barrett continued. "The experiment started off right. Miguel used telekinesis to move the ingot in all directions and his level of inflection increased gradually." He ran his finger over the rise in the magenta line. "Everything was fine until here. The records of inflexor activity are correct for the entire preliminary process for telekinetic movement." Barrett looked at Castillo. "That is, the warm-up," he added, "But they disappear when the process of transmutation begins. With the gold."

"Are you suggesting," Gorlov asked, looking at the graph, "that Miguel stopped his inflexor activity when he got to the point of touching the ingot?" He made a circular motion with his hand on the paper, as if trying to surround the mess of colored lines on the graph. "Not all of the variables we have measured show that tendency."

Monica turned her attention to the colored lines, a tangle of nearly thirty different variables that mixed with one another on the page like a child's drawing. Vladimir was the true expert. Monica didn't doubt that he could interpret all of the gibberish about variables and tendencies and gradients better than anyone. She respected his opinion, but there was a possibility that he was biased now out of a boastful defense of his experiment.

"Correct, not all the variables show that," said Barrett. "But the quantum differential doesn't fall to zero if the subject's inflexor activity stops."

"And could it not be the case," Gorlov said, "that Dr. Le Fablec simply is not a Midas-type inflexor?" Monica's eyes widened. "It might be that he is not able to turn his imagination into reality," Gorlov insisted, his face blank.

Monica watched the others fidget in their seats. Even Castillo appeared to have let one of his masks slip. His self-assured expression creased, and his fingers stopped drumming on the table. He tightened the knot of his tie. But Monica didn't care about Castillo, or any of the others. *Vladimir!* she told herself. He couldn't possibly fall now just because of one failed test.

"I haven't analyzed all the data thoroughly," Barrett admitted. He shifted through the pages like a frightened schoolboy, mumbling. "But I think the subject has not managed to imagine it. And if he hasn't imagined it, he couldn't have… The graph…"

Gorlov picked up the folder and looked at the graph. "We must analyze all of this material carefully, Eugene," he said, closing the folder and leaving it on the table. "I don't understand why you're so insistent that Miguel could not imagine the transmutation. This data is not…"

"He told me," Barrett interrupted. "'I thought it was impossible.' Those were his exact words. Monica and Fred were there."

"It's true," Monica said, looking at Fred, who nodded emphatically.

Vladimir stared at her blankly, more so than usual. It was like his glasses, which he had not changed in decades, had finally instilled in him a definitive unfeelingness. Monica thought that he always looked at her angrily whenever he did so intensely. And right now, he was looking at her very intensely.

"Monica," Gorlov said, "you know that the impressions given by the subject can be wrong."

"Yes, but when I asked him what he felt in his brain when he tried the transmutation, he told me—"

Gorlov interrupted. "I suppose he said he didn't feel anything."

Monica thought she heard a Russian accent in his words. It hurt her to face him like this. She didn't want to do it, but the data was what it was and there was no avoiding it. She had to expose it all.

"I'm an inflexor," said Monica. "When you don't feel anything, it's because nothing is happening. I think Miguel believed that transmutation was impossible, so he didn't truly desire it. He didn't imagine it – he didn't dare. We can't determine if he's a Midas because he hasn't carried out the experiment. This test… has proved nothing." The last sentence hurt her as much as if she had slapped Vladimir. A full-armed slap with an open palm, resounding, public. "I'm sorry," she added.

Gorlov said nothing for a few seconds. No one said anything.

"There is nothing to be sorry for," he said finally. His Russian accent was very pronounced, his words slow. "We're not here to feel sorry for ourselves or apologize for our discoveries. We're here to investigate." The scientist fell silent again and looked at everyone in the room one by one. "There is one piece of data which indicates that Miguel stopped producing points of inflection when he got to the transmutation, but it is inconclusive. We don't know if he didn't want to do it, or if he couldn't do it. That's the reality. Let's see…"

Gorlov began a series of detailed explanations about theories, mathematics, the uncertainty of the variables… everything he could to defend his hypothesis. The tension, his Russian accent, echoed around the room. Monica couldn't bear to see him like this, trudging through mathematics to find an excuse that would clean the image of his experiment. It was ridiculous. He seemed afraid to continue investigating. Or maybe he was afraid of failing. Monica looked away so she could stop listening to his explanations. She didn't want to listen to him, couldn't listen to him.

Monica saw the black folder on the metal table. She hadn't had time to properly analyze the material, and thought in that moment that maybe she could find an answer. Barrett wasn't very imaginative. He was a good laboratory leader, yes, very meticulous, but he wasn't very clever when it came to searching for oddities. She decided to look it over. It was the best thing to do to escape Vladimir.

Discreetly stretching her arm out, so as not to interrupt the explanations, Monica grabbed the folder. She opened it and searched for the page Barrett had shown, looking at the lines, the variables. The magenta line of quantum differential fell to zero the moment Miguel touched the ingot. That variable was not internal to the subject, it was a measure of quantum inflexion outside him. It didn't show anything about what happened in Miguel's head, only what he produced outside himself, which showed up on the sensors. The consequences, not the causes.

Vladimir was right. That line by itself, its bright color standing out against the other lines, could mean that Miguel had abandoned the experiment before even trying transmutation, or that he had tried it and failed. The failure of the experiment or the failure of the Midas. Monica looked at Gorlov. He was still arguing with Barrett, his Russian consonants echoing sharply against the metallic walls like spitfire. Almost convulsively, Gorlov removed and put back the cap of a fountain pen Monica had given him for his last birthday. An expensive gift, a display of affection for him. *He'll destroy it soon*, Monica thought. But he was right, they needed something more, a measurement, proof of what was happening in Miguel's brain right at the moment when he stopped.

If there was a way to take measurements of inflection inside the brain... she thought. But that wasn't possible.

The head. His head. There was something.... Monica looked in the folder for the graph of cerebral frequency. She used to always look at it after experiments. A single page of results with her name on it in the black folder. It was a simple gray-blue graph taking a rudimentary measurement, barely important, but it belonged to her. The proof of her catalyzing effect on Miguel's wishes. As she remembered, a small chill ran over her skin, the same shiver she felt when she produced points of inflection with him. Yes, she told herself, Miguel had to be a Midas. If he wasn't, how could she explain that shiver, that spasm in her brain that she felt when she was his catalyst? She felt in him an unattainable power of inflection. She had felt it in so many experiments she couldn't possibly be wrong.

Gorlov tapped the metal table with his pen, causing Monica to shudder. Barrett silently removed a page from the folder Monica was holding and slid it over towards Gorlov. "You see?" Gorlov said when he received the page. He continued unleashing his Russian consonants in his seemingly endless, tedious scientific speech.

A disappointment for his pride in science, Monica said to herself as she flipped through the folder again in search of her cerebral frequency graph. She looked up with wide, unfocused eyes to the empty space between herself and the golden wall of the anti-inflexor room. The hum of the quantum distorters bore down on her, the static making her hair stand on end. Monica recalled Castillo's words. *Is it normal for an inflexor to enter an inflexor-proof room?* And then it came to her: she was the only inflexor who could access that room! She chewed on her lip.

Inflexors weren't part of the team of scientists. Monica was an exception. She had been a researcher since the beginning, Gorlov's right hand. But Miguel.... They had only told him he would be a researcher in order to motivate him, in order to achieve the Midas Effect. If he didn't achieve it, what interest would the Project have in an aerospace engineer? Miguel barely knew anything about the disciplines they used there. They would only allow him to be a guinea pig, like Vincent, like the rest of the inflexors. She had been lying to him just for that end. Monica bit down harder on her lower lip. She felt no pain, but saliva began to build at the back of her throat. *I've been lying to him just so he would become a lab rat. He'll hate me*. Both of Monica's legs began bouncing automatically. Gorlov tapped the table once more with his pen, as if he wanted to drill into the surface. Monica swore she could feel the pen's taps on her temples. Suddenly, images began flashing in her mind – Granada, the restaurant in San José, the Mirador in the Alhambra where she met him, how they kissed, the maroon sofa, the breakfast he made, how they talked naked after sex. Images that dissipated, faded away forever. *It can't be!* She was drowning.

Miguel is a Midas! Monica assured herself as she looked down at the cerebral frequency graph. She removed it with such force that the page tore, the sound attracting everyone's attention.

She looked back at them without a word, holding the page in her hand and biting her lip. Her legs stopped moving until Monica took a breath, and they returned to their rhythm. Everyone turned back to Gorlov.

Monica studied the graph she had taken out, although she wasn't all that interested in it anymore. There was nothing there that could save her. The gray-blue line showed a rhythmic oscillation, much like how her legs moved. Her test for inflexor activity, constant, monotonous, to amplify Miguel's thoughts. The typical catalyst effect. All normal. Miguel would hate her, that was the only thing that wasn't *normal*.

She was about to close the folder and put it back on the table when an idea came to mind, as quickly as a magician's trick. Perhaps Miguel's frequency…

Miguel's frequency? Monica suddenly noticed the rush of adrenaline in her veins. Pushing away her own cerebral frequency graph, she searched for Miguel's. They also measured his cerebral frequency, and that… That could explain… As she searched, she felt a tiny pinch in her brain, as if her inflexor instincts were predicting what she would find. If there was a peak… Monica thought of her gold crucifix. She wanted to touch it, but she had to keep searching. The pads of her fingers seemed to burn. Miguel's cerebral frequency. The explanation. A peak. The frequency…

"Ah!" Monica let out a noise when she found Miguel's graph.

There it was. The peak.

There was a maximum in the gray-blue line just before the drop, and then a small increase in cerebral frequency. It was so simple, so stupid how that explained everything. Monica rubbed her eyes, as if her discovery were a mote of dust that would disappear. But the graph didn't disappear. The answer was there.

"Have any of you seen Miguel's cerebral frequency curve?" Monica said. Her tone of voice rose above Gorlov's wordy nonsense. He stopped as everyone stared at Monica.

Barrett took the folder from her hands, adjusting his round glasses as he analyzed the graph. His serious expression took over his entire face.

After a few seconds, he looked at the middle of the graph and saw Miguel's peak recorded in gray-blue ink. His small eyes widened considerably like he was seeing a magic trick. Wordlessly, he handed the folder to Gorlov, who took it and nodded slowly as he read. It seemed he didn't need to search for what Monica already found. Fred stood and approached the scientist, also looking at the graph. Castillo did not move.

"I don't know how you overlooked this," said Gorlov, looking at Barrett. "I don't know how I overlooked it either," he added. He stared at the page for a few more seconds before shaking his head. "I can't believe you didn't see this, Eugene."

"He's a human being. He made a mistake," Monica said.

Gorlov turned his head sharply to look at her. "I have never doubted Eugene's efficiency," he said. "Or my own. And I know we're human beings." His Russian accent had disappeared completely. "Everyone makes mistakes, but it's a strange coincidence that the two of us have made the same mistake." Gorlov's stare from behind his glasses remained fixed on Monica. "You know I don't believe in coincidence," he said.

"I don't understand it either," Barrett added. "I had already seen this graph before. But, there is the answer."

"Well," Gorlov said, "there's nothing more to talk about. The experiment failed. Eugene, we'll look over this more slowly."

Fred placed a massive hand on Gorlov's shoulder and said, "We'll find another way."

Monica was certain Vladimir didn't need encouragement. His experiment had failed, but the Project went on. That was the important thing. Miguel was still a candidate.

Miguel! Monica remembered suddenly that he was all alone in that dark room of the mini-clinic. And she had left him in such a pitiful state. She should go up and check on him, help him recover. Her watch told her she had… ten minutes. But she had to go through the exit controls on level -5, take the elevator, go through the controls on level -2…

Gorlov opened his mouth to speak, but Castillo interrupted before he could. "Could you explain what's going on?" he asked. His level tone echoed loudly around the metal walls of the anti-inflexor room.

Everyone turned around to face him. Castillo pressed his lips together in a firm line, his face a far cry from his usual smiling masks. He looked at everyone in turn, leaning back in his seat with his arms folded, as though he despised them.

***

Castillo despised that cohort of cryptic scientists. He felt the muscles in his crossed arms tense. They all seemed to enjoy using their jargon about quantum inflexors and neural variables. He had only understood one thing in the whole discussion – that Gorlov had failed. But Miguel… Nothing proved that Miguel was a Midas. He loosened the too-tight knot of his tie.

"Don't worry about it, Walter," said Fred, sighing as he returned to his seat. "It's better not to go into too much technical detail when scientists start arguing. They'll tell us about it another time, in a language we can understand."

"I would prefer to hear it now," Castillo said, crossing his arms even tighter.

Fred's enormous face wrinkled, but Gorlov extended a hand to Barrett. He began explaining immediately.

"The peak in the blue graph means that Miguel abandoned the experiment before trying to transmute." Barrett showed the page to Castillo. "It's a jump from low-frequency alpha waves, the mental state in which something is imagined clearly enough to produce quantum inflection, to high-frequency beta waves, which don't work when it comes to creating images which then become points of inflection. Then, the frequency increases before stabilizing in the beta zone…"

Castillo began to open his mouth to stop Barrett from becoming mired in his own explanation. It was like he was speaking in a dead language. Dead and buried, Castillo thought. He hated Barrett and his explanations, which he never fully understood. He looked at Monica and saw that she was smiling.

She seemed to enjoy seeing him there, not understanding a word, like the idiot she thought he was. He was sure that smug, spoiled brat of Gorlov's was laughing at him. He had known plenty of other harpies like her in Yale. Monica looked at her watch, shook her head, and interrupted Barrett.

"What Eugene is trying to say is that Miguel left the mental state capable of producing inflection before even attempting transmutation," Monica said. Barrett nodded. "The cerebral frequency shows that. He never got to imagine the lead turning into gold. He left before he could enter the… *imaginative* state, let's call it, so you can understand," she added before checking her watch again.

It no longer mattered what snooty little Monica thought. He recalled that they had explained to him that the exercises had to be designed to prevent that – to prevent the inflexor from doubting their ability and stopping their imagination. That was why the inflexors did warm-ups and inductors were used in the chambers. Of course, Castillo would not have trusted a staging of a mythological king turned into a children's story. Adjusting the knot of his tie, he placed his hands on the table and spoke once the felt the cool metal on his skin.

"Could we repeat the experiment?" He guessed not.

"No," Barrett answered. "It wouldn't be any use. If Miguel doesn't believe in it, and he has already broken the induction in a chamber once, he'll do the same thing every time we try it. No, this experiment isn't useful to us anymore. And honestly, I can't think of anything different to substitute it. Turning lead into tin and things like that. Bah! If we try that, Miguel will think we're making fun of him. No, I can't think of anything."

Monica once again checked her watch. Leaning over to Barrett, she spoke in a low voice. "I'm leaving in five minutes."

Castillo watched her. It appeared she was planning to leave without solving the problem.

In that moment, Gorlov began collecting the papers and putting them back into the black folder. He was getting ready to leave too, it seemed. The knot of Castillo's tie felt too tight again, but he didn't touch it this time.

No one is leaving here until we find a solution, he told himself. He was lifting the index finger of his right hand, about to prohibit them from leaving, when Gorlov placed the folder on the table. He passed his hand over it as if flattening it and said, "There is an alternative plan."

Everyone straightened in their seats, foreheads creased as if they hadn't heard the Russian correctly.

"What plan?" Castillo asked immediately. His index finger was still lifted.

"I'm not sure I want to use it," said Gorlov. "It's dangerous."

"What plan?" Castillo repeated. His tie now really was too tight.

"A dangerous experiment?" Barrett asked. "It goes against the policy of the Project to place a subject under examination in danger,"

"Miguel isn't the one who is going to be in danger."

Castillo used his pointed finger to loosen his tie. It seemed to him that Gorlov, without expressing anything in particular, could not avoid the gravity of the situation affecting the look in his eyes. That must have meant that there was a serious alternative. A new possibility! Castillo breathed deeply, mouth closed, in silence. *What plan?* he wondered, but he managed to keep himself quiet.

"Who's going to be in danger?" Monica asked.

Gorlov looked her in the eye. "You."

His Russian accent was sharp as he went on, while Monica bit her lip worriedly as she looked at him.

"You don't have to do it," Gorlov added.

"Tell me what I have to do and then I'll decide."

"We have to put you in a life-threatening situation so he'll save you using his abilities."

Monica looked at her watch and then back at Gorlov in a rapid movement. "We'll do it."

The two stared at one another silently.

Castillo broke the anxious silence. "Can we do this?" he asked. He looked at Monica, and then at Gorlov. No one wanted to answer, but he insisted. "Maybe Miguel won't believe in it. We've already tried getting him to imitate a hero from a story. Now he'll have to try to be a… comic book superhero? Save the heroine with his superpowers or what?"

"Like a comic book character," Barrett repeated quietly, slowly, his eyes squinting as if he were mulling the idea over.

"Yes, something like that, but suggested beforehand," Gorlov said.

They're all crazy! Castillo thought.

"We also need the person in danger to have an emotional connection with him." Gorlov looked at Monica. "Miguel's motivation is essential."

"Life-threatening…" said Fred. "Vladimir, you know we can't risk…"

Castillo could not believe it. They actually wanted to do it!

"The danger Monica will face won't be real; it will be pretend," Gorlov responded. "Monica will have to trick him, be a decoy. The true risk lies in that we don't know how Miguel will react. He could respond violently, out of control, with perhaps dangerous consequences. Monica will be there, in the middle of the points of inflection, amplifying them, without even knowing if what she is amplifying puts her life in danger. That is the risk."

Castillo wanted to say something, resist, stick out his index finger again, when Monica spoke. "Have you designed the procedure yet?"

"Basically," Gorlov said. "Yes, the essentials. Some of it still needs to be worked out, of course."

The damn Russian always seemed to be one step ahead of everything. He had already been working on Plan B. Castillo tightened his tie again.

"Okay, let's do it," Monica said. "I have to go now, Miguel will be waking up soon. What should I tell him about what happened today?"

Castillo observed her silently. Monica seemed to want to smile. Maybe, he thought, she was relieved to have found a way to compensate Gorlov for the failure of the experiment. Or maybe it was because she found another opportunity for Miguel, but now she would have to lie to him. No, it was much more than that. She had to lie to her boyfriend, the love of her life, or some similar sentimentality. She was in love with him, that much was sure – Roth watched them very closely. Yes, he was certain – and now she would have to lie to him in a life or death situation. Women could lie very well. That was something he knew all too well. But Monica… She wouldn't just be keeping some information hidden from Miguel, like she had been doing until now. This time, she would have to set a trap for him, a good trap. And be a decoy.

"When he wakes up, tell him there was something wrong with the yellow sheet," Gorlov said. "Tell him we should have described the atomic process of transmutation so that he could imagine it and recreate it. Tell him we've collected a lot of data and his research will continue once he has fully recuperated. Soon, in a few weeks."

I already planted the idea of atomic reaction before, Castillo remembered. The Russian had just stolen his idea. He improvised well. Or maybe he wasn't improvising. Maybe he had already thought all of this out. That old, sly Soviet fox.

However, Monica... No, he definitely couldn't trust her fully with the success of the experiment. She could fail. She *would* fail. Unless he fixed it first, of course. Castillo reached for his phone in the inner pocket of his jacket. He didn't want to take it out, since there was no coverage there and it would startle everyone, but touching it calmed him. Perhaps there would be an opportunity if he intervened. He had to think of something.

A comic book hero, he thought.

CHAPTER 19

Beside the keyboard was a comic. A quick tapping had attracted Miguel's attention towards Jagdish's keyboard. The Indian was writing something at high speed. Miguel didn't know Jagdish liked comics.

He and Jagdish were the only ones left in the Department of Systems Engineering, August having cleared out the campus. Miguel brought a page over to Jagdish and said, "This should solve the problem from last week."

Jagdish stopped typing, taking the page and looking it over. "That's great," he said, smiling, his eyes fixed on the page he had been given. Then he looked at Miguel. "I hope you don't completely abandon me when the new guy comes."

Miguel smiled back. "Well, you can always come visit me at NASA Ames."

"Yeah, yeah." Jagdish seemed to be in a hurry as he started writing again.

"You like comics?" Miguel asked, picking up the one on the table.

"I collect them," Jagdish replied without looking at him. He continued typing. "I love these old ones. This one's a classic, Iceberg Man."

Miguel had never heard of Iceberg Man. He flipped through the comic. It cost a dime, with black and white illustrations of frowning villains with wicked smiles, and screaming damsels in distress. And Iceberg Man, the hero, in hypermuscular poses. On the first page, Iceberg Man had to defend a young woman from an attacker. He wasn't wearing his superhero outfit. Instead, he wore a suit that turned him into an anonymous passer-by. He found himself up against one of the age-old dilemmas of a superhero. *Do I save the girl and reveal my identity, or let the bad guy get away with misdeeds right in front of me?* Iceberg Man was gripping his shirt like he wanted to rip it off. Miguel turned the page and saw that the hero had not ripped off his shirt, but was staring with furrowed brows and wide eyes right in the direction of the attacker's pistol. The next panel showed a broken line coming out of his eyes towards the gun. The gun appeared to freeze across two more panels – first the barrel, then the grip. The attacker, who stared open-mouthed as his eyebrows shot up so high they nearly left his forehead, dropped the pistol, which shattered like glass when it hit the ground.

"He freezes things with his eyes," Miguel said.

"Not exactly. He turns them into ice," Jagdish said, not looking at Miguel. "He can turn anything into frozen water, but he has to touch it with his hands. This issue is unique – Iceberg Man turns something into ice without touching it, just by using his mind."

"I see."

"The attacker's pistol at the beginning, did you notice? It's the only time he does it in this superhero's entire storyline. A small error, but a jewel for a collector."

Miguel looked at the scene again. *Just as well I didn't turn the lead ingot into gold*, he thought. *They would have called me Gold Man*. He smiled again before returning the comic to Jagdish.

"I'm going," he said. "I'm having dinner with Monica. Good luck with the program."

"You really are lucky. Someday you'll have to tell me how you managed to flirt with her," Jagdish said, his smile bright.

Miguel left, and thought Jagdish was right about his luck. Monica, he remembered, had helped him a lot since his small failure with the stupid lead ingot. Her help was unconditional. She had helped him even when he had gotten impertinent about the white NASA coat. Yes, he was very lucky.

When Miguel left the engineering building, he looked back. Soon his new job in NASA would take him far away from the university. He would miss it here. Through the window on the first floor, which looked onto the department, he saw Jag. He appeared to be typing something on his phone. Miguel waved at him one last time. Jag saw him and waved back, phone in hand.

***

Monica sat on the bench where she used to meet with Miguel, below Tower Hall. At this hour, the campus was almost entirely covered with the shadows of buildings, but it was still very hot. Suddenly, the lawn sprinklers turned on, causing Monica to jump. She immediately put away the yellow page she had been reading.

Before taking it out again, Monica looked around. The university was deserted. It smelled like dry grass at the beginning of August. Then she finished reading the yellow page. It was Miguel's next experiment, Vladimir's alternative plan. She memorized it.

There would be no chambers or inductors this time. Miguel would have to do it all himself. And Monica. The two of them, without any help from machines. She would have to make an effort to detect the inflection and amplify whatever he did. It was not easy.

When Monica looked up, Miguel had appeared at the bottom of the avenue. When she saw him, she put the page away again in the back pocket of her jeans. She smiled, then, as big as she could without feeling like vermin. Her teeth tried to nibble at her lip, but she contained herself. Nibbling would have caused her to stop smiling. Monica forced herself to maintain that fixed smile of reunion, like the kind you'd see in a television show, when her phone vibrated in her pocket. Miguel was already very close. Taking it out, Monica saw it was a message from Jagdish. *Ok! Iceberg Man on the move*, it said. She deleted it.

***

"Ready?" Miguel asked as he reached Monica. He noticed her putting her phone in the back pocket of her tight jeans. She was wearing the tight olive-green t-shirt he liked so much, with her navel visible. She looked incredible – all curves, her Italian-actress hair swinging with every movement. "So, tell me, what are we celebrating?"

Monica looked at him, her eyes shining. She said nothing and kissed him. It was a long, intense kiss. Unexpected, too. When the kiss ended, Miguel looked at her dazed, and then looked around. It was unusual for her to kiss him in public, especially like that, least of all at the university, even though it was deserted. But he loved it.

"What was that for?" he asked.

"For the same thing I'm taking you to dinner. On a Friday just like this, four months ago, we left the university and got dinner together and… ta-da! That's how everything began. I want us to go to the same restaurant. I want us to repeat…" Monica's eyes widened as she bit her bottom lip, very tense. Her lip seemed to want to escape her bite and stretch into a smile. "…everything!" Monica said.

Miguel smiled back. He saw Monica's golden crucifix from the corner of his eye. It shone the same way it had the first time she brought him to the restaurant. Below the small crucifix, the neckline of her tight t-shirt showed the beginning of the gap between her breasts. Miguel pulled Monica closer and kissed her again.

When the kiss came to an end, Miguel wrapped an arm around Monica's waist and they left the campus.

A four-month anniversary, thought Miguel. *We're like two teenagers*. He couldn't imagine Monica liking all those things. Going back to that modern restaurant, leaving the dishes half-eaten, playing with the chocolate dessert, kissing endlessly. And afterwards, teleporting back to San Francisco for a roll in the hay like two lascivious perverts. Miguel caressed the curve of Monica's waist, touching the space on her hips left uncovered by her olive-green shirt. Her skin felt humid, perhaps due to the heat from the day, or maybe because of the traitorous water of the sprinklers. Her body. Miguel caught the faint scent of her sweat. He recalled the moment Monica's black thong fell around her leg, the first time she stripped in front of him. A shiver ran over him from his throat to his feet, thrumming in his muscles.

They returned to the designer restaurant, left the dishes half-eaten, played with the chocolate dessert, and kissed like two teenagers. Between bouts of laughter they reminisced on their first date, and solemnly promised each other, between solemn giggles, to repeat that first night. And that entire weekend.

Monica wanted to pay. Miguel watched her as she signed the credit card note. He liked to watch her when she did things like that – serious, diligent, decided, sure, with her long, wavy hair pulled up behind her right ear so that it wouldn't annoy her when she wrote. The rest of her hair fell freely over her other shoulder, and her lower lip was always caught between her teeth. Monica looked up and Miguel noticed she had chocolate on her upper lip. *Just like our first date!* They kissed again.

By the time they left the restaurant and headed back to the university parking lot, the sky had darkened, but some daylight still remained. Miguel tried to hug Monica, but she let go of him.

"I have to buy milk," she said.

Miguel opened his mouth and looked at Monica as if she had just told him she planned to buy a nuclear warhead. *Milk? But it's time to go home! Sex. Lots of it*, Miguel thought, mouth still hanging open.

"We have none left at home. There's a store just there," she added, pointing to a one-storey building. Right beside the door was a sign with the words "OPEN 24h" in blue, yellow, and red neon lights. Flashy colors, like Superman's suit, Miguel thought.

Sure, he could go along with the daily routine, and all the little details – the damn milk! – were necessary, but did it have to be that day? Miguel didn't want to start a fight. He wordlessly followed after Monica towards the store. He couldn't remember if there had been a store there before, and inwardly cursed whoever decided to put it there.

Monica entered the store, and Miguel wanted to wait outside, but the sign, blinking alternately in red, yellow, and blue… it seemed to dissolve his romanticism, his excitement, everything. He walked inside and stood beside the open door. At the back, Monica looked at a bottle of milk. *What is she looking for now?*

Miguel noticed the cashier behind the counter on his right. A gray-haired man in his sixties smiled at him. He seemed to be of Asian descent.

"No, I'm not looking for anything. I'm with her," Miguel said.

The Asian man kept his wrinkled eyes and his smile on him. Miguel decided that persistent smile was even more unnerving than the multi-colored blink of the neon lights. He turned around to look outside from the door. The street was empty. There didn't appear to be anyone in all San José, except for those two. And the Asian cashier, of course. There were no cars either, just a black truck with tinted windows parked on the pavement at the bottom of the street.

***

Castillo got out of the monitoring truck along with the actor disguised as a homeless man. They got out on the side of the vehicle opposite the store, and Castillo looked around to make sure no one could see them from there. Barrett, inside the truck, told him that the man acting as the cashier had just sent the message. Monica and Miguel were already inside the fake store.

The homeless man wore a torn oversized shirt, almost a rag, and a cap as grimy as his long hair. The beggar's disguise was complete. Castillo held up a mirror so the actor could add some last-minute touch-ups to his make-up. He looked at the actor's eyes as he worked. Something, perhaps the eyes, was out of place with the beggar's appearance. He hoped Miguel didn't notice. This man did not seem to be a very good actor. In fact, Castillo thought, he must have been one of the worst in Hollywood. A poor man aspiring for glory, short of funds. Of course, if he were strapped for cash, he'd do just fine.

Castillo looked at the truck. Barrett was inside, concentrating on a screen, wearing large headphones. Barrett wouldn't be able to hear him. Then, Castillo looked at the actor and said, "Don't let Monica go."

"I won't," said the actor.

"And if he doesn't react," Castillo added, voice low, "if he lets you go without confronting you, you hit her with the pistol."

The actor pushed the mirror in Castillo's hand out of the way and looked up. "That's not in the contract," he said. "We haven't practiced that."

Castillo held the mirror up again and smiled without looking away.

"She's not a professional actress," the actor insisted. "She won't know what to do, or why she's being hit."

Castillo tightened the knot of his tie without moving his face. Then he removed a long envelope from the inside pocket of his jacket. "Two thousand dollars," he whispered.

"I already got my money. I just have to hit him, right? Not… very hard."

"I'll give you two thousand more if you hit her for real. Come on, we'll say it was a misunderstanding. That's what television is like, we all know that. It's a show. You have to make it seem real."

The actor looked over at the camera inside the truck. Then he took the envelope, opening it and looking inside it quickly, and tucked it into a pocket in his filthy disguise.

Castillo climbed back into the truck silently. He closed the door and watched as his actor walked along the pavement, head low, with the unsteady walk of a vagrant.

***

Miguel saw a man appear behind the black truck at the bottom of the street. Going by his appearance, he looked like a bum. It was unusual to see homeless people in San José nowadays. In San Francisco, sure, there were dozens of them, but in San José… *Where did this guy come from?* Miguel wondered.

Once the man had made it far enough up the street, he began crossing the road in the direction of the store. Miguel watched as he walked, downcast. As the vagabond approached, the scarce light of sunset lit up the neon sign as it flashed from blue to red to yellow, to blue. Miguel could see him much more clearly. He was dressed in rags like a typical bum, but his face didn't quite match up with his clothes. He was white, with clear eyes and a striking face. His beard was a few days old, but it was well-groomed. He didn't have the typical appearance of a bum. His cold stare and determined gait as he neared the store didn't quite fit either. The man no longer walked unsteadily, and his blue eyes fixed on Miguel. That wasn't how a homeless man behaved. He didn't seem to…

The shabby-looking man entered the store, took out a gun, and struck Miguel in the face with it, sending him to the ground.

Miguel fell onto a cookie shelf and saw Monica, out of the corner of his eye, his vision blurry, turn around while the cashier raised his hands.

By the time Miguel managed to stand up, still dazed, the attacker had an arm around Monica's throat and was pointing the gun right at her temple.

Miguel looked into her eyes, which were already brimming with tears. He noticed she still had a tiny smear of chocolate on her upper lip. *Son of a bitch!* He remembered her excited look from just a few minutes ago, in the restaurant, and when he looked at her now… Miguel's pulse throbbed in his now-bloody cheek. *I'll kill him*, he told himself. No, no, no! He had to think of something!

The cashier had emptied the register onto the counter and raised his hands again. He smiled strangely, like he was nervous. Miguel looked back at the attacker and reached behind to the back pocket of his trousers.

"Don't move!" the attacker yelled, pointing the gun at him before bringing it back to Monica's temple.

"I'm not doing anything, okay?" Miguel said. He thought his heart was about to jump out of his cheek. "I'm just looking for my wallet." He held up his wallet. "Take the money and leave us alone. We don't want any trouble."

"You, bitch, take the money from the counter and this guy's wallet!" the attacker said, pressing the gun even harder onto her temple.

Monica collected the money in a paper bag. Miguel didn't take his eyes off of the attacker. He clenched his jaw. He didn't like Monica being hit, or being called a bitch. And he certainly didn't like anyone pointing a gun at her. His palms began to itch. They itched badly, but he didn't scratch them. Instead, he squeezed his hands into tight fists. He could see Monica's gold crucifix. The attacker must not have seen it, Miguel thought, or else he would have taken it. Miguel would not allow that.

"Get away from there!" the attacker shouted at Miguel.

The crucifix. God wouldn't help them. The gun looked real. The shining barrel, huge compared to Monica's head. Miguel took a step back, his hands half-raised. The attacker went outside, still holding onto Monica.

"This bitch is coming with me!" he shouted from the door. The neon lights illuminated the two of them. Blue, red, yellow…

Miguel felt helpless. Helpless and angry. Furious. He was sweating. His cheek seemed to burn, and so did his hands. But he didn't move, not even a muscle. *Dead!* was the only thing he could think.

The attacker took a few steps away from the store. "If I see any cops within the hour, she's dead. Tell the Chinese guy! You, keep the cashier quiet, or your bitch is dead."

Miguel could taste the blood coming from his cheek and suddenly noticed his brain starting to react. He felt the first pinches of inflection like a dull spark inside his head, and looked at the attacker as if he wanted his eyes to jump out of his face and slam into him.

***

Monica stared at Miguel's eyes. They were half-shut, tense, as if infused with hate. He must be furious. He'd act soon, she thought. She felt her phone vibrate in her pocket – the signal. The first invisible waves of quantum inflection must have started radiating from Miguel's brain, picked up by the sensors installed in the fake store. The vibration announced a message from Castillo. Monica imagined the monitoring equipment in the truck showing a graph with a magenta line that climbed higher and higher, just about to reach a level marked with the letters M.E. *Midas Effect.*

Monica searched for the inflection, concentrating a little, trying to capture it and… she felt it, then, in her own brain. Miguel's wishes. It felt so clear, the electric buzzing in the center of her head, like always. She started amplifying it almost automatically. It was easy. With Miguel she could do it without barely concentrating. And she was glad she didn't need to concentrate, because she could have to talk to the false attacker while producing her catalyzing effect.

The actor held the gun to her temple painfully and Monica remembered the scene from Iceberg Man in the comic Jagdish had prepared. She didn't want a gun turned to ice to burn her skin.

"Move the gun away from my head a little bit," Monica said quietly, teeth gritted, her terrified expression undisturbed.

But instead of doing what she asked, the attacker yelled, "Come on, bitch, you and I are going for a walk!"

Imbecile! she thought. It seemed he had decided by himself to overact. The actor pulled her back, which made her lose her balance. She almost fell over.

Idiot. Monica let herself be pulled, lifting her head up to stop it from hurting when he pulled. Then she saw the black clouds that had gathered over the city. They took over almost the entire sky and devoured the last bits of sunlight from the west. The sky threatened a powerful summer storm. If Miguel didn't act soon, the inept actor wouldn't know how to react to a rainstorm and would ruin everything. Then Monica looked at Miguel, pointing to the gun with her eyes.

***

Miguel saw Monica looking at him strangely, her eyes glued to him. He followed her stare and looked at the gun. In that moment he recalled the scene from Jagdish's comic – there was the attacker, the damsel in distress, the gun and… the superhero.

That image unleashed his imagination. Miguel visualized the black and white panels, remembered how Iceberg Man used his powers with his mind, from a distance, and in his head formed the idea that he could do anything he could possibly imagine. He was an inflexor. Iceberg Man could turn anything into…

Death. Miguel could only think of death. He concentrated on the attacker, who was inching away from the store with Monica. Miguel felt his brain start to boil. The darkness in the sky covered all of San José. He looked up and saw the clouds. They looked blacker than night.

He had already seen those clouds before, that darkness. In his imagination. They were his.

A warm wind swept across the street, cooling Miguel's bloody cheek. That wind was his, too. Miguel concentrated on his anger. And it started to rain. The droplets were enormous, like in a rainstorm. As the first drops fell, Monica looked up while the attacker lifted the gun and…

He hit her.

A clumsy hit, with the butt of the gun colliding with her temple. Miguel felt the impact on his own head, but not on his temple. He felt it inside, deep inside. Then he felt Monica's fear, her hatred, like a wave of inflection that combined with his own, his own hate, to multiply his power.

The attacker's mouth twisted. He gritted his teeth as if a sudden, intense pain had gripped him, and he let go of Monica. He seemed paralyzed. Monica stepped away from him, frowning at him with compressed lips as she touched her temple. She looked at his gun and cocked her head as if expecting to see something other than a pistol in his hands.

Miguel did not think about the fact that the thief was no longer grabbing Monica or pointing a gun at her. *Death*, he repeated to himself. The attacker raised his gun, about to strike again, and Miguel's brain boiled. He felt a strong pinch in the center of his brain. Then the clouds collided. A flash of lightning lit up the city, while a lightning bolt struck down, clean and silent. Monica looked into the attacker's eyes.

And the lightning bolt hit him.

Fat drops of rain fell over them, drenching them, and the smell of wet earth mixed with the smell of electricity and burnt flesh.

An exaggerated, unnecessary rumble of thunder boomed above them.

The thunder passed. The attacker lay on the ground, rigid, his mouth twisted.

Miguel had killed him.

Monica gripped her gold crucifix. She seemed unable to move, staring at the man with wide eyes. Miguel approached her, but her expression didn't change. She looked at him as if she didn't know him, as if he were the man with the gun.

The black truck at the bottom of the street hummed to life and sped over to where they were. It screeched to a halt on the other side of the road. Miguel and Monica looked at it. A sliding door opened and Castillo leaned out, motioning with his arm for them to get in. No one spoke. They ran over to the truck and entered quickly.

Inside the vehicle were quantum sensors, cameras, and monitoring equipment. Miguel looked around. *What is this doing here?* he wondered. But that didn't matter. Monica was what mattered. The attacker was about to kill her. He tried to hold her hand, but she pulled it away.

"Monica…" said Miguel.

Monica didn't answer, keeping her eyes firmly on the front seat.

Miguel looked towards the back of the truck. He saw Castillo. Barrett was there too. Castillo was staring at a graph on a computer screen. He was smiling. *I don't understand…*

Miguel looked back at Monica. She was soaked, like he was. She looked confused, like he was. "Monica, that man was about to—"

"He was an actor! And you killed him! You fucking killed him!" Monica screamed.

CHAPTER 20

"You are a Midas Effect," Gorlov said.

Miguel looked at the Russian and pressed his lips together. *Midas Effect*, he thought. *Another term for not telling me what's happening. Setting more traps for me so they can experiment on me. More lies!* He wouldn't speak. They were the ones who had to tell him everything.

Everyone important was there – Gorlov, Barrett, Fred… Castillo wasn't there. And Monica. Monica was there.

He had not seen her over the last few days, since the attacker. Miguel had not seen anyone, in fact. He had been sedated most of the time, kept in one of the dark rooms of the mini-clinic on level -2. They had done tests on him, kept him either asleep or semi-conscious, and had only allowed him to wake up completely that morning to attend the meeting on level -5. In the room with golden walls.

It looked like the interior of a golden sarcophagus. It produced a feeling similar to that of static electricity. It gave Miguel goosebumps. An anti-inflexor room, they called it. A mechanism of quantum distortion, something which Miguel could neither understand nor was the least bit interested in, surrounded the room. It stopped common inflections from coming in or going out. Common inflections? They had never told him about common inflections. Nor had they brought him to this room before. Nor had he ever gone down to level -5 before. They hadn't even told him the truth about what was on this level. They had told him very little of what was true. *Anti-inflexor rooms, quantum distortion, Midas Effects…!* Miguel revised all of the new terms they had mentioned to him in less than five minutes. He didn't know anything about the real Project! All they had done was lie to him! He squeezed his jaw shut even tighter. And Monica was there. He looked at her, but she avoided looking at him. Monica. Lied to. He had been lied to by everyone. Everyone. Red-eyed guinea pig with a twitching nose. Miguel fidgeted in his seat.

"And just what the hell is a Midas Effect?!" He looked at Monica as he asked the question before turning to Gorlov. He shut his mouth.

"A Midas Effect is a quantum inflexor with abilities far superior to what others are capable of," said Gorlov.

Miguel stayed quiet. He noticed his breathing had sped up while Gorlov spoke. New powers. He tried to hold his breath inside his body behind his pressed lips. *Far superior abilities*, he thought. They had been lying to him for too long.

"You told me that inflexor abilities were limited to classic paranormal powers," Miguel said. "That was what you told me the day I went to your office, when you all tricked me into joining the Project. About the visible spectrum, enclosed abilities, all those lies."

Gorlov's face did not change. Miguel supposed that if Gorlov wouldn't show any kind of emotion, he certainly wasn't about to show shame. That is, if he felt any shame. Miguel doubted it.

"A Midas Effect is something very serious," Gorlov went on. "Its existence cannot be divulged. And you were only a candidate. We couldn't tell you about it without having checked if you were the Midas we were looking for. Never before have we had a Midas in the Project. We don't even know the true extent of the ability. Had it been dangerous—"

"Dangerous? I killed a man!"

As he said it, Miguel relived with startling clarity the memory of the attacker's decomposing body, his dead, twisted expression, scorched on the asphalt, pelted by fat raindrops, like the sky was spitting on him. The storm Miguel had created, alone. He looked down at the palms of his hands. There was no blood on them. The blood had been a comfort, he thought, because then there was some human proof of what he had done, a gun to shift some of the blame onto. But there was nothing. Just him. He was the gun.

"The experiment did not turn out the way we hoped," Barrett said.

Miguel turned around immediately, narrowing his eyes again as he shot Barrett a look like he wanted to slit his throat.

Barrett swallowed some saliva and moved back slightly. In his fleeing, the wheels on his seat squeaked on the metallic floor. A whiny squeak. Barrett was afraid, Miguel realized. He must have thought that he'd be the next one to die, that Miguel would soon start launching lightning bolts at all his enemies.

What kind of monster have I become? I am a murderer. Miguel shifted his gaze to the wall in front of him. He imagined the golden surface warping, breaking apart like aluminium foil, and that behind that underground wall in the SSR, a dark, toothed, horrendous monster was coming to devour him. But in reality, he was the monster. He felt a pinch in the middle of his head and flinched. He blinked.

The wall was fine. His "far superior abilities" hadn't brought forth the creature of the abyss. Not yet, he thought. His sweaty palms burned, and he brought them to his face.

The others stayed silent. Miguel rubbed his eyes. Monster.

"Miguel," said Monica. Her voice sounded distant, sweet. Deceitful.

Miguel moved his hands away from his face. He refused to look at Monica directly, but he turned his head in her direction to show he was listening.

"You've already tested the limits of your power," she continued. "We couldn't tell you the whole truth; we had to take certain precautions—"

"Precautions? Lies," Miguel interrupted, still not looking at her. "I killed a man, and it's your fault." Hearing himself say it made Miguel feel a little better. If they had gone to so much trouble to prevent something dangerous that had happened anyway, then they must have shared some of the blame for the actor's death. And for Miguel's monsters.

Gorlov spoke then. "Miguel, I don't see any need to keep insisting that the experiment got out of control. You have dedicated your entire career to science, I think you can understand this. The most dangerous subject of our entire investigation – you – were totally unknown to us. We've done whatever carried the least risk. You must understand that it's very difficult to control an ability that is unknown even to the subject who has it."

Ability, Miguel said to himself, looking down at his hands. He no longer imagined seeing blood on them. He shook his head. "And what ability do I have?" Miguel asked. "Have you analyzed the data? Do you really understand the danger or do I have to kill another actor in order to test my own ability?"

He looked at each of them one by one, looking for an answer, but none seemed prepared to speak. Maybe they wanted to continue lying to him to protect him. Too much protection! Perhaps he should threaten them with some lightning to make them talk…

No, not again! Miguel squeezed his eyes shut as tightly as he could. The monster.

Gorlov waited a few seconds before responding. "The test has shown that your ability goes beyond what we thought we could achieve in one try," he said. His Russian accent had returned. Was he angry? *What right did he have to get angry?* Miguel asked himself. "The mathematics tell us it is infinite."

Infinite? Miguel began scratching his palms. He felt the scientist's as of yet unspoken words coming toward him like a bulldozer about to destroy all the lies, all the truths, the knowledge, whether it was true or false, that had already entered his mind.

"You can turn anything you imagine into reality. Anything you want. Everything," said Gorlov.

The world spun and flipped upside down under Miguel. Vertigo. The anti-inflexor room fell quiet. Miguel only heard a deafening buzz that seemed to come from the golden walls, the ceiling, the floor. The quantum distorters making his hair stand on end. A buzz that was drowning him.

Miguel suddenly felt his dry mouth, his pulse throbbing rhythmically in the half-scarred wound on his cheek. His palms hurt from all the scratching. He looked down at them. They looked like someone else's hands, hands he had never seen before. It was like the infinite power Gorlov spoke about could come out of those hands. Infinite. No, he couldn't understand what it meant, how far it could go, or… what for, to what end. He felt dizzy. He had just landed in a new life, lost, with an ability he couldn't comprehend, or even feel strong enough to control. His hands, they were so strange now. Maybe they were right. Maybe it was best to keep reality a secret until everything had been checked. Or until it was controlled. Both.

"Regarding the actor," Gorlov said, "nothing can bring that man back to life. What we must do is study the data and find the best way to control your quantum inflexor ability. No one wants a repeat of what happened a few days ago."

"Accident?" Miguel said, still looking at his hands, although something else apart from the Russian's words grabbed his attention.

"Yes," Gorlov replied. "If you think you're a murderer…" He stopped himself. "If anyone here thinks that," he looked through his glasses at everyone present, "they are wrong. Your ability is a weapon, and we put the weapon in your hands. If you had known that just by wishing it you could kill that man, you most likely would have wished for something else, correct?"

"I don't understand," said Miguel. He *could* understand it, really, but he wasn't listening. He was still looking for something in between what the scientist said. *I can wish for anything, and it will become reality*, he thought.

Gorlov kept talking. "You're like a monkey – if you'll pardon the comparison – with a gun, harassed into defending yourself from the annoyance by throwing the gun. If, coincidentally, the monkey pulled the trigger… Giving a monkey a revolver and harassing it could lead to death. An accident… Do you understand?"

Gorlov and his impeccable comparisons. But Miguel heard one more sentence in his head. *Nothing can bring that man back to life*, the Russian had said. That was it!

"Yeah, yeah," Miguel cut in. "I get it, but did you say we can't bring him back to life?"

Everyone looked at him, frowning simultaneously. Miguel took in their doubtful expressions, breathed deeply, and said, "I can."

All except Gorlov smiled. They appeared moved by what seemed to them like the innocent proposal of a little boy. He must have said something stupid, surely. It couldn't be that easy, if no one had asked him to do it. Miguel felt small, like a boy offering to save his father's company with his piggybank savings. Coins, a little pig. Juvenile.

"Well? Can I do it or not?"

"Do you want to try performing miracles?" Gorlov asked.

"I suppose there's some problem I don't know about, but if I can do anything just by willing it… What I mean is, I can wish the man back to life."

"No, it cannot be done," said Gorlov.

Miguel felt like someone had thrown the coins from the piggybank in his face. "I don't understand," he insisted. "If I can imagine a lightning bolt and make it reality, surely I can imagine that man leaving his grave."

Gorlov stuck a hand out to Barrett, who presented a black folder. "This is the secondary effect of the storm," said Gorlov, taking a satellite photo out of the folder.

Miguel looked at the photo. There was a spiral formation of clouds with a hole in the middle.

"That is Hurricane Laura. You created it."

Miguel frowned and looked up at Gorlov.

Monica leaned over the meeting table towards Barrett's black folder. She rifled through it before taking out a folded-up page. Unfolded, it took up most of the table. It was a map of the west coast of the United States, Central America, the Caribbean… To the south, it showed the coast of Brazil. Concentric lines, like isobars on a meteorological map, covered the map, superimposed on the land, the ocean, the islands. The world.

"It's an isoinflexor map," Monica said.

"With this, we monitor the activity of all the inflexors on the planet," Barrett added. "These are global estimates done with information about predicted reality based on millions of data points and reality transformed by inflection. Our spy satellites send the data to the monitoring posts on level -4, where…"

They've been watching us, Miguel thought. *Watching the inflexors. Level -4. They're spying on us.* He pressed his lips together.

Gorlov lifted two bony fingers from his right hand and pointed toward Barrett, who immediately stopped talking. "Now is not the time to go into technical detail," said Gorlov. Then, he looked at Miguel. "Quantum inflection, as you know, moulds reality. It changes it. The residual effect of that change extends to the entire universe to adapt it to the modifications produced." Gorlov passed his hand over the map. "The isoinflexor lines show how the residual wave is distributed over the surface of the Earth. Sometimes there are vertices of secondary inflection. In this case, there have been changes all over the world, and off-planet as well. And some of them were important."

"Hurricane Laura," Miguel repeated.

Gorlov sat up straight and pointed to a spot on the isoinflexor map near Brazil. There, the lines were close together.

Miguel stared at the map and the satellite photo. Along the Brazilian coast, where Gorlov was pointing, the photograph showed the eye of a spiral cloud formation. The hurricane. He hadn't just killed a man in California.

"But, the South Atlantic isn't a hurricane zone," said Miguel. "It's impossible."

"It's not impossible," said Gorlov. "The inflection that caused the lightning bolt caused many other changes, but specifically – here, the lines that prove it – it created a meteorological instability here. And the water has gotten warmer here." He pointed at the photograph. "All that created Laura. Category 3."

Miguel looked at his hurricane in silence.

"There were no deaths in Brazil," Gorlov said, "but that's the real effect of the storm you produced a few days ago."

"Meteorological impact," said Miguel.

"Quantum impact," Barrett corrected. Miguel turned to him. "It's not a readjustment of meteorological parameters. Well, if you change the weather, of course meteorology will adapt, but that's nothing. It's the waves of inflection that cause the residual effect and they can cause big changes at points where they reorganize and concentrate. Look." Barrett pointed again to the point where the lines concentrated on the map, south of Rio de Janeiro. "The gradient here is nearly as high as in San José, where the original inflection took place. See? That caused the hurricane. Anything else could have happened – an earthquake, a new virus, a meteorite… But, given that your original inflection had meteorological effects, the effect imitated the original. Normally that depends on the stochastic variables of the process, which, in this case—"

"I get it, I get it," Miguel said. He was in no mood for Barrett's long-winded explanations. "The residual effects of quantum inflection used to bring the man I killed back to life would be devastating. Right?"

Everyone nodded, with their heads and their eyes. Except Gorlov.

"They could be devastating, or they could not," he responded. "They could even provide an abundant harvest in an area ravaged by drought. Anything. The problem is that we don't know how the effect of an inflection needed to revive someone will extend. We also don't know how to stop it. It's an uncontrolled process. A very high risk for all of us."

Miguel once again looked down at his hands. They started to look his again. They were still full of power, but now he started seeing blood on them. They were full of power and faults, of incontrollable, unknown workings. Like tools he didn't know how to use.

"But if you didn't have it under control," Miguel said, "why did you trick me with the actor?"

"Because the gold experiment failed. *That* was controlled," Barrett answered. Miguel stared at him. "A low-intensity phenomenon, like typical abilities. We can simulate their effect. Parameters of inflection have been well-studied, characterized in mathematical models..."

"The MIDAS-000 experiment? That stupid thing about turning lead into gold?"

"You couldn't do it without generating a Midas Effect," Gorlov replied.

Miguel shook his head. He could hardly believe he had been so close to freeing himself from being a murderer. That damn experiment! "Fuck."

"It was for your safety," Monica began to say.

"And the only thing you could think of was getting someone to provoke me by pointing a gun at your head?" Miguel shouted, looking at her as if she were the only one to blame.

"You were supposed to turn it into ice, like Iceberg Man!" she screamed back. "Jagdish's comic."

No one spoke. Monica and Miguel looked at one another, both breathing heavily like they wanted to spit the air out through their noses. Miguel looked into Monica's eyes – dark purple eyebags were visible below her gray-blue eyes. It seemed she, too, was tired. Miguel hadn't noticed until now.

"So, Jagdish is in on this too," Miguel said, almost to himself. He looked back to the map without seeing it. "Well, it was a stupid trick. Turning things into ice was the last thing on my mind when I saw that bum pointing a gun at you. If I couldn't turn lead into gold, how the hell was I going to turn a gun into ice?" The last words were said in a whisper.

"I'm also to blame for that man's death," said Monica. Miguel looked at her again, at her dark purple bags. "I amplified your will, gave it strength. I amplified that lightning bolt, you know that."

"You thought you were amplifying something innocuous, that you were helping Iceberg Man turn things into ice. I truly wished for that man to die." Miguel looked at the others. He expected them to tell him what to do now, but he didn't know. He couldn't know.

"I think Miguel should rest now," said Fred. "The past few days have been very hard for him."

Miguel stared at him. Fred hadn't said a word during the whole meeting. He was the only one who hadn't tried to convince Miguel of anything. *He's the most human*, Miguel thought.

"Miguel," said Fred.

"Yes?"

"Can we count on your discretion with this matter?"

Of course, confidentiality! Miguel told himself. *That's the only thing you're worried about right now. Very human, yes, but a CIA agent to the end. Nothing more. Like Walter, the CIA. Where is Walter now? All this is disgusting.*

"I don't want us to argue over your future participation in the Project," Fred continued. "Monica will tell you everything important. But I do need to know that you won't go talking about what happened here." Fred pointed at the metal walls. Miguel looked at them strangely. "It's an inflexor-proof room. Not even a telepath can hear us. Only we know what really happened, and what was discussed in here today. Well, Walter knows, too. He wasn't able to come."

And what do I care about Walter? "I won't say a word," said Miguel. "I swear on the Bible. Is that enough? We'll talk about it another time; right now, I'm exhausted."

Fred looked at him with a sunken expression, like a wounded bear that hunched over to protect its abdomen. "Yes, it's better if you go," he said. His voice was serious but soft, barely making it out of his enormous body.

Miguel stood and made his way to the door.

"Monica, go with him," Gorlov said. "He shouldn't drive with the sedatives still in his system."

Miguel paid no attention to him, but he stopped when Monica stood up. There, beside the door, was a small bookcase, golden like the walls. On it were maps, yellow pages, blocks of steel and pieces of equipment he didn't recognize. And a grayish ingot. Miguel frowned before looking at the scientist.

"It's the same one from the MIDAS-000 experiment," said Gorlov. "It's still lead."

Miguel stared at the ingot. He grimaced disgustedly. Then he touched it with his finger and the ingot shimmered with the opulent shine of gold. "Not anymore." And he left.

***

Monica watched him from the corner of her eye as she drove. Miguel didn't look at her.

"You shouldn't talk to Fred like that," she said when they exited onto Route 101 on the way to San Francisco.

Miguel did not respond.

"Swearing, laughing at the Bible. You know he's very devout. His father is very religious. He's a good man, Reverend Windhorst, from Illinois. Fred has always defended you—"

"I'm tired of holier-than-thou believers. His faith didn't stop me from killing a man," Miguel replied, looking at her. His tone told Monica he was talking about her, too.

Miguel crossed his arms, pressed his lips together and turned toward the window.

The heat, the freeway. It wasn't the place to talk about his future. It was best to let Miguel organize his thoughts first. She had to be practical. That would avoid unnecessary confrontation. When they got to San Francisco, maybe at home they could talk…

An hour later, as they entered the apartment, Miguel seemed to find what he wanted to say.

"This is a set, right?" He knocked on the wall, as if waiting to hear the hollow sound of plasterboard.

"This is my apartment," said Monica, "where I've lived for the past few years. My home. And yours now, too."

Miguel stared at the walls and ceiling as if seeing them again for the first time. He looked at the chairs, the table, the sofa. He seemed to hesitate. Finally, he sat on the sofa. "It's a farce. This whole life," he said, looking at the ceiling again.

Monica took a chair and placed in front of him with the back of the chair between them. "We've already told you this. You've seen how dangerous you are. We had to investigate you, control you as soon as possible. That's what we've done." She bit the right side of her lower lip and began to shake her leg rhythmically. Miguel kept his tired gaze on her. "There were sensors all over the apartment, microphones, cameras. We installed them when you came to live here. We had to watch you.

The rest is a home like any other. There's nothing like that here anymore."

"Us meeting in Granada wasn't casual either, was it? You were controlling me with your satellites, your isoinflexor lines. My whole life in the United States is controlled by the Project – my job at the university, Jagdish, Dr. Branson… everyone's involved, aren't they? Like you."

Miguel's expression did not change when he referred to her, as if the role of fake lovebird that was assigned to her didn't matter to him in reality. His gaze returned to the walls as his hands squeezed into tight fists. Maybe all he needed was a slight impulse to explode – protests, swears, insults. That was what he needed, something to relieve the tension, to let them both confront each other. The movement of Monica's leg sped up. If they didn't, they would never get past this. And Monica wanted Miguel to get past this, to return to normality. As if the lives of two inflexors – not just any inflexors, but a catalyst and a Midas – could ever be considered normal.

Monica breathed slowly. She still had her initiative, her intelligence, her sense of practicality. She could do it. She could gain Miguel's respect. And now she had something else: the truth. Now she could give it to him. Tell him, involve him in what they knew and what they didn't know, in the danger that surrounded the Project. Her leg kept hitting the leg of the chair, producing an intermittent pain in her knee. The truth hurt. She might even provoke him with it… Of course!

"Do you like the power you have?" Monica asked.

Miguel left the world of walls and looked at her, but didn't respond. He sighed, his breath loaded with disgust, and shook his head very slowly without looking away from her. "This is about the Project, isn't it?" he replied. His mouth twisted as if he were swallowing something bitter. "You want to know if I'm going to collaborate with you, if I'm still interested. You need that info, of course. The only thing you care about is the Project! Nothing else! You can all go to hell!"

Monica's leg fell still and stuck to the chair as if magnetized. She had done it. "I can imagine how you feel," she said.

"No, no, you can't! That's the thing: imagine." Miguel looked at the walls again, wide-eyed. "I'm scared to imagine, to think, to want anything. It could become reality, don't you realize?"

"Of course."

"Not everything I think is noble! I'm not a saint. Damn it! How am I going to control this power if I can't even control myself?" His fists rested on his knees. They seemed to want to squeeze out all the air trapped inside. Miguel's chest inflated and deflated as if he were fighting against the whole weight of the world on every inhale.

"In the Project, we will help you control it," said Monica. "That's why we brought you here."

"You don't know what it's like! You don't know!"

Monica did not respond.

"Damned. You're all damned, for letting the demon out," Miguel went on through gritted teeth.

Monica got up from her chair and sat beside Miguel on the sofa, looking at him with her whole body. She tucked one leg underneath her, like she always did whenever they spoke together naked after sex. She took his hand between her own. "You're not alone."

Miguel lifted his eyes to her. Monica thought his breath stopped for a moment. "You lied to me," said Miguel.

Monica kept her eyes on him and said, "My feelings are real. They always have been. The rest was just work. Our work."

Miguel's breathing finally calmed, and his hands relaxed. He was looking at her now. The truth, Monica remembered. That would save them. There were barely any walls between them now. It was time. She squeezed his hand so he wouldn't let go, and said, "You haven't answered me yet."

Miguel leaned back, surprised, but left his hand in Monica's.

"Do you like the power you have?"

"Your work again?" Miguel blinked but didn't move away. His brow wrinkled as if he were plotting something. "Monica, I hate your hyperpractical act, you know that. And now you're taking it too far."

"Do you like it?"

"I haven't thought about it," said Miguel. But Monica knew that he had. His power frightened him, he had just said so. And if it frightened him, then he would also know if he liked having it. Miguel turned his head slightly to the left and looked out the window. "I don't know."

"Okay," said Monica, and she smiled.

"Why do you ask?" Miguel said. He looked at her again and frowned.

The truth, Monica repeated to herself. They would be allies. "The aim of the Project is to help you control the Midas Effect…"

"To investigate me," Miguel cut in.

"And investigate you, of course. But the CIA could have other plans."

Miguel tilted his head. Monica felt him squeeze her hands.

"Plans to use you."

"Use me?"

"You already know the ultimate secret of the Project – the Midas Effect. You're ready to know everything Vladimir and I know. And what we don't know, of course." Miguel opened his mouth to speak, but he didn't interrupt Monica. "The plans of the CIA could depend on you, on how good you feel with your ability." She lifted Miguel's hand and kissed his palm. "That's why I'm asking you if you like your power. We're in danger."

"The CIA."

"Castillo."

"Walter?"

"You have every right to doubt my feelings. But think about it. Do you think the CIA loves you more than I do? No. They could hold more danger and deceit than you've ever experienced before."

Miguel stared at Monica's hands, which still held onto his. "Where is Walter?" he asked.

"In Washington D.C., or in Langley. He never says exactly where. It's all the same. In the hallways of the powerful."

"Langley?"

"Langley, near Washington. The headquarters of the CIA."

CHAPTER 21

Walter Castillo enjoyed hearing the clear, rhythmic sound of his own footsteps on the waxed floors in the buildings of Washington.

The Capitol Building, the Pentagon, Langley. Power. He had just passed the emblem on the marble floor in the CIA headquarters in Langley: the eagle, the sixteen-pointed compass, the shield. He loved that emblem. He strode with purpose down one of the corridors, gripping his black briefcase firmly. Inside were his plans, as well as information about Miguel. Castillo smiled, looking toward the sunlight filtering through the white curtains on the windows to his left.

The deserted corridor widened on the left to form a rectangular area with two doors. Seated at a desk between the doors was a young woman, her short red hair pulled tight and flat on her head. She asked Castillo to identify himself and he showed her his CIA credentials. The young woman stood and asked him to follow her. She opened the door on the right and gestured for Castillo to enter. He flattened the lapels of his dark blue suit, tightened the knot of his maroon tie, and walked in.

The room was dark, barely lit by halogen lights in the high ceiling and the light of a projector screen. A narrow table of dark wood, like the wood that covered the walls, stretched out before Castillo. The people seated at the table looked like wax figures, their faces frozen as they read the reports in their hands. Gray envelopes, gray folders, all with the words CIA – TOP SECRET printed in red on the cover. As Castillo entered, the light from the corridor windows shone in the statues' glasses. They seemed to come to life, turning to face him. Their serious expressions would have been better suited to a wax museum. The redheaded secretary closed the door behind him, and the light nearly disappeared.

"Please allow me to introduce you all Walter Castillo," said William Whitaker, the Director of the CIA. "He's the agent in charge of this operation."

Castillo gave a brief nod as greeting. "Thank you," he said, placing his briefcase on the table. He sat in the only seat available, nearest the door, and saw that Roth was sitting beside him.

Roth stood as Castillo took a seat. He had sent the agent a few days before to prepare the presentation, and everything seemed ready. He was a good agent, Roth. Castillo gave Roth the CD, who walked away with it.

The computer was on the opposite side of the room, near the projector screen. Castillo did not like being so far from the picture. He would have preferred to be right beside it, to be able to stand and point out details when necessary, to showcase his ability with conviction. But he couldn't do anything about it.

While Roth operated the computer, Castillo looked around at the other people. The majority of them were over fifty. The darkness inside the room made it hard to see, but he could identify several generals at a glance, some big fish from the Department of Defense and various agents from high places in the CIA. Director Whitaker was silent, and in front of him was… Wella!

Wella Anderson. *No way!* How long had it been? He stared at her, trying to see if it was really her.

As cold as ever, Wella tucked a lock of straight, blonde hair behind her ear and adjusted her dark, plastic glasses – perhaps they were mahogany-colored, designer, no doubt very expensive, like the gray pearls in her ears. *Are those her usual pearls or are they new? New, surely*. She didn't even look at him.

But what was Wella doing there? Of course, she was in politics, like her congressman father. She had gone far since her years in law school. She must have come as a representative of the Secretary of Defense. She held a high position, he had heard. Castillo hadn't seen her since Yale. More than fifteen years ago. She hadn't changed at all. Castillo smiled slightly – at least she had made it in time to see his triumph.

In that moment, the projector showed a photograph of Miguel and everyone turned to see it. Castillo adjusted the knot of his tie.

"This is the subject," he said, his voice level, sure. "He is what the Project refers to as a Midas Effect."

He began explaining what the Project was and the plans they had to utilize what they found out. He explained some, but not all, of the details of the operation, just the scientific basis that supported the Project. Castillo also mentioned other less relevant ideas, such as how they had identified Miguel as a candidate. To catch their attention, he showed various videos of the experiments that were developed in the cover building of the SSR Center, in NASA Ames. Of course, he didn't mention the other cover building they had with NASA facilities in Hampton, Virginia, in the exact same state. Whitaker had already given him instructions regarding what he could and couldn't say. And Castillo always followed orders.

The videos had everyone in the room watching open-mouthed. They showed tests of telekinesis, extrasensory perception, telepathy. Castillo informed them that the same could be done by many other quantum inflexors hidden away in the Project, in San José, in California.

"But Miguel Le Fablec," he said, "is not like the other inflexors. He's special. He's like a god."

Everyone turned their heads away from the screen and towards Castillo. Now he had everyone's attention, even Wella's. He breathed slowly through his nose, trying not to grin at having drawn in all those big fish. Then he stood, unable to keep himself there any longer, far from the screen, and continued talking as he walked towards it.

Castillo began almost frantically showing data, photographs, videos of Miguel's most important experiments. He explained them while pointing out the most important details, his tone of voice rising and falling like a television presenter.

His audience seemed to stop breathing when he showed them the image of the broken steel block. Castillo witnessed Director Whitaker's smile from the corner of his eye as he murmured something into the ear of a military general beside him. It was General George Rosmouth. Castillo knew him. He had been Whitaker's colleague. Naval Academy, Marine Corps. He was a personal friend of the president, so they said.

The presentation ended with a video of the simulated robbery. Castillo explained the trap they set for Miguel and the projector showed in slow motion how the lightning bolt hit the fake attacker. A light illuminated the room so brightly that everyone was forced to look away. After, on the screen, the man with the gun lay dead on the ground. Thunder rumbled over San José. The room remained silent.

Everyone seemed too afraid to blink, to break the silence Castillo had left.

The projector turned off and the light from the small halogen lights intensified slightly. Castillo thought the meeting room must have been designed to be sinister, and that there would be no more light than this. There wasn't. There didn't seem to be any questions. Everything was perfect, he thought. His plan *and* his presentation.

"And how do you know that the lightning wasn't natural?" asked Wella Anderson suddenly. She took off her glasses and pulled her neat, straight, blonde hair behind her ears. "It could have been a coincidence," she added.

Did that daddy's girl think he and the Project's scientists were imbeciles? Castillo wasn't about to give her any more explanations than he already had. Not to her. If a general, someone with criterion, asked, he'd give them an explanation, but not to that little girl, that overambitious politician who was only there because of her surname.

"Co… in… ci… dence," Castillo said slowly, squinting at Wella. "My time in the CIA has taught me that coincidence is how the naïve refer to how people like us manipulate their lives."

Everyone except Wella smiled. That wasn't true, of course, but it was a nice phrase, and it answered her and insulted her at the same time. Castillo delighted in Wella's plain, frozen expression.

"No, there was no coincidence in this experiment," he added before the acid of his response corroded the beautiful collaborator from the Secretary of Defense. "Everything was rigorously documented."

She squinted at him like she wanted to strangle him. Tucking her hair behind her ear again – although it hadn't moved from before – she put on her glasses without looking away from him. She was furious. He knew that look very well. Monica Eveleigh did the same thing with her hair sometimes. Women were all the same. But Wella was very beautiful with those designer glasses.

"Good," she said. Her tone was dry but seemingly satisfied, like she was content with the response. Castillo smiled inwardly. She was still as cold as ever, he thought. "Then that man is an incredibly powerful weapon, isn't he?"

"Of course," Castillo replied. "But the CIA's plan is not to use him as a weapon. On the contrary—"

"Right," interrupted Wella. "And does the president know the CIA's plan?"

"We did not consider it opportune." Whitaker's immediate intervention sounded like a seamless continuation of Wella's words. Castillo was grateful for the director's agility. "Not for now," he clarified.

"May I ask why a plan of this magnitude is being kept from the president of this nation?" Wella asked. She appeared to be asking Whitaker, but she looked at Castillo.

He kept quiet. He knew that her efforts to make him uncomfortable were among the lesser of the dangers in the Yale madwoman's arsenal.

She finally turned to Whitaker for his response.

"A few days ago, the Midas Effect was just a postulated theory. Now, it has been proven physically for the first time in the subject from the video. It's obvious that there are still many tests to be done to determine its usefulness in the plan Agent Castillo has presented to us. When everything has been checked, of course, we'll notify the president. We'll only move forward with his approval. Believe me, Miss Anderson, we don't want to bother the president with unbelievable plans based on a scientific hypothesis the government has spent a lot of time and money on without producing anything useful."

Wella Anderson did not respond. For a moment she looked at Director Whitaker like she understood much more than what he had said. Then she removed her glasses and brushed her hair back again.

In that moment, someone slammed their folder closed. Everyone turned to him. General Rosmouth.

"Why have you gathered us here, then, Bill?" Rosmouth asked, looking at Whitaker. "If there is still no operation, it's a useless waste of confidentiality."

"I've gathered whoever will be involved," said Whitaker. "The preparations… We'll need your collaboration when it begins. Everyone's collaboration. We cannot tell you something that important the moment we begin."

Rosmouth looked at the folder. He kept his mouth shut, but his lower lip stood out on his face as if a hamburger was coming out of his mouth. His breaths through his nose were audible throughout the entire room. He grimaced before saying, "Understood."

Castillo realized there had been more tension in the clipped words between Rosmouth and Whitaker than in harpy Wella's questions.

Whitaker closed the meeting. Everyone went about placing their reports in the top-secret envelope inside their briefcases before leaving silently, in an orderly fashion.

Castillo waited to collect his disc. He was just about to leave when he saw Wella looking at him fleetingly as she collected her things.

He walked over to her. At the end of the day, he thought, they were old friends. They knew each other well – they had slept together. A long time ago, now, of course. Castillo straightened his suit and then fixed the knot of his tie. "Long time no see."

"No kidding," she said, not looking at him. "I have to go. I'll see you soon." Then she looked at him and smiled one of her practiced smiles. She slid her gray envelope into her mahogany leather briefcase, which matched her glasses. The leather must have been as soft as her skin.

I hope not, Castillo thought. *Idiot.*

Whitaker got his attention.

Castillo turned and looked at the director. Beside him was General Rosmouth, still seated with his hands on top of his report. Rosmouth was staring at him.

"Please, Castillo," said Whitaker. "Please tell us. You have lived with the scientists of the Project for months now. Do you think Miguel Le Fablec will work? Please be sincere, we don't want you to sell anything to us."

"I'm sure," Castillo answered, looking at Rosmouth. Castillo thought he was the one who was really asking. Rosmouth stuck out his bottom lip again.

"Well, have a seat," said Whitaker as he stood and started gathering pages left on the table. "We must resolve some issues with General Rosmouth, and I'd like for you to be present." Whitaker looked through each of the papers he collected. Castillo knew he was a neat freak.

Wella Anderson left the room. The three men looked at her and she flitted her fingers as she went, like she was playing piano scales in the air. Castillo knew that gesture. To him it had always seemed like a cheesy thing that rich girls did.

Roth followed Wella out and pulled the door shut behind him. The dark, wooden door closed softly, giving the three men some privacy.

"Did you have to call that bitch?" Rosmouth asked as soon as the door shut.

Castillo nearly choked trying to contain his laughter. Whitaker also swallowed.

"For God's sake, George!" the director exclaimed. "It must have given you an ulcer, trying to keep your military talk back."

"I can't stand that asshole Anderson or his daughter," said the general.

"Well, I need her to put this operation forward to the president. That's why she's here."

"I could have done that. John trusts me, you know that."

Castillo breathed heavily, his nostrils flaring. He felt so much bigger than usual there, with the big fish who called the president by his first name.

"That's exactly why I don't want you to say it to him," said Whitaker. "I want him to find out through official channels, not through a friend. And I don't want to implicate you, I need you somewhere else."

"Anderson's daughter could hinder you more than help you. I can't wait to see what story she goes off with to the Secretary of State! He trusts her… Ha! They're sleeping together, of course he trusts her."

"Alright, yes, they're sleeping together. And what of it? I need her. I don't give a fuck about her sex life," Whitaker replied. His tone – calm, always under control – didn't fit his words.

The general smiled. So did Castillo, who thought that all three of them coincided in hating Wella Anderson. They were all in the same boat.

"I love when you get all military, Bill," said Rosmouth. "It reminds me of those days in Annapolis. What a time!" He looked at Castillo. "I envy you, Agent. Right in the thick of it. Bill, the old fox, and I used to be like you. Do you enjoy it?"

"Very much, sir."

"Yeah," Rosmouth continued. "But I couldn't have done that presentation."

"Sir?"

"Not then, not now, to be honest. You, however, were like a peddler selling spaceships. A good agent, from what I've heard, and a good soldier too. And from what I've seen, a good salesman." Rosmouth stuck out his bottom lip and nodded, as if to himself. "Back in our day, this job wasn't so complex. We didn't have to sell anything. There were the Russians, and us… and the missiles, of course. Nothing else. The world was so much simpler back then. You're as complicated as the wars of today."

"Yes, sir."

Whitaker quickly picked up a few more pages, as if he didn't intend to leave even a single mote of dust for the cleaners. Then he stopped and said, "We'll be jumping into action soon."

"With what you told us today?" asked Rosmouth.

"It's a plan we've been preparing for years." Whitaker pointed at Castillo with the paper he had in his hand. "And he will make sure it's a success. I'm certain."

Castillo swelled. He felt like shouting *Sir, yes, sir!*

"I'm not so sure that plan is a good one," said Rosmouth.

Whitaker left the pages on top of his briefcase and stared at the general.

"Too pacifist for my liking," Rosmouth added. "You know me. Damn it, I have to agree with that bitch Anderson! This is too big. We have to tell the president. This is…" He opened the folder like he needed to see something inside, but he flipped through it without looking at anything in particular. "This has worldwide implications beyond any other operation in any other country. It's total control of the planet… Are you planning on waiting until it's over to tell the president?"

"I'll remind you that I haven't started yet."

"It's still too big."

"George," said Whitaker. He was quieter now. "I'm not going to start the operation *without* the president." He looked at the general with wide eyes, as if trying to show the general his thoughts.

Rosmouth stared at him in silence. He closed the folder with a thud. "I hope so."

Castillo adjusted the knot of his tie. It was like the room trembled every time they faced off.

"Will I have your military coverage when we inform the president?" Whitaker asked.

"Yes."

"Right now, I need your logistic support to start the preparations. You have men in Egypt, right? The agreements with the Egyptian government..."

Rosmouth looked at Whitaker, sticking his lip out again before taking it back.

"You can count on my men for the preparations," he said, waiting a few seconds before continuing. "But I also have two aircraft carriers loaded with marines in the Red Sea. If you start this of your own accord, I will send the F-18s to blow up every last thermal inflexor."

"Quantum inflexor, sir," said Castillo.

Rosmouth spun to face him. "I don't care what they're called!" he yelled, sticking his lip out.

Castillo fixed the knot of his tie.

Whitaker smiled. He picked up the phone and dialled a number, reciting a code.

"I'm going to order the preparations for the operation to start," Whitaker said to Rosmouth, covering the mouthpiece of the phone.

Rosmouth looked at the gray folder again. He bit his lip and smiled almost imperceptibly. "The only thing I like is the codename of the operation. It's very symbolic, like the ones we used back in the old days."

"I know," said Whitaker. He handed the phone to Castillo. "You can do the honors," he said. "You deserve it."

Castillo felt his pulse speed up and his pride swell. He took the phone. "Yes, sir!" he said.

He looked at the general once more, who observed him with his head slightly lowered and his lip out of place on his mouth. Rosmouth gave a firm nod.

"Initiate Operation Messiah," said Castillo.

CHAPTER 22

From the door of the wind tunnel, Miguel was entranced by the space vehicle prototype. It was white, like an angel from above, and looked like something from another planet, or from another time. From the future.

It was a whole ship. Not a to-scale miniature, or a part of the fuselage. It was the vehicle itself, loaded with sensors for the aerodynamic tests in the tunnel. The largest wind tunnel he had ever seen.

A NASA worker, dressed in white overalls with the agency's logo on the chest, was taking measurements with a laser device and adjusted something on the base of the three hydraulic supports. They were thick, like the columns of a temple, and kept the vehicle a few meters above their heads. The man moved between the columns, measuring with a red laser and picking up tools from a small table with wheels that looked like it belonged in an operating theatre. Miguel approached him.

When Miguel reached his side, the worker started turning some small wheels with a key the size of a pen. He squinted as he turned the key, slowly, very slowly, as though he were tuning a piano. Or a church organ, Miguel noticed. He must have been balancing the hydraulic columns.

Miguel lifted his hand to greet the organ tuner. He would have told the man that Walter Castillo had arranged to meet him there, the subdirector of the SSR Center, that he had a pass and everything, but the man wasn't interested in anything but his laser beam and his tiny tools. Miguel decided to keep quiet as he looked up at the ship.

He couldn't help but open his mouth as he looked up. The test section of the wind tunnel was the size of a cathedral. And the ship hanging over him was like a baldachin over an altar, the hydraulic legs like marble columns supporting it. Miguel had never seen an aerodynamic test with a real vehicle before, only with to-scale miniature models – and he never would again. There were no gigantic tunnels like this outside NASA.

The great NASA, he thought. Soon they would begin the tests on the prototype of the ship from the future. In another time, it would have fascinated him. Now, the image he had of the space agency before joining the Project seemed naïve, almost ridiculous to him now. Everything was much smaller after seeing the secret basements of the SSR.

He recalled the structure. Level -2, a dark lab, the induction chambers. Level -3, the offices of the scientific team, white meeting rooms. Level -4, global monitoring posts, the screens showing isoinflexor curves, the whole planet on watch there – from there they had detected him over a year before. Level -5, the anti-inflexor rooms, machinery. Inconceivable technology, even for the great NASA. Everything hidden and in production down there, just a few steps away from the canteen building, a few dozen meters from the wind tunnels.

Miguel was glad to have finally seen it. Castillo had insisted. *You have to show him everything there is in the basements. The truth, all of it. Put an end to the distrust towards the Project*, he had said to Gorlov and Barrett.

A cracking sound led Miguel's gaze away from the hanging ship towards one far end of the tunnel, where the cone of compression was. He saw another worker's white overalls shine far away in the darkness. The man must have been using something like an electric soldering iron. Sparks flew near the wall. Spot welding, Miguel thought, surely to install a sensor in the entrance to the tunnel. He lifted his head up again to the ship.

When the smell of electricity reached him, Miguel studied the holed surface of one of the craft's double vertical stabilizers. The two stabilizers were joined near the top by a type of a horizontal stabilizer, incomprehensible to Miguel. Together they formed an empennage that looked like a spoiler on a sports car. He calculated the distance from the empennage to the canard, near the droop-nose. The smell of electricity. Another soldering spark crackled in the air, but Miguel kept himself concentrated on the ship. That vehicle had to fly in the upper levels of the atmosphere, and would take off from an adapted Boeing-747, he thought. Why did it need a canard? The smell of electricity again. The design made no logical sense, of course. Two small directional thrusters, at the back, below the plane of the horizontal stabilizer, or what was supposed to be the horizontal stabilizer. More of the electric smell, another spark. Damn welder. The delta wings were small, too small. The ship all together was like a squashed crow's beak. Where were its flaps? A white crow. Electricity. Lightning! Burnt flesh! In that moment, the ship disappeared from his mind and in its place came the image of the actor, the false attacker, with an open mouth and bulging blue eyes, twisted on the ground. Dead. Electrocuted.

Miguel felt a wave of nausea, but managed to contain himself. He leaned on one of the hydraulic legs to stop himself from collapsing. The organ tuner looked at him wide-eyed. Miguel took his hand back from the column and leaned on the tool table, nearly falling over.

The dead attacker's face was still there. The illumination in the tunnel was scarce, yellowish. There was no other way, he told himself. That was how they had to do it. The Iceberg Man experiment. There was no other way to prove that he was a Midas. Miguel shook his head like a wet dog, the fleas, the pain, the nausea.

"Please don't touch the hydraulic legs," said the organ tuner. He had a surly, dejected look. "Are you okay, sir?"

"Blood pressure," said Miguel, sweating. "Sorry, sometimes I get dizzy. It'll pass… I'm meeting Walter Castillo here."

But the organ tuner was no longer paying him any attention. He began collecting his tools very neatly, everything in order. Every note, every octave had found its place in the harmony of the cathedral. It seemed to be the only thing of interest to him. It was his job, of course, Miguel told himself. He had no reason to see electrocuted actors. Miguel let go of the tool table and the organ tuner pushed it away.

Not even a week had passed since he left the clinic on level -2. They had already warned him he could become dizzy. A week and a half since the incident with the actor. Miguel still felt nauseous below his throat. There was no other way, he repeated to himself, looking at the welder. There were no more sparks. The worker wasn't there either. He must have left through another door. All Miguel could see was the dark space inside the immense tunnel, like an empty cathedral. He still felt dizzy. The smell of electricity had gotten stuck in his nose. Where was Walter?

When he got to the wall, he put all his weight on it. He remembered Castillo suggesting to him, in a very quiet voice, that they meet in the tunnel. It was when the visit to the SSR basements had ended, after Gorlov, Barrett, and the others had already left. He must not have wanted the others to find out about their meeting. But the tunnel wasn't a secret location. It wasn't even protected like the anti-inflexor rooms on level -5. Whatever Castillo had to tell him must not have been very confidential. The welder appeared again, like a ghost in white overalls, from the darkness of the cone of compression. He was facing Miguel.

"We're going to start this up in ten minutes," he said. "You can't stay there."

Miguel straightened from against the tunnel wall. The workers there were some of the meanest he had ever met. The welder left through a nearby door. On the arm of his white overalls, the NASA logo shone as if new.

Miguel decided to follow him, to wait for Castillo outside the tunnel, when Castillo appeared through the door the welder had left through. He was smiling, greeted the welder and fixed his tie.

"The NFAC!" said Castillo excitedly, looking up with open hands and spread arms. "The National Full-Scale Aerodynamics Complex. One of the few wind tunnels in the world for real scale tests." He slapped the wall with one hand, like a rajah proudly slapping the back of his favorite elephant. "Eighty by one hundred and twenty feet in the test section." About twenty-four meters in height by thirty-six in width, Miguel calculated. "A truck could fit in here. Two, even. And we have another smaller NFAC in the complex. And transonic tunnels, supersonic tunnels, hypersonic tunnels, regulated temperature ones, pressurized ones…"

"They showed me nearly all of them when I visited the center for the first time, the day I was captured. Vincent's welcome, the telepath, remember?" said Miguel. He thought he felt another wave of nausea, but he recovered.

"Vincent, of course."

"There was an F-18 here."

"It's the largest tunnel in the world."

Castillo clapped Miguel on the shoulder and began to walk towards the bottom of the tunnel, towards the diffuser and the thrust section.

"Tests for commercial planes, acoustic models, natural scale vehicles…" Castillo continued selling wind tunnels while Miguel followed him. "Aerodynamic research programs. The Department of Defense tests all their jets here."

Then Castillo removed something from his jacket pocket. It looked like a remote control from a distance. He touched a button and the space for the thrust section illuminated with blueish light, like the afterlife. Six huge fans appeared in front of them. Three columns of two ventilators each, with blades larger than a person.

"The drive fans," said Castillo, taking big steps towards the blades. "Forty feet in diameter each, fifteen-thousand horsepower per ventilator."

Miguel followed him. If someone connected those immense fans in that moment, the two of them would go flying and end up torn apart, pulverized by the blades. There were noises, like small cracks in the ceiling, and the walls, all around. Miguel rubbed the palm of his left hand. "Why did you want to meet me here?" he asked, and then stopped.

"Do you like it?" Castillo asked, lifting his hands and turning around in a circle, as if all of this was his.

"You want to sell me a wind tunnel?"

Castillo laughed. Then he said, "Not to you, to your brother. Damian?"

"Daniel. Dani."

"Dani. I want him to come here. Everything's already arranged. The best aerodynamic labs, the best wind tunnels in the world."

Miguel's palms had stopped itching. Castillo had arranged Dani's grant there. He did it! He could have hugged Castillo in that moment.

"He'll be able to continue studying aerospace engineering in the University of San José," Castillo added. "That's sorted too. Everything."

"I… I don't know what to say."

Castillo placed his right hand on Miguel's shoulder and looked him in the eye. He looked like a Latin gangster offering his nephew a promotion. He was missing a little bit of gold – chains, rings. Miguel smiled.

"You're a Midas, Miguel." Castillo's tone lowered. "The only objective. The most important thing in all this commotion we have inside the SSR. I know you need your brother close. I told you I know from experience. You need contact with someone from the outside, or you'll get lost. I'm sure of it." He looked at Miguel very intensely. Miguel's smile slid off his face. "I'm doing my job."

"Thank you," said Miguel.

Castillo turned wordlessly to look at the fans. He said, "Look at those blades." He pointed at them. "They could cut us into pieces if someone clumsy activated the tunnel right now. Of course, you *are* a Midas. You would save us."

Miguel looked back. The air still smelled burnt, electric, in there. He had already tried to save someone once, he thought. Monica. A dead man! The pressure in his veins dropped again and his stomach churned.

Castillo grabbed his arm. "Let's get out of here. I just wanted to show you what I did for Dani. If you're in agreement, he can start at the beginning of next year."

"I'm sorry," said Miguel. "My blood pressure, sometimes I remember and…"

They walked in silence. The cracks became more frequent. When they reached the exit, Castillo stopped beside the door. "One other thing. I haven't been able to talk to you alone since the accident." Castillo always referred to the actor's death as an "accident." He placed his right hand on Miguel's shoulder again. It was warm and firm now. "I don't want the scientists to hear this, since we're a team" – he looked outside – "but I didn't agree with the experiment. The superhero trap, you know what I mean. I'm sorry. I'm so sorry."

"It doesn't matter now." Miguel looked at the spaceship. He still couldn't look anyone in the eye when he remembered that he killed a man.

"I could have stopped it," said Castillo. "That ridiculous comic book scene, the danger. I warned the actor to be careful, but it was impossible to control everything. He overacted, I suppose. I should have stopped him…"

Castillo seemed to be the only person willing to admit his guilt for the "accident." His words were calm, slow. Believable. Everyone was supposed to be a team, he had just said. But no one trusted Castillo. The CIA. He represented the Agency. The light from the test section turned off, leaving the two men at the bottom under the blue lights Castillo had turned on. It was a cold, distant light.

"They're about to do a test now, in the tunnel," said Castillo. His hand remained on Miguel's shoulder. "I'll ensure everything is under control from now on. No more risky experiments. No more tricks. That's also my job: to protect you."

Protect us, Miguel told himself. Monica had warned him that the CIA wanted something. But Walter hadn't done anything wrong. He was bringing Dani over to research prototypes of white spaceships like angels bathed in blue light. To the cathedral of wind tunnels. Miguel looked at the prototype, its incomprehensible aerodynamics. Walter was doing his job. He was a professional, that was all. And a spy.

"Walter," said Miguel, looking at his face.

Castillo removed his hand from Miguel's shoulder and adjusted the knot of his tie. Its maroon color turned into a purple so dark it was almost black under the tunnel's blueish light.

"Does the CIA have plans for me?" Miguel asked.

Castillo smiled, a blue smile. Then he opened the door of the tunnel. "The world has plans for you!" He left the tunnel. "It would be best if we left," he added.

Miguel left after him. The orange light outside, like a sunrise after a blue night, brought his blood pressure back up. He began to breathe more easily. Another worker, also in white NASA overalls, hurried over to them.

"You're not allowed to be here!" he shouted.

CHAPTER 23

From the hill where the SSR encampment had been settled, Castillo could make out, to the east, the ochre plain of the desert. He contemplated it for a few seconds. Rocks, dust, some thick bushes. The horizon was full of liquid reflections produced by the hot midday air.

"Even at the start of October, it's still hot in Nevada," he said, returning to his work. He adjusted an electrode that had fallen from Monica's forehead. Neither she nor Miguel looked at him. "But it's nothing compared to the summer months. It's fine now," he added. But he wasn't fine. The experiments weren't yielding any results.

Monica and Miguel, sitting beside each other, stared at the same plain. They looked as if in a trance, barely blinking, like they were completely absorbed in a play. Their bodies were covered in electrodes, while cameras and quantum sensors focused on them from various poles and tripods that surrounded them.

Castillo looked at Barrett, in the higher part of the encampment. He noticed Barrett moving his finger to his lips and nodded with his small head.

Silently, Castillo began to walk over to him.

"You'll break their concentration!" Barrett hissed when Castillo arrived.

Castillo looked at Monica and Miguel, unmoving where he had left them fifty feet downhill. From where he was, he couldn't see their faces. "They can't hear me; they're in a trance," Castillo responded quietly. He tapped his watch twice with his finger. "If there are no results in the next ten minutes, I'm stopping the experiment. We've already risked too much. Ten minutes."

But Barrett wasn't interested in paying him any attention. He was staring at a screen over his round glasses and typed something on a computer.

Castillo turned back to the dry plain to the east of the encampment. He had had to swallow a lot of desert dust like this in his life to get where he was. The son of a Cuban dissident with a fondness for rum, another Hispanic making his way in Florida. He wasn't the son of a general or congressman. He was not Wella Anderson. Castillo grimaced as he remembered his last meeting with her in Langley. Soon that arrogant woman would see how far he'd gotten. Alone. He didn't want her getting involved in his plans. General Rosmouth could be right – Wella would sell them to the Devil to climb one more step in politics. Castillo used the sleeve of his field uniform to wipe the sweat of his brow.

Barrett was typing on several keyboards now, jumping from one to another as if he had four hands. He seemed tense. Everyone was. Perhaps that was the reason why the experiment was failing. Everyone was annoyed. Castillo had forced them to carry out this test in the remote, rocky desert. It was the first time that the CIA required an experiment, and the scientists were not happy that the agency wanted to get into their test tubes. But what did it matter? It looked like it was going to fail. They would have to try it again later. There was barely any time left.

Castillo looked at his watch. Steel hands moved too quickly over a black face. They had already been there for two hours with no results, and in fifteen minutes a satellite would pass by overhead taking photographs. In fifteen minutes, the encampment had to be gone. The best thing to do was call the helicopters and disappear. But there was still…

"Ten minutes until we abort the mission," he said, "starting in three… two… one…"

"Don't be stupid," Barrett replied.

Castillo swung his head around to stare at the scientist. Insubordination was not something he expected from Barrett. He didn't tolerate it from anyone. He looked around, but there were no soldiers underneath camouflage netting. The troop that had been installed in the encampment were underneath the shade of two transport helicopters, two Black Hawks and an enormous Chinook. They were far away, about a thousand feet away, at the base of the west slope of the hill. From there, no one could hear them.

"Nine minutes," said Castillo, turning his back to Barrett to stare at the desert. He breathed slowly. "And don't talk to me like that. I'm tired as well. Don't forget, this is a military operation."

"It's not that."

Castillo turned around quickly. The scientist's voice, almost entertained, along with his flea-like face and his small smile, announced news. The success of the experiment.

"It's going up, look," said Barrett as he pointed at a monitor. "Inflection."

Hurriedly, Castillo approached the table and looked at the screen. The magenta line of quantum differential rose steadily. Soon it would reach its maximum. Miguel and Monica were doing it!

Suddenly, a gust of hot wind hit Castillo's face. He stopped looking at the screen and looked out at the plain. Nervously, his eyes darted back and forth over the area. Stones and bushes, nothing more.

"I didn't mean to offend you," said Barrett.

"Yes, yes, alright."

Barrett pointed to the screen again. Castillo saw that the magenta line of inflection was about to enter the Midas Effect zone.

"We're almost at the limit," said Barrett. "We're about to witness a miracle."

A miracle! Castillo forced himself to keep his eyes on the empty desert.

Empty.

And the desert wasn't empty anymore.

A blink later, the plain was filled with soldiers, trucks, tanks, helicopters, as if they had always been there. Battalion upon battalion of infantry and artillery from the U.S. Army began moving toward the small SSR encampment. A sudden roar, the clamor of an army in movement, reached them as though all the stones of the desert decided to explode at once.

Both Barrett and Castillo stared open-mouthed. An immense dust cloud rose from the army and rushed toward them.

"Position Alpha-Charlie," said a metallic voice on the radio. "This is Position Echo-Delta. All good in the encampment, sir? Over."

Castillo turned to face the other side of the hill, where the lieutenant and his men were. Position Echo-Delta. The soldiers had left the shadow of the Black Hawks and were looking nervously to the east. They had surely seen the dust cloud and heard the noise of the approaching army.

"Alpha-Charlie here," said Castillo. "Copy. All good here. Over."

"What's that noise, sir? We're seeing a dust cloud coming from the east. Sounds like a whole army is about to fall on top of us. Over."

A whole army *was* about to fall on top of them. "Nothing, lieutenant. We'll go ahead with the plan. Over."

"Are you sure, sir? Over."

"We'll go ahead with the plan, Echo-Delta. Over."

"Copy that. You have five minutes left, sir. Over and out."

Five minutes. Enough, Castillo thought. He turned around and observed the desert army through his binoculars. All of the details were perfect – Abrams and Bradleys tanks, Chinook helicopters from the rotorcraft division loaded with rear-guard men, Apaches flying in vanguard formation, armored divisions, artillery and infantry brigades. Nothing could differentiate the army from a real one. Nothing distinguished the virtual soldiers from the soldiers of flesh and bone that skittered around three helicopters behind them.

"A Jeep is coming," said Barrett, sticking a finger out at the plain.

A Jeep? Castillo perked up. That wasn't realistic, the army didn't use Jeeps anymore. Castillo focused his binoculars on a vehicle approaching in vanguard formation.

He smiled. It was a khaki-colored Humvee. It was a flat vehicle, with wheels spaced far apart, perfectly. On the roof of the vehicle was a TOW anti-tank missile launcher.

"It's a Humvee," Castillo said, still looking through his binoculars. "Miguel has done very well," he added, smiling at Barrett. Barrett shivered.

The Humvee skidded to a halt some two hundred feet in front of the encampment. The skid sent a small dust cloud into Castillo and Barret's faces. Both of them squinted through the dust, licking their lips. Their mouths tasted like dirt! Castillo wondered if it was real dust or if the inflexors had created it. Everything seemed so real.

The soldiers exited the vehicle and saluted to the encampment. When Castillo saw the salute, he began descending the east slope. The soldiers from the Humvee appeared to be waiting for him to come closer. He had to see them up close; those were his instructions – see the miracle up close. As he passed by Miguel and Monica, he saw they were still in their trance. Miguel squeezed the yellow page of instructions in his hand.

He would congratulate him when it was over, Castillo thought. He continued heading down between the rocks while he observed the soldiers from the vehicle.

They wore desert combat uniforms, covered in camouflage, as were their helmets, bulletproof vests, and M-16 rifles. They reminded Castillo of his days in the academy, the maneuvers in New Mexico. His mouth was dry, and his throat was tight with emotion. He tried to loosen the knot of his tie, but there was no tie in his field uniform. The same uniform as the men in front of him. He approached a sergeant who appeared to be the highest-ranking soldier in the Humvee.

"Sergeant Cruz, at your orders, sir," said the soldier, standing at attention.

Sergeant Cruz was sweating. Castillo stared at him. Sergeant Cruz smelled. He smelled like sweat and dust, like everyone else marching through the desert. Like Castillo himself had smelled when he had done the same thing that the fake soldiers were doing now. He could hardly believe they weren't real. *But they have to be fake. They weren't there before*, Castillo thought as he watched and smelled the Hispanic sergeant who looked like he had just stepped out of Little Havana, from the same street Castillo had come from. He smiled slightly, proudly. The sergeant's sweat was the aroma of his success.

Castillo stuck out his hand. "Give me your hand, Sergeant," he ordered.

The sergeant's face crumpled. He looked at his companions as if he didn't understand why an intelligence official wanted to shake his hand in the middle of a military camp. The soldiers stood to attention while the sweaty sergeant approached Castillo and took his hand.

The sergeant's hand was warm and slightly wet. His grip was firm on Castillo's hand. The sergeant smiled, and Castillo thought it looked like Miguel smiling at him.

The metallic voice on the radio spoke again. In the background, Castillo heard transport helicopters. "This is Delta-Echo, sir. The mission has ended. We're picking them up. Over."

"This is Alpha-Charlie. Copy that. Proceed. Over and out."

In that moment, Sergeant Cruz and his soldiers, the Humvee, the attack helicopters, the armored tanks, the artillery brigades, all disappeared.

The army disappeared.

The dust disappeared, and so did the noise of war.

And the smell of sweat.

Everything. Everything disappeared.

Castillo observed the empty desert for a few seconds, not breathing. Stones and thick bushes. Nothing more. Mission completed.

Then he looked at the steel hands on his watch. Five minutes left before the CIA surveillance satellite passed overhead. A satellite that would have shaken even the highest official in the Pentagon, had it seen the army advancing in the middle of their country. But now they wouldn't see anything – at most, three transport helicopters disassembling a small scientific encampment in the Nevada desert.

Castillo climbed the hill slowly. He smiled, tasting victory, the dust and sweat that remained on his palate and in his nose. He had barely taken a few steps in the direction of the encampment when he saw soldiers from his transport troop on the summit, real soldiers. They must have climbed the west slope at a run. The orders were to pack up the scientific encampment in less than five minutes. They had to do it quickly, of course, but he was sure that their curiosity to see what had happened on the other side of the hill had pushed their legs to climb the hill faster than any order could have. Castillo stared at them, gasping for breath as if they had no lungs, their creased faces showing their disappointment in finding an empty plain. Empty.

The soldiers started packing up the encampment, glancing over sporadically at the desert, as if they couldn't admit to themselves that there was nothing there. There had been so much there, Castillo thought. There had been the first of miracles. He smiled.

The two transport Black Hawks appeared, then, from behind the west slope. They landed on the summit, on both sides of the encampment. Castillo saw Barrett approach one of them. The scientist looked at him and gestured with his hand to the helicopter where it had landed before gesturing for Castillo to hurry up. He was holding a briefcase with all of the data and computers he needed. The soldiers helped Barrett, who was showing them the rest of the material. He seemed to be giving them instructions. The soldiers had to pack up everything into the third helicopter, which would also carry the whole troop – a Chinook, similar to the ones that had just disappeared, but real. Nothing would differentiate it from the fake Chinooks. The soldiers moved quickly. Castillo arrived at the top and entered the Black Hawk with the scientist.

"Well done, Eugene," he said, shouting to make himself heard above the noise of the rotor. He clapped a hand on Barrett's shoulder. Then Castillo looked through the window to the second Black Hawk carrying the SSR medical team. Monica and Miguel had removed their electrodes and silently entered the helicopter. Castillo smiled again. There were his quantum inflexors, he thought as the Black Hawk with the medical team took off. His new weapons.

***

Monica's excitement grew as the helicopter took off. It was a feeling she couldn't quite figure out, somewhere between panic and euphoria.

The medical team had laid them on two gurneys, checked their physical state, and then left them alone. Monica's shirt was drenched in sweat. The heat of the desert, she supposed, breathing deeply. Miguel's scent of honey and old oak was there. He must have been sweating as much as she, his scent filling the soundproof cabin. Monica felt a jolt of excitement beneath her stomach.

She always felt it when she amplified a Midas Effect. It was like an inexplicable adrenaline, almost sexual in nature, that sparked in her brain for minutes after the inflection. It filled her head and body with extreme but opposing sensations. Or maybe it was just that she needed Miguel now and the rough, maroon sofa, and sex in their apartment.

"That was amazing," said Monica, looking at Miguel as she lay on the gurney. "So real! And without any neural inductors!"

"I don't need inductors anymore," said Miguel. He was looking at the ceiling of the helicopter. "I can do it by myself."

"You still need me, at least. Right?" she asked plaintively.

Miguel turned over. They smiled as they looked at each other, each laying in their own little bed. "I like the push you give me," said Miguel. "I can feel how you amplify me and I take the leap. It's like a trampoline."

Monica pursed her lips and blew a kiss to where Miguel was.

"Did you like the detail of Sergeant Cruz's sweat?" Miguel asked. "I got the idea from our visit to the barracks in Arizona. There was a soldier who smelled like that… Castillo was stunned."

"I was more impressed by the image of the army. It was enormous. The whole plain was full. Thousands and thousands of them. Incredible. I've seen you create a lot of things, but the virtual army… I don't know…"

"It was like any other illusion," said Miguel. "More of the same. I can do much better things than fake little soldiers. I can make little soldiers out of lead. Or, even better, out of gold. I am Midas!"

Miguel laughed like an ogre from a children's story. Monica looked at him, serious. She wasn't laughing. "What's wrong?" Miguel asked. "I was joking."

"I don't like it when you joke like that."

Miguel frowned.

"Your ability isn't a joke," Monica insisted.

"I know."

Miguel turned over again until he was face down, no longer looking at her.

"If I had that power…" Monica started.

"But you don't."

Monica was about to protest when someone opened the door to the soundproof cabin. The roar of the helicopter entered along with the face of one of the doctors. She and Miguel gave him a thumbs up. The doctor and the noise disappeared as the door closed.

"I thought you liked the idea of a virtual army," said Miguel. "You encouraged me to do it. 'It's the ideal weapon, it dissuades the enemy without producing casualties. It's harmless. A weapon for peace!' You said something like that, or was it Walter who said it?"

"It was Walter."

"But you agreed."

"And I still do. It's just that…"

"Sometimes I don't understand you."

"I've always been honest with you—" Monica started to say.

"Always?" Miguel interrupted.

Monica closed her eyes and breathed heavily. She turned to lie face up and pressed her lips together firmly. That wasn't fair! Why was he bringing that up now? Yes, she had had to lie to him during the capture, and while they had checked that he was a Midas, but… "I have always been honest when it came to my feelings," she said, looking at him again.

Miguel did not respond.

"I don't like your attitude whenever we finish these experiments," Monica said.

"This again."

"Yes. It seems like you enjoy exercising your power."

"What do you want me to do? I can't avoid having these abilities. You guys were the ones who discovered them. And as well as that, I only use them for your research, and to… Look at the fake army. A weapon that doesn't kill. Isn't that an advancement?"

Monica looked at him firmly. It was obvious Miguel did enjoy his power. "You could also create real armies, right? You know how dangerous it is…"

"That's ridiculous! I'm not going to create an army! Who said anything about creating armies? I don't know where this is coming from." He shook his head. "I don't know if my attitude changes after the experiments, but you… I can't talk to you. You always make sure I'm not allowed to enjoy it."

"Did you enjoy it too in San José—?"

Miguel spun his head around to look at Monica. She didn't dare continue speaking. She felt how his fury, shining in his narrowed eyes and tense lips, put an end to any agreement, to the euphoria, to the adrenaline she felt whenever she produced inflection with him.

A new argument. Another one. They repeated themselves more and more frequently after the experiments. No, she couldn't bear this much longer.

"It was an accident!" Miguel shouted. "An accident caused by your negligence! It was your fault!" He turned to stare at the ceiling. Crossing his arms, he said, "You become insufferable."

CHAPTER 24

This is unusual, Castillo thought. Fred wasn't usually late. He didn't like the delay. Gorlov had gathered them half an hour before in the anti-inflexor room. Everyone had arrived except Fred. Castillo shifted in his metal seat.

Barrett, seated opposite him, was going over some graphs with Gorlov. They showed the data from the virtual army experiment in the Nevada desert. That had been a month ago.

"You are correct, Vladimir," said Barrett. "Miguel's residual inflection spreads from the moment Monica begins to amplify it. It's that incongruence again."

"It has happened in all of the experiments," said Gorlov. "Look at the graphs."

Barrett glanced over various pages and his small head nodded. "I see," he said, looking back to the graph in his hands over his glasses.

Castillo observed the two scientists. He smoothed out his tie. It looked like they had a serious problem. *An incongruence*, they had said. They were always so cryptic. He tried to pay more attention to what they were saying.

"We have never measured Midas Effects," said Gorlov. "It's very difficult to establish the behavior of the variables without a pre-established frame of reference. These measurements, however, violate the uncertainty principle."

Gorlov showed Barrett one of his notebooks. He opened it to a page where various equations had been written in blue pen.

The Russian and his stupid obsession with colors. *Mathematical formulae in blue*, he always said.

"No, it's not that," said Barrett. Out of the corner of his eye he looked at the equations and returned to the graphs. "It's because of Monica's catalyzing effect. It confuses everything. The crossing effects of Monica and Miguel's points of inflection fail to comply with the system of fundamental equations of quantum disruption. We still haven't resolved the Henk integral in the case of two inflexors..."

Damn scientists! Castillo thought. Meetings with them were a waste of time. Despite his degree in science, he almost never managed to understand what they said. He didn't trust them. Although, he had so many things to do now... If only Fred were here to help him. *Where the hell is he?* Castillo inwardly grumbled.

Barrett suddenly went wide-eyed and looked at Gorlov with a terrified expression, as if he had just discovered that the papers he had been reading contained his death sentence. "What if we've been wrong from the start?" Barrett began.

Castillo looked on amusedly. After a few minutes, their discussions became quite dramatic. Sometimes they were funny, so innocent with their equations and blue formulae.

Barrett pointed something out to Gorlov on a graph. He stared with an exaggerated sobriety, his finger drifting over the data as his mouth screwed up like he was about to whistle.

"No, it can't be..." Gorlov trailed off. "This is a replica of Miguel's inflection."

The door to the anti-inflexor room opened with a metallic sound and Gorlov immediately fell silent, as if some idea of his would slip out the door. He turned to the doorway.

"Sorry I'm late," said Fred Windhorst, turning his huge body slightly to fit through the narrow doorway.

"Are you alone?" Castillo asked.

"Yes," Fred answered. "I had to take a call for you. It was urgent."

Castillo took out his phone. They would have called him if it were urgent… Of course, he didn't have coverage. No radiofrequency signal could enter or leave the anti-inflexor rooms. He smiled. The scientists had managed to gloss over all of it with their chatter.

"You have to go," said Fred. "Someone called Jack Harper, from HQ, is in San Francisco."

Whitaker! The name Jack Harper made him cough, which he managed to ease by loosening his tie. Not even Fred knew that codename. Whitaker wanted to see him. And he had come to California, in person. It must have been very important. Castillo stood up. "I have to go," he said.

"Who is Harper?" Fred asked, sitting down beside Barrett. "I don't know him."

Castillo looked at Fred. He couldn't tell him anything, of course. Then he looked at Gorlov, who was observing him with a hard but vague expression from behind his massive glasses. It was like Gorlov was looking into him, like so many other times.

"A bureaucrat," said Castillo, holding Gorlov's gaze. Then he turned to Fred. "I have some explaining to do regarding the SSR accounts."

"No one said anything to me about it," said Fred.

"It's paperwork, nothing more," Castillo insisted. "A mistake I made on my last visit to Langley. Now I have to write up a report."

Castillo walked over to the door and turned around before leaving. "What was that you were discussing when Fred arrived?" he asked. "Something important, some discovery?"

Barrett squeezed his lips together and turned to look at Gorlov over his round glasses.

"We have discovered more incongruencies in the data," said Gorlov. "This time in the desert experiment. That is why I've gathered you here."

Castillo looked from his watch to Gorlov. Perhaps he should listen to what he had to say, although he doubted he would have time to ask for clarification. Barrett spoke then.

"It's because of Monica's residual inflection. Once she amplifies Miguel's quantum transformations, it generates a diffuser effect. Logically, the equations of quantum disruption aren't designed for that singularity in the outlining limits, and the Henk integral." Barrett seemed almost possessed by some blabbermouth demon from mathematical hell.

"Alright, alright, alright," Castillo snapped. "I don't need any explanations right now. I'm sorry, but I'm in a hurry." He looked at his watch again and pressed the fingerprint scanner at the exit. The light beside the door turned red as the door opened. Castillo hurried out, mentally cursing the scientists one more time.

***

Gorlov sat staring at the light beside the door. The small red bulb was the only remnant of Castillo's presence in the anti-inflexor room. Suddenly, the light turned green. The agent was outside. It was like a traffic light changing for Gorlov. He had to move fast in the small window of time he had been given. Turning to Barrett, he said, "We're finished here for now, Eugene. You can go."

Barrett wordlessly began collecting his papers and organizing them in his briefcase. Gorlov and Fred watched him without speaking.

"Bye, Fred. Vladimir," said Barrett as he finished.

Fred smiled at him and waved with his stone colossus hand. Gorlov did not respond. He didn't look at Barrett. He was looking at Fred, at his reactions.

When the door shut behind Barrett and the light turned red again, Fred looked down at his hands as if discovering in that moment that they were twice as large as anyone else's. He said, "Eugene talks a lot, explains a lot. And Walter really was in a hurry."

Gorlov said nothing. Fred continued.

"I know you're worried, Vladimir, although no one could tell from your face. I've been around you for so long, I can't help but notice. You old fox! You still make the same faces you used to make in Leningrad." He smiled nostalgically, like he was watching a film in his hands of the two of them as young men during their years in the Soviet Union. "Everyone thinks your only expression is that stony, constipated Bolshevik look, but I see much more in your face than any of them think."

Gorlov remained silent for a few more seconds before speaking. "We have problems we must explain about the effects brought about by Miguel. An incongruence in the data. Something is wrong."

"Yeah, technical problems. There always are."

"No, no, it's something else. Nothing adds up."

Fred said nothing. He didn't move, but he did look at Gorlov from the corner of his eye. Gorlov went on.

"From the very first Midas tests, the data hasn't been the way it should be. It justifies what happens, yes, but it is wrong. All the experiments are full of incompatible, inexplicable data. It is as if we know nothing about inflexors. It is as if the fundamental equations are completely useless."

Fred looked at his hands again. He seemed to not be paying any attention.

"All these problems," the scientist concluded. "And now, on top of it all, Walter."

Fred jerked his head up like someone had yanked his hair by the roots. His eyebrows created a vast, cavernous wrinkle in his forehead. "Walter?"

"I gathered you all here to give you details," said Gorlov. "The incorrect data, the incongruencies, whatever it is. We need help. But… You see it. Walter has more important problems to attend to."

"Castillo works for the CIA, Vladimir. *I* work for the CIA."

Gorlov slowly shook his head. "Do you remember the concentration of inflexors we detected two years ago near the NASA Center in Hampton, Virginia? The CIA must have something there, a parallel lab, a replica of this one. Perhaps this one is of no use to us anymore. You know how—"

"I don't know anything!" Fred boomed.

"Of course not," Gorlov snapped. "But listen, we all suspect – that includes you, Fred, don't deny it – that Walter wants something. Jack Harper? Come on, that's a codename. Even your grandson could have made up something better."

Fred breathed deeply, slowly, his broad Soviet chest inflating. Looking at his hands again, he said, "I preferred the job in Leningrad."

"Fred…"

"Fighting with Sergei, preparing your escape… I had every support from the CIA then."

Gorlov's memory produced a sparklingly clear image of Fred Windhorst the day they met in the Soviet Union, thirty years ago. At that time, Sergei Krushenko followed him everywhere, watching him. Sergei was his young, personal KGB spy, of an age with Fred. Fred nearly killed Sergei. He was like a machine back then, acting as he was programmed. Luckily, Fred didn't kill him. Thanks to Sergei's help, he was able to leave the country. Part of him understood Fred, who had dedicated himself to paperwork since his mission in Russia. He had spent too long managing the Project for a shark like Castillo to come along and take everything for himself.

"Sergei," said Gorlov. "Where is he now?"

Sometimes Fred updated him about Sergei. Now he was an arms trafficker, a gangster, but Fred seemed to miss the criminal. Sergei had once been his rival, but the two of them had become good friends after saving each other's lives.

"He steals guns, you know that," said Fred. "Gone to waste. It's all gone to waste." He placed his enormous hands on the metal table and shuffled to stand. "Shall we go? The static in the anti-inflexor rooms gives me a headache."

"Be careful with Walter," Gorlov began to say as he stood as well.

"What does Monica think of the incongruency in the data? She's your best analyst."

Gorlov froze and looked at Fred. It was clear he did not want to confront his problem with Castillo. First Sergei, now Monica. Fred didn't even want to hear about Castillo.

"She has not yet had a chance to look at the data," Gorlov replied. "Right now she is dedicating herself to the experiments. To being Miguel's catalyst."

"I haven't seen her in a while."

"I'm worried about her too." Gorlov left behind Fred. "Now, I miss our days in Leningrad too. It's all problems here lately. Monica isn't well."

***

Monica removed the last electrodes from her chest, near her breasts, and cleaned off the sticky gel with a towel. The gel was hard to get off. It was like a troll's drool all over her body. She tossed the towel onto the metal shelf where the clinical equipment was kept. Then, she looked over the records on the medical team's screens. All was normal, it seemed.

Monica tried to get up from the gurney, but the effect of the sedative used for the medical exam had not yet dissipated. She felt a wave of dizziness and sat down. Then she saw him, in the distance. Was it him? Vincent? Had he returned?

She rubbed her eyes – her eye sockets hurt, as did her eyelids and tear ducts – and looked again.

Beyond the glass door of the medical room, Vincent moved in the blackness of the lab. She saw him appear in the shadows of the chambers. Against the black of his overalls, his pale face seemed to float in the air, like the lonely head of a beheaded ghost. As he neared the soft light of the control panels, the rest of his body became visible.

He looked taller, fresher, younger. Monica had not seen Vincent since his telepathic welcome to Miguel. June. Already more than four months ago. Vincent had been outside, according to what Barrett had told her, away from the Project, resting. Monica touched her temples, the wet skin of her forehead rough where the electroencephalograph helmet had been.

"Are you alright, Dr. Eveleigh?" The doctor spoke by means of an intercom.

"I can still feel the sedative," said Monica.

"You shouldn't move for the next ten minutes. You should rest."

I won't move from here for the next ten years, she thought. "Okay."

Her eyes hurt from so much time spent living underground. Always on level -2. From the chambers to the clinic, from the clinic to the chambers. Always underground, like technological moles. Her and Miguel. The tests, the physical inactivity; it was all starting to get to her. And Miguel was unbearable.

Monica once again looked at the medical tracking monitor above her gurney. Curves represented her vitals. Her mood wasn't there, on those graphs. Her mood, lower and lower. It was becoming more and more difficult to get close to Miguel. The "Great Midas." He had gone from behaving like a Hollywood superstar to acting like a jealous, spoiled brat. She, too, was an important inflexor, as well as the best researcher in the SSR. But there she was, acting as a guinea pig for Miguel's tests. Did he not realize that everyone was sacrificing themselves for his damn tests? Monica tugged off the electroencephalograph helmet, the sudden movement pulling on her hair. *Stupid thing!* She was about to smash it against the ground.

Monica tried to calm herself. The heart rate monitor had climbed to one hundred beats per minute. Fine, so she wasn't a "Great Midas," but she could still do amazing things. Her heart rate lowered to ninety. Her life's research was waiting for her after all those tests, she told herself.

Barrett had told her that the Midas inflection study was progressing in leaps and bounds. Data, data, and more data. Everything was going well, except that they couldn't explain some of the results. Typical stuff from any investigation in uncharted territory. Monica breathed slowly. Her heart rate had stabilized. Yes, soon it would be over.

As well as that, she mused, Castillo hadn't bothered anyone with his military fancies since the virtual army. Everything was in order. Perhaps the sacrifice of being a mole for a few months was worth it. It had to be worth it. Monica looked away from the multimodal monitor and looked outside.

Level -2 was so dark.

She lay down and watched Vincent. He was talking to a worker. Seeing his black overalls, his hair, shiny and perfect as always, was like seeing an old friend from school, or from times gone by. More peaceful times for the Project and inflexors. Hopefully he saw her and came to talk to her. It would be so comforting to hear stories from the world up there. The breeze of the Pacific, the offers in the supermarkets, the sprinklers at dawn, the raucous grumble of exhaust pipes on Market Street, the potted petunias on her windowsill, tourists taking photographs of the Golden Gate Bridge and eating disgusting crab on the docks of Fisherman's Wharf, the maroon sofa and its rough fabric... Monica breathed slowly, deeply. Had her petunias shrivelled up?

Vincent looked at her from the control panel where he stood. His eyes fixed on her and his pale face broke into a smile.

Then, as if he had read her thoughts, Vincent began walking toward the medical clinic. His strides were firm, long, decided. Monica thought that he hadn't changed at all. He still had that gift of anticipating someone's needs. Vincent came closer. His smiling face had perfect features and a sharp, symmetric profile, as if made by a computer. *A happy telepath*, she thought as Vincent opened the door to the clinic.

"Moni!" he exclaimed.

Three strides were all it took for him to reach her bed. Monica sat up a bit as Vincent hugged her. He held her softly, delicately, like he was afraid to break her or only hug her with his mind, almost without touching her. But still, such a warm hug. Vincent still smelled like baby soap.

"Vince," said Monica. She smiled, and her eyes hurt with the movement.

"You don't look so good. Are you okay?"

"A battery of experiments," she said, gesturing with open hands to the entire basement. "It's only for a few more months. Nothing a good inflexor can't handle, you know."

"The tests with Miguel Le Fablec, I suppose. You captured him, right?"

Monica nodded. Sitting up further, she lifted her legs onto the bed and hugged them to her.

"He was terrified when he let me into his head to talk to him," said Vincent. "Was he the type of inflexor you guys were looking for?"

Monica couldn't talk to him about Miguel, or about anything he was doing, or about, of course, the type of inflexor he was. Vincent sat down beside her. He smelled so good, like a child fresh out of a bath, so fresh, so vulnerable.

"What have you been doing this whole time?" Monica asked. "Tell me something about the outside."

"Taking a vacation. Egypt."

"Egypt?"

"Pyramids and temples, you know. Stone gods, a lot of gods everywhere. And sun, of course, a perfect sun on the beaches of the Red Sea. Diving, incredible coral reefs. You have to rest, get out of here every now and again."

Monica imagined Vincent nursing a beer under the shade of a palm tree in a hotel beside the pool, deciding which temple, which pyramid he would visit, bathed in light and wobbling shimmers from the pool, the sea breeze dispersing his baby soap scent throughout the whole garden and between the palm trees. She inhaled slowly through her nose.

"One of the pharaohs," Vincent continued, "Akhenaten – I saw his statues in the Museum of Cairo – had a face like mine. Weird, straight. Uglier than me, of course." He winked. "A really weird guy. He introduced monotheism, or something. They killed him, of course. He must have been an alien."

"You're not weird."

Vincent made a shape with his mouth, like a wrinkled half-smile. He said, "I am, a little bit."

Monica smiled too, and her eye sockets began hurting again. *If you met the Midas...* she thought. "There are stranger things than being a silent telepath with the face of an alien pharaoh," she said. They both laughed.

Monica's eyelids stung. She squinted her tense eyes, her face twisting into a pained expression. Vincent touched her cheek with the back of his hand.

"Poor thing," he said. "Eugene once had me in here for four months. He carried out experiments endlessly. You begin to really hate this basement."

He was so beautiful, Vincent. It was like he had a supernatural halo. Monica told herself it must have been because of his alien ancestors. She let her eyes go unfocused as she looked at his shiny black hair, so perfectly styled, as he spoke in his calm voice. One time, Monica recalled, shortly after they adopted him into the Project, they went out together. Dr. Eveleigh, she remembered, in charge of one of the first telepath experiments, and him. They went out for dinner in Sausalito, and Vincent tried to seduce her at one of the lookouts on the Golden Gate Bridge. He was so smooth, so quiet, so elegant, that she nearly gave in. But she didn't. She was a professional. That would have been breaking the rules of the SSR. And back then, she didn't break the rules. Everything was so easy with Vincent. The smell of babies filled her lungs and her memories. Everything was so complicated now. Rules, Monica thought, were there for a reason.

Suddenly, Vincent's hand disappeared from her cheek. Her vision came back into focus and she saw that Miguel had just opened the door. Vincent had his back to him, but he turned with a ready smile, as if he had seen him coming. Vincent always saw things before everyone else did.

Two purple eyebags hung under Miguel's eyes. His hair, slightly dirty, was longer than usual, falling into his face. Miguel looked at Vincent, without moving from the doorway. "The doctor told me you weren't feeling well," he said.

"I was just on my way out," said Vincent as he stood. "Take care," he said to Monica, and winked.

Vincent and his baby soap scent left the clinic, along with a nod in greeting to Miguel. Miguel stood to the side to allow Vincent to pass, watching him leave from the doorway as Vincent took large, sure strides in his impeccable black overalls, his hair gleaming.

"What was that guy doing here?" said Miguel, without moving.

"It had been a while since we saw each other. He came to say hello. Vince is a good guy."

"Vince?"

Monica straightened in her bed. She stood and found she was no longer dizzy. She walked slowly, tiredly, toward Miguel. He continued staring after Vincent.

"He's scary," he said. "What's that smell?"

CHAPTER 25

Walter Castillo drove his black Pontiac Solstice into the underground parking lot. It was the agreed meeting point if Whitaker ever got in contact with him. A shopping mall in the suburbs of San José. He recalled the exact location of the parking lot and went down. Basement 2, Lot C-22.

Along the way, he had thought of many hypotheses about what had brought the director to San José. He had even thought that maybe, during the desert test, the satellite in the end had actually passed over sooner than planned and taken a photograph. Castillo descended through two levels and parked beside a large SUV, a black Cadillac Escalade with tinted windows. It was possible that the satellite had seen them and the virtual army. He would have to explain why he had taken such a risk, why he had pressed until the last minute. He activated the automatic opening of the back of his sports car, grabbed his black briefcase, and entered the backseat of the SUV.

Whitaker was there, in the backseat. Two other men in black suits sat in the front. Whitaker said nothing. He tapped the driver's shoulder and the Cadillac started moving.

"How is everything going, Castillo?" Director Whitaker asked when they left the mall.

"The experiments continue as planned. We've passed all of the recent tests, and the virtual army test. They worked perfectly. One of our own satellites nearly spotted us, but they didn't... did they?"

"No, no one has spotted any army. Except me, of course. The recordings you sent me."

Castillo observed the director. Whitaker wasn't looking at him, instead choosing to read the road signs. A big blue sign announced that the SUV was about to enter Route 101 towards Los Angeles. Something worried Whitaker. The knot of his navy-blue tie was twisted, loose, his top button undone. Castillo adjusted the knot of his own tie and said, "You will have noticed that Miguel can make us see anything. An entire army! That's what we need to start the operation. You should have seen it. The soldiers… They even smelled like sweat—"

"Yes, yes," Whitaker interrupted. "But I didn't call you here for that."

Whitaker turned to him, and Castillo couldn't help but focus again on his dishevelled tie, although this time he managed to contain his habit of fixing his own. He looked him in the eye.

"Agent Castillo," said Whitaker. His light eyes, as calm as ever, seemed to be able to penetrate his mind and convince him of anything. "If everything is in order here, you must begin Operation Messiah. You must go and bring your scientists and inflexors immediately."

"I don't understand. The plan was to start in two months, when—"

"Wella Anderson has already started," Whitaker interrupted again.

"Wella?"

"Yes, the congressman's daughter, the assistant to the Secretary of Defense. She was in Langley when you presented. Don't you remember? She is the one who—"

"I know perfectly well who she is. I had a… an affair with her many years ago. At Yale."

Whitaker stared at him with one eye slightly squinted. The Cadillac joined the highway, the acceleration causing the two men to lean back.

"She's a hyena," said Castillo. He considered himself ambitious to a point, but she was like a vampire, always ready to suck the blood out of anyone who came closer than a mile to her.

Whitaker shifted again in his seat and looked outside, his head shaking from side to side as he looked at the trucks and cars in front of them. "Well," said the director. "Wella Anderson is trying to get herself a good position, and her family is powerful. She has more adequate projects than Operation Messiah to use our funds for. She'll sell my head to the president to get it, too. The funds, the position, everything. She's a good shot."

Castillo expected no less from her. As they overtook a huge red truck, Whitaker turned his head to look at the vehicle. Wella. She had used him to get closer to the collective of Cuban dissidents in Florida, one of her first small waves in the political world. Whitaker started giving small slaps to the beige leather of the seats. The backs of the seats had some dust on them, which the director could not tolerate.

The leather of the Cadillac was soft, Castillo thought, good quality. The kind of thing that belonged to the inner circle of the powerful. During his years at Yale, Wella had an upholstered Mercedes convertible with identical beige leather. Soft, like the skin behind her earlobes, always adorned with two gray pearls. *This is the closest I've ever been to the upper class's soft skin. To power. To those who play with our budgets*, Castillo thought as they overtook another truck. The upper part of the cabin of the truck was filled with headlights and some kind of painted goddess of war. The goddess brandished a shining, ornate sword and had enormous, nearly naked breasts.

"I counted on her because she was a good link to the White House," said Whitaker, turning his head to look at the truck's headlights. Or the warrior's breasts. Who knew? "That's what I told George Rosmouth. 'My best contact with the president is Wella.'"

Whitaker squeezed his left hand into a fist on the beige leather seats as tightly as if he were strangling a rat. Castillo remembered General Rosmouth's jutting lip. The general also would have strangled a rat.

"I thought Wella Anderson would be interested in being on our side and wearing the medal of our success," Whitaker added. He smacked the back of the seat twice. Castillo had not seen any more dust. "But she's not about to wait or risk anything. That ambitious girl" – *ambitious bitch* was what Castillo heard – "wants all the glory."

Whitaker's gaze, full of calm, returned to Castillo. His blue eyes were cold. Castillo thought the director could have slit his throat without the slightest change in his expression. He focused again on the loose navy-blue tie. He was about to tighten it so the director could execute his enemy with all of the elegance his position required.

But there was something more. Something underhanded in their movements, Castillo knew it. That was why Wella had jumped into action. She was actually making use of the cracks in his plan. Perhaps if he did the right thing, she wouldn't have a chance to put them in danger. Flattening his tie, Castillo looked at Whitaker and said, "In any case, we must inform the president before we begin, isn't that so?"

"Don't be naïve, Castillo! You sound like Rosmouth!" Castillo leaned back. "Of course we'll inform the president before we begin, but not now. We don't have results yet. Don't forget, we're just a species of traitor that spends federal money on war plans that the president isn't aware of. Shark bait like Anderson!"

Uh-huh. I'm not that naïve, Castillo told himself. He again imagined General Rosmouth's lip, protruding as if in protest of what Whitaker was about to do. Castillo understood. They were going to begin without authorization, without hesitation, to avoid the political workings of an overambitious adversary – Wella. No hesitation. Castillo nodded and Whitaker continued.

"Once we have the first few successes, the president will be delighted. Then he'll have the opportunity to give his approval. And he will."

At that moment, Whitaker touched the driver's shoulder. The Cadillac took the first exit off the highway while Castillo reached for a briefcase in the back of the car.

This world disgusted Castillo. Politics. But if they didn't do what Whitaker told them to do, that bitch would bleed them all dry, that was for sure. What alternative did they have? Castillo noticed the SUV turning left over a bridge and turning around to Route 101, which they had just left, towards the lanes on the opposite side. They were already returning. Castillo hated changing plans. It was all like a game of ambition, his own up against Wella's. But he… his mission… No, he told himself, the mission wasn't only for him. His mission made sense, had ideals. Did lying to the President of the United States fall under his ideals? No, of course not. That damn bitch! She came back into his life and turned everything upside-down.

The car began to retrace the route it had taken. In a few minutes, they would arrive at the mall where they had met. Soon, Castillo thought, he would be alone with his instructions. There was no time to react, or think, or see what the right thing to do was. The mission, he reminded himself, had to start now. Above the president. Stupid rich girl! Yes, of course, Operation Messiah was above everything else. It was the best idea mankind had to protect all of humanity. It had to be more important than everything else – politicians' ambitions, his own ambitions, Wella's and Whitaker's, too. Above the president. Castillo touched the knot of his tie before adjusting it again, looking at the director's dishevelled tie.

War plans. He repeated Whitaker's words to himself. The Cadillac left the highway. That wasn't right. He hadn't expressed himself well. The plans weren't war plans, even though there were soldiers.

"What's happening with the soldiers?" Castillo asked.

"Nothing. General Rosmouth will cover us. For now. You just make sure the Midas is ready and in place. I'll take care of George." Whitaker took out a gray envelope from his briefcase and handed it to Castillo. "Here are your orders and the secret codes you'll need. That's all. Any problems in the SSR?" Whitaker looked at him again with his light eyes.

"No, sir," said Castillo, taking the envelope.

Whitaker turned toward the window and observed the mall they had left just a little while ago. "Good," he said.

The sun began to set, and in the distance, the first Christmas lights were just about visible. They were heading straight for it – stars, angels, light-up reindeer. Symbols of excitement for half the world, Castillo thought as he watched the blinking lights. Then he looked down at the gray envelope containing instructions that would initiate Operation Messiah, and put it away inside his briefcase.

CHAPTER 26

Miguel looked at himself in the mirror of the elevator that brought him from level -2 to level -3. The latest meeting announced by Castillo caught everyone by surprise. He had just gotten up and, like every morning, greenish bags hung under his eyes. He disliked his underground guinea pig look. Castillo had left instructions the evening before; he wanted to speak to everyone on the office level whenever the inflexors woke up. Listening to Walter would be refreshing.

Monica went down with him, but they didn't speak. Miguel looked at her from the corner of his eye, her image reflected on another mirrored wall of the elevator. She, too, was looking at her own eyebags, poking the skin under her eyes with a finger. She looked tired, as he did.

The two of them had practically lived in the medical units on level -2 for months now. For their security, they had been told. They did experiments and medical tests, more experiments and more tests. Miguel touched his own eyebags. The skin was oily. Descending to the white, well-lit rooms on level -3 could only mean that Castillo had another experiment. More experiments, more tests.

Although, if it was a CIA test, at least they would be able to leave, like they had with the army test in the desert. Repeating something like that would be nice, Miguel thought. He smiled slightly, pushing his eyebags up against his eyelids. They had had to leave several times in order to prepare the desert test. Seeing, memorizing, touching, smelling the real soldiers and tanks. *Leaving*, Miguel repeated to himself as the elevator stopped on level -3. He brought his hands up to the long hair falling over his face, greasier than he would have liked, and pushed it back.

"You first," Miguel said to Monica. She smiled at him uninterestedly as she stepped out of the elevator towards the soldiers and doors.

A few short minutes later, after passing through the security controls, they arrived at the white meeting room. As he entered, Miguel saw that only Gorlov and Barrett were there. Barrett seemed nervous. He polished his round glasses like he wanted the glass to disappear, looking everywhere at once. Miguel waved without much enthusiasm and sat beside Monica. Without his glasses, Barrett looked more like a gremlin than usual. "I don't like this meeting," Barrett said to Gorlov, almost inaudibly.

Gorlov shot Barrett a quick, possibly disapproving glance. They must have feared some game of Castillo's. What did it matter? Miguel was too tired. He wanted to see Walter. Fred walked in, then, and must have noticed Miguel's fatigue. He gave Miguel a cavernous smile and sat beside him.

"How are you feeling?" Fred asked, covering his shoulder with an enormous paw. His hand was warm. Fred always felt warm to Miguel.

"Good. Tired." Miguel yawned.

"I'll get you some coffee," said Fred, standing up. He left and walked towards the offices. Miguel said nothing. He covered his face with his hands and rubbed his eyes.

"What's wrong?" Monica asked.

"Another experiment."

"When we were in the helicopter, you seemed excited by Walter's experiments."

"Yeah. I don't want to talk about that again," said Miguel, pushing back the hair in his face. He hated touching such greasy hair.

"We haven't spoken since then," Monica insisted.

"We haven't seen each other since then!" Miguel replied. He had tried to answer quietly, but his reply came out louder than he intended and grabbed the scientists' attention. They turned to Miguel. Fred returned with two mugs of coffee. Two white mugs with the red and blue NASA logo. *NASA! A magnificent trap!* Miguel told himself. Fred stood frozen in the doorway, looking at Miguel.

"I'm fed up with these experiments!" Miguel shouted. "We don't have a life! We've been locked up in here for months!"

Castillo entered the meeting room in that moment. He was carrying a bunch of papers and rolled-up blueprints under his arm. He dodged the giant and his mugs of coffee as he walked to the white table, smiling all the while. Miguel supposed Castillo must have heard him yelling about his life as a lab rat. It was no laughing matter. Miguel had been serious.

"What's so funny?" Miguel spat. "I want out of these basements. I have the right, don't I?"

Castillo said nothing. His smile stayed in place. He unfolded a map over the entire table. Miguel looked at it, his brow furrowed, his eyebags aching. The map showed the Red Sea, the Sinai Peninsula. The Nile.

"We're going to Egypt," said Castillo.

CHAPTER 27

"I'm sorry," said Miguel.

He needed to make things right with Monica after their latest arguments. He needed her, now that they had finally left the rat cage that was the SSR Center. Miguel needed to share his excitement with her, the energy the journey gave him. Egypt.

Monica, seated beside him, looked out the window on the jet that was taking them to Cairo. She didn't move, or look at him. *She must be tired*, Miguel thought. Ten hours in a Boeing 747 that had brought them to London, the transfer… Everyone was exhausted.

Miguel looked around. Gorlov and Barrett were asleep, or so they appeared, lying back in their seats a few rows back. Fred, in the same row as Miguel on the other side of the aisle, was reading some papers. He looked out the window every now and then. Alone. Castillo wasn't there. He had left for Egypt a week before. There was no one else in the passenger cabin of the Bombardier. The CIA wanted them to fly in a private jet from London. Isolated from the rest of the world. From the silence, it was like they were all isolated even from each other and themselves.

"What are you sorry for?" Monica asked suddenly. She covered herself with a blanket and turned to look at Miguel.

"I haven't treated you very well recently," Miguel replied.

"No," said Monica.

"No?"

"No, of course not. What do you want me to say? You've barely said a word to me. Not exactly what a girl dreams of her boyfriend doing." Seeing her there, wrapped up in her seat, made her seem small, weak, defenseless.

"I'm a little confused."

"Very confused," Monica said.

Miguel noticed her tense expression. He wasn't expecting those answers. He began rubbing the palms of his hands. Miguel hadn't apologized just to start another fight. He breathed slowly and said, "I feel great when I produce Midas inflections. I can't avoid it, it's like a drug. I feel this euphoria—"

"I also feel that euphoria during inflection, but when we finish, we start to come down from it and it disappears in a few minutes. Every time I feel it less. I suppose we must be getting used to the Midas Effect."

Miguel picked up a pair of earphones from the seat pocket and focused on wrapping the wire around a finger. He had thought that the euphoric feeling was something exclusive for a Midas, exclusively his. He never spoke to her about it. They didn't speak much lately. "Maybe it's because you're not a Midas," said Miguel. "You only amplify inflection. I feel it in its totality."

Monica looked at him seriously, a small wrinkle appearing over her right eyebrow. "I can feel nearly everything you feel," she said. "It's inevitable. When I amplify your wishes, I feel them and make them mine automatically. I feel your feelings as well, as if they were my own. I only have to think of it, and there they are. I think it's some kind of residual inflection. Doesn't that happen to you?"

"Sometimes, yes, if I concentrate, I can see what you feel. But I try not to do it. It's... like going through a door, I don't know."

Monica smiled. Miguel saw her from the edges of his vision as he continued wrapping the wire around his finger. She seemed content to be sincere with him after so long, after so many arguments. Her greenish eyebags were still there. Tiredness lay on top of her smile. "If we told Vladimir, I'm sure he'd find a mathematical formula to explain it," she said.

"I suppose so." Miguel had wrapped the length of the earphone wire around the index finger of his left hand with no gaps, like the bandages around a mummy. He began unwinding it, slowly, before winding it again around the index finger on his right hand.

"I haven't felt a euphoria in you different to the one I feel," said Monica. "More intense, yes – you're the Midas, of course – but the same. After is different. Like now! You're doing it again."

Miguel stopped winding the wire and looked at Monica.

"You're doing it again," she insisted. "What you're feeling right now isn't euphoria."

"You can tell what I'm feeling?"

"It's… vanity."

Miguel yanked the cable roughly, breaking it with a loud snap. *It's not vanity*, he thought, but he said nothing. His mouth tightened. He placed the broken earphones in the seat pocket and looked around. Fred looked up just then from his reading and his gaze met Miguel's. The two men smiled at one another and Fred raised his eyebrows quickly in greeting.

"How are you?" Miguel asked, raising his voice so he would be heard above the roar of the engine. "Tired?"

"Fine," Fred replied. He did not seem fine.

Miguel turned back to Monica. "Fred isn't doing too well," he said quietly to Monica. "He hasn't said anything, but he's exhausted. Castillo is in control and no one in the CIA has bothered to inform Fred. He doesn't deserve that."

"Don't change the subject," said Monica.

"Talking about that puts me in a bad mood."

"You're enjoying your power. You feel good using it. You like your power, just admit it."

Miguel retrieved the earphones from the seat pocket in front of him. He saw the broken, frayed cable and twisted it between his fingers.

"There's nothing wrong with that, I suppose," Monica continued. "But you should be conscious—"

"Yes, I suppose I do. I like it."

"It's dangerous, you know that."

"I don't know, but…" Miguel once again began to feel like a child enduring a stern talking-to. He hated seeming like a child. And Monica made him feel like that, always lecturing him.

"You're proud of your power, but insecure."

"Maybe." Miguel took the wire in his hands and started pulling it tightly, trying to break it again. He had liked the sound it made when it split before.

"Look at your reactions. We're all worried about whatever Walter has planned for us, what he wants to do with the Project, with the Midas Effect, with you, and you're acting like a schoolboy." Miguel yanked the wire. "What if he wants to create virtual armies that control the Middle East, or kill an enemy leader with a lightning bolt? That's most likely what he wants, war plans. Did you think he wanted to search for the treasures of the pharaohs? Look." Monica looked into Miguel's eyes as if she were reading his thoughts. The earphone wire in his hands broke again with a snap, but neither of them paid it any attention. Miguel didn't look away from Monica. "Look at how you feel when I talk to you about Egypt."

Miguel remembered how, since Castillo had spoken to them about Egypt, he hadn't stopped imagining himself creating miracles in the country of the pyramids. Wearing a khaki linen shirt, shorts, and an explorer's pith helmet, Miguel saw himself in the desert, using his power to discover the technological marvels of the pharaohs. Things like that. They had crossed the Atlantic in a Boeing 747 like the one that had brought Miguel to California. A jumbo jet that transported him again to his fantasies. How could he not dream? But it was just that – a little bit of fantasy.

"I like the idea. That's all."

"You only care about your adventure. How exotic it is, full of spies and secret missions. God, sometimes you're like a child!"

"You treat me like a child!" Miguel exclaimed, throwing the pieces of wire on the ground. He turned to check if Fred had heard him, but he appeared to be concentrating on whatever was going on outside the window. Nothing. *At thirty-thousand feet, nothing is happening outside*, Miguel thought. Fred had surely heard his outburst, but was pretending he hadn't so as not to get involved in the argument. *Poor Fred*, he thought. Miguel, at least, could argue with Monica over the secret world they lived in, even if she ended up getting on his nerves with her Catholic mother attitude, always chastising him like a little boy who splashed in the bathtub. Suddenly, he remembered something.

"Vincent uses baby soap," said Miguel. He looked at Monica again. "*That* is childish. What were you talking about in the clinic?"

"Vincent has nothing to do with this."

"You two seemed very close."

"You worry me," Monica said slowly. "Your power is starting to become stronger than you." She kept insisting. It was like nothing else mattered to her. What did she want? He was worried, too. But he was trying to save their relationship, to find once again the North American woman with full, bitten lips and tight jeans that had tackled him with a map and a reflex camera in the gardens of the Alhambra. The woman he shared an apartment with on Russian Hill. The woman who opened the windows for him two at a time every morning. But they were so far from San Francisco, from their sunny campus in San José. He had to get her back. "You can't control it, you like it too much," she insisted. "I can tell from your feelings."

Monica kept her eyes on him. Curled up, she continued rummaging through his feelings. But she wasn't treating him like a child anymore. He needed her.

"Yes, I like it when I use my power. I like it a lot, but it also scares me. I can feel that I'm not controlling it." Miguel began scratching the palms of his hands. "Sometimes I think about the man I killed, you know? And I'm scared. I'm scared to think, to imagine, to want. Anything could turn into reality, and... You already know, my desires aren't always..."

"They're like anyone else's. No one controls their desires."

"Rage. It was rage that made me kill the actor. What will happen next time I'm furious?"

"Your desires are human, they're normal, we can all—"

"I'm afraid of my desires!" Miguel's exclamation came out strangled. He breathed deeply.

"Like King Midas," said Monica. "His wish backfired on him."

"Yes." Miguel looked at his hands. The scratching had turned them red, red with blood that wouldn't go away, that he couldn't make go away. "Like King Midas. You all picked the perfect name for this curse." Monica lifted a hand out from under her blanket and took Miguel's hand. "His sin was greed. Mine is wrath, for now. Do you see what I'm saying? What will the consequence of my next sin be?"

Monica looked down at Miguel's hand held in her own on top of the blanket. She caressed it slowly, almost without touching it, as if she were petting a tiny, frightened lion cub that could bite her at any moment. Monica had already seen his feelings, Miguel remembered. He needed to know what hers were, her deepest ones. He concentrated.

Confusion.

Desire.

Fear.

And…

"You pity me?"

"Nothing is wrong with you, I know that," said Monica in a rush. "But you're human, and you sin, and you have faults, just like every other human being. Except that you also have the power of…" She gripped Miguel's hand tightly.

"Pity," Miguel repeated.

"I've already thought about it a lot," Monica went on, "since they told me about the Midas Effect. I believe in God – you know that – and I can imagine His power. But, of course, He is perfect. I imagine He can control His power. What I can't imagine is…" Miguel felt a wave of pity sweep over Monica's face, her body. She looked like she was about to cry for him. With her free hand, Monica touched her small golden crucifix. "How can a human being live with the power of a god?"

CHAPTER 28

If God has ever been here, he left a long time ago, thought Miguel. He watched the tourists and the pilgrims swarming Saint Catherine's Monastery as they ascended the stone steps of Mount Sinai: in the gardens, in the church, everywhere.

The burning bush was not as impressive as he thought it would be. It didn't burn, nor was it a bush. It was simply a shrub. From the lookout on the monastery walls, Miguel saw a pilgrim approach the shrub and stealthily tear off a leaf. Nothing happened. No lightning bolt struck him down. He looked at Monica, who was also watching the thief. She shook her head.

Monica turned to him and smiled. Miguel liked her archaeologist costume: her tight, sleeveless khaki t-shirt beneath an open khaki shirt. It was similar to his own archaeologist costume, except his own did not include a tight t-shirt. He looked around – there was no one on that platform above the wall. He kissed her. Quickly.

And she kissed him back.

They broke apart and looked around.

Monica began buttoning up her khaki shirt, hiding the t-shirt as well as any trace of the gap between her breasts. She bit her lip. Miguel watched her, thinking about how magnificent she was.

Several days had passed since they had arrived at the encampment, which was what they called the group of rusty hangars and dilapidated buildings beside an oasis on a stony plain in the Sahara Desert, between the Nile and the Red Sea. They had done nothing all week – no experiments, no medical tests, no reports. All they did was sunbathe and wait for Castillo to return from a mission. It wasn't so bad being there, on vacation with Monica beside the Oasis of Al-Hakim. But the scientists were nervous. Monica fastened the button on her collar before looking at herself and unfastening it. She fastened it again. She seemed nervous too, biting her lip almost constantly, having taken an interest again in sex almost excessively.

Miguel smiled. That same morning, before leaving for Saint Catherine's Monastery, they had a roll in the hay in the dusty barracks. Had it not been for the Jeep they had requested from Castillo's agents, they would have been late to the helicopters. Miguel picked up Monica's scent. It was similar to that of the desert soldiers but sweeter and at times more intense. He remembered the sweat from the sex that morning, and the dust and the sand from the ground in the barracks on Monica's naked body. Desert sand on her ass, her hips, her breasts, her nipples. The memory aroused him, causing his stomach to clench. The sand itched again on his back and thighs, the same way the rough fabric of the maroon sofa did in San Francisco. Miguel could have thrown her down then and there and repeated everything from that morning, right in front of all the pilgrims and monks and CIA agents who guarded him like a golden idol.

Monica finished fastening her buttons. "I have to cover up to go back where the monks are," she said, tying her hair up in a ponytail. She really was gorgeous. And, even better, they had not had any more arguments. "Will we go back down?" she asked.

"Let's go."

"Walter better have something important to tell us after making us waste the whole morning here."

Miguel didn't mind Castillo making them wait, but he didn't respond. Monica had good reason to get angry. Castillo had left them there all morning. Maybe he had wanted them to settle in before he told them why they were in Egypt. And he had accomplished that. Everyone had found themselves forced to invest their mornings in visiting the settlement in order to escape boredom – Miguel and Monica, Barrett, Gorlov, Fred, the CIA agents, the other SSR scientists Castillo had brought to Egypt, and the new scientists. No one knew where the new scientists had come from, and the scientists themselves did not say. Everyone pretended to be pilgrims, dressed in khaki.

Monica arrived at the far end of the platform at the entrance to the tower.

Pilgrims, Miguel thought. He smiled and said, "You haven't wasted the morning."

"What?"

"When you get back to Houston to see your family, you can tell Father O'Brien that you went on a pilgrimage to Saint Catherine's Monastery."

Monica shook her head silently and began descending the stone steps of the tower.

Miguel followed her, still smiling. He was sure Castillo would have something big to tell them. If not, why would he arrange to meet them there? The burning bush, the Orthodox monks in their black tunics, cylindrical caps and long beards. CIA agents disguised as archaeologists were everywhere in the fortified monastery beneath the mass of granite that was Mount Sinai. It had to be something big.

"Be careful with these steps; they're worn down," said Monica as she stepped.

Miguel descended carefully. According to what Castillo had told him, they were going to Egypt to carry out a new secret test for the CIA. But all of it – the display of means, the personnel – couldn't have been just for that. They had set up a replica of the SSR Center in the encampment at Al-Hakim. They even had a hidden anti-inflexor room in a rusty hangar.

A pair of young tourists crossed them on the snail shell-shaped steps. Miguel pressed himself against the outer wall to let them pass.

The helicopters, he recalled, were magnificent. They looked brand new. That morning, four Sokol helicopters had collected them very early at the encampment and transported them across the Red Sea to the monastery. Castillo spared no expense.

When they reached the bottom, another helicopter appeared. Miguel expected it was another one of Castillo's. It flew above the sacred mountain. Another Sokol.

At that moment, the church bells in Saint Catherine's Church began to ring. It was a strange, quick peal, with three high notes followed by one low, quick note which seemed to mark the end of each section. Then, as if driven by the bells, dozens of bearded monks began herding the tourists and pilgrims out of the area. The monks drove everyone out from the church, the mosque, the chapel, the cells and offices – every single building in the monastery. They even seemed to evacuate the hospice.

Miguel looked at Monica, who shrugged. They moved as if to join the tourists, but a man disguised as an archaeologist placed his hand out, palm down, telling them not to move. He wore dark sunglasses and had cropped hair and gnarled arms like the slips of an aircraft carrier. One of Castillo's agents. Miguel spotted more clones of that iron man in nearly every corner of every building in the monastery. They all had their arms crossed, eyes hidden behind sunglasses. None of them moved. The bearded monks passed by in their black tunics without looking at the agents. It was like they were invisible, despite being as large as Goliaths.

"What do we do?" asked Monica.

"Quiet," Miguel answered.

None of the monks approached them, or anyone else dressed as an archaeologist. Miguel and Monica pressed themselves against a wall and remained there, watching the parade of pilgrims leave the sacred land. The thrum of the Sokol's blades faded into background noise.

After a few minutes, the CIA and SSR scientists were the only ones left. Then Castillo entered the monastery's walled enclosure alongside a monk with a thick, gray beard. Vincent walked with them.

"What is Vincent doing here?" Miguel asked Monica quietly.

"How would I know?"

"He's your friend."

Monica did not answer.

Castillo led everyone to the building containing the hospice. Almost all the CIA agents stood watch by the corners, except for some who helped Castillo gather the scientists who were scattered around the grounds.

They climbed a few floors and the monk with the thick beard – he looked identical to a photo Miguel recalled of Mendeleev – led them down a corridor with a row of balconies full of arches. The balconies looked onto the monastery's buildings, as well as the valley where the pilgrims had once been. Miguel looked out at the views. They reminded him of something. He bumped into Monica when the monk stopped, as did everyone else.

Mendeleev opened two thick wooden doors that lead to a large room. Inside was a huge table and about twenty seats of wood so dark it was almost black. *The meeting room. The moment of truth*, thought Miguel. A projector had already been installed in the table, and one of Castillo's agents connected it to a laptop.

As everyone took their seats, Miguel neared one of the room's five windows. They were very tall. From there, he couldn't see the monastery anymore. Instead, he saw the narrow gardens and their stone borders, cypress trees, orchards and olive trees. It was like the view from any other lookout in Granada, only drier. It had its charm. Granada, Miguel thought. Thinking of it was like verifying his reunion with Monica to himself. Far away, he saw the cemetery. A few hours earlier, they had visited the ossuary, which had hundreds of monks' skulls piled up there. That was not like Granada.

The monk with Mendeleev's face, who had been closing all the windows and shutters, approached Miguel and closed the window in front of him. Miguel stepped back and let the monk work. Close up, the monk looked even more like Mendeleev. Miguel remembered the periodic table in Cyrillic that Gorlov had in his office. Then, the monk went to the door, where Castillo was. Everyone was seated now: the SSR scientists, the CIA agents, the inflexors… Vincent sat at the end of the table.

As he sat beside Monica, Miguel observed the telepath. His straight, dark, carefully-styled hair, his pale, angular, perfect face. No one had told them that he would be there. Vincent didn't look at him. He didn't look at anyone. He studied a blank piece of paper on the table, lost in thought, as if he could read something on it. A small shiver ran up Miguel's spine. Vincent was as sinister as ever. Miguel could smell Vincent's goddamn baby soap scent. It filled the vast room and clung to the walls, the table, and the solid wooden seats. Miguel rubbed his nose. The monks wouldn't be able to remove that smell even with all the incense in the world. He visualized in his head the mountain of skulls and hoped that Walter had everything under control.

Monica shot him a look, darting her eyes over to the door. Miguel saw Castillo talking to Mendeleev, handing him a thick envelope. The monk made the sign of the cross with two fingers on his right hand held out towards Castillo. Then he stroked his thick, gray beard and closed the door behind him with a sound not unlike the creak of a ship's keel.

Everyone there was isolated in the coolness provided by the monastery's walls, which were more than a meter thick. Miguel saw Gorlov, Barrett and Fred talking to each other. Gorlov coiled and uncoiled a quill. If he continued like that, he would end up flooding the table with blue ink.

Gorlov did not let Castillo out of his sight. He nodded along to whatever Fred was muttering about and said, "Well, Walter, would you mind telling us what has brought us to Egypt with such urgency?" His Russian accent was very clear.

Castillo placed his fists on the table and looked at everyone, one by one, with his eyes half-closed as if he was about to reveal to them the last secret of the pyramids. Miguel loved his commercial poses.

But Gorlov's question, of course, was reasonable. Castillo had given no explanation in San José, only directions to where they were now – which flights to catch, passports, identities, contacts. Nothing about the experiment that had brought them to Egypt. If it even was an experiment.

"A god," said Walter Castillo, very quietly.

Miguel's palms began to itch.

"That is what we are here to make – a god," Castillo continued, in an even quieter voice. He pointed to the monastery walls. This was a house of God, after all.

"Do you want Miguel to burn the bush again?" Gorlov exploded. "Or revive an Ancient Egyptian god, or some similar nonsense? I knew it!" he shouted. The inkwell flew out of his hands, leaving several drops of blue ink, like royal blood, splashed across the table. His Russian accent crashed into his English, producing consonants like ridges in his mouth. "I knew someone would try this someday! I told you, Fred," he yelled, looking at Fred, who said nothing. Gorlov looked at Barrett. "Someone in the CIA has had the stupidity to try searching for esoteric meaning in our research, and to try using the Midas to give life to whatever tremendous foolishness lies unexplained in history. What are you thinking? That we'll find extraterrestrial gods who built the pyramids four thousand years ago? So they can give us their war technology? So they can tell us which planet they're from? Or maybe you think we'll invoke Yahweh on his bush for the tourists. Idiots! Which imbecile thought to mix mythological superstition with science? All that hurry for *this*?! All that secrecy? If that's the policy we're using to manage the Project…"

Castillo, without taking his eyes off Gorlov, as if he were interested in listening to him, opened his briefcase and took out some thick, gray envelopes as big as folders.

While Gorlov continued insulting the CIA, Castillo pounded twice on the table quickly, calling the agents who were standing at the door. They began distributing Castillo's envelopes. Miguel recognized one of the agents – he had shown them the anti-inflexor room in Al-Hakim. Roth, or something like that. He didn't have swollen arms like the others, nor did he look like a thug. He didn't talk too much in Al-Hakim. Miguel didn't even want to think what it would have been like to have this meeting in the metallic anti-inflexor room in the desert. It was hot in there.

Roth, or whatever his name was, placed one of the gray envelopes in front of Miguel and continued handing them out.

Once Gorlov's rage had subsided, Castillo asked everyone to open their envelopes. Inside, there was a folder of the same lead gray. The cover displayed capital letters in bright red. TOP SECRET – OPERATION MESSIAH.

Miguel rubbed his palms on the wooden table.

"We're not going to be carrying out an experiment on pseudoscientific speculations of Egyptology," said Castillo. He spoke slowly, calmly. "None of that. This is the first practical application of quantum inflexors. It's a scientific application about controlled and tested effects, whose objective is to support a CIA plan on a global scale." His voice dominated everyone, including Gorlov, who was now focused on his quill. No one else moved. "In these folders are the details of the operation. For now, I have a brief video explaining it."

He turned off the light and turned on the projector. The words "Operation Messiah" appeared in red on a white background, bathing everything in the room in a pink light. Castillo paused the video. "I'd like to clarify something before starting the video. This operation is not related to a war strategy but to a peace strategy. We intend to create a new world, and this will be the peace that sustains it."

To Miguel, the slogan seemed closer to an electric appliance advertisement than the grandiloquence Castillo wanted to give it, but it unsettled him all the same. Then the video began. It was no time at all before the details that verified the project's grandiosity appeared onscreen.

The video showed plans to create a new religion.

Miguel thought it something that, if taken out of context, would seem an extravagant, ridiculous stupidity, even if it was to be taken seriously. No one interrupted.

The video explained that a new Messiah would come down to Earth to unify all religions into one belief. First, Judaism, Christianity and Islam, and then other major religions would join. The theological details were meticulous. Miguel, at least, thought so, although he didn't understand much of it. He looked at Monica from the corner of his eye whenever anything religious was mentioned, just to see if she was scandalized or surprised, or laughed at a mistake. But there didn't seem to be any mistake. If there was, Monica's face didn't show it.

Operation Messiah was the first step in a larger plan of universal religious unification. It consisted of representing a mixture of the prophet of the Son of God, who would travel through various Middle Eastern countries recreating the wonders and lessons of Moses, Jesus and Mohammed. Miguel began scratching his palms when he heard the list of idols… He did not dare call them idols. Not even his atheism afforded him the luxury of thinking that amalgam was an irreverent joke. Irreverent and incredible. The supposed Messiah would start imitating Moses, since the three major religions accepted him as a prophet, according to the video. He would divide the Red Sea, climb Mount Sinai – which was also sacred ground for the three major religions, said the video. Then, similar to the life of Jesus, he would travel to Jerusalem, climb a mountain, proclaim himself the Golgotha, die there, and come back to life. *Incredible*, Miguel thought. And, to finish, he would travel to Mecca, find the mountain cave named Hira, where the Archangel Gabriel would appear to him, as he did to Mohammed, to ask him to unite all God's people into one.

Believers will kill whoever tries these imitations before taking the first step, Miguel thought.

However, it gave the impression of being something that had been years in the making, like theological machinery, organizational, even institutional. Of course, it left Miguel feeling overwhelmed in just a few minutes. He looked back at Monica, who still showed no doubts on her face. Her gaze remained fixed on the video until it ended.

Castillo turned off the projector and turned on the light. He circled the large wooden table and began collecting his papers.

No one spoke. No one seemed able to. Everyone watched Walter Castillo collect his papers, looking as if they wanted to run away. Although everyone knew there was very little left to say, they seemed to want to hear more. More Messiah.

Miguel fidgeted in his seat. He dried the sweat on his face with his hand. Even though the thick monastery walls left the room cool, he was sweating. He picked up the lead-colored envelope and the sweat from his hands immediately left marks on it, like it was his signature.

"The theology looks all figured out," said Miguel.

Castillo looked up from his briefcase to Miguel. He smiled. Miguel continued. "That's the what of the plan. What about the how?"

"A god, Miguel," said Castillo. "We're creating a new world, and we need a new god."

Miguel's hands itched considerably. The wood of the table was rough. Castillo straightened and looked Miguel in the eyes.

"We ask you to be that god."

Miguel felt his breath leave him in a rush. He gripped the edge of the dark table tightly. He knew it, had suspected it ever since Castillo started talking about the operation. He had understood that they had not been brought there to revive Egyptian gods, or to bring in a virtual army to the Middle East, or to do more experiments. He knew he was the new Son of God, the new Messiah. He couldn't breathe!

Castillo finished collecting his papers and headed for the door. It was like he had just offered Miguel a new job at the local university and didn't need to wait for a response. Everyone's eyes followed him.

"I have to go now," he said. "I must supervise the work on one of the emplacements. I'll be back in five days, and we'll meet again. I'll leave you some time to think. I think you'll like some time to reflect on what I've just shown you. And on your participation in this," he lifted his hands up like a preacher in a trance, "*new world*."

He left.

CHAPTER 29

New world. New god, Miguel repeated to himself.

As Castillo left, the light of midday entered the room and illuminated everyone's faces. They were all looking at Miguel. Silently. The room's inexplicable heat pressed on his chest, as did the frowning stares. Miguel could feel their eyes on him, feel their reactions. It was like they were waiting for him to smack the table, to make them tremble, laugh, or run, perhaps.

"I don't know what to do," he said in a faltering voice. "I don't know. I need air." Grabbing the gray folder of Operation Messiah, Miguel stood and quietly walked towards the door. He saw Monica do the same. No one said anything. By the time he arrived at the door, Castillo had already disappeared. Miguel turned around just before he left and found that everyone's eyes had followed him. "I need air," he repeated, and hurried out.

After a few short minutes, he and Monica had already passed the bush, the bearded monks, Mendeleev, and the entire monastery. They boarded one of the Sokol helicopters and asked the pilot to bring them back to the encampment at Al-Hakim.

Miguel didn't say a word for the entire journey. *A god, a god*, he repeated to himself as he began to leaf through the contents of the gray folder. The timidity with which he started to read quickly turned to avarice. Until they landed.

"Let's go for a walk," said Monica as they left the helicopter.

The comfortable shade of the inside of the helicopter gave way to the blinding heat of the sun as they stepped out. Miguel closed his eyes and took a breath of the warm air that blew through the desert. He felt it dry his face and evaporate the sweat that ran down his back. The memory of Castillo's video came to mind again, his words like a balm, everyone's eyes on him as Castillo finished. The tepid desert breeze was much more refreshing than the thick, stuffy air of the monastery, filled with eyes. He looked at Monica. She squinted, blinded by the sun, much like he was.

"Somewhere quiet," she added. "In the Jeep."

"After you."

Monica approached the vehicle they had left behind that morning in the shade of a nearby hangar. She hopped into the driver's seat while Miguel sat in the passenger's seat. He smiled seeing her so resolute. This was the same Monica as always, and he needed her like this right now. She helped him act, decide, in surety.

Before starting the car, Monica opened the glove compartment and took out a cap. She fixed it to her head with vigor, pulled down the visor and turned the ignition. With a 180-degree turn of the key, the Jeep roared to life, sending up a cloud of dust and stones toward the dented hangar walls. The Jeep jerked forward.

A short while later, they passed through the barriers of the old Al-Hakim encampment. They passed by a clinic, a building of dull brick and peeling paint, and Miguel contemplated it. He knew that beyond that feigned appearance of ruin was a replica of the medical clinics on level -2 with equipment more technological than NASA's basement. Nothing was what it seemed in the corner of that desert. Everything, he now knew, was prepared for him.

Monica gestured with her hand beyond the palm grove of the oasis to the first visible hill outside the encampment's perimeter of broken fences. Miguel looked at the hill, truncated on its upper part on a small plateau. He nodded. He liked the hill. It was like a desert lookout. He and Monica had gone there several times over the last few days. He remembered his reunion with her, their reconciliation, the sex.

The Jeep neared the hill, jolting forward to the control post of the encampment. Miguel and Monica showed their passes to an Egyptian soldier, who said something in Arabic to another young man in uniform standing in a hut beyond the dust cloud. The second soldier lifted a barrier with his hands and the Jeep took off, leaving another dust cloud.

Miguel turned around in his seat as the vehicle began clattering. He watched the control post. The soldiers sat down again in the shade of their hut and lit their cigarettes. Miguel thought they could have taken a gold sarcophagus out of there without anyone giving them a second glance.

"We're supposed to be archaeologists. That's our cover, right?" Miguel shouted over the hum of the motor and the crunch of the dirt. He kept his gaze turned back.

"That's what Castillo's agent said, Roth," Monica replied.

"Why are there soldiers everywhere?"

"I don't know. CIA things."

"Does the CIA control us with Egyptian soldiers?"

"How would I know? Castillo, all his secret plans, he'll know."

Another Jeep exited the encampment. Narrowing his eyes, Miguel could just about make it out behind the vehicle's dust trail. "They're following us," he said.

"I suppose they don't want you to lose that," said Monica, looking at the folder Miguel held. "They don't want you getting robbed. You should have left that in the camp; it's top secret. You should know these things..."

I'm a Midas. No one can rob anything from me, Miguel thought. He looked at the folder. He liked its dark gray cover, the red lettering. From what he could tell from the references, the folder was just a summary of volumes and volumes of specifications and plans. A colossal work of religious, institutional, and political engineering... Something worthy of a pharaoh, of course.

Having crossed the palm grove of Al-Hakim, they drove off-road and began ascending the rocky terrain of the upper part of the truncated hill. They soon arrived at a point where they could no longer continue in the car, about two hundred meters from the summit. Monica got out of the car and took off her shirt, throwing it into the Jeep, before straightening her sleeveless shirt and beginning the climb. Miguel followed her, the pharaohs and volumes of Operation Messiah whirling in his head. The Jeep that had been following them stopped at the foot of the hill. Two men – supposed archaeologists in khaki outfits identical to that of every other supposed archaeologist – got out, sitting in the shade of the car with their arms crossed. They stayed watching Monica and Miguel.

"From the CIA," said Miguel as he looked down, breathing hard. Then, he continued the climb.

By the time they got to the summit, they were soaked with sweat. Monica removed her cap and began fanning herself with it. She shook her head, letting her messy hair fall loose. Miguel watched how her Italian-actress hair moved. She looked the same in Granada, he thought, the day they had met, when she was disguised as a tourist in a cap. She looked as sensual as she did back then. More so, probably. Her sleeveless khaki shirt clung to all her curves. Sweat coated her back, shining in droplets on her neck, her shoulders, her collarbone. Even her small gold crucifix was wet. Miguel noticed Monica's gentle scent. He remembered the sex they had that morning, a buzz running through his legs. His stomach clenched, as did his thighs.

Then he felt the rough texture of the folder under his fingers.

The gray folder. His mission. A god.

The buzz caused by Monica's wet shirt disappeared.

Monica stopped fanning herself. She sat on a rock near the edge of the plateau. She looked out onto the desert with a serious expression. Miguel sat beside her and looked out as well. Towards the east were barren, stony plains, ochre hills, and a jagged blueish line that spoke of flat, arid mountains just beyond.

"This reminds me of the desert scenery in Nevada," said Miguel. "The virtual army."

Monica didn't respond.

Miguel recalled the image of battalions of false soldiers, the tanks, the helicopters in the desert. They had appeared out of nowhere. He breathed deeply and let the air out slowly, almost as if he were whistling. Then he imagined a new army, an army of loyal soldiers who followed him and listened to his teachings, and adored him. Him, preaching on top of a hill like this. He could almost see them as they proclaimed him the new Messiah. The only. *We need a new god.* Those were Castillo's words.

"What are you thinking?" Monica asked.

"Nothing," said Miguel.

"What Walter told us—"

"Look." Miguel cut her off, pointing at a paragraph on a page in the folder. Monica looked where he was pointing. "It's like the virtual army test. It's a good plan," he said. "First, I create a crowd of virtual followers. Then, real followers will join – at first, they'll be people who are curious or crazy, but then people who are less crazy will come and join my doctrine. After that, I start performing miracles. I cross the Red Sea with all of them, like Moses. Exodus 14: 16-30… See? There." Miguel pointed to a spot on the map.

"Yeah," said Monica, looking between the map and Miguel.

"It has to start in Egypt, of course. Here is where it all started. Well, nearly everything. Look, it's written down in this paragraph. Quotes everywhere – the Old Testament, the Torah, the Qur'an… It looks believable."

They looked into each other's eyes. There was a fine wrinkle above Monica's right eyebrow. Miguel began leafing through the folder again.

"Did we really come all the way up here for you to study those papers?" Monica asked.

"What?" Miguel replied as he unfolded another map.

"Does this whole Operation Messiah seem like a good idea to you?"

Miguel didn't reply. He was looking at the map.

Monica yanked the folder out of his hands. Miguel followed the movement with his eyes and looked up at Monica, his mouth half open.

She looked serious, her blue eyes obscured by her deep frown as she prepared to reprimand him. Tell him off like a child, Miguel thought. Again. Just like she had been doing before arriving in Egypt. *Not again*, he said to himself. He could almost hear the accusations coming out of her mouth, even though her lips were still tense. A moment ago, he would have complied with any kind of sexual game she proposed on that same rock. But now…

"I asked if you like the idea of Operation Messiah," Monica said.

"I don't understand."

"Are you going to do it? That's what Walter wants us to decide."

Of course I like the idea, Miguel thought. "I looked at you during the video," he answered. "You seemed to like it."

Monica looked out at the desert again. She shook her head. "It would be the most amazing thing in the world if some beliefs could reconcile. Some people—"

"Yeah. But you don't think I can do it," Miguel said, taking the folder back from Monica.

She let him take it back easily and place it on his lap. They looked at one another. "You're nearly a god. I already told you on the plane. But—"

"I don't see anything wrong with—"

"You haven't thought about it, right? No, I suppose you haven't." Monica's eyes narrowed. She concentrated on Miguel like she wanted to send her convictions to him through the air. Miguel let Monica's feelings into his head. He felt her fear, a concentrated fear that he could almost touch, solid, inside her. He shivered without looking away from Monica. "It would be a mockery of all believers," she said. "And of God."

"God…" Miguel repeated. She was a believer. *Religion. Of course*, he thought. Was she offended? No, it couldn't just be that.

"You're not a god. You are human, and you know it. You're going to end up doing something bad, making a mistake."

I'm not God, Miguel told himself. *Just a man, of course.*

"And it would mean the domination of humanity," Monica continued. Miguel could feel her fear much more clearly now. And her pity. "Mankind will stop being free if you intervene. You'll end up controlling destiny. It's an abomination. And that's if you manage to control your power. And your own destiny. You're not God," she insisted.

Miguel looked away. He concentrated on stopping himself from feeling what she was feeling, seeing what was inside her. He didn't like it. He looked at the horizon again, the desert that he had already filled with armies and could fill again with followers. *We need a new god.* Castillo's words resounded once more in his head.

"Your friend Vincent liked Operation Messiah," Miguel said suddenly.

"What does Vincent have to do with—?"

"He came with Walter. Your friend is one of his."

"He's not my friend!"

"Yeah."

Miguel caressed the gray carpet on his legs.

***

Gorlov closed with a slap the gray folder Castillo had given to him a few hours earlier. He decided he had already read enough.

The interior of the anti-inflexor room at Al-Hakim felt like an oven that would toast their brains in no time at all. Gorlov lifted his head, dried the sweat from his temples with the back of his hand, and looked at his companions. Fred and Barrett were also sweating profusely.

But he was convinced they couldn't talk outside. Castillo was counting on Vincent. And if Castillo had a telepath, he would also have inflexors capable of extrasensory perception who would hear everything that was said outside the room. They had to stay in the oven.

Gorlov left the gray folder on the table. Barrett, seated in front of him, had removed his small round glasses and was cleaning them with a cloth. As he did so, he looked around at the golden walls, at the roof, at the floor, everywhere. He began to look like a rat in a cage.

"Eugene!" Gorlov shouted.

Barrett flinched. He stopped cleaning his glasses and looked at Gorlov with widened eyes. Then he said, "This is a real anti-inflexor room, right?"

"You've already seen the walls, and the machinery outside."

"What if they've disconnected it?" Barrett put on his glasses.

"We would know, Eugene. We would be able to tell – the buzz, the static, the goosebumps…"

"But if I were in the CIA—" Barrett suddenly shut his mouth and looked in Fred's direction, his small eyes looking above his round lenses.

Gorlov watched Fred as well. Of course, the CIA. But Fred wasn't like the rest of the CIA.

Seated at the far end of the rectangular table, Fred contemplated the papers in his grayish folder, breathing loudly through his nose. The muscles of his face noticeably tightened over his jaw. His father's round, town-reverend face, that once looked fixed into Fred's features for years now, had almost disappeared.

At that moment, Fred looked up and said, "This is why Walter wanted us!" He held the folder up high, keeping it flat, at a level with his tense jaw. "For this nonsense!"

Gorlov felt an impossible, ancient cold that seemed to come from the winters of his past. Fred's blue eyes looked lost, as if in some distant, snowy evening in Leningrad. That same expression. A droplet of sweat slid down the scientist's temple. It wasn't warm in Russia. Gorlov saw in his mind the image of Fred pointing his Colt at Sergei's head. That cold expression – the one he had seen on the young North American Secret Service agent he had met in the Soviet Union – had returned to his face.

"You're in the CIA," said Gorlov. "You cannot talk about one of their operations like that."

"I am not part of this operation!" Fred's voice sounded like thunder. "I am not part of any of them! If it weren't for the fact that I do the paperwork in San José, they would have let me go years ago." He hit the folder against the table. "Castillo is the one in charge here, you know that. And what he's doing… This is dirty work. It is. This war operation hasn't been approved by the president." Fred gripped the folder in both hands and stared at it. He looked like he was seconds away from ripping it to pieces.

"It's not a war plan," said Barrett in a high, timid voice, like a child.

"It's something very similar, Eugene, believe me," said Fred, softening his booming voice. "I know how Washington works. An operation like that… There would be footprints, movement, in the Pentagon, in Langley, in the Capitol, everywhere. In the White House itself. And there's nothing. I still have my contacts. They're all too calm. No, this is dirty work, I'm telling you."

Gorlov agreed. But he also knew that nothing was ever completely dirty or completely clean when dealing with operations as ambitious as placing a new god in the world. He shrugged and said, "It may be that they intend to inform the president when they have results. Just after starting, at a point where the 'boss' can make the final call. Or it seems like he can. That's how I would do it."

"The president will never authorize this." Fred gestured again with the folder.

Gorlov shook his head slowly. "Fred, you and I have worked for our countries' intelligence services." Fred frowned and his forehead filled with cavernous wrinkles. "We both know the interests that move our politicians, as well as anyone else in the upper echelons of society. Do you really think that this mission would be rejected for noble reasons? Come now, Fred!"

Fred seemed to clench his jaw, looking down at the folder. Then, he rolled it up. His large hands engulfed the roll like a wrecking pincer in a junkyard. He huffed laboriously through his nose once. He looked at Gorlov and pointed the roll at him.

"Maybe that's the way you think in the Soviet Union," he grumbled. "You were all atheists in the Party. But in my country, we believe in God. You know that. There are millions of believers there, and all over the world too. The faith of humanity usurped by test-tube gods? Do you think the president will authorize that? It's… it's blasphemy! You tell him, Eugene."

"I'm not very religious, Fred," said Barrett. "But Vladimir, he's right. We're a country of believers."

Gorlov looked at Barrett silently, and he shook his head again, slowly. They couldn't possibly be so naïve. "I'm not going to argue with you about religion," he said. "I believe you'll agree with me in that we cannot allow—"

"Of course I won't allow it!" Fred yelled. "I'll tell the president. I'll go right now—"

"Fred!" Barrett cut him off as Fred rose from his seat.

"What?" Fred looked at him and froze.

Barrett pushed his glasses up on his nose with his index finger. "There's something…" Barrett began, looking at his lead-colored folder with the corners of his mouth pointed downward, as if he were looking at something worthless. "I don't know, do either of you really think this could work?" He looked at Gorlov. "The president isn't an idiot. Okay, I agree that he can be ambitious, but this world peace that Walter is selling, do you really think we can get it just by making a new god?" Fred watched him wordlessly, leaning his head to the left. Gorlov nodded. "What I mean is, when this new Messiah's religion is created – if it *can* be created at all – sooner or later it will split into factions. Schisms, splits, dissident groups, heretics, separatists, new creeds, saviors, the enlightened, prophets in the Messiah's pocket who will later denounce him—all of them with a thirst for power. They'll create their own religions. That's what has always happened, throughout history." Fred straightened. Barrett pushed his glasses up again. "Don't you see? When Miguel disappears, his own religion will split into groups. Lots of them. And between all of them, they'll soak the world in war and irreconcilable hordes. Not to mention the economic and political wars. A universal creed to achieve world peace?" Barrett smiled his small rat-like smile. "No." He elongated the vowel disdainfully. "No one would ever believe that, much less the president. It's so juvenile, believing that a god will unite humanity." His smile grew. "Impossible."

There were a few seconds of silence after Barrett stopped talking. It was unusual for him to express himself so eloquently, Gorlov thought. He never spoke of any ideas of his beyond his calculations, his equipment, and his colored graphs.

His ideas. Wrong ideas, Gorlov told himself. The heat inside the metallic room intensified for a few moments. He felt another droplet of sweat slide down his cheek and along the black plastic of his glasses. He thought about removing them but didn't. He felt a need to hurriedly end the discussion. Soon the heat would make it hard to breathe and they would have to leave.

"All wars are economic, Eugene," Gorlov began, staring at Barrett. "But this new god could change things." Gorlov saw Fred straighten, his cavernous wrinkles accompanying his frown.

"Fred, I don't mean to offend you, and I don't want to argue about theology. Let me explain."

Fred crossed his arms over his chest like two wooden beams. Gorlov picked up his gray folder and searched the pages. When he found the page he was looking for, he left the folder open on the table. He turned the text toward Fred and Barrett and pointed at a paragraph with a bony finger. The two other men leaned over the table.

"The Midas subject will be an immortal god," Barrett read out, "whose presence and miracles worked will heal splits in his religion, his people, and all of humanity. And he will live for centuries, the necessary time to find another Midas who can continue his work when he decides to voluntarily rest…" Barrett nodded. "I hadn't seen that. If he's immortal, perhaps there's a chance he'll survive."

"It's still blasphemy!" Fred boomed.

"*Voluntarily!*" said Gorlov, pointing at the paragraph Barrett had just read. His wrinkled fingertip hit the word "voluntarily." Fred and Barrett looked at the paragraph again. "Do you think anyone would live for centuries *voluntarily* doing what he considers *good* for humanity?" Gorlov asked. "Only to pass the work on to the next god? *Voluntarily?* Another god doing his own *good*?"

Fred looked at him in silence, leaning his head again. Barrett removed his glasses once more and began cleaning them, still looking at Gorlov.

"Castillo must have some way to control the Midas' will. I don't know how, but he must have it. He cannot risk Miguel exercising his own will. No one builds a missile and launches it without navigation control, right?"

"He's going to control everything," said Barrett. His eyes widened considerably, as if he could see the end. His hands stilled.

"Of course," said Gorlov.

"He's going to control Miguel," said Fred.

"And if your president won't use him," Gorlov added, "Castillo will. Do you think he'll keep his weapon in a dusty hangar like the ones outside? He'll use him to control humanity, until someone manages to wrestle control from him, someone else who will use him for the same end. Until he dies and someone else inherits his control, or robs him of it. Always control. Power. Control of the power of a god. A god!"

"A religion," said Fred in a low, quiet tone.

"A god, Fred, a god."

Silence reigned for a few seconds. The temperature climbed, the quantum distorters prickling their skin. The room's gold walls seemed to emit microwaves to cook them with.

"Many kings and a Midas to grant their wishes," Gorlov continued. "But one day, one of those foolish kings will misstep and ask the Midas for something whose consequences are not well calculated." Barrett and Fred watched Gorlov carefully. "And he will destroy the entire universe," Gorlov concluded.

Fred pressed his rolled-up folder between his hands until it crumpled and folded in on itself. The heat seemed to congest his face, but his small blue eyes remained cold. His vision was unfocused, anchoring him somewhere in the infinity between himself and the metal table in the anti-inflexor room.

That expression, thought Gorlov. *Those snowy days in Leningrad.*

He felt his sweat dampening his cheek where it met his Russian glasses. He lifted them slightly to dry his face and saw Barrett do the same. Gorlov closed his folder. On the lead-gray cover, he saw the words TOP SECRET printed in bright red beneath the emblem of the CIA.

The eagle, the sixteen-pointed star… the CIA. It was unlikely that the Agency would let Fred act of his own accord. Gorlov looked at his friend. Fred had placed the gray roll of paper on the table without any hurry and placed a hand inside his jacket. What was certain was that Fred would not be able to get near the president, or anyone else who could stop Castillo in time. *Miguel.* He was their last hope.

"We must convince Miguel to refuse to collaborate," said Gorlov. "The entire mission depends on him."

Barrett sat up in his seat, looking at the bulge of Fred's hand in his beige, wrinkled archaeologist's jacket.

"Convince Miguel, yes. Or Walter," Fred muttered slowly, almost in a whisper, with his hand hidden and his eyes still lost in thought in the anti-inflexor room.

Gorlov watched him. He could guess what Fred was looking for in his jacket. He could even guess what Fred was thinking. Fred finally relaxed.

"It's very likely," said Barrett, before he coughed and touched his throat, "that Miguel has already convinced himself." His rat-like smile returned to his face and disappeared again. His hands fiddled with his glasses. "He's a good boy, don't you think?"

Gorlov shook his head before looking back at the bulge of the gun inside Fred's jacket.

CHAPTER 30

Miguel watched him from behind – his dark, slim silhouette, his hands behind him. Standing silently above the flatland that was used as a helipad, Vincent seemed to be looking out at some distant point on the horizon. To the north. Miguel began walking towards him. Alongside the barriers to the right, several Egyptian soldiers lounged about a guard post. No one else would be there then, in the early hours of the morning.

Sunrise in the desert was cold—very cold. Vincent had already warned him when they spoke the previous evening. *The jacket*, he remembered suddenly, but this wasn't the time to go back and search for a forgotten jacket he had left in his room. Miguel shivered as he rubbed his arms, left uncovered by the short sleeves of his khaki shirt. Despite the cold, he tried to convince himself that the invitation to go and scout out locations was a good idea. What he needed now was a new perspective about Operation Messiah. He shivered again. He was not about to turn back for a stupid linen jacket. Besides, they might find him.

Miguel had had to almost sneak out of the building where the SSR team slept. If the others knew he was going to go for a helicopter ride with Walter and Vincent, they wouldn't understand. Castillo was an enemy to them. They considered his plan close to diabolical. *A war plan*, Fred had called it. Yes, in a way, it could be considered a peaceful invasion of the whole planet. But an invasion nonetheless. Miguel was now just a short distance from Vincent, who was still entranced by the uneven line of the horizon. Another shiver. It worried Miguel too, of course, the idea that Castillo or the CIA, or Vincent – why not? – or everyone together were only trying to control him and his power for their own ends. Gorlov had tried to convince him of it, but his explanation was just another scientific theory of his – very simple, understandable, but full of lies. Miguel was not convinced. *I'm a Midas. Nobody can control me if I oppose it*, he told himself.

He placed his hands in his pockets and felt yet another shiver run through him. In that moment, as he took the next step, he kicked a stone that rolled along the ground, near Vincent, but the telepath didn't turn around. It was like he was greeting Miguel with his back. Vincent was strange. He was kind of scary, like always. Everyone, in fact, had tried to scare him.

But now, everyone was asleep. Except for those two.

"Hi, Vincent," said Miguel. "He hasn't arrived yet?"

Vincent turned around calmly, looking at Miguel as if he had seen him coming with an unseen eye on the nape of his neck.

He can't help it. He looks so sinister.

"Good morning, Miguel," Vincent replied in a soft but firm voice, like he was speaking directly into Miguel's ear. Or inside his head. "He'll be here soon. Walter is very punctual."

They know each other well.

Vincent stood watching him without speaking. His eyes were too dark, like an alien's. His pale face looked like it belonged to a gothic angel. He smelled like baby soap. "We can talk through telepathy, if you want," said Vincent. "I heard you've mastered the technique."

In your dreams, Miguel thought. "Yes, well," he said, "I can do it, but I'd prefer not to use telepathy. I don't like using inflection outside the Project. You know, outside experiments," he lied. He loved playing outside experiments, but he wasn't about to say that. *Inside my head again?* he asked himself. *No way.*

"I understand." Vincent turned back to the horizon. It was like he could see Castillo's helicopter, even though there was nothing there.

"Besides, I'm still recovering from the shock you gave me in the chamber," said Miguel. He gave a fake, nasally laugh, just a little one. He thought that joking about it was a good way to start a civilized conversation with that dark inflexor who smelled like babies. "When you welcomed me into the Project, remember?"

"It was the scientists' idea," said Vincent, still looking at the horizon. "They designed that experiment to lure you in. I didn't mean to frighten you." He smiled without moving his gaze.

Suddenly, Miguel thought Vincent had lost his sinister look. His smile had completely transformed his face, turned it into someone else's. Now, all Miguel could see was a young man made of straight, beautiful features posing calmly as he contemplated the desert in silence. In that moment, Miguel understood why Monica had found him so attractive once. She hated him now for allying with Castillo.

"What are you thinking?" Miguel asked.

"You don't want us to talk through telepathy, but you want to know what I'm thinking?" Vincent said, his smile growing. He looked at Miguel.

Miguel felt his face burn with shame. *What are you thinking?* he asked himself. *That's the kind of thing girls ask their high-school boyfriends. Why the hell did I ask him that?*

"I'm thinking about Operation Messiah," Vincent answered quickly. "I haven't been able to think about anything else since Walter gave me the details."

"Neither have I," Miguel admitted. He began to like talking to Vincent. He felt freer, more relaxed. He felt like no one could pressure Vincent – he could think and draw his own conclusions. And Vincent didn't pressure Miguel either.

"You must be proud of your mission," said Vincent.

"Proud?" Miguel had not heard that until now.

"I'll only be a support for some effects of telepathic transmission. It's the only thing I know how to do. But you… I envy you." Vincent turned back to the distant horizon to the north of the encampment. The smell of baby soap caressed Miguel's face like a cool breeze.

He envies me, Miguel thought. He looked northward too. The sun's rays grew very slowly to the east, already illuminating the part of the horizon they watched. The sun would rise soon. A black dot appeared on top of the uneven line where the land met the sky. Miguel paid it no mind. He saw Vincent place a hand over his eyes like a visor and squint.

"Why do you envy me?" Miguel asked.

"Your mission," said Vincent without looking at him. "You are a means of creating a much more just world, without holy wars, or crusades, or chosen people, or gentiles, or infidels. None of that."

Miguel shivered.

"A world," Vincent continued, "with one true religion that doesn't differentiate between men. A religion created with intelligence, controlling every detail, scientifically designed to unite all people."

Miguel felt the hairs on his arms stand on end. The cold was to blame. He placed his hands back inside the pockets of his khaki trousers and tried to find where exactly on the horizon Vincent found those words. In reality, he thought they sounded like they were taken out of one of Castillo's pep talks. But Miguel liked hearing them. He thought that maybe he could feel proud of himself, too, if he achieved what Vincent described. The black dot had grown now into something much more visible. He was a Midas, a Midas Effect. He could make it possible, an idyllic world. He could do anything he could imagine. It was his duty.

"I'm a believer, y'know? Methodist," said Vincent, as if he had just remembered.

Miguel's eyes widened. *Methodist?*

Religion. There it was again, he thought, shaking his head. He hadn't expected it from Vincent. But there it was, just like everyone else. Once again, religion came up against him. A true religion, they would tell him now, but surely, not like everyone else's. It would be one that had been programmed and prepared meticulously. That was what they had just told Miguel. Vincent had managed to distract him very well with his praise. Another swindler trying to indoctrinate him.

The telepath raised his right arm and pointed at the black dot in the sky. Miguel didn't want to look. He looked at Vincent and grimaced. He was already tired of running into other false, unique religions, like Operation Messiah. Always pointing to him like a sinner. Barrett told him that he would disregard all other believers in the world if he agreed to join Castillo's plan. Fred told him it would hurt him if Miguel disrespected his faith, the faith that his father had preached in order to help others. Gorlov told him that religion had only ever helped the powerful to control others. *As if other religions don't care about people!* he thought bitterly. *Control them, sure!* Monica told him it would be an insult to free will and God. *But everyone has a different god! Gods that enslave them!* Miguel felt an urge to spit onto the sand. *People who have two versions of the same god and reject the other's version are more insulted! Hypocrites! But sure, they have their own pompous, secular institutions that coddle them and negotiate what is or isn't offensive. Ha! What are they going to do? Not let me join the club?*

Miguel was sure that any believer from any religion, creed, schism, branch, or sect would join the chorus of accusers who pointed their fingers of blame at him like spikes. Everyone would try to convince him that their multiple true religions, their multiple true gods, were more real than him. He didn't want to endure more holier-than-thou religious reprimands. He began scratching his palms inside his pockets.

Miguel concentrated on the black dot on the horizon, which had turned into an enormous Sokol that was nearly on top of them. He supposed Vincent would tell him now what he could expect from a Methodist who smelled like baby soap. He wasn't quite sure what a Methodist was. It didn't really matter to him, of course. The helicopter was falling on them. They didn't yet feel the wind from the blades, but Miguel was sure it would hit them in that instant.

"I'm a believer," Vincent repeated. "And I believe that you are the Messiah."

Miguel felt the gust of wind from the helicopter on his face and chest. It was a violent, deafening gust that blew into his mouth and nose, pushing him back, almost causing him to lose his balance. The wind made him feel something like a change in the matter of his body. Like a revelation. *You are the Messiah.* Vincent's words hit him like the wind from the helicopter.

***

Castillo watched them from the window in the helicopter. Vincent and Miguel were on the helipad. Miguel was covering his face.

Perfect! Castillo thought. This was what he was waiting for, to be able to talk to Miguel without those scientists around. Vincent had done well; he seemed to have convinced Miguel. Or maybe Miguel was willing to let himself be convinced. Even better.

The helicopter landed and Castillo opened the door. He leaned half his body out of the helicopter. He knew they wouldn't be able to hear him. With one of his hands, he grabbed a handle and used the other to motion for them to get in. Vincent looked at Miguel and pointed at the vehicle, before walking towards Castillo with his head low. Miguel followed, covering his face.

Once they had boarded the helicopter, Castillo handed them both thick helmets identical to the one he was wearing. Vincent and Miguel put them on immediately.

"Hello, Miguel. I'm happy to see you're coming with us," said Castillo into the microphone of his helmet. "We're about to go see the place where you'll cross the Red Sea. You'll like it. How is everything at the camp? A lot going on these days?"

"You dropped the bomb and then you left." Castillo heard Miguel's metallic voice in his headphones.

"I thought it would be better if I left and gave everyone time to think. Don't worry, everything will calm down. Big changes are always scary at first."

Castillo deliberately assumed it was a given that Miguel would agree to join the plan. In fact, he intended on treating him as if he had already said yes. That was his sales strategy. Miguel needed security. From the reports he had received, he knew that the museum of old, scientific glories as well as his girlfriend had invested this entire time in chipping away at the little security Miguel had left. Castillo would show him, beyond the desert, the place of the first miracle. That would be more convincing than sermons from the scientists.

The helicopter flew over the small, arid hills to the northeast of the encampment. After a short while, they arrived at a flat, sandy area. From there, they could see the sea. *The first miracle*, Castillo told himself.

When they reached the beach, he gestured to a long stretch of water that penetrated the land to form a bay with a narrow point. There, the helicopter reduced its speed until it hovered in the air.

"The Gulf of Suez!" Castillo heard his own metallic voice through his headphones. He pointed out an outcrop that jutted out along the shore, at the end of a small beach. "Some Greek and Hebrew historians believed that it was there that the Israelites crossed when they fled Egypt. Others think they went a little farther south."

"I believe the report mentioned something about Flavius Josephus, Herodotus—" Vincent began.

"Doesn't matter," Castillo said sharply. "The rock at the edge of the beach is a good place to part the sea. It's very effective."

Miguel was entranced by what he saw below. He stared out at the rock and the sea. Castillo supposed he was imagining himself up there, parting the sea like in a Hollywood blockbuster and guiding his followers through the area he had cleared. He smiled.

"There are about six miles to cross along the narrow part, right at the mouth of the bay," Castillo went on. "The other side is the Sinai Peninsula. It's the perfect place to evoke images of Moses and his chosen people. We've done a submarine study. The bottom of the bay has a lot of sandbanks – see them there beneath the water? – and the rest is no accident. The inflection you generate should push the sea a little towards the coast and create some mental dykes. The path will practically jump up out of the water. It's easy."

Miguel turned to him suddenly. He said nothing, but his face seemed full of doubtful creases inside his helmet. He must be expecting more explanations, of course. Parting the sea…

"Yeah, yeah, I get that it's not that easy," said Castillo. "We'll explain everything to you, everything you need so you can imagine it – submarine topography, sandbank report, dyke location. Sure, parting the sea isn't what you've seen in movies. It's much more complicated, of course. It's a true conundrum of the engineering of the imagination."

Miguel nodded wordlessly.

The helicopter flew over the bay as Castillo continued giving details. Vincent asked questions every now and again, but Miguel didn't say a word. Castillo supposed that having an opinion about the plan meant he was really part of it. It didn't matter that Miguel wasn't part of it yet – his face, along with the interest he showed in looking at everything, told Castillo he was convincing him. And he hadn't even gotten to the best part yet.

They descended and the helicopter landed on the beach. Vincent and Miguel got out first. When Castillo removed his helmet, he felt the smell of the sea and fresh air of the shore clear his head. He inhaled slowly through his nose, smelling the breeze calmly. He loved it.

"We've done several tests here," he said. "With telekinetic inflexors. They managed to open dry corridors the size of a tank. I walked along one of them up to there." He threw a rock into the sea and it sunk beneath the waves about fifty feet from the shore. "More or less," he added. "We have a quantum sensor submerged near that point. And many more all over the bay." Miguel looked at Castillo, brows furrowed. *You'll talk*, Castillo thought. Then he said, "What for? To control secondary effects of inflection. We don't want to move a little bit of water here only to cause a tsunami in South Africa."

"And is everything okay?" asked Vincent.

"No part of what happens here will generate problems in other places. At most, there may be a small storm farther south. It depends on the day we choose to perform the miracle."

Castillo saw Miguel look skyward at the mention of a storm. *Perhaps he is looking for a black cloud*, Castillo thought, *like the ones he created in San José when he took down that actor*. But the sky was totally clear. Brilliantly blue, clear. It wasn't a dangerous sky.

Castillo approached Miguel. "No one will die," he said slowly. He looked into Miguel's eyes as he sat on a rock, legs spread. He brushed some dirt off his khaki trousers. "I really don't like these clothes," he added before looking at Miguel. "Don't worry, everything here is under control."

Miguel sat in front of him on another rock. "Here?" he said, breaking the silence.

Castillo did not smile outwardly; they were talking about serious things. His face, serious now, did not move. But on the inside, he felt like hugging Miguel. He had done it! He forced himself to breathe slowly. "Yes," he answered. "What I mean is, there won't be a repeat of San José."

Miguel turned his head and looked out at the sea.

***

Miguel looked out at the sea. Anywhere was a good place to try and escape that memory. He still couldn't look anyone in the eye whenever he thought about that actor's death.

"I already told you in the wind tunnel," he heard Castillo say, "I was always against that test."

Miguel made an effort to look at him.

"That was not the right way to stimulate your abilities," Castillo continued. "But I couldn't stop it. Everyone insisted on it – Vladimir, Eugene, Fred..." Castillo hesitated. He didn't say Monica's name. "Everyone. You're not at fault for his death, but it won't happen again. Everything is under control here, trust me."

Miguel tried to decide if Castillo was telling the truth or if he just wanted to attract Miguel to his cause. Walter had never done him any harm, far from it. He had been the only one who worried about him, right from the very beginning. *Dani*, he remembered. Castillo had told him he'd bring Dani to NASA, to the wind tunnel. All that and more.

"It's different now," Castillo continued. "This isn't an experiment to collect data to fatten up the studies in the Project. No, the Project wouldn't make sense without some sort of benefit for humanity. The risks it has faced ever since it was set up, and its consequences, including death, would be an insult if they were only used to fill out reports and feed the vanity of brainy scientists." Castillo rose, as did his voice. "The Project needs an objective, and now there *is* an objective, something much more ambitious than the Project itself." He spoke quite loudly and looked back and forth between Vincent and Miguel like he was at a pulpit. "Something to pride ourselves on, a legacy for our descendants – utter peace!"

Castillo had completely absorbed their attention. Vincent looked at him with his mouth half open and Miguel could barely move. He felt like he needed to continue listening to him, hear more about the miracle they would perform. Castillo went on.

"The power of the Midas Effect cannot be wasted. We must use it for the advancement of humanity – an organized, controlled religion. Think about it. It may have been the case that Christ, Muhammed, Moses, the other prophets and saints of all the world's religions were quantum inflexors, even Midas Effects. I think that's the best explanation, perhaps the only explanation, for most of them. They could have been normal people or gods; it doesn't matter. The chaos these religions have sown can be redirected. The other Midases were interpreted and used by religion. The new Midas will be directed down a rational, infallible path, by science—"

"Vladimir says that science can't sustain a god," Miguel interrupted. "That it's impossible to control an infinite power like mine. That we'll use it wrong."

"Vladimir knows a lot about quantum physics and neurons, but he's not very well-read about modern theology. Philosophers, physicists, and computer engineers reinterpret the universe and God today. Teilhard de Chardin, for instance, is a compatriot of yours. He is a French theologist, paleontologist, philosopher, and Jesuit priest. It's all in the report—"

"Pierre Teilhard de Chardin, of course. The Omega Point."

"The Omega Point, yes. Man becoming God as a natural step of evolution. And the physical world harmonizes with the spiritual world. Man controls matter. *You* control matter!" Castillo walked closer to Miguel. "Look at you. Now we have an Omega Point, a Midas, a new Messiah—call it whatever you want. You are omnipotent. You cannot fail. You are the seed of a new, infallible, scientifically-controlled religion that will serve the world. By God!" Castillo looked up at the sky. "Even He has to agree with this plan. You" – he looked at Miguel – "are His emissary. His archangel."

Miguel felt a shiver on the tops of his shoulders and thought wings were about to sprout from his back. He could not speak.

"Think of the lives you'll save," Castillo added in a much lower voice. He breathed slowly, keeping his gaze on Miguel. Miguel felt the prick of his wings all over his body. "Think… about… it."

"I think we'll go see other locations," said Vincent. His strained words barely reached Miguel over the sound of the rotor. Vincent stood and followed Castillo.

Miguel slowly lowered his head and looked at the water at his feet. The waves lapped at the rock where he was, forming a round puddle on the sand of the beach the size of *a baptismal font*, Miguel imagined. Something in that small haven, its calm waters, caught his attention. *A piece of the Red Sea*, he thought. *Part the sea*.

He felt the sun make his skin itch. It seemed to accelerate the growth of his wings. The Red Sea. He could try it, just a small test. Something any telekinetic could do. Nothing important. A tiny miracle. Why not? He didn't need to be in an induction chamber in the SSR. Imprisoned, always watched. Neither did he need a yellow page telling him how and when to breathe. He could breathe whenever he wanted. Miguel dipped his finger into the puddle until he touched the sand at the bottom. He concentrated and soon felt the buzz in the middle of his brain.

The water began flowing away from his finger until a cylindrical hole formed around the point where his finger touched the sand.

You are the Messiah. Those were Vincent's words. *You are His emissary. His archangel*. Castillo's voice rang in his head. Miguel inhaled convulsively and removed his hand from the puddle.

The parted waters rushed to fill the empty space he had created.

He stood up, watching the miracle waves in the puddle. In the Red Sea. His wings itched. His head hurt with a sweet ache. The rotor of the Sokol roared as if it were about to explode, and the hot air that blew hit his face again.

Miguel hung his head to avoid feeling the air and the sand. He finally entered the helicopter, which took off immediately, before he could even take a seat. Miguel arrived at his seat, feeling dizzy – maybe it was just the sudden take-off. Castillo was smiling at him. Vincent was, too. His smell of baby soap seemed to fill the cabin of the Sokol. With some difficulty, Miguel put on his helmet and pressed the communication button.

He breathed deeply once more and closed his eyes. The smell of kerosene and a baby bath. An explosion and the birth of a new world. *His* world. He felt so good there. It was like the helicopter was his home. They were his family. The image of his finger parting the water came back to him. Sharp, terrible. A miracle. Then he heard his own metallic voice through his headphones. "I think I'll accept the mission."

CHAPTER 31

When Miguel got out of the helicopter, the first thing he saw was Monica, who was coming towards him in the Jeep. He couldn't quite see her expression behind her sunglasses, but the closed, straight line of her mouth, like she had just had a molar removed, told him she wasn't happy. The dust cloud that followed her was like a sandstorm, waiting to be fully unleashed by her when Miguel told her of his intention to join Operation Messiah. The Jeep screeched to a halt, throwing up a huge puff of dust.

"Just where the hell have you been?" Monica said angrily, giving the vehicle a jolt. She turned to him with her chin held high. "I've been looking for you all morning. What were you thinking, disappearing like that?"

"I got up early, everyone else was asleep—"

"I thought something had happened to you. I searched the whole camp, the barriers, the hangars, the guard posts, the entire oasis, the hill…" Monica must have come straight from the truncated hill. Her neck and chest glistened with tiny drops of sweat, and there were patches of sweat all over her sleeveless khaki shirt. She smelled like a desert soldier. Miguel took in her scent.

"I went for a helicopter trip," Miguel explained when Monica fell silent.

Monica looked over Miguel's shoulder at the Sokol behind him. She would see Vincent and Castillo too. She would know who he had been with.

The storm.

Monica removed her sunglasses with a sharp motion. Without moving her gaze from the helicopter, she twisted her lips like she wanted to spit, mentally calculating the distance between herself and the vehicle. Then she turned her blue eyes on Miguel. "I see you've made some new friends."

Miguel didn't want to fight. He didn't want to have to endure a storm. "I'm not talking to you if you're going to be like that," he said slowly.

"Have they convinced you to play their game yet?" The disdain in her voice dripped from every syllable.

"Maybe," Miguel replied. He started towards the encampment, turning his back to Monica. He didn't want to hear any more reprimands.

When he got to the Jeep, he turned around to face Monica. She gave him a curious look, somewhere between rage and confusion, as if what he had just said to her was an insult in some unknown language. She frowned again. Miguel saw the small, deep wrinkle above her right eyebrow, like the eye of a hurricane.

"I'm taking a shower. We have a meeting in the anti-inflexor room in an hour," said Miguel. "Talk to Walter." He turned again and left. He hated storms.

***

An hour after Monica's attempt at a tempest, Miguel arrived at the anti-inflexor room.

The dusty hangar where they had installed it was empty except for the enormous golden cubic structure of the room, the generators, and the control teams. All of it piled together in the middle of the hangar, full of echoes. Two of Castillo's men controlled access to the area. Two other operatives kept the contraption functioning. Miguel watched them as he completed the entry protocol. All of those men would soon become part of his team, he thought. And many more. The first door to the compartment opened, giving him access to the entry hall.

When the second door opened, Miguel saw that everyone was already there. Gorlov, Monica, and Fred – the Project – were seated at one end of the rectangular metal table, while Vincent and Castillo – Operation Messiah – sat at the opposite end. Standing behind Castillo were two more agents: Roth and another man who looked like a bodyguard. Both were disguised as archaeologists.

Castillo had already removed his khaki clothes and returned to his dark suit, white shirt and navy tie. As elegant as always, he was dressed for his big moment, despite the heat between the gold walls of the anti-inflexor room.

Miguel placed himself in the middle. He chose one of half a dozen seats that separated the two groups, placed his gray operations folder on the table, and sat down. He lay his hands on the cool, metal surface of the table and interlaced his fingers. In a few minutes, it would get very hot. He hoped they would finish quickly.

Castillo began his speech at that moment. "I have gathered you here today to make a decision," he began. "In reality, to make a historic decision." He stood up and started walking around the table. "You already know the details of Operation Messiah…"

Castillo wasn't saying anything new. He gave more technical, organizational, institutional, and sociological details. He talked about some of the ideas that he had mentioned to Miguel by the Red Sea – some philosophy, the evolution of species, the Omega Point again. All reasons why Miguel would be considered a true Messiah. But most of all, he talked about humanity, what he called "the Great Advancement" and "Utter

Peace." Miguel felt his pride buzz every time Castillo talked about that.

Castillo continued for just over half an hour. No one interrupted him during that time. "There are no cracks," he stated when his discourse came to an end. "The operation and the plan are all secure and all details are under control."

There was a moment of silence. During his talk, Castillo did not break his stride around the room, until he came to a stop behind Miguel, placing his hands on his shoulders. Miguel felt warm pressure on his archangel wings. Castillo spoke again.

"I am sure that your past few days of studying the folder and reflecting have served to help you understand the extent of making your decision. The right one, I hope. There isn't much time. We must begin soon. If all of you agree to join this 'great advancement of humanity,' Miguel will start preaching to a large group of virtual followers next week. A subtle but convincing press campaign will bring the news of the true Messiah to the four corners of the world. And in less than three months, we will have a crowd of real, loyal believers crossing the Red Sea, parted by Miguel's miracle."

"And what makes you think we're going to agree to this foolishness?" Gorlov asked. His words, tinted with a thick Russian accent, sounded angular, like his glasses, like the look in his eyes. He didn't look like himself. Ever since they arrived in Egypt, he had somehow become harder.

"Do you think utter peace, the alliance of all people, is foolishness?" Castillo asked.

"Your cardboard Messiah won't achieve any of this 'utter peace.'"

Miguel clenched his jaw when he heard Gorlov call him a "cardboard Messiah." *How dare he?* Gorlov must already consider him an enemy. Those scientists, he thought, had manipulated him, lied to him, played with him, just to make him carry out those stupid experiments. They had even made him kill a man. And now that he was useful for something outside their useless labs, they rejected him and insulted him. *Cardboard Messiah!* he repeated to himself. Miguel looked away from them, choosing instead to look at the wall in front of him, chin lowered.

"You have already read," said Castillo "that we have an outline of continuity, revised and agreed upon by our experts." His voice managed a new tone. Now he sounded more like the moderator of a televised debate. His voice was firm and convincing, but musical at the same time. "We've been preparing this for years." He removed his hands from Miguel's shoulders and once more started walking around the table. "Everything has been researched in order for him to survive – the technological basis, the likely agreements with major religious institutions…"

Castillo's voice was seductive, hard to escape. When he passed by Gorlov's group, Miguel turned to his voice and found himself looking at Fred.

Fred Windhorst, as enormous as he was, with his formidable hands resting on his wrinkled operations folder, as if caressing it, was looking down. His eyes seemed lost in some sad future he was imagining.

Fred is a believer, Miguel reminded himself. *His family, his father, his whole life has been spent close to God, and now his country is asking him to abandon it. How will he explain it to Reverend Windhorst? Will he lie? No, he can't. It's just a little collateral damage.*

"The new church we will create," Castillo went on, "the New Scriptures…"

"The new world order!" Gorlov shouted.

Everyone turned to look at the scientist, except Miguel. He was still looking at Fred.

"Come on, Vladimir," said Castillo. His melodic voice retained its firmness. "Of course there will be a new world order. And, of course, the United States will control that order. But if that brings peace and wellbeing to all, why are you so committed to rejecting it? What bad is there in it?"

There *was* bad in it. Miguel no longer paid attention to the discussion. He didn't want to listen to it, having already had it with everyone he knew in the encampment. Something else held his interest now: Fred. There was something about him. Fred didn't hate Miguel, or offend him. He was just sad. A fuzzy idea picked at his brain like it wanted to elbow its way out of his thoughts. *There's something I'm doing wrong.*

"Because it won't bring about any peace," Gorlov argued. "It will only bring control. I don't know if you're a hypocrite or a simpleton, or both. Religion is just an excuse…"

Monica! The thought struck Miguel. Over the last few days, all they had done was fight over whether the plan was right, whether it was just, whether it served to do anything. Just like how Walter and Vladimir were arguing now. But, really, how would she feel if they carried out a plan that went against her beliefs, her world, her God? That went against what she called free humanity? He knew it. Miguel knew very well.

"Vladimir, I don't think you have thought enough about this plan," said Castillo as he paced behind Miguel.

He knew it. Fear, pity in Monica. So much of it. He was certain. Miguel saw Castillo from the corner of his eye at the far end of the table, beside Vincent and the archaeologist bodyguards.

"I think we should continue to work on it. I think I can still convince you," Walter was saying. "All of you."

Miguel stopped listening to Castillo's voice and looked at Monica.

"I suppose you all maintain the same stance. Perhaps for different reasons, but the same stance. And I understand that…"

The look in Monica's eyes made Miguel's determination fall to pieces.

She didn't look angry, the way she had been during the last few days in Egypt. She didn't seem to want to scold him or fight him. None of that. The storm had passed. She looked at him with a blank expression, similar to Fred's: lost. But she wasn't staring into space; she was looking at Miguel with dull, blue-gray eyes. Monica looked like she was about to either burst into tears or ask him who he was, as if she didn't recognize him. Her fingers never left her small gold crucifix. She gripped it tight, determined not to fall into a well where Miguel couldn't find her.

"What interests us now is Miguel's decision," said Castillo.

Miguel recognized the pitiful look she had given him on the flight to Cairo. Her eyes narrowed as if she felt a sharp pain in the middle of her forehead. When she told him he was a human with the power of a god. A sadness as large as the jumbo jet that had transported them there.

"It doesn't make sense to discuss anything without knowing our Messiah's decision," Castillo went on.

I'm not a god, Miguel thought. And he remembered how much damage he could do, how much he could hurt himself, and he saw in Monica's eyes how much he was hurting her. He wavered. He doubted the goodness of that plan. *I'm not a god*, he repeated. And he concentrated on seeing her feelings, on feeling them inside himself.

"Miguel," said Castillo, "do you want to be the god the future needs?"

A wave of sadness coming from Monica flooded his head, pushing him back like the wind from a helicopter, almost throwing him off-balance. The sadness was like sand in his eyes, in his nose, in his mouth…

"Miguel," Castillo repeated quietly.

The sadness was drowning him.

"Miguel?"

"No," Miguel answered, still looking at Monica, in a barely audible voice. Then he turned to look at Castillo at the far end of the table, feeling like a child who dared to contradict his teacher for the first time. "I… don't know," he added.

He saw Vincent seated beside Castillo. He was smiling at Miguel. Miguel picked up his innocent, baby-soap smell. He seemed so sure. Vincent touched his own head with a finger and then pointed at Miguel's. Miguel nodded.

Miguel, said Vincent telepathically. *You are the Omega Point, the archangel, the Messiah.*

"You don't know?" Castillo asked. His television moderator tone never faltered. His voice expressed neither surprise nor anger. Miguel kept his eyes on Vincent. "I thought you had already decided to collaborate on the operation."

I can't... I don't know, Miguel thought at Vincent. *There's something... wrong*. He looked at the gray folder as if he would somehow see what was wrong printed there—a spelling mistake in the title, something that had obviously gone unnoticed until now. But he saw nothing.

It's you, Vincent insisted. *Utter peace. It's all fine, you know that, you've read it. You know.* Vincent looked at him. He was still smiling.

All fine. I'm the only one who can do it, Miguel thought. *No, I can't. I... No*. He turned and looked at Monica again. She would understand.

Except Monica was staring at him now open-mouthed, eyes opened wide. Beside her, Fred made a strange face. His jaw was tensed, and his right hand reached inside his jacket.

Now! Miguel heard Vincent's telepathic voice yelling inside his head. But he wasn't shouting at Miguel.

Miguel turned his head just in time to see Castillo and Vincent take out slim, white pistols and open fire.

The two bodyguards also took out their own guns. Theirs were matte black and thick, with filed edges. They weren't white like Castillo's and Vincent's.

White guns? thought Miguel – just as he felt the impact of a dart in his chest.

The dart squeezed his chest, its tip like a wasp's sting. Then he felt his body relax. And he began to feel tired, very tired.

But it wasn't a physical tiredness. It was like he was dreaming. A mental stupor. He began feeling the same thing he had felt for many days after a long day's work – he just wanted to stop thinking. Just watch the television, disconnect, tune in to something that didn't require any brain power. That was what he wanted.

And he didn't think.

After a few seconds, he came to a semiconscious state. He began to smile. He was fine like that. He watched what was happening in the room, in no hurry. He watched everything as if from the outside looking in, like he was watching an imaginary television show he wanted to get hooked on. The CIA agents took an old-looking gun out of Fred's hands. Walter and Vincent left their guns on the table – theirs were very modern, like they had come right out of a film about spaceships. It was funny, very funny. Miguel looked at the guns, which looked like laser cannons, and smiled. He liked stories with spaceships. *Or was it Dani who liked them?* he wondered.

Your brother likes spaceships, Vincent told him. *You like guns and adventures*.

Miguel looked at Vincent. He was smiling at him. He was smiling and talking to him inside his head. He liked Vincent. He smelled like a baby just out of the bath. He used to scare him, but Miguel couldn't remember when. He was so tired. He didn't want to remember anything. At the other side of the table, far away, infinitely far, he saw his other friends. Fred had his hands up. *Fred looks like he's going to dance. I like Fred. He's nice. He's big and sweet like a brown bear. Why are they pointing those guns at him? They must be playing cowboys*. Gorlov. *With his stupid face that never says anything. He never says anything!* And Monica. *She's smiling and looking at me. I like smiling. She's smiling like me. She has a white arrow in her shoulder. It's small and white. Like mine. I don't want this arrow*. Miguel pulled the dart and removed it. *Aaagh! It burns!* And he threw it away from him.

***

Walter Castillo watched the small ceramic dart crash against the gold wall of the anti-inflexor room. The sound, like a bomb exploding, caught everyone's attention.

"Nobody move," said Castillo. He had neared the far end of the table where Fred and Gorlov were, and he picked up Fred's old .45 Colt. "Relax, Miguel,"

Miguel smiled at him.

"What have you done to him?" Gorlov asked slowly. His accent was so thick he may as well have been talking in Russian. "*Sukin syn!*"

Castillo understood the insult but paid it no mind. Miguel, on the other hand, seemed to find the outburst funny. He laughed and clapped. Monica did the same.

"He's left them stupid," said Fred.

"No, nothing like that." Castillo pointed the Colt at him. "They're too valuable. I need them. At least, I need Miguel."

"The darts?" asked Gorlov.

"I've administered a drug that stops them from solidifying their desires. It makes it hard for them to think. They can't concentrate on their own wishes."

"A drug," said Gorlov slowly. He seemed calmer, his accent less noticeable. He looked through his enormous glasses at the table, as if he would find there the answer to an enigma he had been pondering for some time. He looked back at Castillo and nodded. "I see."

Castillo smiled as he approached Miguel to check on him. He knew the Russian was probably the only one who would appreciate his ideas.

"What has he done to them, Vladimir?" Fred asked. "I can still take down these two brats with my bare hands!" Fred moved his giant hands and Castillo's agents took a step back, despite the fact that there were two of them and they were armed.

At sixty-five, Fred was still in shape, Castillo knew, but above all, Fred remained a hulk with the strength of four men. It would not do to provoke him any more than necessary.

"You can go," Castillo told his men. "I control Windhorst and Gorlov."

"But, sir…" said Roth.

"Fall back!" Castillo shouted. "That's an order. What we're about to discuss is secret." He lifted the Colt and showed it to his agents. "Everything is under control," he added in a friendlier tone. "Wait outside."

The two agents put away their automatic Glocks and left the anti-inflexor room.

Castillo took a seat beside Miguel, who smiled at him as he did so, and said, "You sit down too, Fred. And put your hands down. I don't intend on shooting you. Until now, no one has gotten hurt. Let's keep it that way." He observed the black .45 Colt, with its wooden handle, in his hands. "A Commander from the sixties. Does this relic still work?"

Fred sat with slow, reluctant movements, like a poorly trained bear. Jerking his head towards Monica, he said, "They seem hurt."

"Walter has found a way to go up against a god," said Gorlov. "I told you he'd have a way."

"What way?" Fred grunted.

"How do you confront someone who can turn their wishes into reality?" Gorlov asked. "Stop them from wishing. Simple." He applauded himself with three slow, empty claps, looking at Castillo. "You've given them a drug that prevents them from wishing. A codeine derivative? An opiate, perhaps? It's an excellent idea. It's like putting them to sleep without leaving them unable to move. A drug! It's almost stupid."

"They're no simple drugs—"

"But if they can't think, how are they supposed to produce quantum inflection?" Fred interrupted. "Why do you want them?"

"Fred, please!" Gorlov exclaimed. "If he has a drug that stops them from thinking, he'll have something else that stops them from acting freely. It's elementary."

"Not so elementary. But yes, it's something similar," Castillo admitted. He took out two plastic boxes from his pocket. "Drugs to stop them from wishing." He hit the table with the box containing darts with a red band. "Drugs to neutralize the effect." He hit with the box in his other hand. Darts with a green band. "The drugs to control their will are in a secure location, of course." He looked at Vincent, who nodded. "All this isn't that simple. The scientists of Operation Messiah have been developing drugs that control quantum inflexors for years. We have another center of quantum inflexor research in NASA Hampton, Virginia. A complex of labs similar to the SSR. We have developed it from there."

"NASA Hampton," said Gorlov. "You Americans are always so cautious, everything in duplicate. What did I tell you, Fred? Hampton."

"Don't make a sword without also making a shield," said Castillo. He enjoyed parading around with his sayings, like a scholarly warrior-king with a beard to his waist. He had already thought of that one a while ago, when they started building the parallel center of inflexors in Hampton. "We wouldn't develop as powerful a weapon as a Midas without preparing some method of controlling it and defending ourselves from it."

"To control it. The weapon," Gorlov stated. "But the idea is very good."

"Vladimir!" Fred exploded, hitting his hands against the metal table. Castillo immediately aimed the Colt at him. "What exactly is good? That these vermin have drugged them to take over the world?"

"Come now, Fred, don't be so tragic," said Castillo. "This isn't a plan to take over the world. We're just trying to make it better."

"I'm sure!"

"It's not my plan either," Castillo continued. "It's your country's plan. *Our* country's. You've worked in the Agency far longer than I have. You know of so many plans and operations that have been carried out for the greater good—"

"Has the president approved it?" Fred cut him off.

Castillo stared at him and didn't respond.

"I still have my contacts, you know?" Fred went on, pointing a thick index finger on his right hand as if he wanted to shoot him. "And I know that this hasn't been approved. Don't talk to me about my country's plan. The president won't allow you to walk all over the faith of the United States with your test tube god."

"He will approve it," Castillo replied, "when he sees the power it puts in his hands. He'll approve it."

"Then," Gorlov interjected, "you admit that this is a plot to gain power."

"Gain power, gain power!" said Castillo, smiling. "Ah, Vladimir, you really do love rhetoric!" he said, opening his arms wide. The gesture brought the barrel of the Colt to rest right in front of Miguel's face. "Always rummaging through words. Power. What is power—?"

Suddenly, Castillo felt a tug on the gun. He turned to Miguel, surprised, to find him pulling on the barrel with an idiotic smile, trying to take the gun.

"Miguel, it's not a toy—!" Castillo began to say.

In that instant, from the corner of his eye, he saw Fred jump over the table while Castillo forced Miguel to let go of the gun. The enormous agent simultaneously grabbed an empty seat to the right and launched it at them at high speed, as if it weighed as much as a paper ball.

The metallic seat flew out of Fred's hands right at Castillo's head. A fraction of a second later, it crashed against him. But he had gotten the gun back. He fired.

Mixed with the clatter of the seat hitting his head and sending him crashing to the ground, Castillo heard the sound of his own shot. The resonance of the bullet, amplified by the metallic, airtight walls, made a deafening bang that almost burst his eardrums. The thundering noise reverberated in his head as he fell back, along with the constant, disordered, clumsy hits from the seat.

Another fraction of a second later, Fred fell on top of him, crushing him with his movements like a crazed bull. His clouded vision only allowed him to see Fred's body colliding with his own and Miguel's.

The pistol escaped his grasp and slid along the room's metallic floor towards Vincent. Castillo managed to see him stand up quickly and pick up the gun before the three bodies pushed by Fred had stopped rolling around.

When they came to a stop, Miguel sat on the floor with slackened muscles, legs spread like a clown made of rags. He was smiling. Fred was lying face down. Vincent aimed the gun at Fred. The Colt trembled slightly in his hand. He didn't know how to use a gun.

Without wasting a second, despite his clumsy, pained movements, Castillo managed to sit himself upright on the floor. He touched his injured head, pressing at a wound that crossed from one side of his forehead to the other. His face burned. It was like the seat had smashed half his brain. He wiped his eyes, which were nearly completely covered in blood, and looked at Fred.

Fucking idiot, he thought, pushing him. His shot must have reached him, but he was surely still alive.

But Fred wasn't moving.

"Fred?"

Castillo touched his neck. His pulse, where was it? A good agent. A good soldier. *My head!* Castillo thought the pain in his head was about to make him collapse. This couldn't be. A good American.

A red stain began to spread on the floor beneath Fred's body as far as Castillo's trousers. Castillo jerked his wet leg back from the stain. The warm blood burned him.

He looked at Vincent. *No! This can't be!* His head could barely endure the pain. Vincent was still aiming the Colt at Fred, ready to fire. Fred, that fucking idiot! It wasn't possible. His head. The gun…

"Stop aiming at him!" Castillo screamed. "He's dead!"

CHAPTER 32

They shot the sheriff! Miguel thought. *The damn outlaws shot the sheriff. I like playing cowboys... and I like guns. Vincent told me so.*

Castillo and Vincent, hunched on their shins in a pool of blood, turned Fred's body over.

The guns! Quick, Flanagan! Miguel got all riled up seeing them left abandoned. He rose with clumsy movements, still smiling. He felt happy playing cowboys in the Wild West. He arrived at the pistols, legs bowed. He was John Wayne. "Hands up!" said Miguel when he had the two white guns in his hands.

Castillo and Vincent spun around immediately but didn't get up.

Vincent still held Fred's black gun. Miguel decided to shoot him first. The dart hit him in the neck and Vincent stayed quiet, on his shins, aiming at Miguel but apparently incapable of pulling the trigger.

Vincent began to smile.

What's he smiling at? He doesn't know how to play cowboys, Miguel thought. *He has to throw himself to the ground; he's dead. His loss if he doesn't know how to play.* Miguel watched as Castillo tried to straighten up. He had shot Vincent with the gun in his right hand. This time, he shot with his left. He felt like a real avenger with two revolvers. The ceramic dart hit Castillo's arm before he could stand up. *Well done, Flanagan!*

Miguel told himself. Castillo stilled, on his knees beside Vincent. He smiled too. No one moved after those two shots were fired.

"General Custer!" Miguel shouted at Gorlov. "I'm turning in these two troublemakers."

Gorlov looked at Miguel silently for a moment. He lowered his hands and stood before walking over to Miguel slowly. He was staring at him like he expected him to shoot.

"Thank you, soldier," Gorlov played along. "Now, hand over your weapons so you can take care of these ne'er-do-wells."

Miguel handed over his two white guns.

***

Gorlov, still confused, took the guns from Miguel's hands and turned to look at Fred. He lay on the floor in a pool of blood. Dead. A deaf, internal thud shook his stomach like a heartbeat out of time. He hunched over. *Too old*, he thought.

The guns! The enemy! Neutralize! Now! He immediately heard the inner voice from the cold days of KGB training in his youth.

He put the guns away in the pockets of his jacket and asked Miguel to sit. Miguel obeyed instantly. He was smiling as he sat. Then Gorlov approached Vincent, who was wearing the same idiotic smile as Miguel, took Fred's old Colt, and hit him on the back of the head. He crumpled in a heap on the floor. Then Gorlov came up behind Castillo and did the same. Castillo fell next to Vincent.

Better unconscious, Gorlov told himself. *Fewer complications*. He put the Colt away alongside the ceramic guns. He looked at Monica, who sat at the far end of the table, smiling. He looked at Miguel, who was smiling from the opposite end of the room. *All under control*, he thought. And he turned to Fred.

He went over to him and leaned down.

He touched his neck.

He waited.

After a few seconds of silence looking at the gold walls of the room, he looked at his wristwatch. One second. Two seconds. Three. Four… Fred's neck had no pulse.

Another convulsion gripped the scientist's stomach. Air. He couldn't breathe in that oven. Too warm for a cadaver. Fred wasn't cold. Gorlov huffed unconsciously. He removed his glasses and placed his ear over the chest of the fallen Soviet monument, trying to hear something inside him.

Nothing. He couldn't hear anything.

The memories suddenly made him clench his fists. The days in Leningrad. Sunday dinners in Fred's house. His wife. His children, who had practically adopted Gorlov as their Russian grandfather. The trips to Illinois for Thanksgiving. Reverend Windhorst… How would he tell the reverend? That poor man would have to bury his son for serving his country, his god. Gorlov ground his teeth. He looked at Fred's enormous hands, like spades. Twisted unusually on the ground. In his blood. "*Niet*," he said.

Slowly, Gorlov lifted his head from Fred's chest. He brought his hand over Fred's eyes, closing them. The cavernous wrinkles in his face almost got in the way. "*Tovarisch*, old friend." And he gripped Fred's shoulder, as Fred himself used to do with his enormous hands. "Damn them all." He stood up, pressing the weight of his age into the metal table in the anti-inflexor room. "I swear to you that I'll stop this madness!" he told Fred's body.

***

Fred is good at playing dead, Miguel thought. *He's really good at playing cowboys. He's my friend. Big, big!*

Gorlov stood and picked up a plastic box full of darts.

Ammunition, Miguel thought. *We'll need lots of ammunition for the Indians.*

The scientist took out a ceramic gun from his pocket and rummaged in the cylinder. The magazine suddenly fell out, as if pushed by a spring. Gorlov loaded two darts with green bands.

General Custer is so ugly! Miguel thought. *With those glasses, the Indians will see the reflection of the glass and they'll catch us all.*

"Relax, Miguel," said Gorlov, resting the barrel of the white gun on his arm. "We're going to play doctors."

I like playing doctors. Professor Gorlov is a great doctor. I like him. He's my friend.

Gorlov fired. There was a muffled shooting noise from the ceramic gun.

My friend.

"Aaagh! Shit!" Miguel yelled, writhing. He felt like he was being pushed towards the television and stumbling into the Wild West movie onscreen. He felt heavy, very heavy, and rigid, like he had become more solid.

He breathed convulsively and began to shiver. It was terribly hot in that room. The desert in the West, metal walls of gold, like a microwave, rattlesnakes, Indians, inside the hangar in the middle of the desert. Another desert. Egypt. The Messiah. A drop of sweat dripped down his nose near his eyes. He shivered again.

Gorlov started hammering the white gun. Then Miguel saw the dart in his arm. A white dart with a green band. He removed it with a pull. Indian arrows. He felt dizzy, and for a moment, his vision faded. He closed his eyes. There was a firefight in the saloon. General Custer…

Monica smiled idiotically. Castillo and Vincent lay unconscious on the metal floor and Fred…

No, no, no! He retched.

Gorlov shot Monica in the arm. She grit her teeth and convulsed, like a spasm. Then she shivered and began to sweat. Everyone was sweating now.

"Can you understand me?" Gorlov asked.

Miguel nodded. His head, his temples, ached horribly.

"Wha…?" said Monica.

"Monica," said Gorlov, lifting her chin with one hand so she would look at him.

She watched him with drooping eyelids and a half-open mouth. After a few seconds, she said hesitantly, "Vladimir?" Closing her eyes, she touched her temples.

"Walter tried to take over your free will," explained Gorlov, looking between Monica and Miguel. "He used a drug. Fred died trying to save you."

Miguel looked at Fred's body. Of course. He knew the story.

"I know!" Monica said. Then her whole face hardened, her teeth clenched. "Shit! The drug… Nothing mattered… Where…?" Her eyes closed. "Father O'Brien… Patrizia?" Then she became conscious again. "Give me the gun," she said suddenly. "Castillo, you son of a bitch! He killed Fred!" Monica tried to stand, but one hand flew to her temple while the other gripped the table.

Gorlov took a step back and covered the bulge of Fred's gun in his jacket. "We're leaving, Monica," said Gorlov. He turned around. "Miguel, I suppose now you understand the real objective of Operation Messiah."

Miguel said nothing. He let another drop of sweat slide down his cheek without moving to wipe it away. Gorlov kept speaking.

"You weren't going to be a god, but a puppet, one who knew how to perform good tricks, like parting the sea or playing dead before reviving—"

"You're right," Miguel interrupted. He felt dizzy, confused. He looked around at the gold walls of the anti-inflexor room. Gold all around. He had been a vain fool. He looked at Monica. She was watching him, but she looked away immediately, as if his stare had hurt her. "I want to go with you," said Miguel.

Gorlov watched him silently. Miguel thought he was about to tell him no, that he was one of the enemy, that he should flee to them if he wanted to flee at all. Yes, of course he wanted to get out of there. But first, he had to talk to Monica. He had to go with them.

"That would be best," Gorlov said, finally. "You're in danger here. We all are." The Russian grabbed Monica by the arm as Miguel stood, wobbling.

"They'll try to follow us," warned Miguel.

"They won't be able to. I'll talk to Eugene before we leave. He can help us without endangering himself. It'll be enough if they're a little clumsy following us at first. By the time we're far away, they won't be able to find us." Gorlov showed them the two white guns, one in each hand, and said, "I'll leave first. I have to neutralize the agents at the door."

"For the love of God! Using that at your age," said Monica. "Let me—"

"You don't know how to shoot." Before entering the compartment, Gorlov turned to Fred. Without letting go of the pistol, the Russian turned his right hand to him. His long, bony hand trembled in the dense heat as he waved goodbye. Gorlov spun around and entered the compartment. The door closed behind him.

Monica remained by the exit, eyes closed, hands on the golden wall.

Then a green light turned on and the door opened. Monica entered the compartment, still wobbling. Miguel grabbed her arm to try and help her, but she jerked it away.

"But—"

"Messiah!" Monica shouted. She looked at him with eyelids partly lowered, but her blue eyes shone like polished metal. "There's your religion."

"What?"

"There's your dead man." Monica spat every word, signalling Fred's body with her head. "The first to die in the name of God—"

"That's not fair—"

"—the new true god. Miguel Le Fablec."

PART 3 – THE FALL

CHAPTER 33

Cairo Airport was packed with tourists. Miguel tried to catch Monica's eye as she stood beside him. When she finally looked at him, she turned away as if suddenly very interested in the crowd of men and women with caps, papyrus scrolls, and backpacks. It was obvious Monica wasn't looking at anything in particular; she was just avoiding him, of course. Miguel didn't insist. He had to talk to her, needed to talk to her, but he couldn't find the words between the crowds moving through the check-in area like disoriented schools of fish.

He, too, felt lost. He would do whatever Vladimir told him. That would get them out of Egypt. Then, maybe he could talk to Monica. He turned towards the shop that stood behind them.

When Gorlov left them beside that airport shop, he had told them not to move from there. Miguel hoped he wouldn't be gone for too long. He leaned back against the shop window and looked at the objects lined up on a shelf beside him. Urns with supposed Egyptian hieroglyphics, alabaster pharaohs, Moorish slippers. He thought about what he would say to Monica when they did get a chance to talk, how to explain to her… that is, if he were capable of explaining it to himself first. To the "true god," as Monica had called him. Miguel saw a clay Anubis on the shelf and realized that he was as much a clay god as that statue.

Midas Effect… The Project… Operation Messiah. He went through the list of secret plots that had once seemed so attractive to him. Before everything that had happened in the last few months, he would have been thrilled at the idea of joining any kind of intrigue with a codename even half as enticing as those. *Idiot!* he told himself.

Miguel noticed the vendor exit the shop and come towards him. His wide smile showed yellow, gapped teeth, reminding him of Walter Castillo's smile. That cheating shark!

"Italian, *españolo*? Anubis good price," said the vendor, picking up the Anubis figurine from the shelf.

"No, thank you," Miguel responded before looking away.

Gorlov returned at that moment. "Come on, quickly!" he said. "There's a flight to Madrid with several available seats. We have fifteen minutes to buy the tickets."

"Anubis twenty dollars," said the vendor, placing the figurine between Miguel and Gorlov.

Gorlov ignored the clay god and grabbed Monica's arm as she was still watching the tourists, pulling her over to Miguel. The vendor began cleaning the figurine with a cloth that looked to hold all the dust in the world.

"I need you to create three fake passports," Gorlov murmured into their ears.

The two inflexors backed away from the scientist and looked at him, wide-eyed.

"What…?" said Miguel.

"Anubis fifteen dollars. Won't go down more," the vendor insisted.

"Take out your Spanish passport," Gorlov demanded. "Study it – the visas, the Egyptian seals of entry… all the details. Then create three identical copies with any three Spanish names you can think up. And our photos. Monica, you amplify his inflection. This has to be fast. We need—"

"Ten dollars, won't go down more," said the vendor, wrapping the statue in a newspaper page as if he had already sold it. "I losing money. Ten dollars, no more."

Miguel and Monica looked at each other, lips parted. He, of course, would do anything Vladimir told him to, he knew he would, but… The vendor continued waving the Arabic lettering on the newspaper in front of his face.

Gorlov looked at the vendor. Miguel thought he would be frightened by the scientist's expressionless face, since he wasn't used to it, and finally leave them alone.

"Five dollars for the figure and three books of postcards," Gorlov said in English.

Miguel was about to ask what he had to do to create three passports out of nothing – if they had to be virtual, what the hell did he expect him to do? – but he closed his mouth and looked at the vendor. Monica did the same.

"I talk with the *españolo*. You don't talk. Ten dollars Anubis and three postcard books. Last price. Ten all," the vendor sentenced.

"Accept, Miguel," Gorlov ordered.

"But…" Miguel took out ten dollars and gave it to the vendor.

"We'll take it like this," said Gorlov, taking everything – the clay statue and three books of postcards – from the shelf.

The vendor narrowed his eyes at Gorlov and disappeared into his shop.

Gorlov gave Miguel the books and said, "Turning these into passports will require a much smaller quantum inflection than it would take to create them out of thin air. The imaginative effort is much smaller, as is the likelihood that Castillo will detect the inflection. Help him, Monica."

Miguel and Monica looked at each other. Miguel nodded. The three of them immediately migrated into a corner where no one would see what they were doing.

Miguel flipped through his passport, memorizing it. Then he looked at one of the booklets – it was full of pictures of pyramids, temples, statues… He felt his brain begin to bubble as Monica's inflection merged with his, amplifying it. *Like my brother, but with typical Spanish surnames*, Miguel thought, and one of the booklets turned into a passport with the name Daniel González Martín. It had his photo. He took the second booklet out of Gorlov's hands. *Gorlov looks... northern?* The second booklet turned into the passport of Iñaki Ugarte Zuloeta, with Gorlov's photo. *And Monica... looks Andalusian.* He looked at her. She was concentrating on amplifying the inflection, but her clenched jaw told him she was still angry with him. An angry, arrogant, resentful Andalusian. Ana. The third booklet turned the Nile postcards into a passport for Ana Montalvo Ortiz.

The inflection ended then.

"Won't they realize these are fake?" Miguel asked as he handed the passports to Gorlov.

"Leave that to me," said the Russian, handing Miguel the Anubis figurine. "Follow me." Gorlov walked with decisive steps, dodging the tourists and their luggage. Monica and Miguel followed silently.

As they walked, Miguel looked at the half-wrapped statue in his hand. Anubis' jackal head poked through the wrinkled newspaper. The clay god. At that moment, a little blond boy ran across the corridor in front of them and called out to his parents in French. "Papa, wait for me!" He wore a NASA cap backwards. Miguel turned to watch the space agency's red and blue logo move further away. A child's dream. The boy disappeared among the sea of travellers. Miguel turned back around and took several quick steps to catch up to Monica, the clay Anubis in his hands. The end of the dream—his life destroyed by that demigod.

"Operation Messiah! Midas Effect! Bullshit!" he spat through gritted teeth, looking at the figurine like he wanted to strangle it.

Then Miguel noticed Monica was staring at him.

"Stupid codenames for stupid games," he said, and threw the figure into the trash.

Monica continued staring at the trash can as they left and later, silently, she looked once more at Miguel.

***

Walter Castillo stood behind Barrett, keeping an eye on what he was doing. Barrett looked over his glasses at one of the monitoring posts' large screens installed in the encampment at Al-Hakim. Eighteen hours had passed since Miguel's escape, and the monitoring room was packed with scientists and operatives. Everyone was searching for Miguel and his inflections.

Castillo looked back at the door. There, two of his agents silently stood and watched what the scientists were doing. He knew that beyond the encampment, in NASA Ames, in San José, and in NASA Hampton, everyone was working for him. The satellites sent their signals to the SSR, which were then processed and sent to Egypt. He had the best people inside and outside the monitoring room. But what interested him most was Barrett and the signal he was staring at.

"Anything new?" Castillo asked.

"It's difficult to know..." Barrett was sweating profusely, fidgeting like an insect in a jar. The signal he was studying had been received less than three hours ago. It corresponded to an inflection produced in a region to the northeast, about a hundred miles away, somewhere near Cairo.

Cairo, Castillo thought. If they had gotten to Cairo, it would be impossible to find the Jeep they had escaped with. And the fugitives would only be three more strangers in the city, small, unrecognizable heads among thousands of milling tourists, like ants. They could take any mode of transport – buses, boats, planes… *On a plane?* he wondered. No, Gorlov wouldn't be so stupid. If they tried to use their passports, they would be found. The desert was the best alternative – if they found a good guide, it could be months before anyone found them in a cave, or a town, or an oasis. Missing. Miguel missing!

Castillo touched his bandage. His hand came away wet, as if the wound he got from the chair was still bleeding. *Fucking guns*, he said to himself, looking at the ceramic gun that lay on the table beside Barrett, one of the guns Gorlov had not taken.

His face wrinkled when he remembered how he had left the guns within arm's reach of Miguel. Even old Fred had better reflexes than him. He was dead now. He was so stupid, attacking Castillo like that when he was armed! Barrett never stopped typing frantically. Fred didn't have to die. Neither did the missing Midas.

Castillo turned his attention back to the signal from the sensor on the screen, near Cairo. It wasn't a Midas Effect. The signal was so small that it would have gone unnoticed, had it not been for the fact that every member of personnel was studying the records. Now, the expansive residual wave was visible on the isoinflexor screen. Three hours after the inflection, the lines of the wave were very clear. The isoinflexor focal point was Cairo International Airport.

"Is it them?" said Castillo, touching his bandage. He winked to hide the pain.

"It's a weak signal," muttered Barrett. "It's complicated. The residual isoinflexors, and of course, the satellite delay…"

On a plane, Castillo thought. His wound throbbed. His face screwed up even more. They must have done something to get tickets for a flight. Barrett continued prattling on about incomprehensible details.

"It's them," Castillo said, rummaging around for a phone inside his jacket, which had been thrown over the desk. "They're at the airport." He grabbed his phone and threw his jacket back onto the table, alongside his bloodstained tie.

Barrett stared at him from his seat. "And if it's not—?" he began to say.

Castillo looked down at him very seriously. Barrett removed his glasses and began cleaning them. "Eugene," he said, keeping his gaze firmly on Barrett. "I'm not sending you back to San José." Barrett put his glasses back on and seemed to tense. "You will come with me and help me find them. Vincent?" Castillo said into the phone. "Cairo Airport. Quickly, they're there… Dart guns, quantum sensors and two agents… Discretion."

Barrett turned back to the screen and typed at high speed, his weasel-like eyes constantly moving. He was hiding something, Castillo thought. He knew Gorlov had spoken to him before he ran. Barrett insisted all they had done was say goodbye. He couldn't trust him. That made him think of Vincent. Could he trust Vincent? He was loyal to him, but he had no experience. Castillo turned to his agents. Standing beside the door, arms crossed, they watched silently behind their sunglasses. Infallible. He could trust Roth. "Roth, go with Vincent. I can handle things here."

Roth lifted his glasses slightly and looked at him seriously, looking not at his eyes but at his forehead. Castillo touched his bandage once more. Beneath it he could feel his wound throb again. Roth was right to worry about him. The pain was as close as he thought he could get to putting his head inside a meat grinder and moving it bit by bit. He could have fainted. Not a single analgesic, they had told him in the clinic; the drug was still in his system.

"I'll be fine," he said. "Vincent," he said to the mouthpiece, "wait for Roth. He's going with you."

Roth nodded and left the room. Once the door closed, Castillo turned to face Barrett. "Everything correct?"

"I already told you before, it's not certain that the signal… When the global wave recorded by the satellite… And the local inflection, as well…"

"Eugene, for fuck's sake, stop spouting bullshit!"

Barrett turned around in his seat and looked at him from below, his wide eyes visible above his small glasses. He barely blinked. Castillo watched his face, his tense posture. He looked so small. He reminded him of his little sister, contemplating from below with wide eyes their father's drunken threats, pulling her braids so hard she sometimes removed clumps of hair. They were just children. Fear, Castillo thought. He didn't like it.

But that was how it had to be.

"Find Miguel," Castillo ordered, almost in a whisper.

Barrett turned his back to him and typed some codes into his laptop. A huge sweat patch covered most of the back of his khaki shirt. Barrett was the best analyst left. Castillo couldn't trust him too much, but he would do. He was too scared. Castillo looked at his watch. The steel hands moved forward firmly over the black face. They moved too fast.

An hour later, Vincent called.

"They were in the airport," Castillo heard from the other end of the line.

"Are you sure?" he asked, but he already knew.

"A vendor recognized a photo of the three of them." Vincent's voice faded in and out due to the noise of the airport. "He looked like he didn't like Gorlov's and... something in Arabic, an insult, I guess. He was sure... They... figurine of Anubis and some postcards."

"Don't move, we're on our way. Hand me over to Roth. Yes. Bye." Castillo and Barrett looked at one another. "Yes, Roth. Can you hear me? Perfect. I want a search done of all passports from all the flights that have departed Cairo to Europe in the last twelve hours. They know we have priority in Langley. They'll ask the European agencies for help. We're looking for three false passports. Gorlov must have gotten them somehow. Goodbye." He hung up without taking his eyes off Barrett. "How did that old fox get those passports?" he asked, not expecting an answer.

"Miguel made them," Barrett replied suddenly, showing a graph on the computer. "I suppose this explains the inflection we detected." Castillo looked at the graph. "This is the signal characteristic of Miguel and Monica when they work together. I finally managed to filter it." Barrett pointed to a peak in the magenta line. He removed his glasses. "Vladimir and I call it incongruence. I tried to explain it to you once in the anti-inflexor room in NASA Ames, remember? You had to go, some Jack Harper phoned you—"

"Yeah, alright. What's incongruence?"

"When Miguel and Monica work together, it's impossible to tell the difference between the Midas' inflection and the catalyst's inflection. They're results that don't satisfy the fundamental equations. The variables—"

"Eugene!"

"It's the signal I was looking for. That's all." Barrett patted his sweaty face with a handkerchief. "And it coincides with the global wave that originates at Cairo Airport. It's them, without a doubt."

Castillo said nothing for a few seconds, staring at the graph. Then, he looked at Barrett. *You only give me the information when I already have it*, he thought. "Come on, grab a quantum sensor and come with me to the helicopter. I might need you in Cairo. I assume you won't fail again in detecting incongruence, right?"

Barrett put his glasses back on as sweat reappeared on his forehead. His head was like a sponge full of water that someone had just squeezed.

In that instant, Castillo's phone rang.

"Go to the helicopter, Eugene. I'll follow you out."

When he picked up, the voice of William Whitaker, the director of the CIA, sounded like a dragon trying to burn his ear, his hair, his bandage, and then his brain. The wound throbbed at the front of his head as if the seat Fred had thrown at him had hit him again.

"Yes, Jack Harper, go ahead," Castillo said into the phone. He clenched his jaw and touched his forehead in a military salute. The bandage was wet with blood.

CHAPTER 34

Sitting on the hood of his yellow Renault Mégane Coupé, Miguel stared at Madrid's School of Aeronautical Engineering. The building's high ceilings filled his head with memories from his youth, when he had studied there.

Two girls and a young man passed by him talking about plane reactors, about the last exam and how Nozzles was going to fail everyone again. Miguel remembered the professor's face, his elongated jaw and comically large nostrils, as round and dark as a reactor's exhaust nozzle. He smiled. Tradition had preserved the nickname.

The students laughed and joked about Nozzles and his nose, which they said could breathe in all the air in the room if he sneezed. They laughed despite being bothered by the first exams of the year, exams which they would almost certainly fail, which would be one of the biggest problems in their post-adolescent lives. A huge threat. But they laughed. Just as other students had, as Miguel himself had in the same circumstance.

He closed his eyes and inhaled the cold December air, the Madrid sun on his face. And for one whole second, he felt no danger.

When he opened his eyes, he saw Dani.

As he saw him come into view, Miguel sensed his right ear, marked with a tiny scar. It was impossible to distinguish from where he was, but he could imagine it perfectly.

Daniel left the School of Engineering loaded with books. Covered by a huge, blue parka, he began scaling the hill leading to the student parking lot. He stopped in front of the yellow Mégane and looked between the books in his arms, the pocket of his parka, and the ground successively. Miguel guessed Dani was trying to find a way to get his keys out of his pocket without having to drop his books on the asphalt, wet from the previous night's rain. Dani would, as always, keep those books in perfect condition until he finished his course.

Miguel broke into a smile. "Need a hand?" he asked.

Dani looked up quickly, as if spooked by a ghost, and stared at him open-mouthed. "But… What are you doing here?" he asked. He approached Miguel with an armful of books and a smile that stretched his face and pushed his ears back. His mangled ear almost disappeared.

Miguel hugged him tightly.

When they parted, Miguel gave Dani a firm slap on the shoulder. Dani left his books on the hood of the car and hit him back playfully on his stomach with the back of his hand. "You never said anything, dude, about coming back to Spain. You're skinnier. No, I don't know, different. Hair's longer." Dani slapped him again on the arm. "Strong, too. What's going on? This is great, man! What a surprise—"

"I'll give you a hand with these books and then we can go." Miguel cut off his brother's endless stream of interjections, slaps, and gesticulations. "I need a favor."

Dani quirked a brow at him, his confused look reminding Miguel very clearly of their father. "A favor? You're the weirdest…"

Minutes later, the two men were in the car on the way to Dani's apartment. He immediately began asking Miguel about his life on the other side of the Atlantic, and Miguel had to recall his first few months in California in order to not reveal any secret details. Everything was so confidential, hidden. Miguel began to feel something like a hole, low in his abdomen, as if his stomach were suddenly disappearing.

Dani stopped his interrogation to watch the uninterrupted speeding traffic on the left, on a road he was trying to merge into. Miguel recognized the avenue but couldn't remember its name. He didn't feel any better being able to recognize a place from his past as a student, a world now distant. His exotic adventure, he thought, the new world he had entered, had separated him from the rest of the planet, from his past, from his family. And that same world threatened him now. The only people who did not threaten him, his only allies, were Monica and Vladimir, and they had rejected him too. The two of them seemed to fear Miguel, to keep him by their side solely because of the danger he posed if set free. Even Monica. Everyone had something to fear from him. Yes, Dani was right. He was weird.

The gap in his abdomen felt like it was pushing his stomach into his mouth. Miguel lowered the car window for some fresh air as Dani merged with the traffic on the avenue. Rapid, impersonal traffic. He felt so alone.

"Why don't we go grab a bite to eat?" Dani asked. "My kitchen's still a mess. It's even worse than the last time you came. We've declared it a war zone..."

I have to get Monica back, Miguel thought.

"They've opened a new restaurant—"

"No, thanks, Dani. I can't stay."

"Come on, man! Why not?"

"I came to see if I could borrow the car." Miguel could hear how his voice trembled, low. He worried his voice would give away that he was hiding something, that his brother would notice.

Dani stopped at a red light and his enthusiasm seemed to come to a stop too. His face went serious as he raised one eyebrow and lowered the other. Dani wouldn't go easy on him. He would surely try to find out what was going on.

"I came here with my girlfriend. I need the car so I can take her on a trip. To the south. I want to show her Seville, Granada..." Miguel lied, anticipating his brother's questions. He had prepared his lie with Gorlov. Gorlov's agreement had been enough for him then, but now he wasn't so sure. "We want to go out tonight. You don't mind not having the car for a few weeks, right?"

"Dude, you come home with your girlfriend and you won't even stay for dinner?"

"Well, maybe we can do that when we come back," Miguel replied, thinking about how to reinforce his excuse. "I came with one of my bosses from the project... Y'know..."

"Holy fuck, man, you came to Spain with your girlfriend and you brought your *boss* along? Are you fucking kidding me? You haven't changed at all. You're a wet fish. I don't know how your girlfriend puts up with you."

She doesn't, Miguel thought. "Seriously, I'll introduce you now and we'll go. It's gotten late and I don't want to hit traffic on the way out of Madrid. When we come back, we'll spend a day with you, okay?" *If we come back.*

"Whatever, you don't have time for me..." said Dani as he shifted into first gear and the car started moving.

"It's not that..." Miguel wished he could have a coffee with him, talk to him, find out if this year in school was any better, ask about what he was doing with his life. He remembered Castillo's offer to have Dani study in San José, a grant in NASA Ames. All lies. Castillo, that fucking swindler. He had to run away from him. He had to get him away from Dani.

When the car turned, Miguel recognized the ancient buildings of Avenida de la Reina Victoria. He searched for the café where he had left Monica and Gorlov. Dani gave him a pat on the knee and smiled.

"Jerk. You owe me dinner. Your treat. In Tontxu, one of the fancy ones, okay?"

"Done!"

"You're going to Seville, huh? You introducing her to Mom and Dad? Your girlfriend."

"Stop there, on the corner." Miguel pointed to one of the buildings, near where Dani lived. "I'll introduce you to Monica and my boss and then we'll go. Do you mind if I leave you here with all that?" He looked behind him at the books piled onto the backseat.

"Fuck, are you in that much of a hurry?"

Miguel got out of the car without replying and entered the café on the corner. Dani got out then and began taking out his books and stacking them on a nearby bench. He grumbled as Miguel and Monica came out but stopped as soon as he saw her.

"Pleased to meet you!" Dani said slowly in English. Monica held out her hand, but he gave her two kisses on her cheeks. "In Spain, we give two kisses!" he said in Spanish.

Monica smiled with her gleaming eyes. It had been days since Miguel had seen her smile. It had felt like years. He was glad Dani had managed it. He wanted to believe her smile came from the memory of the time Miguel taught her the Spanish custom of greeting someone with two kisses, in Granada, many months ago. When everything was fine.

At that moment, Gorlov joined them. Dani shook his hand with a guarded expression, as if he were greeting the dean of the university.

"Dani," said Miguel, "I'm sorry, really, but we have to go right now. I'm sorry to take away your car like this."

"It's robbery."

"We'll see each other again in a few weeks, okay? I'll call you. Can I borrow your parka? I didn't bring my coat."

"You're incredible," said Dani as he took off his parka.

"Do you need anything?" Miguel asked. He felt wrong leaving just like that.

"Go on, hit the road already!" said Dani, clapping him on the back. Then he hugged Miguel quickly.

Monica and Gorlov got into the car silently. Miguel got in after them. "Take care," Miguel said to Dani from the driver's seat.

"Yeah, sure."

Miguel turned the key and began circling the avenue to the north. He spotted Dani in the rear-view mirror gesturing for him to turn right there, at the first change in direction. Of course, Miguel knew that the best thing for travelling south would be to turn there and turn in the opposite direction. But he didn't turn. He kept going straight.

***

Walter Castillo stopped to sit on a bench in Madrid-Barajas Airport. He looked at his watch as he sat. They were wasting too much time. They had had to wait there for the new agent to arrive, for the green light to follow Miguel through Europe, for Whitaker to open their accounts so he could hire some fucking cars.

Controlled! That's how he felt.

But he was finally in Madrid, in the bright, clear terminal. Following Miguel. Some light on his problems.

He was taking out his notes from his briefcase when he saw Vincent and Barrett approaching. They sat on either side of him. Castillo looked at his watch again and noticed that it had been fifteen minutes since he had sent Roth and Kells to hire some cars. They would be another while yet, he supposed.

Time, he repeated to himself, looking up. The third agent, the newbie, was standing beside the bench. He never separated from Castillo. His pachyderm arms, his fat head with close-cropped blond hair facing right. Whitaker had sent him. He said he was called John Smith.

They've run out of names at Central, so they're turning to absurd ones, Castillo had thought when he heard the agent introduce himself with the typical code name.

The director said he was sending the weightlifter to "help him." Castillo adjusted his tie. His version was that Smith – or whatever his name was – had been sent to control him, bring him back to the United States and put him in front of a war council if he lost Miguel, or if he fell into enemy hands. If he lost the Midas. The wound on his forehead throbbed and Castillo touched the bandage. Everything seemed in order in his head. He just had to get Miguel back, he made himself think, and the rest of the injuries would heal themselves.

He looked at Barrett to his right as he studied a quantum sensor. Castillo turned his neck, looked at the sensor's screen and saw that there was no inflection nearby. Barrett turned on the portable SSR signal receptor. Castillo noticed the isoinflexor lines over a map of Europe on the screen. The data from the SSR arrived without issue. The map didn't show the residual effect of any inflection worth caring about. Everything was calm with the inflexors, he thought. Too calm.

"I don't know how we'll find them now," said Barrett. "I don't think they'll go around producing inflection, so we can follow them."

Castillo didn't answer. He turned his attention back to his notes. He flipped back and forth through several pages before turning on his laptop.

"Why did you request the passport report from Central?" asked Vincent. Castillo lifted his head and looked at him, seated to his left. Vincent kept his eyes on Agent Smith, who was walking very slowly away from them, as if taking a stroll through the light of the terminal. "They've complicated matters for us now. This guy isn't going to do anything other than bother us."

"We can't change it," Castillo replied, flipping through his notes again. He hated wasting time complaining about the inevitable.

"I could have searched for them," Vincent insisted. "I definitely would have found them in some airport. I just would have had to investigate the flights a little and discard some of them." He lowered his voice as Agent Smith's steps brought him closer. "I could have looked in the airports for suspicious flights. It wouldn't have been too much work—"

"Since when do you have extrasensory perception abilities?" Barrett asked.

"I'm in NASA Hampton's parallel Project, you know? Since about a year ago," Vincent answered. "They trained me there."

"You never told me," said Barrett. "I was your SSR researcher."

"It was a secret…" Vincent returned to his conversation with Castillo.

Where is that report? The sunlight that entered through the enormous windows fell onto them. It reflected onto the computer screen, making it so Castillo couldn't see it very well. He soon found another codenamed report among his notes. *Here!*

"NASA Ames' Project is secret too," said Barrett.

"Yeah, but Hampton… the CIA, you can imagine."

Castillo typed on his keyboard. At that moment, Smith stopped in front of him, his huge shadow, his gorilla neck, blocking the sunlight that shone on his screen, which allowed Castillo to see clearly. "I have it!" he said.

Barrett and Vincent, on either side of him, as well as Smith above, looked at the screen. Castillo slowly read what he himself had written months before. Dated April first, the screen read *Daniel Le Fablec, brother of Miguel Le Fablec*. Below was a photo and an address. Avenida de la Reina Victoria, Madrid.

CHAPTER 35

Over half an hour had passed since Miguel's Renault had passed through Perpignan, having crossed the northeast border into France. Miguel knew that highway well, although he had never driven on it at night. He looked out at the black countryside through the passenger seat window. It was the same road his father used to bring them on vacation to Nice. Except now, they were no pit stops every two hours like back then. And they weren't going to Nice. Or were they? He didn't know where they were going. Gorlov wouldn't say. They barely spoke. They drove at the maximum legal speed, with just a few short stops to refuel, let Monica take the wheel, or pay the toll bridge.

A new toll appeared at the end of a straight line. They must have been near Narbonne. Miguel remembered that there was an exit to the west that led to Toulouse. Monica lowered the window, paid, and pulled over to the right as soon as the barrier lifted. As she did so, she got out of the driver's seat and Miguel left the passenger's seat. They switched places without speaking to one another before starting the car again. Miguel sighed, gripping the steering wheel.

"We haven't rested since we left Madrid. We've gone nearly five hundred miles without stopping," said Miguel. *We haven't spoken either*, he thought. "Do I take the exit for Toulouse?"

"No, to the north, parallel to the coast," said Gorlov from the backseat. "We'll rest in a hotel near Montpellier or Avignon."

Miguel smiled when he heard Gorlov pronounce the French words. Of course, the Russian's abrupt French was better than silence. Montpellier was about sixty miles away, Avignon about one hundred and twenty. In Avignon was another crossroads of highways, where they could go north to Lyon or east to Marseille, Nice, or Italy.

Nice, Miguel thought. He remembered the beach, the park with enormous pine trees where he played with Dani, the streets they would get lost in whenever they didn't want to be found by their grandmother, Monsieur Parvais' hotel, the Secret Hole Club, he and Dani arguing. He had not gone back there since his grandmother died. He saw the souvenir shop that belonged to the old couple near the Marché aux Fleurs. He was so close to home.

He fidgeted in his seat, feeling like his bones were poking at his flesh. Silence and darkness. Monica appeared to be dozing in the passenger seat. He looked at her from the corner of his eye. They had to talk, of course, when a Russian spy wasn't in the backseat.

"*A-vi-gnon*," said Miguel, enunciating slowly. "That's how you say it, Vladimir." He liked hearing himself speak French. He looked at the fuel gauge, which displayed an orange light. They would have to refuel soon. At least he could use some of his grandparents' language.

"I don't speak French," said Gorlov. "I don't know how to pronounce the names of those cities."

"You haven't told us which city we're going to."

Gorlov did not answer.

"That's not fair," Miguel insisted.

"What is fair does not matter. Vincent must be searching for us mentally. He could find us by accident. You could think about the destination too strongly. You're both tired from the trip, hoping it will end soon. There is a mental technique that Vincent has mastered. It's not exact, but he can enter your mind during the transitory phase between sleep and waking."

He had finally managed to push Gorlov into a conversation. Even though it was yet another one of his endless technical explanations, he preferred it to silence. "Couldn't Vincent enter your mind and find out?"

"I'm not an inflexor. Vincent will be looking for inflexors. He's looking for you. For you and Monica."

Monica shifted in her seat. Her eyes were closed, but Miguel knew she wasn't fully asleep.

"This is no way for a Midas to travel," Miguel commented. "Why don't we do something less exhausting? Travel through space, teleport ourselves, something like that. I'm still omnipotent, right? That way, we could get rid of Walter and Vincent once and for all."

"Don't be foolish!" Gorlov scoffed. "I cannot calculate what kind of residual wave an inflection like that would have. You could destroy the planet doing something like that. Or not, I don't know. I don't have the measures here to calculate it. You know that."

Miguel *did* know that. But he was still a Midas. "I could calculate the consequences without the help of the SSR computers," he said.

"It's possible," Gorlov admitted, "but it requires a genius intellect to comprehend and control residual effects from those inflections."

"Right."

"Do you really think yourself capable of folding space? Do you have the knowledge needed to control it?"

"I don't know." Miguel scratched his head before pushing his hair back.

"You think so?"

"Even so, this journey is exhausting. I hope you know where we're going."

"You can't do it if you don't believe in it..."

"Yeah, yeah, alright..."

"We're going to Mulhouse," Gorlov said suddenly. "It's a stepping stone along our route. That's all I can tell you right now."

"Mulhouse?" Miguel narrowed his eyes like he was trying to read an imaginary map on the windscreen. He seemed to be able to see the map better once he had overtaken another car. Of course, to the northeast. "The German border."

Gorlov said nothing.

"We're going to Germany, aren't we? And what do we do there? Maybe we'll see some scientist from the old regime, right? An old friend of yours from East Germany. Will they help us hide? Stuttgart is near there, Freiburg, Munich. Maybe they have a secret formula to stop our inflection being detected so the CIA will stop following us. Is the scientist in Germany or Switzerland? Switzerland is close too, Basel—"

"This isn't a game," said Gorlov. "Stop being stupid. This is very serious."

With the scarce light inside the car, Miguel could make out the scientist's eyes in the rear-view mirror. He imagined they wanted to burn through his glasses like a laser, bounce off the mirror and reach him. Gorlov's expression remained as blank as ever.

"I ask you not to take this situation so lightly. It's serious." The consonants took on a thick Russian accent, confirming Miguel's suspicions that Gorlov was annoyed.

I'm the one who should be annoyed, he thought.

"I'm not taking it lightly," he said. "But this trip from hell is driving me crazy. No rest, no destination—"

"We have a destination."

"—no conversation, like we're enemies, like we hate each other for what we are…"

"I still have contacts. They will be able to stop Castillo. A war council—"

"I'm fed up with contacts! I'm tired of wars, and spies, and secret organizations, and all those so-called 'stupid things' that I lived so well without before now…" Miguel was almost shouting now. Gorlov went quiet. "… and codenames for secret projects, and secret missions, and everything being a secret!" Miguel realized that he had gone from protesting about the trip to complaining about the true source of his worry – his life, his power. "No, I'm not taking it lightly," he said. "I know how serious it is to be a Midas. I know better than either of you." He tightened his grip on the steering wheel and shook his head slowly. "I wish I wasn't a Midas," he added in a whisper.

At that moment, Monica opened her eyes and turned to look at him. Miguel saw her from the corner of his eye. Then he realized they were nearly on top of the truck in front of them. He overtook it and concentrated on the lines on the road.

He looked back at Monica, who was still watching him. He held out his hand without taking his eyes off the road. He hoped she wouldn't rebuff him. The last forty-eight hours had felt lonelier than Miguel thought he could ever feel. He was a weirdo, a loner, misunderstood even by those best acquainted with his strangeness. Monica watched him carefully. Miguel could feel Gorlov's eyes on him from behind. He couldn't even understand himself. He didn't know where his blinding delusions of power and divinity had come from. A lonely divinity in their paradise. No, he didn't want to be alone again, not for all the damn gold King Midas could offer him. He would change everything just for Monica's hand.

And Monica took his hand.

For almost half a mile, inside the car reigned a stony silence, loaded with stares, drowned by the thrum of the Mégane's engine as it continued down the highway.

A bright red and green sign appeared on the right of the highway indicating they were near a hotel from the Ibis chain. It seemed lonely. Miguel guessed it must have been in the middle of a field in the south of France. There would not be many hotels over the next few hundred miles. What did it matter? Monica was with him. He had her hand, finally.

But Gorlov broke the silence. "Take the first exit, Miguel. Maybe we should rest. Follow the directions to the Ibis."

Miguel had to let go of Monica's hand to change gears as he took the exit. After about six hundred miles, the damn Russian decided they needed to rest. Since the day Miguel had met him, the scientist had never once had good timing.

***

A few minutes later, they had unloaded the small amount of luggage they carried, and Miguel was speaking in French to a receptionist at the small hotel.

Miguel looked at Gorlov and Monica, who both nodded at him. He turned back to the receptionist, a woman with very dark, short hair and bangs. She looked at him through long, mascara-coated eyelashes. She reminded him of one of Dani's French girlfriends.

"Three rooms," said Miguel in French.

The receptionist typed something on her computer and handed him three magnetic key cards, one for each room. Her pink lips stretched into a smile. It was like she was amused by the idea of Miguel not being able to sleep with Monica.

"It's better to stay in three rooms," said Gorlov as they walked to their rooms. "I don't trust you two. I don't care about your feelings, your love, your hatred. But I don't want you producing any inflections. Walter would find us and he would be here before we woke up."

"Yeah, yeah," Miguel replied.

Gorlov continued his sermon. "Remember that we came here in your car, exposing your brother and putting him in danger, so that you didn't have to produce another inflection to find a mode of transport. Don't ruin it now."

"You already said that," said Miguel, dragging out the words. "We'll sleep separately." Miguel opened his door and threw his backpack inside without turning on the light. "I'm going to get some air."

Monica, who had been about to enter the room beside Miguel's, stopped suddenly and turned around. Miguel watched her hair sway as she turned her head. "I thought you were tired," she said.

"I am. I just need some fresh air."

"I'll go with you."

Gorlov stared at her, expressionless, silent.

"Just to talk," she said.

"Do what you want, but be careful. Keep in mind there are many lives at stake. You are directly responsible for the future of this planet."

"We're going to talk, Vladimir," said Monica quietly. Her voice was firm. "Not drop atomic bombs."

Gorlov entered his room, shaking his head. He said nothing.

***

The carpet in the bedroom looked rough. Gray and rough. Gorlov shivered as if it were cold, but it was hot. The entire hotel looked neat – the furniture was new, the room was spacious, and everything smelled faintly of disinfectant. Gorlov's hands were cold.

He approached the bed and left his small suitcase on top of it before sitting down on the edge of the bed. There was a white phone on the bedside table. Gorlov looked at its cold, modern design silently. He placed his hands on his legs.

He was so thin, so old now, looking down at his bony hands on his khaki archaeologist's trousers. *Still wearing that!* he told himself, like a sharp, vivid memory of what he had created. The desert, the false gods. A monster, that's what he had created. The formulae, the equations of the Midas Effect written in blue ink in his notebooks, flowed through his mind.

If Fred were still alive, the two could have commiserated over having wasted their lives searching for a naïve idiot, only to give him the power of a god, before serving him on a silver platter to a legion of overambitious, soulless beings. His whole life had been spent working himself to the bone on research, only to create a new war machine. Nothing more.

He looked back at the phone. Graham Bell, at least, had managed to invent something useful for humanity. *Not like me. My inventions…*

Gorlov remembered one of his first inventions in Russia. There were other objects that could help him now, but he needed somewhere to hide and give him time to think of something, run tests, look for a way out. Sergei had everything he needed.

He picked up the phone and dialled a number.

After a few seconds, a tone rang. Then, a feminine voice, in Russian.

"University of Leningrad. Office of Professor Vladimir Gorlov. Please leave your message after the tone," said that outdated, impossible voice from some computer limbo where his office was stuck in 1980. Immediately, a beep.

"Sergei Krushenko," he said, "it's Vladimir Gorlov. Call me at this number." Then he hung up.

Gorlov slowly removed his shoes and noticed the tired pain in his legs. An old man. But saying Sergei's name out loud had left an echo of his youth, of times when he studied the first inflexors in the Soviet Union.

He remembered Sergei Krushenko's broad, smiling face, his green eyes, the day they said goodbye for good. In Freiburg. His melodic laugh belonged in a Russian military choir. Irina was still alive then. She never saw California, never even left the Federal Republic of Germany. She had chronic bronchitis and her heart, weakened from Russian winters, failed before she could see the Pacific sun Fred had promised her. But Gorlov could not fault Sergei or Fred. They had done everything they could to get to the United States as soon as possible.

Gorlov placed his shoes in the wardrobe and sat back down beside the phone. The cold in his hands and feet as well as the rough carpet kept him in the past. Sergei owed him his life. They would have exiled him to Siberia years ago after the robbery of medical teams in the university. He lied for Sergei, although he knew the KGB had sent him to watch him – his own personal spy. Back then, Sergei was just a boy, disorientated by the decadence of the regime, of the Party, by changes that multiplied chaotically in the country. A thief, but one who deserved an opportunity far from Siberia.

Gorlov had given it to him. And Sergei betrayed the KGB, and the KGB kicked him out of the Soviet Union. In all probability, that had been the last straw for Sergei. He joined the mafia and became one of the biggest arms traffickers in the world.

The telephone rang suddenly. Gorlov's heart leapt into his mouth, but he didn't move.

He turned slowly. The white object Bell had invented. He let it ring twice before picking up. "Gorlov," he said into the mouthpiece.

"Vladimir!" a baritone voice replied on the other end of the line. "Hahaha! Professor!" He seemed to sing in Russian.

"Sergei," said Gorlov. "I see this old KGB line still works."

"Everything that's paid for still works, Vladimir, you know that."

Of course a Russian mob boss would have a direct phone line between spies from the past. It was likely that Sergei used it now for his agreements with traffickers and thieves all over the world. If he used that line for organized crime, Gorlov thought, he should have deleted the message from his department at the University of Leningrad. But Sergei had always been nostalgic.

"I need help," said Gorlov.

"Are you okay? Is it the CIA?"

"Something like that. Can you hide me for a while? You're still in Bratislava, right? I need somewhere safe to get in contact with some people."

"Vladimir," came Krushenko's deep, quiet, musical voice, "you can ask me for anything. I owe you my life."

"Come now, Sergei, enough of that."

"Do you know what I did with all the material from your lab?" Krushenko asked suddenly. "They had all the machines on display as relics in the old Leningrad Museum of the History of Religion and Atheism. I still have one..."

Fred had given him the news of the robbery many years prior. Someone had broken into the cathedral the Party used as a museum, and they had taken a spacesuit and its equipment: a rudimentary anti-inflexor cabin, a failed attempt at a quantum inflexor that looked like a ship's cannon, a distorter made with valve amplifiers, things like that. That could be useful now, Gorlov thought, but he didn't know how he would use it. Fred suspected it had been Sergei. *A damn thief. Nostalgic, too. You know him*, Fred had said.

"Yes, I assumed you would. I might need that equipment, but what I need more is a safe place to hide. The CIA—"

"Say no more," Krushenko cut him off. "You can count on it. When are you arriving?"

"In a few days. I'll call you when I'm close."

"Old friend, I'll chill a bottle of the Party's special vodka for you. For old time's sake."

"I'll call you," said Gorlov.

"I'll be waiting."

The line cut off. A concise message between spies needed no more protocol.

Once he had hung up, Gorlov stood and slowly walked over to the bathroom, almost dragging his feet on the rough carpet. Before entering, he looked at the phone again. It was quiet now.

Then he approached the sink, turned on the cold tap, removed his Russian glasses, and wet his face with water as cold as the pipes in his apartment in Leningrad.

***

Castillo and Vincent stopped in front of Daniel Le Fablec's apartment door and rang the bell.

"Open up, this is the police," said Castillo. He spoke in Spanish, trying to cover up his Cuban accent. "We believe Miguel Le Fablec has been kidnapped. We'd like to ask you a few questions." Castillo placed his fake Interpol badge at the peephole.

Suddenly, the door swung open and Daniel appeared. He looked at them seriously.

"National police, we're working for Interpol. Can we come in?"

"Kidnapped?" Daniel asked in a faint voice.

Castillo and Vincent went as far as the living room, sitting on a sofa filled with books in the middle. Two other people joined them. Castillo assumed they were the other students Daniel shared the apartment with. They appeared alarmed, shy around the police officers on their sofa. They did not cross the doorway into the living room.

Castillo adjusted the knot of his tie. With the slightest turn of his head, he looked around. Books, magazines, a cardboard pizza box on the small table in front of the sofa. Everything was very disorganized. He took out a picture of Miguel.

"Is this your brother?" he asked, showing Daniel the photo.

"Yes. But I just saw him this morning."

Castillo looked at Vincent. What was Miguel doing with his brother? Had he warned him about them?

Miguel hasn't warned him. Dani wasn't expecting us, Vincent told him telepathically. Vincent's words crashed into Castillo's head as if Vincent had tried to push out every other thought. The wound on his forehead throbbed and Castillo thought the pressure in his head would cause it to split open again.

He looked back at Daniel, touching his bandage, and said, "A gift from the kidnappers." Daniel's face screwed up, his eyes on the bandage. "We nearly caught them two days ago. We could have prevented the kidnapping, but... You said you saw your brother today?"

"This morning. He was going on a trip. He told me. When did they kidnap him?"

"He said he was going on a trip? Did you notice anything strange?"

"I don't know..."

"Was he with strangers? Try to remember, it's important."

Castillo spotted Daniel looking at Vincent from the corner of his eye and looked away quickly. He supposed that Vincent intimidated Daniel, like he usually did with everyone who saw him for the first time, and wondered if bringing him had been a good idea. He could only guess what Daniel was thinking, trying to see if he was telling the truth. But that could be done later, when they had him. Right now, they could scare him.

"They were in a hurry!" Daniel said suddenly.

"Good."

"He was travelling with two people, but..."

"Go on."

"The people he was travelling with weren't strangers."

Castillo moved his right hand inside his jacket. There he kept the photos of Monica and Gorlov. He saw the students staring at him. Maybe they thought he was about to take out a gun. He took out his fake Interpol badge along with the photos, placing them on the pizza box.

"One was his girlfriend," Daniel was saying. "I didn't know her personally, but Miguel had sent me pictures of her by email. I have them here, on my computer, if you want to see them..." Castillo gestured with his hand that it wasn't necessary.

He put away Monica's photo. "I didn't meet the other one. Miguel said it was his boss. He looked like an old man. Too old to kidnap anyone."

Castillo showed Daniel Gorlov's photo.

"Yes, that's him," said Daniel.

"He's very dangerous despite his appearance. And he's never alone. Of course, it's not easy identifying his co-workers."

"But I was alone with Miguel in the car," Dani replied, looking up and to the right as if remembering that moment. "No one was watching us. He could have told me then."

"They must have threatened to kill his girlfriend. That's why they took her."

Dani's eyes narrowed. He said, "Yeah, of course. Miguel was acting weird. Very weird."

"Weird?"

Daniel looked at Gorlov's photo again. Then he returned it to Castillo. "My family can't afford to pay a ransom," he said.

Castillo put the photo away and readjusted the knot of his tie. Daniel wasn't as stupid as he looked. "Your brother has made a huge scientific discovery in San José State University," he explained. "Something related to armaments for hunting or something – the Americans haven't given us details, of course. The kidnappers want to control that discovery. Black market for guns, very dangerous. Those people would slit the throat of anyone in this room for even a trace of a rumor of what your brother has invented."

The students looked at one another. One began biting their fingernails.

"Where did they go?" asked Castillo.

"They said they were going south."

"South. Good."

"No! That's it! Miguel said they were going south, but then he started driving north. Yes, yes, yes…"

Vincent smiled, which Castillo noticed from the corner of his eye. He shot him a frown, and Vincent's face went blank again. Castillo turned back to Daniel.

"It's not unusual for kidnappers to give wrong information," he said. "It's an old trick to give police the slip, although it's not very effective. Now we know where they're going." He looked at Vincent and nodded. They both stood up. "Would you mind coming with us to the station? We have a few more questions for you. You alone." The two other students were still staring at them from the doorway. "We might need you to come in later, so please don't go anywhere tonight."

They nodded silently.

Daniel followed Castillo to the front door, where he stopped suddenly. "Can I ask," he said, "why they want the car?"

"What car?"

"Miguel came to ask me for the car. Don't international gun traffickers have cars? I don't get it."

Castillo observed Daniel in silence, maintaining his serious police face. Now he understood why they had come to see Daniel. The car was a clever trick of Gorlov's to find a clean mode of transport. No payment, no credit card, no robbery, no inflection. But the Russian must not have counted on Castillo talking to Daniel. Their gamble had backfired – instead of escaping cleanly, now it would be much easier to locate them. Daniel stood in the hallway with one eyebrow raised and the other lowered. It was like he didn't believe anything, like he had just realized there was no kidnapping and they weren't really the police. The damn car complicated the explanations they had to give to get him out of his apartment. Castillo tightened the knot of his tie. He was a professional. He could lie to a simple student.

"They must be using Miguel's car so they won't have to steal another one," he said. "We suspect they want to move Miguel out of the country, and, logically, they won't want to do that with a stolen car."

Daniel looked at Castillo in silence. Castillo was about to open his mouth to speak again, when Vincent told him, *He believes it.* Once again, Castillo felt the telepath's thoughts pushing his own right out of his head through the wound on his forehead. He didn't touch his head this time, breathing slowly.

Daniel moved closer to the door and picked up the coats hanging on the coat hanger. He turned back around to his two roommates. "Can I borrow your parka?" he asked one of them. "My brother has mine."

CHAPTER 36

It's too cold out, Miguel thought, buttoning up the parka Dani had lent him. He didn't remember it being so icy in the south of France in December. Of course, he wasn't often there in winter.

He and Monica walked through the small garden that surrounded the hotel. Outdoor lights along the edges of the path, like mushrooms at the edge of the lawn, lit the way. At the end was a stone wall covered in ivy and, beyond that, the parking lot.

The ivy reminded Miguel of Tower Hall, of his encounters with Monica in San José. Right now could be his next encounter with her, the one he needed. He could talk to her. Finally.

They ambled down the path, untouched by the cold. The light from the mushrooms illuminated Monica's hair. Miguel looked at her before looking down at her shirt, at her chest. It was too cold to go out wearing only a blouse. Against the backlight he could make out her nipples. Suddenly, the image of their maroon sofa in San Francisco came to mind. Sex with views of the slopes of Russian Hill. The warm sunrise in California. Without NASA, without the CIA, without secret labs. Just the two of them. He wanted to touch her. The light from the mushrooms illuminated her from below as if she were on a pedestal. Perfect. A goddess. Like him.

Miguel was about to move closer to her and hold her against him when the path ended and the light of the pedestal disappeared.

Monica, without stopping, walked beyond the ivy wall and entered the parking lot. Only a streetlight illuminated her now with its scarce, white light, almost weak.

The Mégane Coupé's yellow paint stood out against the other cars. Monica approached the car and sat on the hood in silence.

Miguel followed her and sat beside her. The air was cold, but the Renault's hood was colder. He needed to talk to her but the parking lot… *If only there were silence.* Any silence was soon broken by the hum of cars that drove along the highway. Miguel thought it probably wasn't a good idea to go out. The cars' headlights lit up the sparse trees and their yellow leaves, separating them from the road. Black poplars, Miguel deduced. Pushed by the wind, their silhouettes of almost bare branches came into and went out of view, threatening like a bad omen.

"My name is Ana on my fake passport," said Monica. Miguel noticed a dry twist to her words, like sawdust. An omen. "It's because of your ex-girlfriend, isn't it?" she asked.

"I don't know, it just came into my head. That's it."

"I'm not Ana."

There was nothing left to say. She *wasn't* Ana, of course, but when she acted like that, she sure looked like her.

"You're not the same as before," she said. A car's headlights lit up the black poplars' silhouettes.

"I don't understand," said Miguel.

Monica took his hand. Hers were warm. "Miguel, getting to know this power has changed you. It's made you different. You weren't like this. Don't you see?"

"But… what are you talking about?" The trees shook their sparse leaves with a rustle. It was like they were laughing. What a dirty trick Monica used – convincing him to go there for another reprimand, so everyone could laugh at him. He jerked his hand back. "I am what I am! Before and now! Why won't you stop attacking me?"

"I'm not attacking you. I want the old Miguel back. I told you on our flight to Cairo – you're a human with the power of a god. That power has changed you. You have to get past it; it... stops you from loving."

"So I can't—?" Miguel saw Monica's crucifix glimmer in the darkness. His face split into a smile. "What about your God? Can He? Oh, of course! He is infinite love, that's why He won't let me join His club."

Monica bit her lip and frowned. Despite the darkness, Miguel could see her expression of disgust, the dip in her skin above her right eyebrow, as if Miguel had just spat his words onto her face.

"Look, Miguel," said Monica, standing up from the car and shivering from the cold, "I could explain to you why God is God and you're not, His infinite love, how we're all part of Him, all of that. But I'm not here to talk about theology."

"Then why are you here? To make me believe you want to make up with me?"

"I thought you had realized that your power is taking control of you! You don't control it! In the car you said..."

I wish I wasn't a Midas. But that had nothing to do with this. They were talking about God, and he had given up being a god for her.

"I left Operation Messiah for you."

Monica was left speechless. Her breath turned into vapour as she exhaled, against the backlight of mushroom lights. Miguel thought Monica finally understood the effort he had made, everything he had abandoned for her.

"You have to give up something more," said Monica.

"More?" Miguel replied. "What more do you want? You're messing with me! You lied to me! A romantic walk, hand in hand! Keep your hand!"

Monica took a step back. "I was wrong," she said in a whisper. "I'm sorry. I didn't want to make you believe anything."

Miguel felt the words hit him among his shouts. Monica turned and walked away. He tried to say something, but he didn't know what. He just watched her walk back along the path of mushroom lights in silence. Monica was getting farther and farther away from him. Monica left.

Another car drove along the highway. Miguel turned to the noise and once again saw the silhouette of the trees.

I didn't want to fight. Shit! he thought, talking to the trees. *Am I going crazy or what?* His mouth felt dry, as if the words he had spat at Monica had burned him as he spoke. He wondered if it was true that his power had changed him. *I'm destroying everything I touch... just like King Midas.*

The trees swayed slightly, like they were nodding.

Miguel looked down at his icy hands. The invisible cold of his power. He placed them on the hood of the car. His left hand felt slightly colder than his right on the metal. It may have been colder than he felt. With his other hand, the right one, he touched the place where Monica sat and felt the warmth from her body, still there with him. He swallowed.

That is the choice, he thought, feeling the contrast between his hands. It was obvious – his power isolated him in a world where he, all-powerful, was all alone in a cold paradise that desensitized him, numbing him and anesthetizing him with his own glory, offering him only more cold. More solitude. And there was the other world, a small, warm one that he could barely feel now. His past. Monica was in the other world. Everything wrapped in cold and power, a small source of heat in a small body. Maybe she could save him.

Another car passed by slowly, illuminating the trees for several long seconds. The wind made the black poplars nod again, making the leaves shudder. Like a great applause.

But what about the Midas abilities? And the power? he thought. *Why do I have to give it up? It's my power. I'm the only Midas-type quantum inflexor. The Midas Effect! The only one in the world. It's me.* His right hand began to go cold again. The little heat Monica had left him was almost gone.

The black poplars stopped suddenly. The cold had returned. He was the only Midas. And he was alone. *I have to get rid of this.* He looked to the trees. "Help me!" he shouted. The empty French countryside swallowed his voice. Not even an echo. Nothing but cold.

The trees nodded unanimously. *To Hell with the Midas Effect!*

Miguel concentrated as hard as he could and wished for his quantum inflexor ability to disappear. If he could do anything he imagined, then he could also get rid of his power. And the trees would help him. Aided by his imaginary giants, he kept concentrating more and more until he felt his brain begin to bubble. And then, the unmistakable pinch, sweet, unusual, in the middle of his head. The Midas Effect.

He could do it. And he felt the inflection, his brain boiling more than ever.

CHAPTER 37

Miguel opened his eyes.

When his vision focused, he saw the young receptionist from the hotel he had spoken with. Her small lips were painted a bright pink. She looked at him with wide eyes, lips parted as if she were giving him a small kiss from above, like she was floating. Her eyes were framed with dense mascara and a black fringe. Her face floated above him. She looked like an angel.

Far away, Miguel heard Monica ask what had happened along with the sound of someone running. Several people were approaching.

"He fainted," said the angel in French.

She won't understand you, thought Miguel. *Monica doesn't speak French*. He tried to sit up, but as consciousness returned to his body, he felt the weight of the morning on top of him.

Miguel gagged, his throat twisting somewhere deeper than his stomach, but he couldn't vomit. He coughed like he was trying to spit out his soul. He was freezing, his body shivering. He couldn't control his weakened muscles as they spasmed. A bitter smell, like something half-digested, hit him. A quick glance downward told him he was lying in a pool of vomit.

His head felt like it was about to explode. Like it had already exploded. *My inflexor brain*, he thought. His head was like a large crater, like the mouth of a pot, with the remains of his brain like dough, floating inside it. He wanted to touch his head, but his hand felt like a hard block of wood at the end of his arm. He could barely move. His hand took some time to reach his head. His hair was wet with vomit, but below, his skull was intact. Inside was his brain – painful but uninjured, he knew for sure.

The middle of his brain felt like someone had slashed it with dozens of razors. But nothing had happened inside. Everything was perfect. Did his ability…?

His quantum inflexor ability was also intact. He could feel it as clearly as he could feel the weight of the frost in the French countryside on his skin.

He hadn't eliminated his power. It was still there.

***

Castillo was looking at the screen of the portable monitor. In the south of France, the isoinflexor curves piled on top of one another. Barrett shuffled papers endlessly from one place to another on the meeting table in the room they had rented in the Hotel Villamagna in Madrid. "What in the world do you have to check right now?" he asked. Barrett didn't respond. He kept typing away at his laptop in a manner that seemed chaotic to Castillo, unmeasured. Vincent entered the room then.

"Are we leaving?" he asked. "Your agents are starting to get impatient."

"Just one more check! The incongruence—"

"Leave it, we're going," Castillo snapped. He began collecting the spread-out pages on the table like he was cleaning up after a party. "Help me with this, Vincent." Vincent began picking up pages too.

"But I haven't checked…" Barrett insisted. "What if it's not them? There's only one inflection here. It's strong, yes, but it's not a Midas-type. It's not strong enough; it cuts off. We might be following a false trail. What if we're getting farther away from them?"

Castillo glared at Barrett. Barrett looked back from below and removed his glasses as if Castillo was about to punch him. *Fear*, Castillo thought. He had no intention of repeating a lesson taught to rowdy children.

"We're leaving. There's nothing left to look for," he said calmly. His tone could have dissuaded a hundred Barretts from continuing with a hundred long-winded arguments. The three of them collected all of the papers and they left the room.

On the way to the car, Vincent dialled a number on his phone and gave it to Castillo. "Yes, we're leaving," Castillo said into the mouthpiece. "Bring him. Make sure he's drugged and put him in your car. I'll see you at the airport. Have you hired the jet? Good." Then he turned to Vincent. "Vincent," he said, showing him a map. They took long strides towards the hotel parking lot. "This is the area where the inflection was produced, near Narbonne. It's not a very large area, the diameter is just over five miles. Focus on main roads. Two highways cut through the area, the A9 and the A61. Start there. They could go towards Toulouse, to the west, or head north. The isoinflexor curves have remained static all night. Wherever Miguel is, he hasn't moved from there. That could be a hotel, or a town. Search the areas near the highways. And the yellow car, a European car—"

"Yes, yes. A yellow Renault Mégane Coupé with a Spanish plate…" Vincent recited.

"Find them."

Once everything had been packed into the trunk, they got into the car. Castillo opened the briefcase containing the ceramic guns to check on them. The car merged with the traffic coming from the Paseo de la Castellana Avenue. The huge trees let sunlight into the car, allowing Castillo to verify the material. He was inspecting the spring of a magazine when he suddenly noticed that Vincent was frowning. Then he pressed his lips together. His whole face tightened. "Vincent?"

"The yellow Renault. I think I have it."

Castillo straightened in his seat as Barrett braked and pulled over. Several cars honked at him.

"A town very close by, near the A9, beyond the fork towards Toulouse. Yes, it's the Renault Coupé."

"They're going north. What are they doing? Are they all together? Let's move!"

"No… They're not in the car."

"What? Find them. They won't get far. Come on, we'll search nearby buildings."

"There are only houses. Let me see, yes, there's one with lettering in the window that looks like a medical clinic. Perhaps—"

"Look inside! Surely—"

"I already am. Stop… Yes! Gorlov's inside, and Monica's beside him. Miguel… is in another room!"

"What is he doing?"

"He's lying down on a bed. He's speaking to a man in French. A doctor, I'm guessing. He's touching his head. I don't know what they're saying."

Without looking away from Vincent, Castillo fixed the knot of his tie before straightening his jacket and squeezing his hands into fists a few times. "Good, good, good. Miguel's head must be hurting from yesterday's inflection. Go back to Vladimir and Monica. What are they doing?"

"Let me see… Yes, they're sitting down. Monica has a roadmap."

"A map? Get a good look at it! What's on the map?"

"Walter, you're making me lose my concentration... The south of France, I think. Nice!" Vincent exclaimed. "Monica has her finger on Nice."

Castillo closed his eyes and touched the bandage that covered the wound on his forehead. It was the first time it had stopped hurting since Miguel escaped. He breathed slowly and looked at Barrett. "Come on, Eugene, a plane is waiting to take us to Nice. Do you feel like visiting the French Riviera?"

***

Monica found the location of the small town they were in on the map. Saint-Rémy-du-Val. It wasn't far from the cities of the French Riviera she had heard about – Marseille, Cannes, Monte Carlo, Nice.

She touched Nice on the map. It wasn't on their route. They were going further north. But she would love to see Nice. Miguel had told her so many times about his childhood adventures with Dani when they spent the summer there with his family. It was almost as if they had returned home, as if he had come to die in the place from his childhood. Monica felt her throat tighten and looked down. The countryside sun filtered through the window, illuminating the entire waiting room. It shone on the white walls of the town's small medical clinic. She folded the roadmap, intent on not getting trapped by Miguel's memories. The sunlight filled her with a happiness she couldn't really feel. She placed the folded map over her right leg, which she began to bounce.

Gorlov was by her side. Calm, very calm. She observed his long, gnarled fingers, which lay still on his lap. His legs were calm. His bony fingers gripped a plastic cup that held coffee from a machine in the waiting room. Gorlov took a drink as Monica noted the stupid, bitter smell of morning coffee, and the breakfasts she made for Miguel.

“Will he be okay?” she asked, biting her bottom lip.

Gorlov didn’t move, didn’t even look at her. He barely moved the cup away from his mouth to speak. “He’s been in there for a while,” said the scientist, keeping his eyes on the door Miguel had gone through to the consultation. “If something serious had happened to him, they would have sent him to a hospital.”

Something serious, Monica said to herself. *Like having destroyed part of his brain in an attempt to get rid of his Midas ability?* It was all her fault. Their last argument. Another tightening of her throat made her cough. Her leg began to bounce faster and her fingers began to drum on the map.

The waiting room was empty. She and Vladimir were the only ones there, along with that unnecessary sun. Miguel was alone inside, with a big-nosed French doctor who had looked at them with disdain. No one would help them. She bit her lip again.

“I have contacts in Europe,” said Gorlov suddenly, as if the silence in the sunny waiting room bothered him, too. “The old KGB.” He was still looking at the door. It was like he was watching an old movie on it about spies and soldiers. But Monica didn’t care about Vladimir’s secret agents and wars.

“We have to help Miguel,” she said.

“If I can pull the right strings, Castillo will sit in front of a war council in less than a week.”

“Will your contacts be enough?”

Gorlov looked at Monica. His enormous glasses reflected the sunlight in the waiting room the same way they used to in his office at NASA. She couldn’t see his eyes behind the gleam, but she imagined they betrayed worry, as well as a tiny amount of tension, almost imperceptible. The KGB. The CIA. They couldn't trust either of them.

"I don't know," said Gorlov.

Miguel won't be able to manage it, Monica thought. Suddenly, she remembered the restaurant in San José. Their first date. She touched her lip to wipe away some chocolate. San Francisco, her life with Miguel, their apartment. The petunias must have dried up by now. So had their love. She drummed faster on the map. Her leg wouldn't stop bouncing. They had forced him to unleash that aberration – the Midas Effect. Them. Her.

"But he wants to be rid of it. The Midas Effect," said Monica. "That could be the solution. It would be—"

"Impossible," said Gorlov. "It cannot be done."

Monica stopped drumming.

At that moment, the white door to the consultation opened and Miguel appeared, accompanied by the big-nosed French doctor. Miguel was squinting as if still in pain.

***

Dr. Miart opened the door from the consultation. Miguel squinted as the light from the waiting room illuminated his face. White walls, white door, white coat... All was white, all was light. It was unbearable.

Among the light, he spotted Monica and Gorlov sitting. They looked nervous. Gorlov looked petrified. Monica was drumming her fingers, biting her lip and bouncing her legs rhythmically. Both of them stood up as Miguel took his first step out of the consultation.

Dr. Miart wiggled his large, hawkish nose and said goodbye to Miguel with exaggerated gestures and recommendations in a thick southern accent.

"Goodbye. Thank you very much," said Miguel in French as the doctor closed the white door. Full of analgesics and showered, Miguel finally felt some warmth enter his body. But all that light… "You're driving," he said to Monica. It was obvious he wouldn't be able to drive, but it was also the only thing he wanted to say. He didn't want to talk; he was exhausted. Monica nodded.

The three of them walked to the car in silence. The car's yellow paint reflected the morning light of the French countryside so brightly it seemed to pierce his pupils. Miguel's eyes were nearly fully closed until he got into the backseat.

Gorlov sat beside him. "How is your head?" he asked once Monica had started the car.

"Better."

Monica looked at him in the rear-view mirror but said nothing. Miguel looked into her eyes. He touched the area above his ears, where it hurt most, but there was no more pain. All that existed in his head was drowsiness and discomfort that almost overwhelmed him. And anxiety. He didn't want to look into the mirror, where he might find her blue eyes at any moment. He looked at Gorlov. "I haven't become a drunk, if that's what you're thinking," said Miguel. His voice, warped from coughing and vomiting, was unconvincing.

"We didn't think—" said Monica.

Gorlov cut her off. "You weren't able to get rid of your Midas ability, correct?"

Miguel straightened. "How did you—?"

"A hangover doesn't hurt in the temporal region. You must have made a gargantuan effort, isn't that right?"

Miguel stopped touching his ears. He didn't answer. He didn't want to explain things Gorlov already knew. The Russian knew everything. His stupor intensified for a moment.

"And despite all that effort, you couldn't do it," Gorlov continued.

"I already told you no."

"I knew it," said Gorlov.

That damn scientist! Miguel wanted to sleep, not answer the Russian's self-satisfying inquiries.

"I don't understand, Vladimir," said Monica. Her eyes followed him in the mirror.

"You see," said Gorlov, touching his glasses as if moving them, but not actually moving them at all, "Miguel has discovered what Eugene and I call the Midas Paradox."

***

"What are they saying?" Castillo asked. He looked at his watch and then at the pilot's cabin of the jet. Pressing his lips together, he huffed through his nose, as if that would make the plane take off faster. "What do you see?"

Vincent, seated beside him at the window, kept his eyes closed. "Gorlov's saying something about a paradox – the Midas Paradox," he said. "Eugene knows what he's talking about. Let him tell you and let me concentrate. I could lose them."

Castillo turned around to see Roth, Kells and Smyth in the back seats with Dani leaning on them as he slept. Barrett was travelling in a seat behind him. He could wait for the damn pilot to get authorization from the damn control tower to leave the damn airport, but he wasn't about to let Barrett keep messing with him. He narrowed his eyes at him and huffed through his nose again. "What is the Midas Paradox?" he asked. "Is it that incongruence?"

Barrett looked back at him with his small, twitchy eyes above his round glasses. He cleared his throat. "No, it's an unproven theoretical postulate," he said finally. "Vladimir and I have been researching it for some time." Then he went quiet and blinked rapidly a few times. He was exasperating, giving only an eyedropper of information. The paradox, incongruence… The little man knew more traps in the Project than all the scientists in the SSR and Hampton combined.

"Eugene," said Castillo, trying to appear calm, "if you don't voluntarily tell me—"

Barrett blinked again, removing his sunglasses and immediately speaking. "The paradox is a critical point for the Midas. I didn't tell you before because it's never been studied in practice. Of course, we've never had a Midas before. We haven't found a complete system of quantum equations that explained the whole phenomenon—"

"Eugene!" Castillo warned, without shouting.

"It's very simple – a Midas reaches the paradox when they reject their power and attempt to destroy it."

Castillo felt a stab of pain in the wound on his forehead. "Destroy it?" he asked. "Can the power be destroyed?" The bandage pressed tight on the wound.

"No," said Barrett. "As with all paradoxes, it is a situation that is easy to enter but impossible to leave."

"Go on."

"A Midas can make anything they imagine a reality, providing they wish for it with sufficient intensity." Castillo nodded and touched his bandage. "They could, therefore, destroy their inflexor ability if they wanted to." Castillo loosened the knot of his tie as Barrett spoke. "But not after using their power. It's greater than their own desire. We don't believe a Midas can somehow reach the intensity of a desire strong enough to counteract the intensity of the power they're using. The mathematics tells us that the system of equations that maximizes the Midas Effect has no solution—"

Castillo lifted a finger. Barrett blinked again before continuing his explanation, without the mathematics.

"The paradox is like this: the more the Midas wants to destroy their power, the more power they need to do it. And the more power they get, the more they need, and so on. It is a vicious cycle. There is no answer to this – the answer is that a Midas can destroy their own power, but they can't make themselves do it. They can and they can't—a true paradox."

Castillo looked up and to the left, searching for the understanding he needed. "Are you sure?" he asked after taking a few breaths. "I don't see why they can't destroy their power. I can imagine it perfectly."

"You don't have that power. No, you can't imagine it because you haven't felt it. Maybe you're visualizing it like a comic hero or something. But an inflexor is a person, not an unshakeable cardboard superhero. They can't wish to be rid of the power of a god. They don't have that ability; it's greater than them. Vladimir and I started to formulate it, and—"

"Okay, okay, forget the formulas." Castillo turned to the cabin door. Why was the damn jet not taking off? He looked back to Barrett. "I admit that a Midas is incapable of destroying their ability – the math, all of that – but tell me, why would they want to? That's what I don't get?"

"There are no concrete reasons, although there could be many. In general, they're related to what happened to the mythological King Midas." The jet began to move, which mitigated some of Castillo's headache. At least it was finally moving. "The idea – and this is just an idea – is that someone with the power of a Midas is very likely to become unhappy, because they can't control their impulses and this produces uncalculated harm. It's like what happened to King Midas, who turned even his drinking water into gold: an imperfect wish. They become a mutant, a misunderstood weirdo who can only live isolated from the rest of the world. The best thing they can do is separate themselves so they don't hurt anyone with a weapon they constantly wield. They have the power of a god, but not the psychology of one, whatever that is. They're a person. The human psyche has no capacity for administering, never mind understanding, such power." Barrett's eyes bulged. He seemed to be proud of his explanation. It was one of the few coherent explanations Castillo had ever heard from him. "I don't know, there are a thousand reasons. We're all happy with a given degree of power. Some have a lot, some have less, but having more than we want makes us unhappy. No, we haven't found a single theorem that establishes that a Midas is destined for unhappiness, but sooner or later, they could be. And then they'll reject their power. And if they do, the Midas Paradox stops them from ridding themselves of it. But none of this has been empirically demonstrated."

The jet arrived at the take-off strip. Castillo turned in his seat with his back to Barrett, and fastened his seatbelt. He thought about what the scientist had just explained to him. The discomfort he felt caused him to start fidgeting. Finally, he turned back to Barrett. "Eugene, Miguel has already arrived at the Midas Paradox, hasn't he?"

"If Vladimir is telling him about it, yes. I suppose he has. That would also explain that strange inflection we picked up tonight." Barrett looked down at his papers, his latest data. "We have to study this inflection," he said. "Nothing makes sense here. A paradox. Miguel must be in bad shape…"

Castillo thought he sounded sincere. But he was in bad shape too. Everyone, he thought, would be in bad shape if Miguel was destroying his ability. He settled into his seat as the plane began taking off. If they were wrong about the paradox…

Castillo felt the jolt of the jet's acceleration pushing him back against his seat. He knew if Miguel could do it, he would certainly destroy his ability.

***

"You cannot do it," said Gorlov.

Monica braked and everyone leaned back. Miguel watched as the acceleration dropped from one hundred and eighty kilometers per hour. He guessed Monica had lost awareness of how fast they were going, absorbed in Gorlov's explanation of the Midas Paradox. Another new misfortune. He was tired. This was all so tiring.

"But it hasn't been proven yet," the Russian added. "If they leave us alone for a few months, we could research it. We have a Midas for testing: you. And we have Monica, our best analyst. Perhaps, with the right measures, I think I can manage something…"

Miguel could no longer fight the drowsiness or the scientist's unshakeable, sour gaze. He closed his eyes. At least Gorlov's unconditional hope was comforting. That, and the analgesics the doctor had given him.

"Somewhere hidden and some basic measures," Gorlov repeated. "That's where we're going."

"Can we get what we need in Germany?" Monica asked?

"Shh! They could be listening. We're not going to Germany."

Miguel heard the last snippets of conversation mixed into his dreams. The paradox. He was Schrödinger's cat. Dead and alive. He could destroy his ability, and he couldn't. A quantum matter wave equation made his black fur stand on end. Dead and alive at the same time. A quantum paradox. A demigod. *Siegfried kills the dragon and becomes invincible after bathing in its blood, except for one place that is left uncovered. Like Achilles, more or less. Siegfried wasn't a cat. He was a Norman, or something like that. Achilles is immortal, but he has a vulnerable heel because his mother didn't think to fully submerge him in the Styx. Achilles was Greek, like Midas. Or was Midas Phrygian? That's more or less Greek. Or Persian? A Persian cat. Do all superheroes have a weakness? Is absolute power weakness in a man? What about in a cat? A cat in a box can be alive and dead at the same time, Schrödinger said so.* Miguel had just enough time to mentally thank Gorlov with a meow for telling Monica to be quiet. But he knew asking Monica to be quiet wasn't out of deference to his mythological, quantum, Chinese dream… What had Vladimir said about them listening?

Miguel succumbed to sleep.

CHAPTER 38

The jet landed on French soil and Castillo felt the knot of his tie finally loosen, no longer choking him. The bandage on his forehead had loosened as well. In just under two hours, the plane they had hired in Madrid had brought them to Nice. They would find Miguel in no time, he thought, as he unbuckled his seatbelt. "Let's go!" he said, turning back to look at his group of followers: Barrett, Smith, Vincent, and the two agents that were taking care of Daniel.

Vincent was the last to leave the plane. He opened his eyes as he descended the mobile staircase.

"You won't lose them?" Castillo asked.

"They've just changed course, near Avignon," said Vincent. He closed his eyes again and grabbed Barrett's arm to guide him.

"Avignon?" Castillo said.

"They're not coming here, Walter. We got it wrong, with Monica's finger on the map. They're going north."

Castillo grabbed a map from Roth, looking at the roads and calculating that Miguel's Renault was just two hours away. That was longer than it would take to leave the airport and hire some cars. It wasn't much of an advantage.

"You have to talk to Miguel when he wakes up," said Castillo, looking at his watch. "They're two hours away. Hurry."

Vincent opened his eyes again and looked at Castillo. Barrett observed the two of them above his round glasses.

"Let's go, Walter," Barrett intervened. "Don't pressure him. He already knows what he has to do."

"They're only two hours ahead of us," said Vincent.

"We can't relax," Castillo responded. "Vladimir has some sort of plan."

Vincent closed his eyes again before taking Barrett's arm. Everyone continued walking along the platform that led to the airport. "I have them again," said Vincent after a few steps. "The yellow Renault, highway to the north. Impossible to miss."

Castillo raised a hand and everyone stopped. "Kells," he said, addressing the agent who was carrying Daniel, "stay here with Daniel in Nice. Find somewhere discrete." Daniel was looking at him with a dopey smile caused by the drug from the darts. Castillo looked at everyone else, ready to follow his orders. Even Smith looked at him attentively with his square face. "Smith, Vincent and I will go in the first car. Eugene and Roth are in the second. Roth, you're in charge of the diplomatic bag and the guns."

They all walked briskly to the platform of the airport parking lot.

Half an hour later, Castillo's group travelled in two all-terrain Volvos at the highest legal speed along the French highway. They were the most robust cars Castillo could hire. He would have used Humvees or even tanks if he could. Two hundred miles of road separated him and Miguel. "Faster, Smith," he said. Smith sped up.

"He's waking up," said Vincent, without opening his eyes.

Castillo looked at the telepath. "You already know what to say to him."

***

Miguel opened his eyes, blinked, and saw Gorlov looking out the window, as expressionless as ever behind his antique glasses.

"What did you just say?" Miguel asked as he rubbed his eyes.

Gorlov turned to him. "I didn't say anything."

"I thought… How long was I asleep? Where are we?"

"A few hours," said Monica. "We've just crossed the Rhine. We're already in Germany."

Gorlov's eyes narrowed minutely – an enormous gesture for him. "Did you hear someone calling you?" he asked, his Russian accent thick now.

Monica looked into the rear-view mirror. "What's wrong, Vladimir?"

"They have found us," he answered.

Miguel tried to sit up in his seat, as if then he would be better able to defend himself.

"He was waiting for him," continued Gorlov. "They must have been following the inflection from yesterday."

Traffic flowed smoothly along the highway, with cars scattered sporadically in front of them. Miguel looked through the back window. No one seemed to be following them.

"They're not here," said Gorlov. Miguel looked at him with lips parted. "They must have used an inflexor with extrasensory perception, a preceptor, to find us," he explained. "And now they have a telepath trying to talk to you."

Miguel quickly closed his mouth, as if the telepath would try to enter his head through it.

"If you've heard him, that means he tried the intrusion technique during the phase between sleep and waking," said Gorlov.

"What do I do? I don't hear anything."

"I suppose he's waiting for you to let him enter your mind. You should talk to him. If they've found us, we can no longer prevent them from following us. We should find out what they want."

Monica looked at Miguel through the mirror. Her wide, blue eyes looked afraid. She nodded twice.

Miguel concentrated. He closed his eyes.

A prickling feeling ran over his brain and he opened his eyes again. He remembered the inflection from the night before. He could not bear that pain again. "After what happened yesterday… I…"

"You don't need to generate a large inflection," said Gorlov. "It will be enough to imagine your mind opening to whoever wants to talk to you. The same thing you did when Vincent spoke to you the first time you went down into the SSR basement. You barely need to concentrate. Relax."

"I'm trying to relax…"

Hello, Miguel. This is Vincent. Miguel heard his voice inside his head.

"It's Vincent," said Miguel. Gorlov blinked as if to say, *I guessed as much.*

What do you want, Vincent?

We know where you are. Please, stop the car and let's talk. We're about sixty miles behind you, on the A36 to Mulhouse.

"They're behind us. They haven't crossed the border yet. We still have an advantage on them, but they know our location. Vincent wants us to wait for them."

Monica kept her gaze on Miguel through the mirror. Gorlov said nothing. Miguel waited a moment for some instructions but no one seemed to want to speak. He felt uncomfortable opening his thoughts to the telepath.

Why should we wait for you? We're running away from you.

Because we have Dani.

Miguel sat up straight in his seat and inhaled sharply, as if he had been winded. Dani's scarred earlobe filled his thoughts. Then he imagined Vincent entering through the ear wound and into his brother's head.

"Stop the car, Monica!" he shouted.

"What?! I can't stop here!"

"Yes, you can! I said stop!"

Monica looked at Gorlov. He nodded and she turned on her hazard lights.

"They have Dani," said Miguel as they pulled into a lane on the right.

If you do anything to Dani, I will find you and I will kill every one of you. Do you hear me, Vincent? The car came to a stop, and Miguel could just about feel a slight pulse in Vincent's mind. Fear.

You should wait for us. We need to talk.

Miguel was already prepared to confront Gorlov. He guessed Gorlov would not want to wait there, that Dani didn't matter to him. He was already opening his mouth to argue when Gorlov spoke. "We will wait. Do you hear me, Vincent?" he yelled, looking upwards at nowhere in particular, like he was talking to a ghost.

Miguel looked at him strangely, as if he hadn't understood a single word. Gorlov wanted to stop. What was he planning?

***

"He's setting a trap for us," said Castillo once Vincent had told him what Gorlov had said.

"So what do we do?" Vincent asked.

"We'll go where they tell us. Keep watching them. Keep an eye on Gorlov. I want to know what he's planning. *We* will set a trap for *them*."

Castillo looked at John Smith, who drove the Volvo in silence. He looked incapable of moving even to turn the steering wheel, like a plastic driver in a toy car. A robot. Castillo looked at the muscular folds of his neck. Then he looked back. The other all-terrain vehicle, driven by Roth, followed them closely.

"Stop at that gas station," Castillo told Smith. "We need to make a plan."

The muscles in Smith's face moved like he was trying to smile, but he didn't.

Fine. If you like action, Castillo thought, *you'll do more than just watch me and my men*. "Vincent, tell Gorlov not to go anywhere public. I already know that trick. I don't want to meet anywhere where there are too many people and police to see us take out our guns. Somewhere quiet, that's what I want. Better if there's no one around for miles."

Vincent stayed quiet. His eyes were closed, but he moved them as if he were reading subtitles on his eyelids.

The Volvo pulled into a gas station and the second all-terrain did the same.

"Gorlov says to meet him in the Black Forest. He asks if that will work."

"That old, twisted Bolshevik! So, he thinks he's Robin Hood and wants to set a trap for me in the forests? Tell him yes!"

CHAPTER 39

Miguel's yellow Mégane continued for a few more miles down the highway parallel to the Rhine. After passing by Freiburg, they took a detour to the northeast along a secondary road that led to the forest. They slowly passed through towns that got smaller and smaller, the farms scarcer and scarcer, as they continued down a road that snaked between the hills. Miguel expected some secret signal from Gorlov, some kind of indication of his plan. But the scientist fell asleep.

Bad timing, Miguel thought. *Always bad timing. Now he's asleep.*

Miguel looked at him a few more times to see if he would wake up but stopped when he knew Gorlov wouldn't. Asleep like that, he looked like the old man he truly was. Miguel looked at his face. The pale light of dusk shone over his wrinkles. His face had softened, like sleep was the only time his face could lose that unchanging tension, that forced expression he always wore. Miguel felt a sudden stab of pity for Gorlov. He had dedicated his whole life to a project he now had to destroy. Did he really have to destroy it? Yes, if he wanted to live and save the planet from Walter's control. He would have to destroy the Project, every part of it. Gorlov had never described it that way, and he probably never would, but he knew there was no other solution. With or without the paradox, the Midas Effect and all inflexors had to be eradicated from the Earth. Miguel may have been a vain, naïve man who had let himself get carried away with promises and childhood dreams, but he was no fool.

Gorlov slept, his head knocking softly against the left window. Whatever his plans were, if he had any, would never leave his lips. They would barely leave his thoughts. Not with Vincent listening.

Does Vincent ever sleep? Miguel wondered. He supposed that Walter must have had him drugged up to prevent him from sleeping, so he could watch them constantly. Walter was capable of anything. Monica veered off the road slightly and the Mégane's back seat jumped as it hit a branch, causing Gorlov and Miguel's heads to painfully hit their respective windows.

"I'm sorry," said Monica. She looked in the mirror and then back out at the road. "I got distracted. I'm a little tired."

"We're here," said Gorlov, sitting up in his seat.

Walter is capable of anything, Miguel repeated to himself. He had Dani. That cheater had pretended to worry about his brother and the only thing he wanted was to use him. Kidnap him. Like he had done to Miguel, to everyone. Miguel saw his smile in his head. He was a hyena who had fooled everyone. No, he had only truly deceived Miguel. How stupid he had been! *Walter, you goddamn son of a bitch!* Miguel squeezed his hands into fists and began scratching his palms. He tightened them until he felt his fingers burn and his brain start to bubble.

At that moment, they drove into a tiny village. In the center was a church with a narrow, angular, black roof. Protestants? More gods. Miguel stretched out his hands to stop the scratching. *Destroy them all!*

No, he couldn't do that. No more inflection. He had to distract himself, stop his desires from firing off before he started killing. At least, he thought, until he got Dani back. He tried to stop thinking about the punches, the scrapes, the bloody wounds on his cheek, and instead thought about the scenery.

Endless forests showed their silver firs, spread out and blackened from the approaching night and its shadows. Shadows and silence. Monica didn't speak either. He had tried to say something to her a short time after Gorlov fell asleep, but she reminded him that Vincent was listening. Yes, sinister Vincent was ruining everything. His presence broke any intimacy. The gothic angel looked scary again.

Another two-faced liar, thought Miguel, fighting to keep the image of Vincent's perfect face, marred by his split, bleeding cheek, out of his mind. The scenery beyond the headlights was very dark. Just like Vincent. And they were heading straight into the darkness. Suddenly, Miguel remembered Dani and the silver firs showed him their sharp, oily teeth, like the roof spires of a church, devouring their enemies. Miguel fought again against those images, against his inner monster. Were they there yet?

In that instant, Monica slowed down and stopped the car near a ditch. In front of them was a small gas station with a white sign that read "Mühlenbach." The sign's arrow pointed to a forest path. Monica took out a map and began unfolding it.

The rustle of the paper seemed to awaken Gorlov. His face immediately regained its hardness, like a spring returning to its natural state. "Yes," said Gorlov, adjusting his glasses to look at the sign. "It's over there."

Monica began to drive down the path. Miguel stared at Gorlov, who was awake now. He waited for a secret sign that Vincent wouldn't notice to give Miguel some idea of what to do.

"I know this place," said Gorlov instead of giving signals. "I used to come here and take walks when I lived in Freiburg. I worked there for just under a year, right before I went to California. The Max Planck Institute, Albert Ludwig University. Thousands of students in the city. The ideal place for research, but the winter was too long for Irina. She was still alive then."

Miguel had never heard him talk about his wife. Monica hadn't told him much either. It was likely that Gorlov hadn't told Monica anything either. Maybe with the threat of death looming so near, the three of them staring down the barrel of Castillo's gun, the old Russian was going soft.

"She died shortly after we got to Germany," Gorlov went on. He looked sad, but Miguel couldn't pinpoint how. "Miguel," he said, looking at his face, "you don't need to kill anyone else. You just need to save your brother, and you can't do that if you kill them."

Miguel looked back silently. He noticed their heads oscillating back and forth, like two roly-poly toys swaying with the uneven surface of the path. It seemed so unimportant, the two of them, so ridiculous compared to the CIA.

"They're going to try and trap me with the darts full of that drug they had in Egypt," said Miguel. "Dani's the bait, right?"

"Yes, I suppose that's Walter's plan," Gorlov answered. He seemed calm, leaning back in his seat. "If they point one of those ceramic guns at you…" He took out his own from the pocket of his jacket and handed it to Miguel. "Concentrate on his darts, on their contents. Turn it into a physiological serum…"

Serum? thought Miguel. *That's all?*

"… that way, if they hit you with a dart, it will just inject you with an innocuous substance. You can do it, you've turned lead into gold. The drug will be much easier. You know the composition of a physiological serum, don't you? Distilled water with a solution of sodium chloride of 0.09%. NaCl—"

"I know the formula for salt perfectly well!" Miguel snapped.

Gorlov looked at him in silence for a few moments. Then he said, "Don't try anything more complicated than a simple transmutation of elements or you'll bring about a disaster. Remember the attacker in San José. Hurricane Laura. No more lightning bolts. Think of the yellow pages we used in the experiments in the SSR. The instructions are to turn the drug into saltwater."

Like parting the Red Sea, Miguel thought.

"The gas light just turned on," said Monica. Miguel could see the tiny orange light on the dashboard. "Do we have enough left? Maybe we should turn back and go to the gas station we saw earlier, at the path entrance."

"No," said Gorlov. "We're not turning back. I don't want to meet Castillo in a place with people. We're already nearly there."

Miguel calculated they had about fifty kilometers of gas left. Getting lost in an uninhabited forest without fuel in the middle of a German winter would be a stupid way to die. They would have to wait for Castillo to find them. Dani was trapped, and they were defenseless. None of it made sense.

"Over there!" said Gorlov, touching Monica's shoulder. "Take that path. There's a clearing with a small prairie at the end. It will be perfect. I used to go there with Irina..." He sat back against his seat and looked out the window. "They were such a happy few months..."

"I won't let them hurt Dani," said Miguel.

"I know," Gorlov answered. "That's why we're stopping."

That's why I'm stopping. He kept his gaze stubbornly on Gorlov. It must have bothered him, because the Russian finally turned to him.

"Vincent sees everything we do and hears everything we say," said Gorlov. "He always knows where we are. It would make no sense to run away. It's better if we hear what they have to say."

Miguel waited before speaking. When it became clear Gorlov would say no more, he asked, "That's it?"

"That's it."

"But shit, don't you have a plan?"

"I already told you Vincent is listening to us," Gorlov replied. "It's here," he said suddenly. "Monica, park the car just beyond the stream." Then he looked at Miguel and said, "I trust you. Don't forget that you are a Midas. You can do everything. *Everything*. Protect yourself with the serum and don't kill anyone. That's it."

The path entered a clearing in the forest. The headlights of the car illuminated an almost circular plain, with high walls formed by silver firs and the ground covered in grass. A stream crossed the clearing, cutting it almost diametrically. A log cabin to the right, beside the trees, suggested that the area was popular among hikers. It was probably some kind of shelter. It must have been cold out. A German winter, Miguel thought, grabbing Dani's parka.

They crossed the river at its narrowest point, which was only large enough to let a car pass. Monica turned the car and left the path, parking it on the grass with the headlights pointing to where they had entered.

Miguel felt his palms itch but he tried not to scratch them. Instead, he crossed his arms and looked at the bridge. It could be an exchange point for spies, if they wanted to exchange Dani for him. Or maybe it was a step, an advantage of the enemy on the battlefield, with the stream as some ridiculous line of defense.

Don't kill anyone, Vladimir had said. Dani kidnapped and in Castillo's clutches. They were coming for him. *I'll kill whoever I want!*

CHAPTER 40

Almost an hour after they had arrived to the clearing in the forest, a car's headlights emerged from between the trunks of the firs. Monica squinted to keep the light out of her eyes. *That must be them*, she thought. Walter and his men. Just one car. The enemy.

Judging by the position of the headlights, very high off the ground, the vehicle looked like an all-terrain, but it moved slowly along the path as if its occupants were afraid the car might hit quicksand. The light from the headlights was broken up by the forest into irregular, ever-changing beams, like it came from the great beyond. Monica felt the hairs on the back of her neck stand up, and she unfastened the last button on the wool jacket she had bought in France. It was very cold in the forest. She looked to the left. There was Miguel. His fury was more terrifying than anything that could possibly come from the underworld. She shivered again.

She looked to the right, at Vladimir. He and Miguel stood on either side of her. The three of them stood in a row facing the bridge they would have to defend. Behind them, the lights from Miguel's small European car were like an infantile attempt to blind their adversary. She and Gorlov gripped the small white guns. They looked like children holding silver toy guns facing Rommel and all the Panzers of the Afrika Korps. Vladimir was the only one who knew how to shoot, but he never stopped fiddling with his gun. He would be dismantling it and putting it back together before long. Monica thought about saying something but decided to leave him alone.

She closed her eyes and visualized the forest around them in her head. She could practice extrasensory perception with small effort. She and Miguel, the two of them together, were strong. That was their true weapon. She remembered the moment the lightning came in San José, the storm, and for a moment, she felt herself grow, like she could crush that entire army with one step. They weren't holding toy guns.

But really, it was Miguel who would be doing nearly everything. Monica shivered again. A god and a demon. She turned up the collar of her jacket and looked at Miguel.

She observed his profile, his brown half-mane almost backlit by the Renault's headlights. It was like seeing him at sunrise at the Golden Gate Bridge, at the lookouts in Granada, his eyes half-closed as if he were sleeping standing up. His profile against the dying light of day. Monica caught his scent of honey and old oak, a mix of warm home and sex that one day had pushed her to him. The headlights illuminated the fog from his breath. Miguel zipped up the parka his brother had given him and shuddered. The tip of Monica's nose was freezing. She smiled when she saw Miguel shiver.

"Are you looking at me?" Miguel asked, eyes closed. He smiled too.

"Are *you* looking at *me*?" she responded.

"Yes. Stop distracting me. I need to watch over the car." He shivered again. "It's so cold here."

"It looks like a light from the great beyond," said Monica. "Walter's car."

"Well, it's from this planet."

"I'm cold too. And scared." Monica's voice was soft, like she was talking to the aerospace engineer she had fallen in love with in San José.

Miguel turned and looked at her with wide eyes, as if her voice had startled him. Monica felt the weight of his gaze. It was him, the aerospace engineer. He had returned.

"I love you," Monica said before turning to face the lights coming down the path. "I don't want us to die or turn into zombies without you knowing that."

The all-terrain came into the clearing and shone its light onto the Renault. The trees lit up as if it were daytime.

***

The lights blinded him. Miguel squinted.

Monica was coming back to him. Or was she just afraid to die? What did it matter? He loved her, and he could show her he had overcome the damn Midas Effect. But not now. Now they had to defend themselves. Defeat Walter! He felt euphoric.

He just had to put an end to Walter and the others, and he had to save Dani. Then, everything would be fine. His palms itched. It was so cold. He was lucky to have brought Dani's parka with him. It still smelled like him. How would Miguel save him? Gorlov had told him he could do it. Gorlov and Monica had just taught him how to use perception. It was easy. If Vincent could do it, he could too, they said. He just had to concentrate.

"It's a Volvo. A big all-terrain," said Miguel when he saw them in his mind. "Inside are Walter, Vincent, and Eugene. They don't have Dani!"

"Calm down," said Gorlov. "They wouldn't risk bringing him if they planned on using him to negotiate. Concentrate. Physiological serum."

"I don't see anything in the forest," said Monica as she opened her eyes.

The all-terrain stopped before it got to the bridge.

"Keep looking," Gorlov told Monica. "Close your eyes and look. Search in the forest. There has to be more of them. Dani could be with the others."

Miguel watched as three people got out of the Volvo. The vehicle's headlights still dazzled Miguel. His thoughts searched out Castillo easily. He had a bandage on his head and a white gun. Vincent was armed as well, and he looked at Miguel even from that distance. Vincent was about a hundred and fifty feet away, but he looked at Miguel as if they were at a table sitting across from one another with his straight, pale features. Barrett didn't have a gun.

"Just three of them," said Miguel.

"Turn off the lights!" Gorlov shouted.

No one responded. Castillo and his men walked toward them, and they didn't seem to want to listen. Did having Dani give them that much confidence? Miguel began to feel his pulse throb in his temple. He began scratching his palms. *Water and sodium chloride, 0.09%. Water and sodium chloride, 0.09%*, he repeated to himself. *That's all it is. Water and sodium chloride...*

"We just want to talk! We are unarmed!" Castillo shouted back, lifting his hands. The car's headlights blinded them, their beams shining several feet off the ground. The only thing to do was to look up to avoid the pain from that light.

"He has a dart gun," said Miguel. "Vincent has another one." He looked up. He could see them with his mind as his eyes defocused on some less painful point above. There he could concentrate much more. *Water and sodium chloride*, he repeated. The enormous trees around him were like a Roman arena. Miguel imagined spectators in the high copse of the firs, shouting at him with their thumbs pointed down. It mustn't have been as cold in Rome. Miguel thought about Vincent and his face struck him as that of an obscene, disturbed emperor, wrapped up in togas and furs. One of three silhouettes on the other side of the bridge. He was armed with a white gun full of drugs for him. Miguel didn't want to look over there; he already knew what they were doing. Drugs. Darts.

Water and sodium chloride. Water and...

"Miguel!" Castillo's silhouette shouted. "Come closer!"

Water and sodium chloride...

"No one's going anywhere!" Gorlov shouted back.

Miguel closed his eyes and saw the water molecules and ions of sodium and chloride floating through the liquid in a solution at 0.09%. It was easy. The ions moved.

"We have your brother!" said Castillo.

I know that, Miguel thought. *Chloride and sodium, ions in the water...*

"You know this war will have casualties, but it can all be avoided!"

Sodium chloride...

"Dani will die if we don't reach an agreement!"

Dani!

The ions disappeared from his head and his nails dug into his palms. Miguel felt the vein in his temple throb like a small metal hammer inside his head. His right foot took a step, as if his body had decided to move by itself.

"There's someone on our left!" Monica screamed. Her voice mixed with one, two, three, four, five, six... several muffled gunshots, almost compressed. White guns. In the forest, to the left, beyond the log cabin.

The composition of the physiological serum had gone. Miguel erased Dani from his mind as fast as he could and looked for the darts that were aimed at them. *Water and—*

A dart, two, three, four, five hit his body like needles. All of them administered their substance. Miguel felt pain, cold.

And a solution of sodium chloride dispersed in his bloodstream.

He looked at Monica, who was staring at him with a frown, her head lolling. She had a dart sticking out of her neck and another in her arm. "They didn't drug me," she said. "But they got Vladimir."

More shots sounded to the left. This time, Miguel located them and transformed them quickly. Two more needles struck his leg and his hip. Miguel grimaced. Those damn wasps… To the right, Miguel saw Gorlov staring at the sky with a dopey smile as if he had gone mad. They must have hit him with an untransformed dart.

Four more shots, this time from in front, from the light from the great beyond coming from the damn Volvo. Two more shots from the left. Monica threw herself to the ground. Three shots from the right.

From the right? Miguel wondered as he hit the ground. More darts whistled as they flew over his head, and he heard others collide with Gorlov. Muffled thuds against his body. *How much of the drug will he resist?* He saw Monica roll to the Mégane. Two darts hit the body of the car above her head with a metallic crash.

Miguel rolled too. The shots multiplied. Three from the right. He couldn't transform so many moving objects. Four from the left. The darts crashed around him and Monica. Two from in front. He managed to transform one just before it hit his shoulder. Another needle. The storm of needles fell around them as the all-terrain continued to blind them. Several more darts hit the yellow Renault Coupe. They would leave holes, he knew. Miguel picked up Dani's scent again on his parka. He couldn't see anything, just darts flying and ions of chloride and sodium.

"I'm with you," Monica whispered. Miguel felt a little stronger with the impulse of her inflection.

"Okay." Miguel could say no more. Another dart transformed. Another needle. In his neck. Another. More shots. Dani. The light from the all-terrain. Another dart hitting the yellow bodywork. Three darts hitting Monica's torso, her eyes squeezed shut in pain. Dani. They would kill him. His parka smelled like him. More darts flying, from the right, from in front. Four shots from the left. Frozen soil. His hands burned. Monica covering her head with her arms. Another needle and…

To hell with all of them!

The headlights of Miguel's Mégane turned off suddenly and the Volvo flew into the air with its ghostly light, flipping in mid-air like a giant's marble.

The last three darts hit the Mégane – one, two, three crashes, and then nothing. The Roman arena fell silent as the all-terrain turned in the air, illuminating the treetops, the last brushes, where the citizens of Rome pointed their thumbs down. Death.

The silence was so intense that, while the all-terrain spun in the air, the only noise was the tinkling flow of the stream, as if at that moment, the clearing was a pastoral picnic area, perfect for new lovers, instead of a battlefield.

Miguel lay on the ground, fists and eyes closed tight. Clenched. Tense. Still.

Only a few seconds passed before the black Volvo crashed back to Earth on the left side of the clearing, very close to the cabin, with an explosion loud enough for an army. It flattened the firs as if its flight could not have been stopped by even the sturdiest trunks.

The light from the all-terrain disappeared suddenly and Miguel rose up from the ground with his right arm, his fingers splayed out in front of him.

After the crash came the clamorous silence from the Roman spectators. Miguel looked up at the stands. Each and every single Roman was looking at him, illuminated now only by the moon, shadow covering most of their pale faces. Their thumbs stayed pointed down.

Then Miguel looked in front of him and saw the scattered, unmoving silhouettes of Barrett, Castillo, and Vincent. Immediately, he pointed at them with his extended hand and the three of them flew up into the air before colliding with three thick trunks, like Napoleonic cannons. Those gladiators could very well be decapitated on those three columns, Miguel thought. Or crucified. Why not? They hung there, their feet about six feet off the ground like they had been placed on hooks.

Miguel mentally searched for whoever had shot at them from the left. He didn't know if he would find them alive. He didn't care. Yes, they were alive. *The son of a bitch somehow survived*, he thought. *Let's see you survive this.*

At that moment, a man with a gun flew into the air, smashing into dense foliage that whipped him. He hit another trunk, hanging there like his companions. He appeared to be unconscious.

Miguel walked forward with his right hand extended in front of him towards the piled-up bodies of his enemies. He stopped on the small bridge. The moon gave them little light, but Miguel could see them clearly. Four bodies that could become four crucifixions. If he was a new god, he would have more crucifixions than the old gods, right? He half-smiled. The only sound was the stream.

"Miguel," Monica whispered behind him.

He didn't want to hear her. He only wanted to think about his work.

"Miguel!"

Miguel turned around to face her.

She looked terrified, her eyes wide and her tense brow furrowed. She looked like she was waiting for Miguel to pounce on her and eat her. "You look like a madman. You're not yourself," said Monica. Miguel felt his face relax. The muscles in his jaw ached, as did his teeth. From all the grinding, probably. The monster. It had returned. "Did you kill them?"

"No."

"They're not breathing."

Miguel remembered he had mentally caught them by the neck. They couldn't breathe, but he didn't think about that when he picked them up. The neck had seemed like a good place to grab. Excellent. The monster came closer.

Miguel concentrated and made the gladiators' arms and legs wrap around the trees without letting their bodies abandon their positions, with their backs plastered to the trees. He did it one by one, with no hurry. Now they looked like skydivers with huge fir-shaped parachutes. Ridiculous. He half-smiled again. Everyone except the unconscious man looked at him in panic.

Terror, right? Miguel thought. Then he let them breathe. The silence was broken by sudden gasps for air, convulsive coughs, almost agonizing whistles from congested lungs, sobs…

Sobs? Miguel paused. *Who's sobbing?*

It was Vincent.

Miguel neared him. There, crying, Vincent no longer instilled any fear. He looked like a weakling, hanging there, gasping between sobs. A whinging fish just taken out of water. Then Miguel smelled the strain of fear in Vincent's body. His sphincter must have ceded to terror; his legs and the tree trunk were covered in his waste. The smell of it mingled with the smell of baby soap, which was clearer now as if trying to mask the fear. *A child*, Miguel thought. Vincent's trembling gave him away.

"Don't kill them," said Monica.

I won't kill them, Miguel told himself. He felt much better now that he could think. The monster was retreating. Vincent's terror, it seemed, had satisfied him.

Monica touched his shoulder and pointed to Gorlov. "Wake him up," she said. "He'll know what to do."

Miguel turned and looked at the scientist, who was still looking up at the stars with an idiotic smile from the drug.

"You... can't... kill... us!" Castillo's words were broken up by spasmic coughs that wracked through him like they were trying to turn his lungs inside out. "In... an hour... they'll kill your brother. If I don't..." Another cough interrupted him.

Dani! Miguel recalled suddenly. Now he was in total control over his enemies. And over the monster, too. But they didn't know he had the monster under control. That gave him an idea – terror. "I'm going to kill you all!" he bellowed, straining his voice so they would hear him.

"If you... kill me, they'll kill... Dani," said Castillo.

Monica was pulling on his arm from behind. Miguel wanted to tell her he was pretending, but no matter how quiet he made his voice, Vincent would hear them. He managed an appropriately enraged face – a tight frown, a clenched jaw, grinding teeth. He said, "Which one do you think I should start off with, Monica?"

"No, please, Miguel."

Miguel cast his wrathful gaze over the row of his enemies. They looked like a little impaled army. The scene had all the cruelty Miguel needed. It would terrify them. He looked for a victim among them. The man he didn't recognize was still unconscious. Barrett would do, but he probably didn't know everything Miguel needed. Castillo… Castillo was untouchable. It didn't seem logical to kill the person who had all the information first. Vincent! He would do nicely. There he was, hanging on his tree, impaled, crucified on its trunk between Barrett and Castillo, the stench of his fear and his bowel movements ruining his scent of baby soap.

"I'll start with Vincent," Miguel announced, speaking to the spectators of the Roman arena. Then he looked at Vincent. "I'm sick of you and your telepathic intrusions." Miguel hesitated, not knowing how to continue his performance. His own voice sounded like an imposter's. Could Vincent read his mind? No, clearly he couldn't. Vincent was terrified. "And I'm sick of you watching us!" Miguel added. "You won't know what we're doing ever again," he said, gritting his teeth as he spoke. That last sentence seemed much more confident and dramatic. He lifted his right hand and splayed his tense fingers as far as they would go, like a magician trying to cast a horrible spell on his enemy. It ended up looking like an entirely too dramatic gesture to Miguel.

At that moment, Vincent burst into a fit of crying and screaming. The mind-reading gothic angel, who once terrified everyone with his ethereal, sinister face, now begged for mercy. Miguel concentrated and created a ring of water vapor around Vincent's tree right at his neck. He knew special effects such as that would not generate significant residual inflection. Now he could think about those details and control them. Controlling his power would bring Dani back to him, he told himself. Gorlov was sure of it.

Miguel closed the ring of vapor around Vincent's neck. The waxing gibbous moon cast light on the firs where Vincent and the others hung. The moonlight made the ring of vapor glow, made it sway softly, thin and flat, its edges sharp like a scythe, giving it a spectral appearance… *Like the skin of death itself*, Miguel thought. He bit his lip to stop himself from smiling. That *would* do nicely. "Goodbye, Vincent," he said. But Walter appeared to have no intention of saving his henchman's life. He wasn't afraid of the ring of death either.

"He won't… kill you," said Castillo. His voice was starting to return to him. "He's already… controlled his fury."

Fucking pig, Miguel thought. It wouldn't be that easy, frightening a CIA agent. He could still kill Vincent for real. Who would miss him? Not Miguel, obviously. Castillo would learn. The monster. Miguel would set it free if his trick didn't work. He clenched his fists and began scratching his palms furiously. Monica was still tugging his arm. She was abandoning him, the impulse of her amplifying inflection losing its intensity, vanishing. Vincent's black eyes widened considerably when he saw the ring of vapor around his neck. He seemed to be the only one who saw the monster. He had always seen so much.

Then Vincent began vomiting up ideas. "Not me, kill Walter!" he yelled between sobs. "Get inside his head!"

"Shut up… Vincent," Castillo managed to say. His tone had regained its authority but not its volume.

But Vincent kept babbling, his attention remaining on the ring that came closer and closer to his neck. "I can't, but you can; you're a Midas. Don't kill me. I can't enter someone's mind unless they let me. But you're a Midas. You don't need me. Control. Yes, that's it! Total control!" He laughed quickly, hysterically. "It's not just entering and seeing. You can control him. His mind is yours; you can do it. Leave me alone. Get inside his head!" He burst into tears again. "Leave me alone, I can't help you. I didn't do anything to you… Him. His head! Get inside it and control it! Get this off me!"

Miguel looked at Monica – she was the expert – and asked, "Can I? The residual waves."

"Yes." She seemed to hesitate, but she looked at him firmly. "I suppose so."

"Help me. I'm going to enter his mind. I won't kill him," Miguel whispered.

Miguel felt Monica's catalyzing impulse, strong, resolved. He concentrated on Castillo's eyes, conjuring all the depth he possibly could. Then Castillo made a strange expression, looking up as if a sudden headache had come over him and he was trying to look at the source of the pain. Miguel looked at his bandage and the wound Fred had given him. He would enter there. Castillo forced his gaze up. Suddenly, he seemed to give up, looking down and blinking like he was trying to get dust out of his eye. He once again attempted to look up and then looked at Miguel. And Miguel felt Castillo's mind.

Leave me alone! Castillo told him. He was so far from the car salesman he used to be. Inside, Miguel noted, he wasn't quite so seductive.

Tell me what will happen to my brother, Miguel demanded.

They'll kill him! Yes, they'll kill him if I don't call within an hour.

Miguel knew he was lying. *They won't kill him*, said Miguel. *Where is he?*

I won't tell you… Nice… Shit!

Your thoughts are getting away from you, Miguel taunted. Then he turned to Monica. "We can't go to Nice now, I suppose."

"Control his body," Monica suggested. "Make him do what you want. He can free your brother."

Miguel went quiet, pensive. He supposed it wasn't enough to enter Walter's mind. He would have to control him and make him do whatever he wanted.

"I'm with you," Monica added.

Miguel nodded. He concentrated again. Castillo let out a small moan and immediately looked at Miguel with wide eyes. *It's about time you got a taste of it too*, Miguel told him. *Fear*.

Castillo freed his right arm from around the tree and reached into the pocket of his jacket to retrieve his phone. He dialled a number. When the other end of the line picked up, Castillo tried to resist speaking, but he eventually broke. "Agent Kells," he said. His eyes went tight as if he were fighting something inside himself. "It's Castillo." Then he shut his eyes tight like he knew what he was about to do would be painful. Miguel focused and Castillo spasmed, his eyes opening and defocusing. He began reciting. "Alpha-tango-three-three-sierra. Alcatraz. Delta-November-eight-four-Mike-Romeo. Delaware."

Miguel tried to memorize the gibberish – secret codes, he guessed – in case it was useful in the future. But he stopped himself – it made him lose his concentration, and he didn't want Castillo to escape him. Neither did he believe those codes would be in use for long once Castillo had used them.

"Yes," said Castillo. Finally, something that made sense. "Mission aborted. Release the hostage and abandon the country. Do it immediately." There were a few seconds of silence. "Negative," said Castillo. "Forget the trails, we'll take care of it. Abandon the country now. He's conscious? Good. Give him money before you leave. Pass him the phone now, I need to talk to him. Good luck." Castillo threw the phone to Miguel before grabbing onto the tree trunk again.

Miguel picked up the phone from the ground. It was Dani, talking so fast he tripped over his words. “Yes, yes, yes… I already know he… Yes, they kidnapped you… And drugged you. I know everything.” Dani’s words came out in a rush. “Dani, listen to me… Yes, okay, listen to me. The people who were watching you, have they left? Just one? Good. Is he gone? Do you see him through the window? He got into a black all-terrain? Perfect. You need to get out of there.”

“No,” said Monica. “They’ll find him if he moves. Tell him to hide. We’ll go find him.”

“Wait a moment, Dani,” said Miguel, covering the mouthpiece of the phone. “He can’t hide. Where would he go?”

“He’s in France,” said Monica. “In Nice. The two of you know that area well. There must be somewhere…”

Nice, of course! Miguel remembered. He saw Nice in his mind. He saw Dani and the pieces of his rocket, the explosion in the park beside the beach. The scar on his brother’s earlobe. Their fights, their games. The Secret Hole Club, of course. Perfect!

“Okay,” said Miguel into the mouthpiece. “Listen to me closely… Yes, I’ll tell you everything that’s happened.”

Dani wouldn’t stop talking. Miguel had to tell him where to hide without anyone else knowing. Castillo was still conscious. Confronting the CIA wasn’t so simple. All of this overwhelmed him. He could drug Castillo so he wouldn’t hear, but he might be needed conscious. Besides that, Castillo’s phone could have been tapped. It was one of theirs, so why wouldn’t it be?

“Do you think they would have watched me as a kid?” Miguel asked Monica.

“Not us. I’m certain of it. But they may have in NASA Hampton, the other lab. I don’t know how long it’s been running.”

“I see.” Miguel delved into Castillo’s mind.

No! Castillo responded. *We didn't exist yet back then.*

"Dani, listen. Shut up and listen to me! Good. Here's what you're going to do. Take the money… Two thousand? Perfect… Go to the place where we used to hide when we were kids, when we spent summers with Mémé in Nice… Yes, of course, don't you know? You're in Nice. Our secret place. Only you and I know it. Don't say its name, the phone line might be tapped. Go there and don't come out. It's dangerous, you know that. Don't go out into the street. Okay… Go now. And get rid of this phone. I'll contact you. In a few days. Yes, they won't find you. Don't come out!" Miguel touched his temples. He swallowed and looked at Monica. "Be careful, Dani," he said, and he hung up.

Then he stopped all his inflections.

The four men collapsed on the ground with a crash like branches falling off the trees. The Mégane's headlights lit up again and the clearing became visible under their soft, artificial light. As the pale white moonlight disappeared, Miguel felt like everything that had happened before had happened in a movie, and now the lights in the theater had come back on. But it was real. Miguel saw once more the fog of his breath and felt the cold in his fingers, his joints, the backs of his hands.

His enemies, crumpled on the frozen ground of the German forest, rubbed their bodies clumsily. All of them tried to loosen themselves up, except for the stocky gunman who lay bent over his neck, the position he had fallen into. Miguel would have to drug them all before he left. But the drug… Gorlov had the gun. "Monica, what do we do with him?"

Monica looked at the scientist, who was walking around looking at the stars. "We have to neutralize the drug. His gun. I lost mine."

"Bring him over, I don't want to move from here. I have to watch these four."

In reality, the four men did not seem very dangerous. They leaned against the trunks of the firs like a bunch of scattered beggars at the door of a church, resting against the columns of a temple.

Monica returned, leading Gorlov by the hand. He allowed himself to be guided like an obedient schoolboy. His dopey smile remained on his face. Miguel searched in the scientist's jacket for the inhibitor darts while Monica took the gun. They loaded it and Monica shot him. His smile instantly faded.

"Irina?" the scientist asked, looking at Monica. "Castillo, the darts… Are we going for a walk?" Then he said something in Russian.

Miguel and Monica sat him down on a nearby fir stump. Gorlov didn't say anything at first, but then he began speaking in Russian as he leaned on Monica's arm. He looked ready to pass out, but he inhaled noisily and straightened. "What happened?" he asked, breathing heavy.

"You got hit by several darts," said Monica. "They drugged you."

Gorlov looked at Castillo and the others. "You neutralized them," he said. "At what cost?"

Miguel assumed he was asking about the special effects. It seemed Gorlov was thinking only of problems as soon as he woke up, after Miguel had saved his life. Always so direct. But in that moment, he was right. They had to hurry.

"Miguel made Castillo's all-terrain fly through the air," said Monica, a clear link of events, as if the car had been just another casualty. The practical and efficient Monica that Miguel liked so much seemed to have returned. "Then he made those men fly and hung them on the trees. He also made a ring of vapor around Vincent to terrify him, I guess—"

"Virtual?" Gorlov asked.

"Condensation," Miguel said.

"Good."

"Then we got inside Castillo's head – I helped Miguel – and we made him let Dani go. They had him trapped in Nice," Monica clarified.

"Anything else?"

"No."

"I also cut the lights to my car," Miguel added.

Gorlov went quiet for a moment. Then he listed off, "Telekinesis, telepathy, a small cooling of the air for condensation – very localized – control of electricity and transmutation of a drug…"

"I transformed as many darts as I could."

"Without any of your lightning or fire or showiness?"

"No, except for the all-terrain. I couldn't contain myself. I destroyed that side of the forest." Miguel pointed to the ruined trees.

"Alright. I don't think there will be a significant residual wave from what you've done. Almost everything was on a very small scale. The telekinesis of the all-terrain… No, telekinesis barely generates any residual inflection. Is your brother safe?" Gorlov asked suddenly.

"Yes, I think so," Miguel answered, surprised by the question.

"Then we must go." Gorlov took the white gun out of Monica's hands. "I'll drug them and put them to sleep. That will give us an advantage." Without waiting for a reply, he stood up from the stump and limped over to the far right of the row of fallen men.

In what seemed like a logical order, Gorlov began shooting and hitting the men over the head from right to left. First it was Castillo – he didn't even look up; he was too busy looking at his hands like he didn't know who he was. Gorlov shot him, and when Castillo began to smile, Gorlov hit him on the back of the neck with the gun. Vincent looked at him seriously, but he seemed unafraid. Gorlov shot Vincent and hit him too. Then it was Barrett's turn.

But Gorlov passed over him and looked at the stocky agent. "Is he alive?" he asked.

"He was when I put him there," said Miguel.

Gorlov shot the agent. Then he approached him and touched his neck. "He's alive," he confirmed, pushing him into a less painful position. "And unconscious. All of them are unconscious."

Miguel stared at Barrett. He was not unconscious.

CHAPTER 41

Monica counted on Vladimir not shooting Barrett. She smiled as she saw the scientist approach Barrett and stretch out his hand.

"Are you okay?"

She and Miguel didn't move from the center of the clearing, beside a fir stump about ten paces from the tree supporting Barrett. The clearing now looked more like a prison yard: the high walls of the firs, the Renault's headlights, the lonely log cabin like a watchtower, the wet, cold sound of the stream, like a sewer through which they could escape. Vincent, Castillo and the other man were left hunched over on the freezing grass, unconscious, each of them stuck to their own tree trunk. Monica shivered and felt the needles from the darts all over her body. It was starting to get very cold in the forest. She ought to remove the darts.

"He was about to kill us," said Barrett, looking at Miguel as he took Gorlov's hand and stood up.

Miguel sat on the tree stump. Then he looked up at Barrett and said, "I'm sorry, Eugene. I lost control. You were with them, you have to understand—"

Gorlov lifted a bony hand suddenly, his palm facing Miguel. Miguel immediately fell quiet. "Can they hear us?" he asked Barrett. "The inflexors at NASA Hampton. Can they see us?"

"No," said Barrett. He touched an arm and grimaced painfully, the expression wrinkling half his face. "Walter only has

Vincent. Well, yes, he has others in Hampton – perceptors, telekinetics, some telepaths – but they have very little ability. All of them need a line of sight." He removed his glasses and checked that they were intact. He placed them back on his face and shivered. "No, no one is watching us right now."

"Good," Gorlov replied. He turned towards Miguel and Monica. "Prepare everything for our escape." Then he removed his jacket and placed it around Barrett. "Tell me, what other means does Walter have…?"

"Eugene is doing very well," Monica said to Miguel. "Come here, I'll take out your darts." She crouched next to him. "Fred would have appreciated his game as a double agent. Poor Eugene. I don't know where he gets all that courage. He's never been—"

"Fred is dead," Miguel said suddenly, gazing at nothing among the trees. "And Dani could be next. Or Eugene. Don't talk to me about spies."

Monica bit her bottom lip. She liked hearing Miguel denounce Castillo and his world. Yes, that was the Miguel she wanted. She looked over the darts in his body, his torso, his shoulders, his back. *Practice!* she reminded herself. They had to get out of there. That's what Vladimir said. Take out the darts first. Then they would talk. They had an opportunity. Suddenly, Monica found herself with much more energy, more self-confidence. *Get out of here. Quick.* Maybe they would have a chance to escape.

She removed one of Miguel's darts and he flinched. "Aaagh!" he gritted out. Monica paid no attention to him. She knew the darts would hurt when removed. She focused on finding them and removing them. Barrett and Gorlov were talking about a discovery, and Barrett looked very serious. Monica couldn't let that distract her. Getting out was what mattered.

"Vladimir," she heard Barrett say, "on my way here, I studied the data from the inflection Miguel produced in the south of France. There's something strange in the latest recordings."

"Systematic incongruence in the data," said Gorlov.

Monica ripped out another dart and Miguel shuddered. There weren't many left. She reminded herself that soon, they would disappear, and no one would find them. What incongruence were they talking about?

"No, no," Barrett was saying. "There was no incongruence in the inflection in France."

Monica looked at Barrett. He seemed to be touching his ribs with his fingers, as if counting them through his clothes. She didn't know of any systematic source of errors in the Project. No incongruence. She pulled out another dart from Miguel's calf, and he jerked as he dug his heel into the icy grass.

"It's logical," said Gorlov. "He alone produced the inflection. Monica was not a catalyst that time. If the two of them are not present, there is no incongruence, you know that. The Midas Paradox, Eugene, that is what's important. The equations you and I began were correct, don't you see? Miguel couldn't do it. It's almost like an empirical demonstration of the paradox."

Monica looked back at the scientists. Barrett was shaking his head, his face tense, his eyes tight above his small, round glasses. Monica tore out two more darts from Miguel's back, and he turned around.

"I'm nearly done," said Monica, turning her attention back to the scientists as she removed another dart from Miguel's right shoulder.

"But Miguel didn't arrive at a paradox," said Barrett.

"The Midas Paradox, Eugene," Gorlov insisted. "Miguel couldn't do it."

"Miguel didn't arrive at a paradox, Vladimir!" Barrett's voice was louder now but still low, and he emphasized every word. "There was no incongruence. There was no Midas Effect. There was no paradox. He didn't arrive at it," he enunciated.

"He didn't?" Gorlov asked quietly. His Russian accent became audible.

Monica removed the final dart without looking away from the scientists.

"I'll do yours now," said Miguel, crouching down beside her.

"No, Vladimir," said Barrett, "he didn't. Do you remember the experiment with the virtual army in the desert? I suspected... That would explain the incongruence. We've been wrong all along."

Monica thought about approaching them when Miguel ripped out a dart from her thigh! *Aaagh!*

Then Barrett looked over at her and Miguel, as did Gorlov. Miguel continued removing needles from her body. Another needle. Monica grit her teeth in pain before smiling at the scientists. Miguel pulled out another dart from her ankle. *Shit!* The pain of it caused her body to cramp all the way up to her neck.

"This changes everything," said Gorlov. He removed his glasses as though he wanted to look at Miguel and Monica with his own eyes. "I must speak with Miguel in an anti-inflexor room."

"Impossible," said Barrett.

"Miguel, you're hurting me," said Monica.

"I can get one," Gorlov responded. "The prototype from Leningrad."

"I'm doing what I can," said Miguel.

"Does that work? Isn't it in a museum?"

"It used to work, yes, well enough. I can get it."

"What about Miguel?"

Miguel appeared to have finished with the torture of removing darts from Monica's body. He threw a handful of them beside the base of the stump. "That's all of them," he said.

"If this is what it appears to be," said Gorlov, "then there is a possibility of destroying the Midas Effect."

"What's going on?" asked Monica, crossing the distance between herself and the scientists with long, purposeful strides. "Can I do something?" Barrett looked at her over his glasses and said nothing.

"Eugene has found an error in the Midas Paradox," said Gorlov.

"I understood that he—" Monica began.

"Can we go?!" Miguel shouted from the stump. "I have to see Dani."

Gorlov gestured with his hand to Castillo and the others, crumpled in a heap on the ground. He said, "Bring them all to the cabin. If you don't, they'll freeze to death before sunrise. Take their phones and guns. Eugene, you go with them. Then we'll leave."

"But the incongruence—" Monica protested.

"We must leave, Monica," Gorlov snapped. He turned to Barrett and placed a slim hand on his shoulder. "Eugene, don't worry if they follow us. If you see a clear signal, give it to Walter."

"An inflection?" asked Barrett.

"Any signal. But don't put yourself at risk. I have my own plans. And another thing – make sure you forget whatever conclusion you came to today. Think about your children, for example."

"My children?"

"Whatever you want! Your conclusions would be wrong. I'll take care of checking everything, okay?"

Barrett began walking towards the cabin, silently shaking his small head. Monica helped Miguel drag the bodies. *Practice*, she made herself think. Vladimir was right. They had to leave as soon as possible. But it wasn't right for them not to tell her what they had discovered. She was a better analyst than Eugene. She could be very helpful if they had to resolve incongruencies, look for solutions…

In just a few minutes, Vincent, Castillo and the stocky man had been moved to the interior of the cabin. Barrett returned Gorlov's jacket and the two shook hands. Monica and Miguel watched from the doorway. Barrett took a few steps back before sitting on the ground with his back to a wooden wall, right alongside his fallen enemies. Then Gorlov took out a ceramic gun.

"Are you going to shoot him?" Monica asked.

"I have to leave him in the same state as the others," said Gorlov, aiming at Barrett. "He's our insider."

"Stupid spy games," Miguel murmured dryly. He sounded tired.

"Vladimir!" Barrett said suddenly. "Before you shoot me. Spies."

"What?"

"Yes, spies. When you leave the forest path, you'll see a gas station. There's another all-terrain, a black Volvo identical to the one Miguel destroyed. Inside it is another CIA agent. Roth. I think you know him." Gorlov nodded. "He'll shoot you with a dart gun when you stop to refuel," Barrett explained. "It was Walter's Plan B. Or maybe it was Plan A, who knows?"

"Just one agent?"

"Yes. One is enough if you're caught off-guard. It's very late and the gas station will be empty. You're almost out of gas. Vincent told us."

"Thank you, Eugene," said Gorlov. "We'll act as if we don't know."

"Good."

Gorlov pulled the trigger and a ceramic dart hit Barrett's torso. Then Gorlov neared him – he was already smiling like a dopey imp – and hit him over the back of the neck with the butt of the gun. Monica thought she saw Gorlov move a little slower than he had with the rest. They closed the door to the cabin and quickly got into the yellow Renault.

"We're going to Nice," said Miguel as he settled into the passenger seat. "We have to save Dani."

"We're going somewhere else first," said Gorlov.

"I don't plan on letting—!" Miguel tried to insist.

"I have a plan to help you!" Gorlov shouted. "But we have to go somewhere else. I need an anti-inflexor room and some other devices. In two days, we can go to Nice. Your brother is somewhere safe, right?" Miguel did not respond. "We can destroy the Midas Effect," Gorlov continued. "Do what I tell you if you want me to help you."

They abandoned the clearing in silence. The battlefield, Monica thought. She looked at the fuel gauge. She remembered that the low fuel light had turned on as they were arriving at the clearing. Now, the fuel light glowed orange on the dashboard.

CHAPTER 42

Miguel took a sip of coffee and mentally went over nearly nine hours of travelling by car from the Black Forest, without stops, except to refuel. He was exhausted. He needed a cup of coffee.

The café was right in the middle of the historical center of Bratislava. The morning sun that filtered through the windows warmed his shoulders. Vladimir was saying something about feeling that same warmth in his office in California. Their cups were slim and white; it was easy to imagine a NASA logo. Miguel took another sip of coffee. It was good, strong, almost like tar. He wanted to stay there. He was so tired of running. He looked at the people inside the café. Slow old people, veterans from Eastern Europe, read their newspapers and puffed out smoke. Young couples spoke quietly. There was no trace of hurry on their faces. Everyone looked like they were from another world.

He was from another world.

But Gorlov had promised him he would fix it. That was why they were there. The Midas Effect. To put an end to his curse.

Gorlov was studying a roadmap. More roads, thought Miguel. Then he looked at Monica as she stared out of a window. She sipped her coffee and grimaced. Miguel smiled, wondering if she would spit it out. If she could, he knew, she would throw it all into a drain, like she used to do in San Francisco.

California was very far away now. He had so much to discuss with Monica. When Gorlov's friend arrived, maybe they would be alone…

At that moment, the door to the café opened. No one moved too much, but men, women, old people—everyone—looked at it out of the corner of their eye before quickly returning to their lives with a general shiver, like a wheat field disturbed by a gust of wind. Miguel turned around to see what had caused such a stir.

From the door, a smiling man advanced towards them. Firm strides, square jaw, very light green eyes, early sixties. Gorlov stood when he saw him. "*Tovarisch!*" said the man in a resounding voice, like a choral soloist from the Russian military.

"Sergei," said Gorlov. The scientist's face seemed to want to smile. He touched the man's stomach. "You've gotten fat." They hugged one another tightly and kissed three times. Gorlov introduced the man as Sergei Krushenko.

During the journey from Germany, the scientist had spoken of him. He told them the KGB had ordered Sergei to watch him, but Gorlov had saved him from ending up in Siberia, which had turned them into comrades, allies. *Friends, you could say*, Gorlov had said. *He helped me escape the Soviet Union.*

"Welcome to Bratislava," said Krushenko. His full-toothed smile inspired more distrust than kindness. "It's a pleasure to have two North Americans in our city." His English was perfect, but his Us and Rs cut through the air like Gorlov's angular consonants did when he got emotional. Before Miguel could correct him on their nationality, Krushenko sat down with them and began speaking to Gorlov in Russian.

According to what the scientist had told Miguel, Sergei was a Russian mafia boss in Slovakia. A mafioso was going to hide them. A thief. They had even stolen Gorlov's equipment from a Soviet museum. But that meant that Gorlov had what he needed to take the Midas Effect away from him. All they needed was there, in Bratislava. Dealing with thieves was worth it if it freed him of the Midas Effect. Miguel sipped his coffee.

A waitress approached the table. Krushenko lifted his head – it was an arrogant movement, as if the café was his – and looked at her. Maybe, Miguel thought, the pair of moustached thugs in sunglasses that Sergei had left in the door had convinced everyone that the café really was his. The waitress, a very young, round-faced girl, also seemed to belong to him. Miguel looked at her neckline, convinced it had not been as revealing when she had served them before. The small gap between her breasts stood out now, almost directed at Krushenko's face. The girl's smile did not look sincere.

Krushenko cast an almost imperceptible glance over her neckline, said something to her, and the waitress left. Then he turned to them and said, "We can't talk here." He invited them to stand with his tight smile as he stood too.

They left and Gorlov got into Krushenko's silver Mercedes. Monica and Miguel were told to get into the Mercedes carrying his two "friends."

Beneath their gray, outdated jackets, Krushenko's moustached "friends" in sunglasses made the angular lines of their weapons bulge. They wore guns on both sides of their bodies, like Mexican bandits. To Miguel, they looked like two discolored mariachis.

Before getting into the car, Miguel looked towards his parked Mégane, so yellow, so bright, practically begging to be robbed. A police officer at the border had warned them that foreign cars had to be watched carefully, that the mafia robbed them, "fixed" them – whatever "fixed" meant – and sold them.

And that was their only method of transport. Their way out, maybe.

"Is it safe for me to leave the car here?" Miguel asked Krushenko as he entered the Mercedes.

Krushenko stopped, looking at Miguel as his forehead wrinkled. Then he let out a sonorous guffaw, as rhythmic as if he had been performing an opera with his impeccable voice. "You're with me!" he exclaimed, lifting his hands. "No one in this city would dare touch that car. You Americans…" He laughed as he got into the backseat of the Mercedes.

Monica and Miguel were swallowed up by the darkness of the interior of the car, provided by its tinted windows. Krushenko's mariachis sat in front. They said nothing, nor did their expressions change. The one with the darker moustache drove while the other smoked a cigarette.

Miguel took Monica's hand. The Russians didn't seem to be able to understand them. What did the Russians matter? "Do you still love me?" he asked. "In the forest, you said—"

Monica spun to face him. She had that familiar gleam in her eyes as they darted over his face. "Miguel," she said, taking his hand. Then she quickly glanced at the mariachis. They kept their attention on the Mercedes in front.

"It's all been for you," said Miguel.

Monica stayed quiet but attentive. The cars entered a wide road full of rails and hanging cables. With the car swaying from the first pothole on the road, Miguel eyed the blurry signs on the ground that indicated the right of way of trams, trolleys, cars, bicycles, motorcycles. The tangle of vehicles and roads was the image of interior disorder, Miguel thought, and the difficulty he had in finding his own path. He looked back at Monica's intense, blue gaze. "In Egypt," Miguel began, "when I was doubting, in the room, when the darts…" He looked at the mariachis, but

Monica nodded in understanding. "I was thinking about you. Afterwards, at the hotel in France, when I tried to destroy… you know… I did it…"

"You did it for me?" Monica finished.

Miguel looked out again through the tinted window of the Mercedes. He had not done it for her. A police car stopped and the officer inside stared at them. Miguel saw from the signs on the ground that they were on a road that was prohibited for cars. The cars had stopped at a traffic light for trams.

"You were the trigger," Miguel admitted, still looking at the patrol car. He loved Monica, but his ability, his power, stopped him from getting any closer to her. "This is very difficult. You don't know what it's like. I love you, but…"

The police officer frowned at the Mercedes. The mariachi who was driving lowered his window and the officer seemed to recognize him. He lowered his eyes, turned the keys in the ignition and immediately drove away. Miguel watched the patrol car as it left. Running away. That was all Miguel was doing, the only thing he could do. Run away from everyone.

"It's the paradox," said Monica. "You heard Vladimir. He'll follow you forever. With or without me. Unless that artefact…" Monica smiled and caressed his cheek. Miguel felt the hair of his week-old beard lightly scratch her hand. Like everything else about him, it hurt her.

The mariachi with the light-colored moustache turned and looked at them from the passenger seat. Monica smiled at him, and he responded by sending them a puff of smoke that filled the entire backseat of the Mercedes before turning back around. Miguel and Monica sat in silence as the two cars continued their journey.

***

The all-terrain was parked alongside the small gas station. It was the secondary road leading to the forest path. When Castillo, who almost tripped as he walked in front, saw the shining black Volvo, like new, it looked like an illusion, or an oasis.

The others – Smith, Vincent, Barrett – must have thought something similar, Castillo supposed, after more than four hours of walking. They had no equipment, no clothes or footwear appropriate for a forest, having already spent a night on the floor of a log cabin in the middle of a German winter, as well as being drugged and beaten by Miguel's telekinetic arms.

Castillo touched his forehead and found his bandage was no longer there. He must have lost it in the brawl, but he couldn't quite remember at that moment. The wound inflicted by Fred's chair and the beating he had received in Egypt seemed like an eternity ago, but they were there, clearly visible, like his new injuries.

He quickened his pace and glanced around to see others do the same. They must have looked like a horde of the living dead, because when the boy working at the gas station saw them, he bolted into the store. Castillo expected them to call the police, but that didn't matter much now. Miguel, who they had already trapped by now, was what mattered.

Although, if they *had* trapped him, Roth would have gone to find Castillo and his men. Castillo sped up.

Then he realized that there was only one car parked there, the all-terrain. *Where's the yellow Coupé?* he wondered, rage fuelling him more than his own strength. *They've escaped! Goddamn it, they've escaped!*

When he got to the all-terrain, Castillo found Roth unconscious in the backseat. He had a dart in his neck.

Castillo imagined, in a fraction of a second, the war council, military prison, Wella Anderson laughing at him with her perfect smile and shiny, straight, blonde hair behind her ears. Two pearls as gray as his prisoner clothes.

When the rest of the zombies got to the Volvo, Castillo was hitting his closed fists against it. He wanted to break it in two, make it fly like Miguel had done with the other vehicle, even though his remaining strength was barely enough for his ridiculous, weak punches.

"They got away," said Agent Smith. Everyone looked at him. Smith didn't talk much. His voice was calm, but neither his voice nor the rags of his clothes offered him any ferocity. He looked like a pardoned gladiator, prepared to kill at the first opportunity that presented itself. The war council.

Castillo opened the door of the all-terrain, picked up a quantum sensor from beneath Roth's head – he barely moved – and handed it to Barrett. The scientist grabbed the equipment with trembling arms, as if it weighed as much as an anvil.

"No, they haven't got away," said Castillo. He got into the passenger seat. "Everyone get in!"

***

The Mercedes cars left the city center and took a left turn before crossing the Nový Most over the Danube. Miguel was thinking that the car full of mafiosos wasn't exactly the best place to talk to Monica.

Minutes later, they had stopped in front of a large building with a façade hundreds of meters long, of simple geometry and architecture, full of lots of windows very close to each other. Miguel thought that all engineering schools were the same. Above the main door was written *Slovenská Technická Universita*.

They got out of their cars and entered the building. In the basements, a seventy-something-year-old bald, thin man was waiting for them. Miguel would have mistaken him for Nosferatu had it not been for the pure white coat.

Gorlov began speaking in Russian with the vampire. Meanwhile, Krushenko told Miguel and Monica that Gorlov had called him two days prior to ask him for somewhere safe to hide for a while. Afterwards, Gorlov had called him back asking for one of his inventions to be turned on again. Now, Gorlov said he wanted to leave as soon as he finished up there.

"I have a family matter I need to take care of," Miguel explained. "I have to leave as soon as we finish up here, but Vladimir might be able to stay."

"Bah!" said Krushenko. "He will go where you go. He was a protective father figure in Russia, and he still is thirty years later."

"We have to leave today," Monica said.

Krushenko showed her his full-toothed smile. "Tomorrow, you can fly in my private jet," he insisted. "I've planned a special dinner for you. I can have the yellow Renault arrive anywhere in Europe in two days, if that's what you're worried about."

The vampire seemed to understand Gorlov, nodding along to his words. Then Gorlov turned back to them. "Everything is ready," he told them. "Sergei has managed to bring me what I had in Russia. And this man is the professor of electrical engineering in this faculty. He studied in Leningrad and knows of my prestige there. He oversaw the construction of the room and its electrical supply, and he has provided everything we need." He looked at Miguel and Monica, gesturing with his hand for them to come closer. "He thinks it's a type of electrified Faraday cage," he whispered to them. Then he looked at Krushenko and said, "Everything is ready for the test!"

"I already told you it would be," said Krushenko. "I found the best engineer, you see. He studied in Russia. The best means…"

Everyone followed the dark corridor to the electrical engineering lab.

"I have a Gulfstream," said Krushenko, placing a hand on Miguel's shoulder. "I have a feeling you know a thing or two about planes. Rolls-Royce Motors. A Mercedes among private jets, right, young man?"

"Yes," said Miguel, but he didn't really understand. In any other moment, he would have loved to talk about the plane, but now all he could think about was what Gorlov had told him on the way from Germany to Slovakia. They would enter a rudimentary anti-inflexor room – the first ever made – and there, they would destroy his Midas ability with a quantum distorter, a prototype Gorlov had once discarded for not having any use. The container would work directly on his brain. Miguel felt his hands begin to itch.

"You could go tomorrow in the Gulfstream," Krushenko went on. "It would be an honor for me…"

But Miguel didn't know if that was safe. The anti-inflexor room, Gorlov had explained to him, would absorb the expansive wave of residual inflection. No one would be able to find them. If they got out alive, of course. *A quantum distorter inside a quantum distortion room.* Miguel wavered. Perhaps, he told himself, that was an effect of the Midas Paradox – he had suddenly lost all interest in entering any room, much less trying out obsolete equipment that could liquify his brain. He made an effort to forget his fear in the poorly-lit corridor.

It lasted until they arrived at the entrance to the vampire's lab and Nosferatu opened the double doors.

The contraption! Miguel thought. In front of them, in the middle of the lab, was an electromechanical monster that looked like it had stepped right out of a black-and-white film about mad scientists. Miguel could feel his blood rush to his legs along with his determination. A stall with a hexagonal base rested with its door opened into the space left by the furniture. The stall was connected by a tangle of cables to various sources of electrical supply, oscilloscopes, and other unrecognizable devices. To the left, a wooden box as tall as Krushenko and as wide as four coffins showed its interior through many small holes. Something like lightbulbs shone inside it. Vacuum tubes!

"Vacuum tubes?" Miguel asked in a whisper. *What year is this from?* As his feet prepared to step back, Miguel looked down and saw something else in front of him, on top of a stool. A helmet.

A snakelike cable that came out of the interior of the stall connected to what looked like a Viking hat without the horns. The helmet in front of the stall, like an offering, seemed to want Miguel to pick it up and put it on. That helmet would fry his brain and leave him a vegetable. He looked up. The vampire in his white coat was smiling at Miguel and pointed at the helmet with a slim, pale finger, saying something to him in his language of the undead. Miguel imagined the professor slurping up his brains through the snakelike cable. He thought he saw the vampire's fangs glisten when he smiled wide enough.

"Miguel!" yelled Monica.

Miguel flinched and took a step back. Then he realized everyone except him had entered.

"Are you okay? You've gone pale."

"What is the helmet for?" Miguel took tiny steps towards the lab without quite crossing the entryway.

Gorlov didn't respond. He began talking in Russian and everyone left through another door on the left side of the lab. A window on that wall showed them entering an adjoining room. The mariachis and Krushenko were already entering the adjoining room when Gorlov said, "You too, Monica. I've told them it's just a test, that they can wait nearby, but not here. This could be dangerous. Go with them." Monica frowned at him. "This place will fill with electric charge when the machines are connected," Gorlov went on, not letting her speak. "Leave." To Miguel, it sounded like a military order. His Russian accent was unquestionable.

Monica left, her lips pressed into a thin line, spinning on her heel. The movement caused her hair to swing. Gorlov took a pair of pliers from a toolbox and began fiddling with something small and metallic he had just taken out of his pocket. A bullet.

"What are you doing?" Miguel asked.

"Nothing's going to happen to you. This is just an anti-inflexor room."

"I think I can feel the Midas Paradox…"

"That's not the paradox. That is fear. If you enter with me, I can help you. Go inside!"

"Are you going inside too? What about the helmet? I thought you would give me more instructions, something… a yellow page about the experiment. What are you doing with that bullet?"

"The helmet is useless; it doesn't do anything," Gorlov whispered, coming closer to Miguel. "Take this and go inside. I'll go in soon." He gave Miguel the bullet.

Miguel looked at it as if Gorlov had given him a trumpet. Or a sweeping brush. Gorlov was gothic and surrealist.

"Sergei gave it to me in the car. We need the lead." That was the only explanation Gorlov gave when he saw Miguel's open mouth. As he spoke, he started turning on interrupters in the coffin full of vacuum tubes.

Miguel entered the hexagonal stall with the bullet in his hand. Inside, the walls of the stall were gold, just like inside the anti-inflexor rooms. He turned the bullet over in his fingers. The bullet had no casing, it was simply the bullet proper. On the bottom, he saw, the copper shell covered a lead center. Lead. Miguel shook his head, stopping himself from thinking about the gold walls, and looked at Monica. He showed her the bullet. Maybe she would know something. Monica looked at him from the door to the adjoining room. Right into his eyes. She paid no attention to the bullet.

"Good luck, Miguel!" she shouted. "I love you."

The last thing Miguel saw in his life, as he knew it, was Monica.

CHAPTER 43

Monica closed the door, sat on one of the room's seats, and glanced at the clock. Then she looked around.

It was a small classroom of twelve desks. She supposed it would have been used to explain experiments to the students before actually doing them in the labs. The professor, whose name she didn't care enough to know, had taken the teacher's seat and was scrawling something on pages he took from a mountain of paper. From the moment she saw him, he looked like a creepy old man, with his glassy, obscene stare. Monica smiled. That little man, far from his role in humanity, had ended up correcting exams, exercises, or who knew what kind of routine task, while the most powerful man on the planet, the only one who could compare himself to God, was being divested of his deity. Monica looked again at the clock. She had forgotten how slow time passed in classrooms.

The mafiosos didn't seem to honor the historical moment they were living either. The man with the darker moustache was cleaning his nails with a small dagger, while the man with the lighter moustache smoked a cigarette. Both of them slumped over their desks, as if they didn't know how to sit in class properly. To Monica, the two of them had looked like alcoholic encyclopedia vendors from the moment she laid eyes on them. Krushenko was the only one who didn't look out of place.

She observed the Russian, who was sitting ramrod straight on top of a desk. He returned her gaze with a smile. His gestures seemed solemn, calm. The hug and kisses he had shared with

Gorlov. The elegant refusal to the waitress' insinuation at the café. In reality, Monica didn't know how a mafioso should look, but Krushenko… No, Krushenko looked like a gentle father of a big family.

When Monica looked at the clock again, twenty-five minutes had already passed, but Miguel and Gorlov had not yet come out. If something was wrong, it would be impossible to know until much time had passed. Everyone would be surprised not to see them return. But then, in all likelihood, by then it would be too late. She began to bounce her leg convulsively, like it was part of some invisible automation that had been caught in a continuous rocking motion. Her fingers drummed without rhythm on the desk. Her mouth suddenly felt dry, and she was seized by an almost unrestrainable need to run out and look for a drinking fountain. But she couldn't leave. Gorlov told her so. She thought about entering the room and looking around. Mentally.

But, of course, Monica's extrasensory perception, her quantum effect, would be detected. Even if it was something small, so small it could barely be distinguished on a sensor, a tiny residual wave… No. She decided to wait. Her leg kept bouncing. She drummed her fingers a little faster. The movements calmed her. Monica began observing the professor again as he scribbled on pages with a red pen. The mafioso with a dark moustache was filing his dagger against a small stone while the other sucked on his cigarette. Krushenko stood with his hands crossed behind his back, like a worried father. He stared hard at the window to the lab. Monica looked at it too. The machine seemed to be functioning. Then she looked at the clock again. Twenty-eight minutes. Her leg sped up in its movement, her fingers began drumming even faster, and she nibbled her bottom lip. She had to see what they were doing.

Monica closed her eyes, focused, and looked for a tiny inflection.

When she managed to see with her mind and approach the room, a block of vague, dark energy dissolved her ability, diluting it until it was unusable. It stopped her from entering the room. That was the anti-inflexor room's quantum distortion effect. She knew it well. The contraption seemed to work. At least, the distorters worked. There was no way to see inside the room. Monica didn't want to insist, since a more powerful attempt would immediately be detected by Castillo. She nibbled her bottom lip again and resumed the movements in her legs and fingers. She opened her eyes.

At that moment, she saw Krushenko's stomach, like that of a satiated farmer after breakfast, moving towards her. His smiling face and tired, green eyes calmed her somewhat. "Are you nervous?" Krushenko asked. His baritone voice seemed to reverberate around the classroom. The operatic tones finally stopped Monica's anxious movements. Krushenko sat on a nearby desk and gave her a protective smile.

"I'm fine," said Monica. She exchanged her drumming fingers for nervous glances at the window to the lab. "Have you known Vladimir long?" she asked.

"I was a boy when the KGB assigned me the mission of watching him." His Russian accent sounded sweeter than Vladimir's. "He treated me like I was his son. He always treats those he loves as if he were their father. Of course, he's always been old, ever since I met him. He'll outlive us all for sure, old Vladimir. I presume you won't be staying for dinner?"

Monica turned her head to the lab. "We're in a hurry," she replied, staring at the gleaming vacuum tubes inside the wardrobe-sized wooden stall.

"We shouldn't sit so close to the glass," said Krushenko. "It won't protect us if one of the lab's old machinery explodes."

Monica thanked the Russian's advice with a smile and began moving her legs again. If there was an explosion, Miguel could die. The thought immediately made her start drumming her fingers again. Krushenko turned around and looked at his men. He said nothing to them. Then he turned back to her. "Your friend must be very interested in Vladimir's research to put himself in a nineteenth-century machine with him."

The mafioso's concern for Miguel had Monica lowering her guard slightly. It was like having someone from the secretive world she, Miguel, and Vladimir inhabited who understood her. Someone she could confide in at that moment, someone whose words stopped her legs and fingers from moving like seismographs detecting disasters yet to come.

"Miguel has something very dangerous, for him and everyone else," said Monica. "But, with luck, Vladimir is going to take it away from him with that 'nineteenth-century machine.'"

Krushenko's smile froze suddenly, like his teeth had stuck together, but the rest of his face wrinkled. Monica thought a sharp pain had overcome Krushenko. She was going to ask him if he was okay, but he stood up and began shouting in Russian. His operatic voice rose in a crescendo to a grand finale. He gestured as if cutting through the air with his outstretched hands.

Suddenly, the two drunken encyclopedia vendors stood and ran to the door. But they stopped before they could get to it and looked back. The professor was shouting something as well and made a gesture of negation with his arms.

Krushenko's thugs did not move, looking to their boss. Krushenko took out a gun from his jacket, an enormous, gleaming pistol. He pointed it at the professor and pulled the trigger.

The gunshot shook Monica like the shockwave from a cannon. She couldn't properly process everything when it happened so fast, but something in her brain latched onto the only thing that mattered: Krushenko would not let Gorlov take Miguel's ability away. And he was prepared to stop the machine, cut the cables, or kill everyone to do it.

The professor fell over his exams with his creepy, old man face frozen by death, his white coat covered in blood. Monica was sure she would have to use her abilities to protect herself. She had to stop Krushenko. Castillo would find them if she produced an inflection, but that didn't matter now. She couldn't let them stop the machine. Monica took advantage of the confusion the professor's death had caused to place herself between the door and the mafiosos.

Krushenko shook the pistol in the air as if telling his men to hurry up. As he turned, he found himself looking at Monica, her small body blocking the door.

Monica lifted her hands, her palms facing them like she was trying to stop an approaching truck. She concentrated on the guns, preparing the hit of telekinesis. She was not Miguel, but she could sweep them away like pieces of fluff if she tried. Her brain was already boiling. She could not let them touch the room.

Krushenko let go of the shining gun and made his men, who had already drawn theirs, do the same. "That madman wanted to kill him, kill Vladimir," said Krushenko, pointing at the professor with his arm, his index finger extended backwards. He looked Monica in the eye. "He just said that Vladimir sent him to prison when he was a student in Leningrad. He sabotaged the machine to kill them inside." The professor's unexpectedly urgent movements before dying had not told a story as opportune as the one Krushenko now narrated. "I had no knowledge of this. We have to disactivate it, the machine," Krushenko continued as he neared Monica. His voice had given up its bel canto, and now Monica could only hear his sharp Russian syllables. "That's why they haven't come out. I love Vladimir. He's like my father, Monica."

Krushenko had slowly come nearer and nearer to Monica until he could almost touch her with his outstretched fingertips. Monica hesitated. *Krushenko is lying*, she told herself. He had just invented that story of students imprisoned by the Party and vengeance maintained by the Siberian cold for decades. Krushenko took another step. He smiled like a kind father. How could that creepy old man in a white coat wait for that distant day to get revenge on his old teacher? In *Slovakia*, of all places? It was Krushenko who had looked for the professor. Krushenko was in the mafia, the KGB. Krushenko knew perfectly well whom he hired. Krushenko would never hire an enemy. He took another tiny step. He could touch her now, but he didn't. He had killed the professor so he couldn't tell the truth, so they could stop the machine. The moustached men did not move. The story of contained vengeance was unbelievable, but Krushenko had made it up so quickly. "I had to shoot him, believe me," said Krushenko as he came closer and closer. Slowly, inch by inch. Monica had known something wasn't right with the machine since… How long had it been? She abandoned her defensive pose to look at the clock. *More than half an hour!* A fierce punch hit her right in the face.

Monica felt a tooth crack inside her mouth while her head spun like it didn't have a neck to hold onto, forced by a type of piston that made her head feel like it was flying. Her body flew backwards, until she was kneeling among the desks and seats.

With the scarce amount of consciousness left from her bruising, Monica watched Krushenko's henchmen run and almost leap over him, like two vultures spurned into action by hunger.

They immediately left the lab and began ripping out every cable in reach. Monica watched them, her left eye swollen shut, from the corner where the body had fallen in a heap among the wood and steel of the desks and chairs. Krushenko's henchmen seemed to have no fear of the electric sparks spat out by the cables. Or perhaps it was that they feared their boss more. The loving father, the inventor of quick lies. Executioner. Monica fought hard to stay conscious.

She lost.

***

Roth was driving the all-terrain. They had given him a dose of the drug inhibitor, making him the freshest of the group. Nearly everyone else dozed. *Even Smith, who's strong as a bull!* Castillo thought incredulously.

But Castillo couldn't sleep, and neither did he want to. He looked at his watch. The black face and steel hands moved smoothly. It still worked, despite Miguel's attack. They had managed to get to Munich in just under three hours. Roth was looking for a hotel near the airport. There they would set up their headquarters. They had to be ready to get on a private jet at any moment. Roth seemed to have decided on the Sheraton; he left the highway and headed towards that hotel.

Castillo stopped looking out the window and squeezed the monitoring mini-terminal in his hands. The screen showed isoinflexor maps transmitted from the NASA centers in Hampton and San José. All they had left was that mini-terminal, a quantum sensor, and a laptop. The rest of the equipment had been destroyed by Miguel along with the other Volvo. What they had left wasn't much, but if they used it well, the equipment would be enough to detect the inflexors. He glanced quickly at the screen.

Nothing. Almost constant isoinflexor lines, unmoving. Castillo couldn't stop looking at the curves, the maps, the data. He clenched his jaw and exhaled noisily through his nose. He cursed Gorlov and Monica and the moment he decided to bring them to Egypt. How would he be able to sleep?

At that moment, a residual wave and its isoinflexor curves lit up to the east of Vienna. Castillo eyed the map of Europe on the screen suspiciously. The signal was very weak. Expanding the image, he discovered that the glimmer he had seen did not come from Austria. It was nearby – Bratislava, Slovakia. He had rarely heard talk about Slovakia. And Bratislava… He knew it was the capital city, but that was all he knew. *What is there in Bratislava? Nothing. It doesn't make sense.* The signal disappeared after a few seconds. Roth stopped the Volvo at the doors of the Sheraton and turned around.

"Will this do?" Roth asked. "The hotel."

"Try to wake these guys up," Castillo grunted. He was still looking at the screen, trying to imagine what Gorlov would want there. The signal was so weak. He clenched his jaw tighter. *No!* he thought. *I won't go to the ends of the Earth for a stupid, clumsy inflection produced by some acne-ridden student who's just discovered their inflexor ability.*

***

An inflexor like herself could neutralize the pain, Monica thought. She could do it, but that would create such a defined residual wave that Castillo would recognize immediately. And she had already risked too much with that small inflection when she tried to enter the lab. She thought she might faint again, but a new wave of pain, like a pinch inside her eye, brought her back to consciousness.

The pain wasn't dissipating. Monica's beaten body burned as she lay on an overturned desk. Rolling onto her side to see what was happening nearly made her black out again, but she endured it.

Then she saw them. Miguel and Vladimir were in the classroom, flanked by Krushenko's men.

Miguel's eyes were hooded as he looked downwards with his shoulders slumped. His whole body was hunched over as if he had no strength. He looked defeated. Monica felt a new pain blossom underneath her abdomen. She couldn't locate where it hurt. She looked for Krushenko. When she finally found his face, the mask of the doting father had been replaced by an armed mafioso. In his right hand he held a white ceramic gun. He observed it, fidgeting with it. He managed to remove the chamber.

"This is where the drug to control him goes in, yes?" Krushenko asked in English. His voice still sounded strong, but it had lost all its operatic modulation. All that was left was crude, careless English, full of Russian consonants.

Monica followed the line of Krushenko's arms with her eyes until they came to rest on his other hand, which held another gleaming metal pistol. It was the one he had used to kill the professor. It was aimed right at Monica's head. The cannon was so close she could see the grooves on its surface. She felt her eyes want to close, but first she glanced at Miguel. Her body began to burn again from the pain.

Miguel kept his eyes on her as he watched her strangely. *He's no longer a Midas!* she thought. *If he were a Midas, there would be lightning or earthquakes or explosions... Miguel's fury. Yes. And everyone would have had their throats slit or been crucified or... He mustn't be a Midas anymore.* Monica tried to smile, when she was painfully reminded of the gap left by one of her incisor teeth when she was punched. The gleaming gun. The grooves of the cannon. She stopped smiling.

Miguel could do nothing to defend them. He looked so tired. Everyone was depending on her. Monica felt herself retch, but the pain inside her body stopped her from vomiting.

Gorlov said something in Russian, which caused Krushenko to shrug and say, "I'll speak in English because I don't want anyone else to know what you tell me." He eyed his minions.

Monica thought she ought to do something, but she didn't know what. Then Miguel began to stare at Krushenko's men.

"And what is it you think we're going to tell you?" said Gorlov in English. His syllables were as sharp as the mafioso's.

"Everything," Krushenko replied. "If you don't, I'll kill her. I want the weapon. I have good buyers."

If I don't get rid of this pain, I won't be able to generate a telekinetic wave big enough. I won't be able to focus. Impossible. Monica was now only paying attention to half the conversation between the two Russians.

"Whoever told you about a weapon lied to you. There is no weapon," said Gorlov.

"We can waste time and wait for this beautiful girl to bleed out from one of her internal hemorrhages," said Krushenko.

Pig! thought Monica. The doting father.

"I'm the weapon," said Miguel. Monica flinched when he spoke. He was so calm.

"I already know it's you, you idiot! Stupid Americans, you think we're all fools."

He's not American, Monica thought. *Shit! I have to do something.*

"Your people sold you out," Krushenko added.

"Someone from the CIA? A mole?" Gorlov asked.

Krushenko's eyebrows shot up. "As soon as you spoke to me, I began moving contacts. There was barely any available information. The secret was very well guarded this time, so it was obvious it was something big. But you know how business is. There are plenty of informers if you know where to look. Paying good money is enough. Come on, how do I activate him? How do I control him?"

But if I get rid of the pain, I won't have the strength to generate the inflection necessary to...

"Who do you think you'll sell the weapon to?" Gorlov asked. "Do you think you'll be able to simply put down something like that? You don't even know what you're dealing with."

Krushenko smiled and puffed up slightly. "I am one of the biggest arms traffickers. I have the wealthiest terrorist groups lined up to buy this. Religious terrorism has really spurred business on—"

"They won't want the weapon once they know what it is," Gorlov said. "This weapon is an offense against God. It's blasphemy, a joke, a parody of God."

Walter will see the inflection. He'll come for us again. God, no! What are they saying about God?

Krushenko's smile widened as if Gorlov had told him some gossip and he could already guess the ending. "Vladimir! Always so naïve," he said. "You don't understand the world. You understand atoms and electrons, yes, but you can't even see the world. Do you think a religious fundamentalist is going to refuse a weapon just because it's against God?" He let out a sonorous laugh. "There is no weapon on Earth that cannot be used to serve God. It could serve any one of them, even if it says on the hilt that it was forged in the very fires of Hell! All they have to do is believe that God himself sent it to them as the sword of God!"

I have to create a telekinetic wave, even if it kills me! Monica gathered all the rage she could muster.

Then, seemingly without reason, Miguel stood up.

The moustached mafiosos looked at him, although they looked incapable of reacting. Monica tried to sit up, but Krushenko pressed the gun against her head. She ignored the pressure of it against her skull – she was close, she felt it. Then she felt her brain begin to boil. But it wasn't just a telekinetic wave Monica was generating.

No, it couldn't be. It was the catalyzing effect. She was amplifying Miguel's inflection. She could feel it as she always had. He was there.

Miguel's serene expression did not change. Before anyone could move, the three guns turned into ice. The three men seemed to have been burned by their contact with the guns and they let go of them jerkily. Monica became aware of the frozen barrel of Krushenko's gun burning her hair and scalp before it fell from his hands.

The guns crashed against the tiles of the classroom, splitting into hundreds of shards of blue ice. Iceberg Man and his powers. The mafiosos sat down, then, placing their hands on their laps. They looked like misbehaving but remorseful schoolboys being punished by their teacher. At this level of an inflection, even Krushenko's face showed panic. He looked at his own hand, red from the ice burn, wide-eyed. Then Krushenko arched an eyebrow, clenched his jaw, and widened his eyes even further. He looked as if a spiked tree trunk had suddenly embedded itself in his stomach. Monica was reminded of Castillo's face when Miguel regained control over himself, and she guessed Miguel would now take control of the mafiosos' bodies. Their faces betrayed their urge to burst into tears. But Monica knew that

Miguel's inflection wasn't inflicting any pain on them. *For now*, she thought.

Miguel should have already been making things fly and unleashing storms. No, none of this was normal. Miguel was either already crazy or repressing his anger until it exploded out of him in a flood, destroying the lab, the university, the entire city.

"Miguel," Monica said in a broken voice. She sat up as she called him. It was painful, but not as much as she thought it would be.

Miguel looked at her as he picked up the ceramic gun from Krushenko's unmoving hand. His look was intense, like he was thinking about kissing her. How absurd.

"What have you done to us?! Don't kill us! What have you done to us?" Krushenko yelled. He was crying. "Monster, monster, no!"

Monica's pain was dissipating. Miguel's work, surely. She watched as Miguel searched unhurriedly for something in the inside pocket of Krushenko's jacket. He removed a mobile phone and placed in the Russian's burned hand. Krushenko stopped crying, his face going blank. The henchmen did the same.

He's going to kill them. He's going to cut their throats, Monica told herself. *Vladimir failed. Miguel has gone mad and Walter will find us from that inflection. We're done for.*

Miguel looked all around the room – the teacher's desk with the dead professor on top of the exams, the desks piled up on one side. He looked at everything with a saintly face, like Father O'Brien's when he gave communion. Finally, he looked at Gorlov.

Gorlov had stood up, his back facing them as he looked through the window at his machine. Monica imagined he was thinking about the technological relic from his past. All destroyed. He seemed not to think about anything else. He showed no interest in whatever would happen to Krushenko.

"Are you okay, Vladimir?" Miguel asked.

"We'll disappear as soon as possible," Gorlov responded, still staring at the lab.

Miguel looked at Monica, and she looked at him too. She was bruised, bleeding from multiple wounds. Inside, she felt fine. Miguel had cured her. *Like a proper god would have done.* "Can you walk?" Miguel asked her.

Monica stood up, limped for two steps, and threw herself against him. "Let's get out of here," she said. She was trembling because she couldn't grab onto Miguel properly. That was it.

Then Monica noticed movement at the edge of her field of vision. With her neck still screaming in pain, she managed to turn her head. Krushenko was dialling numbers on his phone without looking at it before raising it to his ear. He began talking in Slovak – or maybe in Russian, Monica couldn't tell. His beautiful voice seemed to be giving instructions, but his eyes remained on the window to the lab.

Once Krushenko hung up, the three mafiosos collapsed on the ground. They looked dead. One of the minions hit his head, leaving a small gash on his forehead. When Monica saw the blood and the twisted bodies on the ground, she assumed Miguel had killed them. She gaped at Miguel, shaking her head.

"They're sleeping," he said. "We're going to Nice in Sergei's Gulfstream."

CHAPTER 44

With his laptop in one hand, Castillo stepped out of the Volvo. Everyone got out of the car parked in front of the Sheraton beside the airport in Munich with clumsy movements and pained faces. Barrett carried the monitoring mini-terminal that Castillo had been looking at for the entire journey, while Vincent had the quantum sensor and Smith the briefcase with the ceramic guns and the drugs. This was their entire luggage.

They had to set up a new headquarters. Administration, logistics, new clothes, rest. Organize the search groups. Put Vincent to work once he was done resting. Roth was already at the hotel reception.

Carrying the mini-terminal, Barrett walked in front of him. The scientist didn't look away from the screen as he walked. That was what he had been told to do and it seemed now that, because Miguel had threatened their lives, Barrett followed orders with more diligence.

Castillo looked at the equipment in Barrett's arms and remembered the signal he had seen in Bratislava. So many incorrect indicators, he thought. At that moment, he was walking alongside Roth, who was waiting to sign the check-in form. He was leaning on the counter as he looked at the receptionist, who was bent over a printer. No one was looking at Roth, he told himself; no one knew what he was seeing. Roth saw everything with exquisite discretion, quite appropriate of an agent of Central

Intelligence. He was so discrete that only another agent would notice it.

Another CIA agent! Of course! "Roth," Castillo called, "who do you know in Bratislava? Have they told you anything?"

Roth immediately tore his eyes away from the receptionist's ass and turned to face Castillo. His eyes floated upwards as if mentally checking a shopping list. He blinked once, very deliberately, and without looking up again he answered, "Krushenko. Sergei Krushenko. These days, he's our main guy in the Russian mafia in Slovakia. One of the biggest arms traffickers in the entire world. He was a KGB agent and a double agent for the CIA. In the eighties…"

As Roth recited facts, Castillo saw Vladimir Gorlov's report in his mind. He stopped in the middle of the hotel reception. Suddenly, a detail sprung to mind – between 1970 and 1980, Gorlov had been watched by someone in the KGB. The reports said that in the end, the agent had helped Gorlov escape to the Federal Republic of Germany. He owed Gorlov a favour, since Gorlov had stopped him from getting deported to Siberia. His name was… Castillo's eyes widened. Sergei Krushenko.

Barrett turned around then. He was looking at the mini-terminal screen, and he looked up at Gorlov above his round glasses. "I have a Midas inflection on the screen," he said. "And the catalyzing effect, incongruence, everything. It's them. They're in…" Looking back at the screen, Barrett adjusted his small glasses.

"Bratislava," said Castillo.

Barrett looked up again, his mouth slightly open. "Bratislava. How did you know?"

"Smith!" said Castillo. "We're leaving. Now." He looked at the others. They were like a group of zombies. He couldn't count on them as they were. "You stay here and rest. I need you refreshed in a few hours. Roth, take care of everything here. And get me a jet."

***

Monica was worried about Miguel. He was calm, too calm. Too absent. And he was avoiding her. She touched her left eyelid. It still ached.

Miguel said something in French to the taxi driver and settled back into his seat while the car left the airport and began driving through the streets of Nice. It was almost morning, and Gorlov had fallen asleep as soon as he had gotten into the taxi. The road followed the line of the coast. It was almost empty.

"I know this city very well," said Miguel, watching the buildings blur through the left window. Nineteenth-century pastel mansions – ochre, yellow, orange – white lintels, small illuminated gardens. Miguel huffed in what seemed to Monica like nostalgia. "My parents, Dani and I used to come here every summer. My grandmother had a shop for tourists near the sea, near the Marché aux Fleurs. Bordeaux wine, Marseille soap, souvenirs."

"You've been very quiet this whole time," said Monica.

Miguel didn't reply.

"What are you thinking about?" she asked.

"My car," said Miguel, keeping his eyes on the streets of Nice. "My yellow Mégane Coupé. It's still there, in Bratislava. That moron Krushenko will carve it up for sure."

Monica stared at him. He couldn't possibly be thinking about his dinky little European car. Not now. If he was, he must have really gone crazy. "Your Renault is all that matters to you right now?"

Miguel turned towards her. He lowered his chin and fixed her with a stare. It was like he was looking into her depths, swallowed up by a hole in the ground. Monica felt herself shiver. "What matters to me is not being able to get rid of this fucking Midas ability."

When Monica spoke, it was barely audible. "Miguel—"

"What matters to me is that I'm tired of running, tired of being threatened, tired of having my brother and my family threatened, tired of having *you* threatened. What matters to me is that I don't know how to protect myself or you two without freeing the monster that roams inside my head, screaming at me to let it out for once and give everyone a good fireworks show – cannon shots, fire, blood, a good explosion of bones. What matters to me is that it doesn't matter how many people I kill, or electrocute, or strangle." Monica looked at the taxi driver. She was afraid he could understand what Miguel was saying, but he didn't seem to. He was whistling a French version of "Blowing in the Wind" that was playing on the radio. "Because there will always be more people waiting to control me and use me. Fanatics, idealists, dictators, tyrants, staunch atheists or religious fundamentalists to the bone. It doesn't matter. I'm useful to all of them." Miguel was breathing heavily now. "Sometimes I think maybe I should have accepted Castillo's plan, accepted my power and sent them all to Hell. Yes, I would have been a good god."

Another shiver ran over Monica's skin from the soles of her feet to the back of her neck, pinching every pore. She felt her pulse throb in the gap where her tooth had been. All her injuries throbbed at once. "I don't think that would have made you happy," she said very softly.

Miguel looked back at the hotels along the coastline. Now there were only huge buildings that left tiny gaps for small houses painted in light colors. Hotel Negresco, Casino. Monica read more luxurious signs. Power, she thought, was drowning the small houses with gardens no larger than a grave.

"I don't think being happy is a possibility for me anymore," said Miguel. "I don't think so."

Monica caressed his hair. Miguel didn't move. The taxi left a roundabout and merged with the smaller streets of inner Nice. Miguel returned his focus to the road. *Midas. What a fitting name you found for this curse.* Miguel had said something like that once to Monica.

As the taxi seemed to leave the city, Miguel looked back at the streetlights. Monica decided to look for something to comfort him. "You've gotten better," she said. Miguel looked at her again, still looking serious. "In the University of Bratislava, you didn't make a fireworks show. You were so good. I was so proud of you when I saw how you controlled your impulses." A trace of a smile appeared on Miguel's face. "You're not as alone as you think," said Monica. "You know that, right?"

Miguel took her hand, moved closer to her, without giving away what he was about to do, and kissed her.

A kiss, after so long. Monica closed her eyes and breathed in Miguel's scent of honey and old oak. A catapult into memory.

She and Miguel, a pair of university researchers sharing an apartment in the steep streets of San Francisco. Monica felt herself run out of air. It was like Miguel was suddenly back after years of being apart. He had returned. Then the taxi came to a stop.

Miguel and Monica broke apart. With small gasps as she regained her breath, Monica looked around and found they had stopped in front of a cemetery. Neon lights announced a nearby hotel. A little old palace with white lintels and sky-blue walls. Cypress trees from the cemetery's stone wall shaded the building.

"We're here," said the taxi driver in French, before going back to his whistling.

Gorlov woke up then and looked out at the headstones while Miguel paid. Then he looked at Monica. She smiled. She felt stupid. The most important intelligence services and mafiosos in the world were coming after them – but Miguel had kissed her.

"You sent your brother to a cemetery?" Gorlov asked.

"We can't go to where he's hiding right now," said Miguel. "It would attract attention. And we haven't slept well since… Germany? France? We need somewhere discrete. This hotel will do, I think."

The taxi driver, with the change in his hand, looked at Miguel seriously. He wasn't whistling anymore.

"Tomorrow," Miguel went on, "we'll get Dani and keep running until we disappear." Monica and Gorlov nodded silently. "That is, if we *can* disappear," Miguel concluded in a low voice, as if talking to himself, as he took the change. Then he pointed to the small place that was the hotel.

***

Castillo and Smith parked along the entrance to a large mansion in the suburbs of Bratislava. The clock on the dashboard showed it was one o'clock. But inside the house, several lights were on – nearly all of them, in fact. An incessant shadowed movement shifted across numerous windows in the main building.

It was an overly angular architectural mix, very modern in comparison to the street's old, wilted mansions, in Castillo's mind. He looked for something to ring or press, but the metal walls had no doorbells or cameras or keypads. The huge front door let him peek into part of an interior garden illuminated by small lights in the grass. Suddenly, a man as tall as a tank, slightly cross-eyed, and as broad as a cyclops came to stand in front of them on the other side of the door. He and his bulky jacket.

This cyclops is armed to the teeth, Castillo told himself. "Your reports were good," he told Smith, looking at the guard who was larger than the agent. "It has to be here." Smith said nothing. Castillo fastened his two top buttons on his jacket before unfastening the third. "We'd like to see Sergei Krushenko," he told the cyclops, adjusting the knot of his tie. "We're from the CIA. Agents Smith and… Brown."

They waited. Castillo guessed the guard from the perimeter hadn't understood a thing. But he also supposed that someone like Krushenko would know that they were in Bratislava since the moment they set foot here. They had done nothing to hide themselves.

The cyclops touched an earpiece he kept in his right ear. Without changing his facial expression, without saying a word, he opened the door and gestured with his palm for them to enter. He then pointed to the main entrance of the mansion, at the end of an asphalt path that surrounded a fountain lined with cherubs.

As they passed the Baroque cherubs – *stolen*, Castillo thought – he turned to look at them. Water flowed from their small jugs. Beyond, in the darkness, at the bottom of the enclosure, there was a single-storey building with chipped walls. It didn't look right coupled with the cubist mansion and Baroque fountain. Castillo supposed they were stables or a garage. Something yellow peeked out from one of the large side doors. The front of a car.

Miguel's Renault! Castillo sent Smith a signal and with a jerk of his head, he gestured to the yellow car. Smith looked, nodded, and continued his march to the mansion.

When they got to the door, a man carrying an AK-47 opened the door before they could even knock. Two other men, armed with Kalashnikovs, searched them. There were armed men all over the house. They guided Castillo's group to a set of double doors that looked like the entrance to a sitting room. In the entryway, two made-up, round-faced young women dressed solely in lingerie seemed to be waiting their turn. They were smoking and playing cards. There, too, were armed men. Castillo smiled at one of the women who was looking at him. No one smiled back. In that instant, someone opened the door to the sitting room.

When they entered, the image Castillo had of the house being a nest of criminals completely disappeared. Inside were just as many doctors as mafiosos. Blocking the exit was a gorilla of a man, similar in build to the cyclops. He was watching a television – large-breasted air hostesses and theatrical presenters – as he cleaned a Magnum. A Desert Eagle 44, Castillo noticed, with a large barrel, large like the gorilla. Near the gunman were two men sitting down, naked from the waist up, being examined by a medical team. Both men wore bandages on their right hands like they had been burned. They both had moustaches; the man with the lighter moustache was smoking while the other watched the television. One of them had stitches above his left eyebrow.

Castillo touched his forehead. Without a bandage, the points of his stitches were exposed. Perhaps that man's head had been split open by a chair, like him. But that wasn't Krushenko.

Castillo continued looking around until he spotted an antique sofa next to a modern, minimalistic fireplace. Seated on it was a man in his mid-sixties. His stomach was starting to protrude. A doctor took his blood pressure and a nurse, who looked like a governess, applied an ointment on his right hand. Castillo saw that it was burned. Had Miguel burned these mafiosos' hands?

Iceberg Man! he recalled. *Ice that burns. A good trick.* Miguel was gaining control of himself.

An artificial fire burned in the fireplace, and the man watched it intensely. A bottle of vodka, of which more than a third was gone, rested on a glass table next to him. The man on the sofa held some of the vodka in a small glass. Castillo could visualize what a fight with Miguel could have done to that man, to his self-possession, no matter how tough he was. "We are Agent Smith and Agent Brown, from the CIA," said Castillo, approaching him.

"I know who you are," said Krushenko, still looking at the fake fire. His Russian accent was filled with forced consonants. "You're looking for that demon. Miguel Le Fablec. He escaped you."

"We're looking for a certain kind of information," said Castillo, leaving pauses between words, like he had something important to say. There were a great many things that could be exchanged for information. He had already prepared his strategy.

Then Krushenko began to shout. "*Poshli vse von otsiuda!*" Everyone – patients, doctors, nurses, thugs – left the room. It was empty after a few seconds. Castillo, Smith and Krushenko were the only ones left.

Castillo touched his tie as the Russian observed him. "They're in Nice," he said quietly through gritted teeth. He downed the contents of the glass in one swallow.

Castillo thought quickly – Miguel had freed his brother there. He must have gone to Nice for him, to protect him. It made sense. Castillo began to improvise, starting with a statement of gratitude. There was nothing left to negotiate. "That information is of great value to prevent a world catastrophe—"

"That son of a bitch got inside my head!" yelled Krushenko. Castillo fell silent. "Fuck! I think he's still there," he said, touching his temple with a finger. "He was able to control my body as if it were his own." Krushenko picked up the bottle of vodka and took a swig that almost finished it off. "It was like… like…"

As if someone had violated you, Castillo thought. *I know it well.* Neither of them finished Krushenko's sentence.

"I want something," said the Russian, staring at him with green eyes clouded by vodka.

It's a bit late to negotiate, thought Castillo. But he smiled. "Of course," he replied. "Let's see what we can do."

Krushenko poured himself another glass of vodka. "Kill him if you find him."

"I'm afraid that—"

Krushenko drank before yelling, "Then I'll kill him myself! I swear it!" Then he smashed the glass against the middle of the fake fireplace.

CHAPTER 45

It was very early. Seven in the morning. Monica was glad to leave the cemetery behind. She hadn't liked the look on Miguel's face when she woke up. He was leaning on the windowsill, looking out at the eternal resting place, his expression subdued as he stared into the distance. Gray angels and mausoleums surrounded by cypress trees formed part of the scenery.

The bakeries, fruit stalls, and fishmongers were preparing for another day of sales. There were just working people on the streets in central Nice. They laughed and joked with one another. Miguel, Monica, and Gorlov arrived at a promenade – Rue Masséna, Monica read. As they passed a bakery, Monica could smell the freshly baked croissants. The scent was pleasant; it reminded Monica of morning routines and freshly made breakfasts. She looked at Miguel and found he had his eyes closed as he inhaled. Then he smiled softly. Perhaps, Monica thought, there was some hope that they could return to normality after all.

They crossed an avenue in the Place Masséna, and once they had crossed several other narrow streets, the Marché aux Fleurs appeared in front of them. The stalls filled with roses, petunias, and yellow tulips, like Miguel's Renault, made Monica feel like they were on vacation, and that everything from that moment on would be for their enjoyment.

"The Marché aux Fleurs," Miguel announced, smiling. "Beyond it is the Place Charles-Félix. That's where my grandmother had her shop. Dani is nearby." They soon reached a dark, narrow street with a small church. Miguel stopped.

"It's here," he said, looking at the yellow front of a small hotel – just three narrow floors – beside the church. "Monsieur Parvais is a friend of my father's. He's the owner. I used to play in the attic with his son when I was a kid. It was full of coat racks, chests, treasure islands, space shuttles, and cavalry regiments. 'The Secret Hole Club,' we called it. In reality, I guess Parvais just pretended he didn't know we were up there."

Monica spotted the attic's round window above the slope of the roof. Miguel's lips twisted into something resembling a smile. "Dani always barged into everything we did, so we ended up having to let him into the club. He was so annoying!" Miguel looked at Gorlov silently before looking at Monica. His tiny smile was still there. "It's a secret place," he added.

A small, sturdy-looking man with a large moustache exited the building.

"Monsieur Parvais!" Miguel called out to him. The man turned around and looked at Miguel, his face wrinkling. Suddenly, he lifted his arms in a huge gesture, as if someone was pointing a gun at him. His eyes went wide and an oval-shaped smile lifted his moustache. "Ah, Miguel, is that you? My God, you've gotten so big!" he said in French.

He and Miguel embraced and began speaking in French. Parvais gave him strong claps on the shoulder after every sentence and shook him lightly almost as frequently. As he left, he gestured to Miguel with exaggerated movements for him to enter the hotel.

"Dani's upstairs," said Miguel once Parvais was far away. "He's renting a room. Parvais told me he thinks he's sleeping. I'll go up alone, okay?"

Gorlov and Monica nodded. “Don’t take too long,” Monica said. She didn’t like leaving Miguel alone.

“Fifteen minutes. I want to talk to him.”

Miguel disappeared into Monsieur Parvais’ hotel. Monica looked at Gorlov, who stared back at her wordlessly. He had barely said anything since they left Bratislava. Looking behind him, Monica saw the road they had come from. Maybe, she thought, she could invite Vladimir for a coffee in the Place Charles-Félix while they waited for Miguel. She felt peckish, wanting to rest for a moment under the sun.

She was about to suggest it when Gorlov, blank-faced, lifted a bony finger and pointed to the hotel. Monica turned around slowly. Miguel was coming back. She looked at her watch – it had only been ten minutes. Then she saw his face – he was grimacing like someone had torn out his stomach. He scratched his palms furiously. His hands were covered in… something red. Was he injured? Monica looked for blood on other parts of his body. “Miguel!” she called out.

“They killed him!” said Miguel, and promptly vomited.

CHAPTER 46

From the small jet they had hired in Munich, Castillo observed the last foothills of the Alps. The pilot had just told them that they would land in Nice in less than thirty minutes.

"Do you see anything?" Castillo asked. He had asked the same question five minutes ago, and five minutes before that, and many other times before that. He knew it, but he had to ask.

"No, I don't see anything!" Vincent spat, eyes closed. "Can you leave me alone already? I can't focus."

Castillo, seated beside him, tried to imagine what Vincent was seeing right now – the streets of Nice, beaches, hotels, shops, mansions. The faces of every tourist and couple seated on the bench of one of those damn lookouts that Miguel liked so much. He put Vincent's visions out of his mind and looked back. Smith and Roth were adjusting their ceramic guns while Barrett watched the monitoring screen. But there was nothing on the screen, Castillo thought. Miguel would not give them any more clues. Krushenko and his ignorant greed had been their last chance. When Miguel found Dani, he would disappear forever. Unless Castillo got there first.

"Let him sleep," said Barrett, without looking up from the screen. "He won't find anything like that."

Castillo looked at the telepath again. Barrett may have been right. He had drugged Vincent, completely exhausted him. He was Castillo's only useful inflexor. And he was still loyal. Loyal to the cause. To a mission. "Rest, Vincent," he said.

Vincent opened his eyes and looked at him.

"I'm sorry," Castillo added.

"You're sorry?"

"For all of this. It's not what you signed up for. What happened in Germany."

Vincent turned to face the window.

"I knew Miguel wouldn't hurt you. It was just a bluff," said Castillo.

"I figured out your plan. I told them how to get all the information out of you, and where Daniel Le Fablec was."

"Yeah. Maybe I would have done the same. Who knows?"

"I thought he was going to kill me."

"This time, we'll do better. I need you to find them. The element of surprise—"

"Do you still think we're doing the right thing?" asked Vincent, suddenly turning back to Castillo. "I don't know. When I saw the end so near – and I really did think it was near – I thought…" He trailed off, choosing to look out the window again. "This isn't worth dying for," he eventually went on. "This isn't a very noble or patriotic plan."

Castillo didn't think himself capable of finding the right words or tone of voice in that moment to convince Vincent. Although, there was still something to show to the world, to ambitious politicians like Wella Anderson. That in itself had to be something good for humanity. "It is our duty to complete this mission," he said. "A mission for world peace."

"Miguel is a weapon. You know that."

Vincent and Castillo observed one another in silence.

"Rest for five minutes," said Castillo. "Then keep looking. We're counting on you to catch them by surprise. I don't want that weapon in the hands of the enemy."

***

Monica looked at the coastline. Old people sitting in a row on blue chairs looking at the sea. Terraces serving breakfasts to winter tourists. They seemed to swallow the pale December sun in spoonfuls.

In the time that had passed since Miguel discovered Dani's body, Nice had filled up with smiling faces and closed eyes turned to the sun, to the breeze. She and Gorlov had brought Miguel to the terraces beside the beach to try and convince him to sit down in the sun and have some tea, but he refused.

They moved quickly between the pleased faces, and Miguel began to climb the hills and steps of a mountain that formed a park along the seaside. Colline du Château, Monica read on a sign. Gorlov stopped before the first set of steps, gesturing with his hand for Monica to follow Miguel.

On the narrow paths leading up the hill, there were stone benches, young people reading, small lookouts facing the beach in a half-moon shape. Places to meditate that Miguel once liked. But he didn't stop at any of the lookouts. He walked without pause along the park paths without paying any attention to the branches and foliage that sometimes hit his face.

When they had almost reached the top, Miguel stopped, gasping for breath. Monica looked back and saw Gorlov following them slowly.

Monica thought about saying something, but just then, Miguel started climbing again. She followed him, her breathing uneven. She wanted to ask him what he had found in Parvais' hideaway. Dani's body, of course. There wasn't much to ask. She tried to remember Dani's face. She had seen him only once, in Madrid, when they asked for his car. He smiled a lot, but Monica couldn't remember his face very well. She recalled how, while

Miguel vomited in the street, she had seen a terrified young man in the attic window. For a moment, she thought it was Dani. She was about to say it to Miguel, but no. She must have been confused. The young man disappeared behind the curtains.

She could barely keep up with Miguel as he climbed, observing him from behind. His hands were still red. His blood, the blood of his family, had been spilt for the Midas Effect. They killed Dani. That was it. Miguel had found him in their hiding spot, where he himself had told Dani to go. Shot in the head. Krushenko's men must have found him, or the CIA. Maybe Dani had tried to escape and…

Suddenly, the climb stopped and a small flat area filled with trees opened in front of them. Monica coughed and looked back. Vladimir would take a while to reach the top.

Miguel, without stopping, went along the edge of a terrace full of people. There was a fir that looked to be a thousand-years-old, sailing boats, as well as several more trees. He walked directly toward the other side of the mountain. Monica followed a few steps behind him.

They eventually reached a lookout. There, on the other side, was a cliff over a small port. Below it were sailboats and a tiny lighthouse at the end of a breakwater. Everything was far below, at the bottom of a chasm. They could go no further.

Dani. Shot in the head. Monica leaned against a stone barrier and coughed again. Now, she thought, nothing would be able to stop Miguel's rage. The monster.

Although her breathing was heavy, she could still smell the sea. It was the city from Miguel's childhood. Perhaps that breeze could placate the monster, Monica told herself. Or not. The fury of a Midas could not be calmed so easily. Wind, sea, views from a lookout, a calm place. Meditate. Miguel was too calm.

Calm? Monica thought suddenly. She realized she couldn't breathe. She recalled the image of the flat area full of trees they had just passed through. She bit her lip. Trees weren't the only thing there.

Monica turned around suddenly. The park was full of tourists, people on walks, mothers with strollers, children running around. If Miguel let his demons out there… It wasn't a lonely forest in the middle of a German winter. Lightning, storms. Beneath the enormous fir was a juggler. He practiced with clubs that kept falling to the ground. Crowds of children ran around, near him, distracting him. *If only*, Monica thought, *I could distract Miguel*. She had to, had to bring him somewhere before the fireworks began.

Miguel stood contemplating the chasm below the lookout, leaning on the railing. Monica sat down beside him. She saw his fists clench as he scratched his palms, his breathing becoming violent. He could explode at any moment. "Miguel…"

"It looks like the Albaicín," he said suddenly. "Granada, right?"

Monica tensed. Without looking away, Miguel pushed back the hair that had fallen into his eyes. He was delirious. He had gone crazy. Granada? What was he saying?

Monica looked down. At the bottom of the chasm was the port, and on the other side were stately buildings with white lintels and pastel walls. Beyond, there were houses perched on a steep slope. Lush vegetation and houses latched onto an almost vertical slope. Yes, it looked like the Albaicín, the view from the Alhambra. Or from the gardens of the Generalife, where Monica had spoken to Miguel for the first time, disguised as a tourist with a stupid reflex camera in her hand.

"I've always liked this lookout. It reminds me of Granada," said Miguel. Then he turned around and wordlessly approached Gorlov, who had reached the summit and was looking around with a hand on his side, gasping like a fish out of water. Miguel was acting strange. Monica eyed the babies in strollers.

Gorlov began talking to Miguel. Maybe now they would leave, Monica tried to convince herself. Vladimir had insisted on leaving Nice as soon as possible. Miguel had refused. If he refused… Vladimir still had the ceramic guns. Darts. Monica shivered. Of course, that was it, they could drug Miguel if he resisted. Get him out of there. Yes, that was a good idea. She watched them talk from a stone bench on the lookout. Maybe they were preparing their escape. Maybe Vladimir could convince him without the need of darts. The juggler's clubs fell again and the children laughed at him. Then, Miguel shook Gorlov's hand.

***

Castillo thought about Vincent's words. The jet was arriving in Nice. They would land in no time. Vincent was refusing his mission, world peace. Vincent was scared, Castillo told himself, that was all.

The sunlight filtering through the windows reminded him of the sunlight that followed him through the corridors of the CIA headquarters. He remembered how his nerves fluttered before entering the office of dark wood where he explained his mission to his bosses. His mission, he repeated to himself. He had everything under control then. He loosened the knot of his tie. Now, instead…

"I have them!" Vincent exclaimed.

"You see them?" Castillo asked.

Vincent kept his eyes closed. "They're in a park. It's some kind of mountain between the beach and the port. They're… Yes, all three of them are there."

"What are they doing?" came Barrett's voice from behind.

Vincent said nothing.

"What are they doing?" Castillo urged.

"I don't know. Miguel is shaking Gorlov's hand."

"They're splitting up!" said Castillo. "Good. We only need Miguel."

"Miguel's going over to Monica," Vincent went on. "Gorlov's staying behind… Miguel is with Monica. He's telling her he has to go. She's saying no, that they can't split up. Now he's looking up and…" Vincent went pale. Drops of sweat beaded on his forehead. Beneath his eyelids, his eyes darted around nervously.

"And what?!" Castillo shouted.

"He found me," said Vincent. "No more surprise."

"What do you mean he found you? That's impossible," said Castillo.

"Perhaps he can," Barrett argued. "Here I can see the wave of an inflection in Nice. It's in the form of—"

Vincent opened his eyes, sweat running down his forehead.

"Don't open your eyes!" Castillo ordered. "What are you doing? Keep looking!"

"He said goodbye."

"Goodbye?"

***

Monica felt Miguel's inflection. He was doing something, and she was amplifying it, like always. It looked like telepathic communication.

"Who are you talking to?" she asked.

"Do you see that Bombardier?" Miguel replied. A small jet was descending to the right of the lookout. Monica stared at it. Miguel had just told her that Nice reminded him of Granada. What would the plane remind him of? That he had to keep running?

"What does the damn plane have to do with it? We can't split up. I'll go with you. You need me; I amplify your inflection. Don't you feel it?"

"It's about to land in the airport in Nice, the Bombardier. It is a CRJ100, I think."

"And?"

"Castillo and the others are coming in on that plane. I've just spoken with Vincent. They'll be here soon."

Vincent! Monica thought. They had found them. Fireworks. Lightning. The babies in the park. "We'll confront them," said Monica.

Miguel looked at her seriously, his chin tucked into his chest. "You know that's not possible. I'd kill them. I could destroy this entire city if I see Walter's face."

"Then somewhere else. I'll help you."

"Then there's the residual waves…" Miguel wasn't listening. He looked out towards the cliff. "A natural disaster, who knows what catastrophe."

"But last time, you controlled it."

"A coincidence. No, too many have already died. I'm not made for this."

"But…"

"Dani is dead. It would be ridiculous to keep going."

Monica looked down, contemplating the height of the cliff. No, she couldn't argue with Miguel. His brother, shot in the head, was reason enough. She bit her lip and began bouncing her right leg convulsively. She couldn't do anything about it if

Miguel wanted to split up from her. Five hundred feet. Monica calculated that must have been the height of the chasm below the lookout.

At that moment, Miguel climbed the small wall behind the railing. Monica looked up slowly, wearily. Then she understood. She stretched out her hands as if she could somehow grab him. "No…" was all she managed to say.

Miguel took something small out of his pocket and threw it down to her. Monica caught it out of the air. A bullet. Then, her mouth half-open, she looked back at Miguel.

"Keep it as a memento," he said. "Vladimir gave it to me before entering the room in Bratislava to take this away from me." He pointed to his head. "The contraption didn't work, you know."

Monica jumped up. *I can stop him!* she told herself.

"Goodbye, Monica. I love you." And Miguel threw himself off the cliff, into a five hundred feet fall.

Monica gripped the bullet as if she were grabbing Miguel and balanced on the railing. Miguel fell rapidly. Monica leaned half her body over the lookout.

She had barely leaned over when she heard the distant, muffled thud of Miguel's body against the ground.

Monica felt a buzzing build up in the middle of her brain, as if her head had entered a cloud of pins. She retched between breaths without looking away from the bottom of the chasm. Miguel's body was down there, twisted into an impossible position.

Miguel was dead.

CHAPTER 47

Castillo was exhausted and short of breath from climbing the steps of that stupid park perched on a mountain. He had already yanked off his tie and carried it in his fist. Smith walked alongside him while others remained behind. Suddenly, he saw Gorlov. He felt the urge to strangle him right there.

The Russian was waiting under a fir tree, far away from the lookout, from the circle of spectators, from the police. Beside him, a juggler was putting his clubs into a bag without looking away from the police tape. Monica wasn't there. Neither was Miguel, naturally.

When Castillo arrived, Gorlov made a tiny gesture with his hand that resembled a greeting. Then he pointed a slim finger at the area the juggler was staring at. He explained nothing; the old man must have guessed that they – Vincent and his extrasensory perception – had seen everything. Castillo ran to the police tape, but a police officer stopped him.

He retreated back to Gorlov. As he did so, he pulled out his phone and dialled a number. "I need access to the scene of a suicide in Nice," he said. "Yes, it happened today. A male with a Spanish passport. In the park." He looked around, trying to find the name of the damn park.

"Colline du Château," said Gorlov.

"Colline du Château," Castillo repeated. Once he hung up, he approached the police officer again and showed them his false Interpol accreditation. The officer spoke in French into their radio. They waited for an answer before nodding and letting Castillo pass.

He looked down over the lookout and saw Miguel's body at the bottom of the chasm. Uniformed men covered him up with a bright, metallic sheet.

Castillo closed his eyes and imagined the hard, steely gazes of the officials on the war council. He exhaled slowly, and the thought occurred to him that air would not be the only thing leaving him.

As he tried to erase the war council from his mind, the officer approached him and spoke in English with guttural Rs. "They are calling from Paris. *Direction Genérale*. They said you can see the forger. You will have to leave through the other end of the park and go around the hill."

"Merci," said Castillo before gesturing to Smith with his hand. The two of them immediately began walking where the officer indicated.

Five minutes later, they were beside the body.

Castillo looked at him, his breathing heavy from their quick pace. The metallic blanket shone gold, as if the nurses knew they witnessed the demise of a king. King Midas, Castillo thought. He felt like everyone was laughing at him.

He lifted his hand slowly.

He coughed.

That bloody, crumpled body had contained the last living god on Earth. His mission, his hopes, his future were all there – ruined, just like that corpse.

Dead.

Castillo told the officers that that wasn't the body they were looking for, and he and Smith left.

He told himself he had failed as they returned up to the park, where Gorlov and the others were. Lost. The Midas.

Miguel. Smith still carried the quantum sensor in his hand. As they walked, he showed Castillo the screen. There was a weak but constant signal. It was like the entire French Riviera was a nest of low-intensity quantum inflexors. Castillo could not understand the signal, but he had no energy to investigate anything concerned with inflexors. He had just lost the only one he needed.

When they got back to the group, Barrett informed him that all of NASA's monitoring centers had also registered a weak global wave like the one on the sensor. Castillo showed the isoinflexor curves to Gorlov.

"I don't know, Walter," said the Russian as he walked away from the lookout. "I suppose it's a residual effect from the disappearance of a Midas. Nothing like this has ever happened before in the Project. We'll study it when we get back."

As they left the park, Castillo turned around to contemplate the spot where Miguel had jumped. Behind it was the port area, with houses dotted along the front of the hill. The view reminded him of something. Some part of Granada, perhaps, when he was watching the supposed Midas, before capturing him and long before losing him forever.

CHAPTER 48

Miguel's death had left Monica in a narcotic, semi-conscious state of limbo. She stared out of the train window that brought her from Madrid to Granada. An army of olive trees streaked past, like they were running away. She was running away too.

Along with the limbo, or perhaps as part of it, the persistent buzzing of a tiny inflection, almost involuntary, left her brain with the constant sweet ache of an inflexor. It must have been her desire to see Miguel alive. An impossible wish that accompanied her from Nice. *Nice*, she repeated to herself. *Miguel dead.*

Vladimir must have suspected that Miguel wanted to kill himself. He had spoken with Miguel before he died. Monica clenched her fists. Vladimir may have even told him to do it. "Your only way out," Vladimir would have said. Monica closed her eyes. The scenery and its millions of olives flooded her. There had to be another way to put an end to the Midas Effect.

There had to be.

But what did it matter now? Vladimir had let Miguel die, and then he gave up. He talked about returning to the Project, he was too old, stuff like that. Monica would not return. Limbo swallowed her senses, barely allowing her to think. She vaguely recalled running away from the park, from the cliff, from Gorlov, from the lookout. She ran until her lungs nearly collapsed and had to throw herself onto the beach to cough and gasp. Then she kept running. She disappeared. Days lost in the south of France. Spain.

Madrid. Run. Disappear among the tourists and backpacked students. Directionless. Her senses dulled by that stubborn limbo. Miguel dead. It was Vladimir's fault for not stopping him. Monica rubbed her eyes. Then she rubbed her entire face. She had to say goodbye to Miguel. Granada would be the perfect place.

***

It was almost night when she arrived in Granada. She checked into the same hotel in the city center where she had stayed when she met Miguel, in April. Just eight months ago. She couldn't bear to stay in the same bedroom, not sleeping, with nothing to do, and she decided to take a walk and clear her mind. Limbo followed her.

When she went out to the street, it was cold and completely dark. She walked until she got lost among the streets full of shops, like an Arabic-style bazaar. *Alcaicería*, a sign announced. She distantly remembered that Miguel had brought her here after taking the photo at the lookout. She stopped and closed her eyes. No, she couldn't remember Miguel clearly. She didn't know why. Limbo.

Monica kept walking. Along the streets full of small shops, Christmas decorations mixed with the Arabic-style decoration of the storefronts. Colored lights, horseshoe-shaped geometrical reliefs, shining angels, stuccos. Monica looked at the mix of symbols and suddenly remembered the arguments over Christmas decorations in her house in Houston. Jesus, Saint Joseph, and the Virgin in Mamma's Neapolitan crib vied for prominence against Santa Claus, his reindeer, and the miles of string lights that enveloped the entire house. Houston's fake snow, the herald angels, Mamma giving her pigtails, Father O'Brien blessing them. Patrizia provoking them with her "crows in cassocks." Monica touched her gold crucifix. God was everywhere. *Miguel Le Fablec, the true god*, she had told Miguel.

She pinched her own arm to wake herself up. She didn't want to think about religion, not his, not her own. True or false. Then she removed her crucifix and put it in her pocket. Now was not the time to talk to God.

She kept walking, but her mind would not clear. She returned to the hotel.

That night, just like the previous night, Monica barely slept.

The next day for Monica began long before the sun rose. The buzz from her memories woke her abruptly, preventing her from falling back asleep. She had gone to bed disorientated and got up disorientated. She would have liked to make some breakfast – eggs, bacon, toast… But there was no one to serve it to. Miguel would have loved it. She couldn't cook there.

Monica left the hotel and looked for somewhere to eat. It was six in the morning, but she found a bar where some men in blue overalls were having coffee. More than one nursed a round glass of liquor.

"Cognac," the waiter told Monica, pointing to the other glasses. "For the cold."

Monica ordered a coffee and a cognac. She thought maybe the liquor could drown out the buzzing in her head. She took a sip, a tiny mouthful, but the alcohol hit her stomach like a drop of acid in her guts. A convulsive gagging took over her body. Her vision clouded, and she felt the acid climb up out of her upset stomach and bore into the middle of her brain. Her thoughts disappeared into the hole and her feelings intensified. She contained her vomit, grabbing onto the table. Then she suddenly saw in her mind the maroon sofa in her apartment in San Francisco. She recalled its rough texture, and the sex she had with

Miguel. And Miguel's lost, dead look before throwing himself off the cliff in Nice.

Monica decided the visions must have been brought on by the cognac. She pushed the glass away from her and took a sip of her coffee, but it provided no comfort. The men in blue overalls looked over at her and smiled. She must have looked like a stupid tourist imitating the locals. Turning her back to them, she unfolded the map of Granada she carried in the back pocket of her jeans.

With the map in front of her, she tried to solidify her plans. She would take the same path she had taken when she watched Miguel. First was the university – the canteen in the school of engineering where she helped him get rid of Ana. Then she would go up to the Alhambra, the Generalife gardens, and she would try to find where they spoke for the first time. Later, she would go to the Mirador de San Nicolás, in the Albaicín, and look out at the view they had shared the day she began drawing him closer to the Project.

The Project, she thought. *I captured him. I put him there.* Monica eyed the cognac. She picked up the glass and took a small sip. It burned a little less. Minor nausea. It was Vladimir's fault. And Castillo. Before she knew it, she had finished the rest of the drink in one gulp.

The limbo remained, but the nausea from the cognac made her feel better. Somewhat dizzy, her vision blurred, with another contained retch, but much better. Then she took out a photo from her backpack. It showed the Alhambra, the Generalife gardens, the Sierra Nevada, and Monica and Miguel. She always kept it with her. With her last drink of coffee and its disgusting aftertaste, Monica managed to stand up and leave the bar.

Her journey gave her no peace. All she saw were fountains, tourists, orange trees, priests. When Monica noticed her mood had not changed and the limbo remained, despite having spent the entire morning and part of the afternoon walking, she felt an urge to return to Texas, to her parents' half-Neapolitan half-American Christmas. But she intended to say her last goodbyes to Miguel from the lookout at the Albaicín. She would make it quick.

She arrived there in no time. The view seemed different to the one she had shared with Miguel. Sierra Nevada was white, like in the photo, but the Alhambra had a cold, scarce light. December afternoons were short. There was no one else at the lookout.

She spotted the stone bench where she and Miguel had taken the photo. She walked over to it and sat down carefully. It was cold. She contemplated the scenery for a few minutes – not very long, since she got tired quickly. She searched for a few words to dedicate to Miguel, to say goodbye, but none came to her. Where had her common sense gone? Damn tourist spot! It was clear Monica would gain nothing by being overdramatic. She could barely decide her next step, as though this was all her life would ever be. Miguel may have been impressed by those poses, goodbyes in thousand-year-old cities, goodbyes sealed with an old rock, but they didn't help Monica. And Miguel wasn't here.

She took out the photo again and looked at it, reading the acronym on her shirt. SJSU. San José State University. A cover for the Project, like NASA. All cover-ups, all confidential. Monica's breath began to speed up. She had pushed him into the secret world where he had died. She had brought him to San José, to the Project.

She wanted another glass of cognac. Her vision focused on Miguel in the photo. She wanted to remember him alive, but she couldn't concentrate. It was everyone else's fault, right? The limbo surrounded her and stopped her from thinking, from noticing her own guilt. But now she saw it more and more clearly. Guilt. She was guilty of Miguel's death. Yes, her. She cursed herself, cursed the Project and quantum inflexors and her comic book powers that only served senile scientists like Vladimir and the experiments of the powerful. The limbo began to dissipate. When she thought about inflexors and remembered she was one too, nausea bubbled inside her. Cognac, she thought. No, she didn't want to be one of them. Never again. She abhorred herself. And, for the first time, she wished for her ability to disappear. She bit her lower lip hard. She wished for every trace of inflection to disappear from her. Her right leg began shaking up and down. The gene, or whatever it was that caused her ability—she wanted it gone. She didn't want anyone to have it. She clenched her frozen hands. She hated that damn blue and red NASA logo, the SSR Center, the Project, the basements, their yellow experiment pages, the dark chambers, the shadowed clinics on level -2, the black folders of results. She hated inflexors and their black overalls. She still felt the limbo, as diluted as it was now. A cold wind moved her hair like a dark angel had rustled it. Her skin broke out in goose bumps, her back, her neck, as she remembered Patrizia and Mamma spitting their hate at one another, between flapping cassocks and crows' wing beats. Monica hated all of them! She wished for quantum inflection to disappear. Yes, that was it. She couldn't bear it. Anguish and hate. Guilt. And she wished for it too, that the stubborn, useless limbo would let her feel. She closed her eyes and concentrated on her firm desire, as if she were a Midas and she could make her wishes reality.

I want inflexors to disappear! she said mentally, her eyelids squeezed shut.

Then she began to feel a bubbling sensation in her brain.

She barely noticed that she was generating quantum inflection that responded to her desire, when it fired off. *I want inflexors to disappear!* she heard inside her head, as if the whole planet wished for it with her.

Suddenly, Monica felt a sharp pinch in the middle of her brain, tiny but unbearable. Too concentrated. Too big. Immense, impossible, unstoppable. The largest quantum inflection she had ever produced. Electricity, a buzzing all over her body, growing. She was losing her vision, her senses, and…

Her brain stopped boiling.

What…?

Monica had the impression that someone had turned off the lights, covered her ears and bound her arms, among many other sensations that had been cut off. It was like she was another person. Someone much smaller. She felt a wave of vertigo almost knock her out. Her inflexor abilities had gone.

Her leg stopped moving. She relaxed her hands. She stopped biting her lip.

When she opened her eyes, she understood. Her incalculable pulse, a sense of emptiness in her throat. It was too cold on the lookout. It was almost night in Granada.

She was the Midas inflexor.

CHAPTER 49

Gorlov sat and waited, completely still. The December sun in California illuminated his office so resolutely, like it did the rest of the year. It was a good place to wait.

Waiting was the only thing Gorlov had done since he returned from France. He acted like he was putting things in order, taking up his research again, but in reality, he was just waiting. He passed a hand over the soft, squared notebook paper in front of him. The equations for the Midas Paradox. Wrinkled fingers on blue formulae. He would not write more.

The phone started ringing. It was the internal line, the one that connected his office to the underground levels. If anyone dared to use that confidential line, it meant a catastrophe was taking place. Gorlov looked at the clock on his desk. Eight in the morning. *Five in the afternoon in Europe*, he calculated.

He smiled softly and felt a small pain in his cheeks, like wooden skin twisting. It had been so long since he had smiled last. It was all over, finally. He let his smile fall before picking up the phone. "Gorlov speaking."

"It's Walter. Please, Vladimir, come down to level -4. We have a problem. It's very urgent."

"On my way."

Gorlov hung up and immediately stood, almost on the verge of smiling again.

Once he passed the security check on level -4, he entered the global monitoring room and found that the problem was much bigger than he had predicted. All the operators watched their screens without doing anything. It was like they had forgotten why they were there.

As Gorlov approached the monitoring screens, everyone stared at him. At that moment, Castillo and Barrett arrived from behind a row of consoles.

"We've lost all signals from the global meters," said Castillo. His tie was askew and he had thrown his suit jacket over a chair. His elegance had vanished, and his voice wasn't selling anything.

"That's impossible. May I?" Gorlov asked one of the operators, who gave him his chair. Gorlov typed something on the keyboard and looked at the screen, which showed a map of southern Europe. There was no signal. Nothing. That was much more than he had expected. He hadn't guessed that Monica would destroy all inflexor ability on the planet. She just had to destroy her own ability. Anyway, it was better that way, Gorlov thought. That way, they wouldn't run the risk of having a new Midas appear one day for Castillo's plans. "There must be a failure in communications," said Gorlov, not expecting anyone to believe him.

"We've checked it," said the operator who had given Gorlov his seat. He spoke very quietly, like he was afraid to contradict the boss's word. "The automatic sampling sensors were checked and they have successfully transmitted signals. All the transmissions are fine, but they're not sending signals. It seems that quantum inflexors have decided not to produce more inflection… today." It sounded foolish, the operator speaking in an almost inaudible voice. "Or that there are no more inflexors out there," he said even more softly.

"Or in here, either," said Castillo, pointing to the monitoring post for level -2.

Gorlov walked over to the post Castillo pointed to. There was no signal at all on the screens. He didn't need to ask if they were carrying out experiments. It was impossible for all the chambers to be unoccupied and unproductive at the same time. "Have you spoken with the supervisor on level -2?" he asked.

"I did, just now," Barrett replied darkly, trying to apply a mask of appropriate solemnity. He had finally managed not to look like a surprised rat. "His direct sensors aren't showing any quantum activity. He's taken all the inflexors out of the chambers. They're saying they can't produce inflection. They don't feel anything, they can't generate anything. Vincent called from NASA Hampton – it's the same thing there. He confirmed that he can't produce even the tiniest inflection."

"Any residual waves?" Gorlov asked Barrett.

"Nothing."

Gorlov removed the glasses that had been with him since Leningrad. Very few people had seen him without them. He looked around at each person in the room. Finally, his eyes came to Castillo and he said, "I think the Midas who died in Nice wished for all quantum inflexors to disappear. And he did it." He went quiet for a few seconds. No one moved. "The weak signal we've been picking up these last few days expanding over all of southern Europe must have been his last inflection. It came into effect today, destroying all quantum inflexor ability on the planet. Even dead, Miguel Le Fablec has defeated us."

No one dared to say anything, or even move. Nobody even blinked. The CIA newbie, John Smith, who had been sitting in silence this whole time, was the only one who moved. He stood up slowly.

"The inflexors…" said Castillo, his voice weak. It was so unlike him.

"There are no more quantum inflexors," said Gorlov.

Smith made two rapid movements with his hand in order to call another agent, one of Castillo's men. Roth. The two approached Castillo, one on either side.

"Agent Castillo," said Smith in an unusually soft voice. "We're done here. We should go."

Castillo didn't even look at him. He kept his eyes, unmoving, on Gorlov as if he hadn't understood a single word he had just said.

"There are no inflexors. Miguel has destroyed them," Gorlov insisted as he stared back at Castillo.

"Come on, Walter," said Roth. He retrieved a pair of handcuffs from the inside pocket of his jacket. "Let's not make this more difficult than it needs to be."

Castillo looked at Roth. He touched the knot of his tie but did not tighten it. He didn't seem to have the strength. Without saying a word, without saying goodbye or stopping to pick up his jacket thrown over the seat, he left the room, guarded by the CIA agents.

"The Project has ended," said Gorlov.

Monica has done well, he thought as everyone began standing up and shaking their heads. He knew his bare face remained inexpressive, as always. Inside, he smiled. His most intelligent student, Monica, whose hair was too thick, who wore shoes too informal for a white coat, had done very well.

***

I am the Midas inflexor, Monica repeated to herself as she stared at her hands. She touched her jeans, staring at her white and blue sneakers as though she didn't recognize any part of her body or her clothing.

What she was doing could only be done by a Midas. And the Midas was her. And Miguel… Miguel had only been a catalyst who had developed his desires.

When the Midas and the catalyst act as one, it's impossible to distinguish which is which. That was what Gorlov had told her during their trip to Bratislava. He was talking about an incongruence in the results. Monica had thought he was telling her about scientific theories because of her insistence on knowing what Gorlov and Barrett had spoken about in the German forest. Or maybe to make sure she didn't fall asleep at the wheel. It seemed so unimportant then. *The wish belongs to both*, Gorlov had said. *The inflection is of both. The parameters, the fundamental equations become useless. There is no way to explain the phenomenon or to assign an inflection to each person. All we know is that only one person makes their wish reality and the other simply strengthens it.*

Monica touched the cold stone of the bench. A rough, alien reality. She was the Midas, not Miguel. She went over in her head all the moments he had generated Midas inflection or approached the Midas Effect. It was easy, since there weren't too many – his meeting with his ex-girlfriend at the University of Granada, the fake attack in San José, the lead ingot in the anti-inflexor room, the tests in the SSR Center, the virtual army, the false passports in Egypt, the fight in the forest in Germany, the confrontation with Krushenko… She was always with him! She had always wished for the same thing. What about Miguel's inflections before they met? No, they were just minor effects, things any catalyst could do. Once, Miguel had told her, he had made something explode into smithereens – nothing important. He had also moved paper, used telepathy, silly things like that.

Everyone had gotten it wrong. The cold wind moved her hair again and Monica shivered. She saw a dry, forgotten leaf at the bottom of the lookout's stone railing. She had to confirm it, that her inflexor abilities had disappeared. She had to make sure of it, she told herself.

She tried moving the leaf with her mind. That was something she could do almost without checking if her abilities were intact. In fact, it was almost a trap – any breeze could move the leaf at that moment.

But the wind did not come. The leaf did not move. Monica did not feel the slightest humming in her brain. Nothing. Monica had no doubt that she had just made her last wish as a Midas inflexor. And her wish had been fulfilled – all quantum inflexor ability had disappeared from the world.

Then she noticed something. The limbo had disappeared as well.

Miguel is dead. The jarring memory, as well as a fierce cold, squeezed her body.

A sudden, unstoppable flood of emotion came to her, overwhelming her. Hate. Distress. Fear. Guilt. And above all of it… Miguel was dead! And she was alone. Alone! The cold, black sky over Granada was like lead. It was heavy. So heavy. She was alone. Soft, flexible lead. It was crushing her. Monica's eyes shut tight from the weight of the metal. She began to shake, and she let her cheeks, her mouth, her nose, her neck sink down.

Minutes later, Monica regained control of her teary eyes. She saw she still had the photo in her hand, wrinkled in her fist. She placed it over her thigh and smoothed it out. When she looked at Miguel, her eyelids trembled again. She could have stopped it. She was the Midas. She couldn't bear looking at Miguel's face. Monica stood up and tucked the photo into her pocket.

Then she found the bullet.

Touching it felt like an electric shock to her fingers. Miguel had given her a bullet before he jumped. She kept it there in the pocket of her jeans.

Monica took out the bullet and looked at it, sitting down again. The light from a nearby streetlight was scarce. It was a caseless bullet, just a projectile made from copper, or some other similar alloy. *Copper?* she wondered. She rapidly turned the bullet over in her fingers and looked at the bottom. The copper sleeve didn't close over the bottom part. Inside, it was…

Monica's throat went dry. A new wind blew, prickling the wet tearstains on her face. Inside, the bullet was made of lead!

Her eyes widened considerably, as though she was trying to breathe through them, and she felt them start to dry out. Miguel couldn't transmute the lead into gold. Not by himself. He wasn't a Midas. And to prove it, all Vladimir had to do was isolate Miguel inside an anti-inflexor room and give him some lead. *The bullet!* Isolate Miguel from her, the true Midas. Vladimir knew! That was why he brought them to Bratislava. *I need to talk to Miguel in an anti-inflexor room*, Vladimir had told Eugene in the German forest. They had discovered it.

Monica stood. *But if Miguel knew...* She tried to think quickly as she began pacing in front of the bench. Her throat felt as dry as the Egyptian sands. *Then it wouldn't have made sense for him to kill himself, except for...* She remembered what Gorlov had told her of the Midas Paradox. *A Midas can make whatever they want a reality, but they can't destroy their inflexor ability, not after using their power. Not after using their power*, Monica repeated to herself slowly.

The only way a Midas can destroy their power is to destroy it before knowing it, she thought.

Monica held her breath. That was what she had just done.

She collapsed onto the stone bench like a puppet whose strings had been cut suddenly. If Miguel could create entire armies using her Midas ability as if it were his own, then he could also fake his own death. He could convince everyone, even Monica, using a virtual body that looked like his own, felt like his own, and even smelled like honey and old oak. Everything. And Miguel could also create a limbo to deaden Monica's inflexor senses and stop her from feeling that he was still alive. Monica had been unconsciously generating a small inflection this whole time. She had helped him without even knowing! And all of that just to… show her how he died.

Miguel's death had caused Monica to hate all inflexors and wish for all of it to disappear, for her ability – everyone's ability – to vanish.

Destroy the Midas Effect.

But Miguel was depressed. That's why he killed himself. They killed his brother, Monica told herself, trying to convince herself that what she had deduced was stupidity brought on by desperation. He had thrown himself off a cliff because Dani…

Dani's alive! Monica realized suddenly. Monica *had* seen him in the attic window! *Stupid girl!* It *was* him! Miguel had lied to her.

The cold air had dried Monica's cheeks, which now felt tight. She was still holding her breath when another breeze broke her from her daze. She noticed she was still holding the bullet. Miguel had given it to her before… jumping?

But he didn't jump.

Monica felt her lips curve into a smile. Jumping. *A very dramatic gesture, very Miguel*. Everything so dramatic. *He'd love to see me now, thinking, looking for answers, pacing quickly with the bullet in my hand. Seeing me…*

Monica turned around slowly.

The lookout was as deserted as it had been when she arrived. She turned more, and then she saw him.

Standing there, behind the bench, just a few steps away from her, was a man. A streetlight behind him showed only his shadowed silhouette. Monica opened her eyes wider to try and see the shadow's face. Her pulse throbbed wildly in her throat. The distant light of the Alhambra reflected minimally onto the figure, illuminating his face. He looked young and he had long hair over his face. His beard was a few days old, and he had Miguel's dark eyes. He smiled.

Miguel's smile.

Monica inhaled sharply, the breath shaking her to her core as her eyes filled with tears. The young man neared her, took the bullet out of her hand and threw it from the lookout. Then he sat down beside her and, with the pad of his thumb, wiped away a tear from her cheek.

His hand smelled like honey and old oak. Like a true god.

"Wish granted," said Miguel.

This book was edited in Madrid, September 19, 2019

What do you think of *The Midas Effect*?

First of all, thank you for purchasing this book. We are extremely grateful.
We hope that you enjoyed it. If so, We'd like to hear from you and hope that you could take some time to post a **review on Amazon**.

Your feedback and support will help the author to greatly improve his writing craft for future projects.
You can follow the purchase link for Amazon review, or just contact the author at www.manueldorado.es or share this book with your friends by posting to Facebook, Twitter, Goodreads or Instagram.

Your review is very important. Thank you.

Printed in Great Britain
by Amazon